Uncommon
Passion

Uncommon Passion

ANNE CALHOUN

HEAT | NEW YORK

THE BERKLEY PUBLISHING GROUP
Published by the Penguin Group
Penguin Group (USA)
375 Hudson Street, New York, New York 10014, USA

USA I Canada I UK I Ireland I Australia I New Zealand I India I South Africa I China

Penguin Books Ltd., Registered Offices: 80 Strand, London WC2R 0RL, England
For more information about the Penguin Group, visit penguin.com.

This book is an original publication of The Berkley Publishing Group.

Library of Congress Cataloging-in-Publication Data

Calhoun, Anne.
Uncommon passion / by Anne Calhoun.
p. cm.
ISBN 978-0-425-26290-0
1. Single women—Fiction.   2. Police—Special weapons and tactics units—Fiction.   I. Title.
PS3603.A43867U52 2013
813'.6—dc23
2013006079

PUBLISHING HISTORY
Heat trade paperback edition / September 2013

PRINTED IN THE UNITED STATES OF AMERICA

10 9 8 7 6 5 4 3 2 1

Cover design by Jason Gill.
Text design by Kristin del Rosario.

ACKNOWLEDGMENTS

I probably could write books without Robin Rotham, but I'm so very, very grateful I don't have to. I must also thank Jill Shavis, Alison Kent, and Kristin Gabriel (who helped fit the puzzle pieces together after I almost stood her up at Starbucks). Megan Mulry talked me off ledges and shared a fabulous week in the West Village when the book was done.

My editor, Leis Pederson, gave me room to roam. My agent, Laura Bradford, guided me from the very beginning. Thank you both for your continuing support.

This one's for Robin Rotham.

As always, for Mark.

Chapter One

When a big black pickup truck zoomed up and parked in the fire zone in front of Silent Circle Farm's educational center, Rachel Hill got to her feet. Latecomers to the silent auction and boutique who feared the downpour threatening to break free of the clouds had been parking in the fire zone all evening. "I've got it this time," she said.

Jess heard her despite the auctioneer's risqué banter and the audience's laughter, and nodded. Rachel swiftly bagged a customer's purchases—produce, baked goods, four felted pot holders, and a jar of the farm's honey—then left Jess alone at the cashier's table. She ducked under the edge of the tent, heading toward the truck.

"Excuse me," she called when the driver's door opened. "You can't park there."

A big, booted foot landed on the gravel as if she hadn't spoken. Thunder rumbled, ominous and slow, through the cool, dark night.

When it faded, she raised her voice, because perhaps he hadn't heard her. "Sir. You *can't park there.*"

Without a word the man slid from the driver's seat and strode toward her. Lightning from the late spring electrical storm split the sky, sound and fury signifying nothing, as her father used to say. In the midday bright moment, Rachel took in details as he strode across the parking lot. Broad shoulders and long legs. Black lace-up boots. Navy cargo pants. A navy polo stretched over broad shoulders and muscled arms. White circular embroidery on his left pectoral. Gun on his right hip.

Even to Rachel, who'd had exactly zero encounters with police officers or sheriff's deputies, the details signaled law enforcement.

White teeth flashed in his tanned face as he tapped a badge on his left hip. "Sure I can," he said when the louder clap of thunder died away.

He glanced into the large, brightly lit tent taking up so much of the parking lot, and then back at her. His gaze skimmed the Silent Circle Farm logo on her shirt.

"You working this party?" he asked.

She nodded. "Yes."

A large crowd had gathered for the Fleeces, Greens, and Bees Organic Boutique and Bachelor Auction benefitting the Gulf Coast Harvest Co-op. The tent held two dozen tables filled with people, eating barbeque made with pork from the Tumbled Stones Farm down the road. Tables along the side wall held baskets brimming with fresh-picked produce. Only the spectacle of the bachelor auction slowed the transfer of produce and goods from the tables to the reusable grocery sacks that held little thank-you gifts for the guests, who'd paid fifty dollars a head to attend the fund-raiser.

It was a party. Rachel wondered if she'd ever find a place where she didn't feel totally alone in a crowd of people.

"Leanne Gunderson?"

"The auctioneer?" Surprised, Rachel pointed her out, still standing in the spotlight set up to show off the bachelors. "Is there trouble?"

"Depends on how you define trouble. I'm her next piece of meat," he said.

Rachel blinked. That glinting, edgy smile flashed on, off, then he set one hand on the gun holstered at his waist and shouldered into the crowd, the white block letters spelling POLICE clearly visible on the back of his shirt. Women eddied away from him, like he was the prow of a ship splitting the ocean, then clustered together to whisper in his wake.

At the sight of him in motion, heat smoldered deep in her belly. Drawn back into the light, she followed him into the tent and took up her place behind the cashier's table. Jess, her roommate in the farm's bunkhouse, rang up another customer's purchases and Rachel carefully bagged them, though now her attention was divided. The police officer spoke to Leanne's assistant, then joined the line of bachelors. He stood straight and tall, legs braced, arms folded across his chest.

"Why would any self-respecting woman buy a date?" Jess said between customers. "That's the question of the night."

Rachel could think of lots of reasons. "Are you going to bid?"

"I might," Jess replied, her gaze fixed on the line.

The auctioneer swiped at her phone, then looked around the crowded tent. "Next up, folks, we have Rob Strong, owner of Silent Circle Farm. He provided the location, and the alcohol."

That got a whoop and a round of applause from the crowd. Rob made his way into the circle of hay bales marking out the stage. Clean-shaven, with his normally shaggy blond hair somewhat tamed, he wore slacks and a button-down shirt, his belt and shoes a gleaming shade of walnut. He looked fundamentally different, something Rachel attributed to the clothes until she realized George the border collie was missing from his side.

"He's been active in organic and community farming for the last ten years, but don't worry. He's not going to put you to work on your date." The auctioneer paused. "Unless you want him to."

Another laugh. Jess leaned forward in her seat. Rachel followed her stare and found Rob—who was watching her, not Jess. He winked. Caught off guard, she blinked and then smiled before he returned his attention to the auctioneer. Then her gaze landed on the police officer waiting his turn just outside the ring of bales.

To find him watching her as well. And unlike the little visual game of tag she, Rob, and Jess had just played, he didn't look away when their gazes met. Rachel's heart thudded hard against her breastbone, and heat rose in her face. His thick brown hair was closely cropped around his forehead and ears. His eyes, fringed with dark lashes and glinting a brilliant blue in the tent's bright lights, held an awareness of her as a woman that was similar to the way Rob looked at her . . . yet somehow completely different. More masculine. Rough, with a hint of carelessness in it.

No man had ever looked at her like that, and the intensity of her reaction made her look away first.

When she dared another glance, he'd transferred that searing gaze to the auctioneer, who was in the process of opening bids on Rob. "Mr. Strong's offering a night out in Houston that includes dinner and box seats at an Astros game. Who wants to start the bidding?"

"Five hundred," came a voice from the back of the tent, but that figure disappeared in a flurry of bidding. Jess was in the thick of it, until the amount shot into four figures. Then she sat back in her chair and brushed dirt from her jeans as the winner pushed through the crowd to claim her prize, an exultant, victorious smile on her face. There was a whisper of bitterness in Jess's gaze as it skimmed over the heels, the flirty sundress, the sleek hair and nails, but she congratulated the winner when Rob escorted her back to the cashier's table.

"All right, ladies, the final bachelor of the night was supposed to be Brian Rogers, brother of our first bachelor, the Lazy R's owner, Troy. But Brian is a member of the Galveston Police Department, and he had to work tonight so Officer Ben Harris has graciously agreed to stand in for him."

The audience offered a round of applause that managed to be both appreciative and flirtatious at the same time. Harris walked into the circle of bales and gave the audience that flashing smile and a short nod. Rachel noted the increase in chatter, the energy spiking in the room. The object of this speculation stood in the center of the spotlight, arms folded across his chest, gaze flicking from face to face as he took in the scene.

Then that smile flicked off and on again. Rachel followed his gaze to the back of the crowd, where a dark-haired woman who'd already purchased one bachelor stood, a bottle of hard lemonade held languidly by her shoulder. A feline smile tugged at the corner of her mouth as she considered Officer Harris. Rachel looked back at the cop and saw the merest shadow of a wink flicker in his eyelid.

Rachel leaned over to Jess. "What do you think?" she asked.

Jess matched Rachel's low tone. "I recognize him. He works security at No Limits, a bar in Galveston, and when he's not breaking up fights in the parking lot, he's using the uniform to get laid. Plus he's got an honest-to-God cleft in his chin," she said. "He's bad news."

So the most overtly masculine slice of humanity she'd ever seen in her life was bad news. That was good news for her.

Like most twentysomethings, Rachel had a *What Now?* list, but unlike other women her age, her list started with basics like *get a driver's license* and *get a car.* She'd ticked off both items several months earlier. Once she realized how computers and smartphones ran the outside world, *get a computer* and *get a phone* had jumped to the top of the list. *Find a job* and *find a place to live* still needed some work—she was still farming, still sharing a room.

The list's biggest items—*get transcripts from state* and *apply to veterinary technician school*—were in progress. Okay, so they were stalled. The email sat in her Drafts folder with the application attached and ready to send. Something about taking that particular step scared her. She was getting better at allowing herself to feel, which certainly helped her identify what she felt. Knowing *why* she felt and how to handle it was something she could only learn through experience.

Jess stood to accept payment from one of the few women in the tent not focused on Officer Harris. An envelope in her back pocket snagged on the back of the folding chair. "Oh, I almost forgot," Jess said, then handed the envelope to Rachel. "This was in today's mail."

Rachel accepted the letter without comment. Yet another letter with RETURN TO SENDER written on the envelope in her father's neat block printing. Over thirty letters written, one a week since Rachel left Elysian Fields Community of God, the isolated religious commune where she'd lived her entire life. She mailed one every Monday, three or four pages containing details about her new life, humorous anecdotes about her days at Silent Circle Farm. How she felt. Who she was becoming away from the only life she'd ever known. The ending was always the same.

*I still love you, Dad. I still want to be your daughter. Please
write me back.*

Love, Rachel

She didn't say she was sorry for what she'd done, because she
wasn't. Her unrepentant attitude didn't matter, because he had yet
to read a single letter, let alone write her back. She breathed through
the sensation dancing along her nerves until she could name it.
Rejection, identifiable by its sting and the way it halted her breathing for a second. Thirty-plus letters into her new life, and she still
felt hurt. The emotion was far too familiar, the price she paid for
leaving the secure world of Elysian Fields. Nothing assuaged it.
She'd tried nearly everything the world had to offer: a variety of
ethnic food, rich desserts saturated with sugar and chocolate, movies she'd never seen, music she'd never heard, books she'd never read.
While the sensory overload occasionally distracted her, it never quite
banished the sorrow of her only surviving parent's rejection.

You rejected him first.

Rachel sat back and tuned in to the auctioneer's banter.

"All right, ladies, I know you're anxious to get to the shopping,
but there's one more man up for sale tonight. Dig deep into those
purses to benefit Gulf Coast Harvest Co-op and all the good work
they're doing to promote organic farming in the region. Nothing
better than a man in uniform."

"Sure there is," Officer Harris said.

Laughter rocked the tent, the switch in energy eddying at Rachel.
Her body got it before her brain did. Heat trickled down her
spine, then a blush flared in her cheeks. When it came to sexual
innuendos, she was usually a step or two behind. She watched Officer Harris scan the women unconsciously pushing closer to the ring

of hay bales, his blue eyes dancing with a private amusement, that scythe of a smile pulling at one corner of his mouth. An unbidden thought rose to the surface of her mind.

The list holds one thing the world has to offer that you haven't tried.

"There you have it, ladies," Leanne said smoothly. "Who'll start the bidding for me?"

"Eight hundred," came from the raven-haired woman in the back.

"Wow," Jess said. Rachel had to agree. Three of the other ten bachelors had gone for less than that, including the bidder's first prize.

"What *exactly* am I bidding on?" the woman added archly.

Harris's smile flashed through the laughter. "Does it matter?"

Heads turned, like two hundred people were watching a tennis match. "I'll let you know afterward," she said.

"Nine hundred," came from another woman.

"One thousand."

"I'll take that thousand," Leanne said, "but hold on a minute, ladies. Let's find out exactly what Officer Harris is offering."

"I'm just filling in for Troy, so I'll follow through on whatever he set up," Harris said. He didn't have to lean toward the mike. His voice carried effortlessly through the tent.

Leanne glanced at her phone. "Officer Rogers offered dinner for two at Gaido's and an evening at the Pleasure Pier."

"Sounds great to me," Harris said.

"And me," the black-haired woman said. "Eleven."

"You've already bought one man!" another woman called from the crowd.

"I can handle it," she said, her gaze never wavering from Harris's.

"I'm looking forward to it," he said.

Rachel heard the words as clear as a bell in her head. *Him. He's perfect for what you need.*

The bidding war climbed by fifties to fifteen hundred, but when flirtatious bidder upped her offer by two hundred dollars, the other woman shook her head in defeat.

"Going once," Leanne said.

Rachel's heart thrummed in her chest. She'd already done the hard part. A date with Officer Harris would be easy, because he'd make it easy, a rakishly charming good time from beginning to end. All she had to do was *buy him.*

The weight of four pages and a business envelope pressed against her back pocket. When she left, she'd never imagined her father would stay angry with her. She was his only child, the apple of his eye, and while he had every right to be angry, she'd thought after a few weeks, he would relent and at least keep the letters.

There was no going back. Officer Harris caught her eye. The smile he gave her, the smile she'd mentally dubbed his *Sure I can* smile, flashed at her, part mocking, part amused, part something her brain didn't recognize but her body sure did. Heat zinged along her nerves, straight through the ball of lead in her abdomen.

Oh.

If you want to cross something off the list, submit your vet tech school application.

No. Do this.

"Going twice," Leanne said, a warning lilt in her voice.

"Two thousand dollars."

Rachel's voice silenced all chatter in the tent. Stares landed like the humidity before a storm on her face, bare of any makeup, on her hair, held back from her face in a thick French braid, on her simple outfit of jeans and a scoop-necked T-shirt representing Silent Circle Farm, but her gaze never left Ben Harris's.

Leanne smoothly kept up her patter. "Two thousand, I have two thousand for a night with Officer Harris. Do I hear twenty-one?" she asked.

Rachel didn't need to turn around to see the response. It was in the way Leanne straightened her back in anticipation of the final bid in the final auction of the night, in Ben Harris's smile.

"Sold!"

A loud round of applause swept through the crowd, covering Leanne's final comments. Rachel made her way through all those people to lay claim to trouble, and did what every other winning bidder had done that evening. She reached for his hand.

"Don't touch me while I'm in uniform."

She froze, then his palm settled warm and hard on her shoulder, his fingers splayed to her collarbone as he guided her not to the table where she'd make payment but back through the crowd, into the darkness of the parking lot. They left behind the noise and clamor of women released to shop, and headed for the truck he'd stepped out of only ten minutes earlier.

His hand didn't drop from her shoulder until they reached the vehicle. He leaned back against the driver's door and considered her.

"Two large?" he said, his demeanor back to cocky flirt. "I don't know if I can live up to that."

Two large what? "I have no doubt you will," she said.

That smile again, the one with so many layers it hid more than it revealed, flashed on, then off, distracting her from her impending heart attack. What was it about that smile? It was somehow arrogant and inviting and hands-off, all at the same time, with an edge underneath it she couldn't quite place.

A silence fell, awkward with the laughter and chatter in the background. He studied her in a way that made her lift her chin and look right back. He couldn't tell. There was no way for him to tell just by looking at her.

"We better set this up now."

"Good idea," she said. "We're open late on Friday nights but we close at six on Saturdays."

"I can't do either," he said.

"We're closed on Sundays," she offered. Sundays, which used to be her favorite day of the week, were now her most difficult day. Rather than spending the entire day in church, she wrote to her father on Sundays, knowing that she'd mail the letter on Monday only to see it returned on Saturday.

"I'll pick you up at six," he said.

"Oh, that's not necessary," she said hastily. The farm lay along a river valley a good ways outside town. "I've got some things to do in Galveston. I'll run errands and meet you at Gaido's."

"For two grand, I should give you a ride."

She'd spent enough time listening to Jess flirt with the Texas A&M boys to know how to answer that. "I'll count on one *after* dinner," she said.

His gaze, focused on entering the date into the calendar on his phone, flicked up to hers, and that smile, that wicked dangerous smile, flashed again.

"Maybe I don't go that far," he said, an odd, teasing lilt in his voice.

Her mouth dropped open in shock.

He gave an amused huff. "Don't worry. I go that far. What's your name?"

"Rachel Hill," she said.

"Phone number in case something comes up."

She rattled off her digits and entered his into her phone. Their phones lit up their faces, giving the whole scene an eerie, unreal glow until the thunder rumbled again, and lightning lit up the sky. Unconcerned, he thumbed away at the keyboard with more dexterity than she did.

Catching her completely by surprise, he cupped her jaw, then kissed her cheek. She froze as heat and light danced under her skin.

"See you Sunday," he murmured.

Rachel stepped back as he got into the pickup, cranked the engine, and swiftly backed out of the lot. Dust lifted in his wake, swirling in the hot night air as she turned and walked back into the tent. Congratulations followed her to the cashier's table, where she pulled out her debit card and ran it through the scanner. Jess stood behind the table, ringing up customers.

"Well, look at you," she said archly as she tucked jars of jam, jelly, and honey into a paper bag. "I never figured you for the type to buy a man, especially one like that. Rob's more your speed."

Rob was watching her from across the tent, his brow furrowed.

"What do you mean?" Rachel entered 2000.00 into the machine, stared at the number signaling the biggest purchase of her life, then pressed OK.

"The whole sweet, innocent thing appeals to Rob. The only thing Officer Harris likes about sweet and innocent is the chance to ruin it."

Perfect, because she'd just bet two thousand dollars that he had no interest in a relationship, no sense that sex was something special reserved for the marriage bed, no inclination to call again. *Virginal* was the word Jess had used one night when all the apprentices went out for drinks and Rachel volunteered to drive when no one else wanted to. The Virgin of Silent Circle Farm, she'd teasingly called her without knowing the truth. Rachel *was* a virgin. Never been to bed with a man. Never been touched below the waist, or below the neck. Never even been kissed, until Ben Harris's mouth brushed her cheek and glancing pressure and hot breath sent sparks along her nerves.

But Jess didn't need to know that. Leaving Elysian Fields meant gaining a measure of not just control over her body and emotions, but also her privacy. She wanted the full range of human experience, and she wanted the option to keep it to herself.

"Rob and I are coworkers," Rachel said, choosing to ignore Jess's comments about the police officer. "And friends. That's all. Want to help me shop for something to wear?"

A Galveston native, Jess knew all about the area's upscale secondhand shops, and had a better eye for fit, color, and appropriateness than Rachel.

"Sure," Jess said with a shrug. "Better pick out some sexy undies, too. Cotton briefs aren't his style."

Rachel walked back to help the other farm employees at the Silent Circle table, the memory of Ben Harris's smile flashing like lightning in her brain.

It didn't matter that Ben wasn't her type. She wasn't going to fall in love with the first man she had sex with. She wasn't going to tie herself down, not after she'd paid so much to get free from that old life. The costs were too high to make that mistake.

But that smile made Ben Harris the perfect man to take her virginity. Rachel wasn't the gambling kind, but she'd lay odds he wouldn't even notice.

Chapter Two

Ben had worked over a week since that ridiculous night at the bachelor auction, a week permeated by the typical things cops smelled. Galveston's ever-present undertone of salt spray, sunscreen, and fish. Gun oil, gas, hot vinyl, the garlic knots the last guy to drive his patrol car ate then sweated out, the faint scent of burning oil coming from the car's engine. Rancid sweat and body odor that could drop a bull at thirty paces courtesy of addicts who hadn't bathed in weeks in an effort to keep the drug from seeping out through their skin. Fear had a distinct smell. So did anger, hatred, rage, and futility. He'd smelled all those things and more, but not even the filtered, cool air blasting from his truck's vents could get Rachel Hill's lingering, indefinable scent out of his nostrils.

He pulled into the parking lot of Gaido's only ten minutes late. Not bad, given that an hour earlier he'd been braced at attention in a very small office with the shift lieutenant and the precinct captain screaming at him loud enough to wake the dead in crypts in Louisiana.

Yes sir, he observed a robbery in progress at a gas station, called 911, then walked into the middle of it.

Yes sir, he was off duty.

Yes sir, he was unarmed.

No sir, he wasn't wearing a vest.

Yes sir, he goaded the robber, providing a distraction for the mother sheltering her young son behind the lids-and-straws counter to bolt out the back door and the attendant to hit the alarm, and *yes sir,* when the robber swung his gun from Ben to the attendant, Ben fucking cold-cocked him.

He flexed his fingers when he got out of the truck. Hitting solid cheekbone, feeling it crack under his fist. *Goddamn.* An adrenaline high smelled like the best sex ever.

No surprise there.

He swung out of the truck, and crossed the parking lot to the front door. The bar to the right of the hostess stand was packed, so he stood in the door, searching for the woman willing to drop two grand on a night with him. When a group left to claim their table, Ben saw his best bet, but slowed his progress through the crowd to be sure, then stopped behind her, absently watching the light glinting off a thick, complicated knot of hair in a dozen shades of brown and gold. She wore a knee-length, sleeveless fitted dress the same bright copper as the bottom of his mother's pots. He inhaled slowly.

Definitely her.

"Rachel," he said.

She turned to face him, and the sight knocked speech from him for a moment, because this woman looked nothing like the farm worker who'd waited until the very last moment to bid on him. In the bar's dim lighting, the skin of her throat and shoulders reminded him of hot nights in the back of a pickup, and sultry eye makeup and mascara turned her pale brown eyes to mysterious, catlike pools.

The combination made him want to bend down and lick her throat before he set his teeth to her neck. Instead he settled for another kiss on the cheek and got soft, sun-warmed skin and another halted breath, just like the one at the bachelor auction in return. Hot blood eddied to his cock.

He was *so* getting laid tonight.

If he didn't crash from exhaustion first. He'd worked until two at No Limits, gone to a party for a couple of hours, slept for a couple until daylight made it impossible to sleep. A simple trip to the gas station for coffee and the newspaper turned into a day at the station, complete with two senior officers taking turns going at him.

Just wait until his SWAT lieutenant heard about this. There would be more hell to pay later, but now . . . now he had Rachel Hill to attend to.

When he drew back, her eyes were wide. He cleared his throat, tried for normal conversation. "What are you drinking?"

"Water," she said.

Usually women had a cocktail in hand by now, but maybe she was dehydrated after a long day outside. He ordered a Shiner Bock and swallowed a good half of it before looking at her again. This time he caught her gaze skimming over his suit, the one he'd last worn for his sister's and brother's weddings. Despite the day he'd had, a two-thousand-dollar date called for a suit. In that dress they'd probably just walk around the Pleasure Pier, skip the rides. Catch the sunset in the Gulf before they disappeared into the darkness of his apartment or hers.

He picked up what was left of his beer and extended his hand toward the hostess stand. "Let's see if our table is ready."

She preceded him out of the bar and into the foyer, where couples sat or stood waiting for a table. Ben checked in with the hostess, who pulled two leather-bound menus from a shelf inside the stand, and led them to a table near the window, overlooking the ocean. The hostess stepped back to let him hold Rachel's chair, and while she seated herself, Ben found himself trying to identify each component of her scent. Heat and sweat, not masked by perfume or the artificially scented shampoos and body lotions so many women favored. Rachel smelled elemental, like the air before an electrical storm. Hot earth and humid air, danger, destruction.

She sat down, flashed him a quick smile over her shoulder at this common courtesy, then laid her napkin in her lap as he seated himself and accepted a menu. He picked up his own menu, found rib eye in the steak section, and closed it again. "See anything that looks good?"

"Everything looks good," she said, still studying the menu.

The waiter showed up and rattled off the specials, then asked if they'd like anything to drink. "Wine?" he said, looking across the table at Rachel.

"Yes, please," she said.

"Red or white?"

"We have a very nice house red that pairs well with the beef medallions," the waiter offered.

Rachel considered the menu again, then said, "I'd like the seafood platter."

She wasn't going to be talked into something she didn't want. He liked that, flicked her a smile. "White wine to go with that, and I'll take the rib eye."

"Appetizers?"

"No, thank you," Rachel said.

Ben held up a hand, stopping the waiter in his tracks. "You were looking at something."

A blush bloomed on that tanned skin, and for a moment Ben

wondered whether he could feel the heat rising under his fingertips if he touched her smooth cheek. In the setting sunlight filtered through the big windows overlooking the ocean, she looked like autumn dusk, a hint of mystery clinging to her tanned skin.

He thought a week between being bought and being had would dull his response to her. No such luck. Unlike a woman picked up at No Limits, he was pretty sure sleeping with the bachelor-auction winner wouldn't be appropriate. But, unlike the last few women he'd brought home, Rachel hadn't faded from his memory.

"The calamari," she admitted.

"We'll start with the calamari," he said.

The waiter confirmed salad dressings, took their menus, and disappeared. Rachel neatly aligned her silverware, sipped her water, then folded her hands in her lap, and it hit him.

"You're nervous," he said.

The bloom on her cheeks darkened from pink to rose. "Yes."

"I'm surprised. You wanted to do this badly enough to drop two thousand dollars on it. I don't bite. Until later, and then only if you ask." His response, a smile to go with the teasing, was as natural as breathing, and to no great surprise, it seemed to settle her down. "Tell me about the fund-raiser."

"That's right. You weren't supposed to be there at all. Why did your friend have to cancel?"

The waiter arrived with the wine, uncorked it, and poured a small amount into Ben's glass. Perfunctorily, he tasted it and nodded approval to the waiter, who then poured full glasses for them. "I joined the SWAT team a few weeks ago," he said as he finished off his beer. "Rogers went to Vice, and he was working that night."

Rachel's eyes widened over the rim of her glass. "We were fortunate you were willing to step in," she said and sipped.

"I beat him out for the SWAT spot," Ben said. "He said it was the least I could do. What's with the bachelor auction anyway?"

"It was a fund-raiser for the community garden initiative. Rob wants to extend it through a program he calls Truck Garden, kind of like a CSA, but one that travels. Last night he raised enough money to buy the truck and renovate it."

"You worked at the farm long?" he asked as the calamari arrived. He gestured to the heaped platter. "Go ahead." Squid wasn't his thing, but he'd eat a few pieces to be polite.

"Just this season, I hope." She transferred a few golden-fried pieces to her plate and scooped out a small amount of the sauce. "I grew up on a farm, but I want to go to vet tech school and work in a vet clinic. What's it like, being a cop?"

That was the number one most common question he got asked at parties, on dates, in groups. Experience taught him no one wanted the real answer to that question. Instinct told him what his lieutenant called *bullshit-death-wish-hero-complex-fucking-crazy stunts* wouldn't impress Rachel Hill, either.

He sat back, beer in hand, and started. "So, last week I'm on patrol, and there's this homeless guy pushing his shopping cart on the sidewalk in the Strand. It's bad for business and someone reports him to 911. I show up. He's stumbling, maybe sick, more likely pub intox. I pull over and start talking to him. He smells like the last time he bathed was in a keg, but the stumbles are from withdrawal because he asks me for money for beer before he throws up. I round up him and his shopping cart full of grocery bags of stuff to take him up to the shelter near the medical center. The intake clerk asks for his name."

Her eyebrows lifted. "Go on."

"He pulls himself upright and says, '*Jesus*,'" Ben said, replicating the drunk's offended, exasperated tone. As if anyone could doubt the presence of the Son of God in a homeless shelter.

The corners of her mouth lifted.

"The clerk's used to stuff like that, so she just goes on. 'Last name?' '*Christ*.'" Ben drew out the word like the drunk had, way past exasperated into *are you fucking stupid?* "'Common spelling?' she asks, quick as a flash."

Laughter huffed from Rachel.

"That's what it's like, being a cop."

She made a little noise that might have been assent, or just an *I'm listening* noise. When their food arrived, she offered a story about an escapist goat, so he kept things light as the meal progressed. Nothing about the risks, the dark alleys or hallways with no backup, the furious tirade from his lieutenant for what he'd done today. Between them they finished the wine. He poured the last of it into Rachel's glass when dessert arrived. An alcohol flush stained her cheeks and lips, and her eyes were the slightest bit glassy as they studied him across the candlelit table. He signaled for the check as he watched the last bite of crème brûlèe disappear between her lush lips.

It was the oddest date he'd been on in recent memory . . . well, the only date he'd been on in recent memory. The first wave of exhaustion hit him. Lack of sleep, adrenaline crash, alcohol. But then they receded, and he found himself wondering exactly what it took to make a flush climb that dusky throat, make those serene eyes close in surrender.

"What's next?" she asked when the waiter brought the bill.

He paused in the act of pulling out his wallet and cut her a glance. "The Pleasure Pier's what you paid for, but lady's choice," he said casually.

She bit her full lower lip, but met his gaze head-on. "I'd like to go back to your place."

Her tone, low and clear, set his radar pinging because the words sounded almost rehearsed, but really, he didn't give a fuck. This was who he was, what he did, because he could do this. Ben thumbed through the twenties and left a small stack in the leather folder, then got to his feet and held out his hand, guiding her through the front door and into the parking lot.

"I'm in the truck," he said, pointing to his black crew cab F-150. "Stay close."

A small green Ford Focus, bearing the dimples of hail damage the body shop couldn't fix, pulled into traffic behind him and parked in one of the visitors' spots when they arrived at his apartment complex. She stayed silent as they climbed up the stairs to his apartment. He flicked on the entry light, then shrugged out of his jacket and draped it over the back of a dinette chair.

Rachel closed the door behind her. He turned to face her. "Want a beer?"

"I'm fine," she said. "Have you changed your mind?"

"About what?" he said, pretty sure he hadn't agreed to anything he would normally change his mind about.

"About going that far."

Never in his life had a woman checked in with him to make sure he was in the mood. "Maybe," he said. Amusement roughened his voice.

She reached past him to set her purse on the table. His cock shifted and thickened as she did. Then she looked at him, as if she wasn't sure what came next. Her hesitation amused him, so he beckoned her close. The play of muscle under the skin of her shoulders transfixed his gaze as her humid, earthy scent rose into his nostrils.

Lust. She smelled like risk, and lust, but he stopped cataloging scents when she went on tiptoe and pressed her full lips to his.

Mouth on mouth, her body aligned with his, heat shot straight to his cock. He wrapped one arm around her waist, holding her against him as her lips barely brushed his. The way her breath heated his mouth made the nerve endings there tingle, made him want more.

He took more, slanting his mouth across hers, dipping his tongue inside to touch hers, then licking the curve of her full lower lip. In the back of her throat she made the oddest, softest noise, somewhere between surprise and pleasure. Even through his T-shirt, dress shirt, and her dress he felt her heart kick hard against her breast.

"Very persuasive," he said when she pulled back to inhale shakily. His arm held her on her toes, kept his erection pressed to her stomach. She wore flat-soled shoes, another oddity in the days of obligatory fuck-me heels, so she had to tilt her head to look up at him. Uncertainty flared in those mysterious eyes.

"Really?" she said.

No need to tell her that tonight of all nights, he was a sure thing. Instead, he held her against him, studying her face, the parted lips, the pulse pounding at the base of her throat. No flirting, no teasing, no tempting. No licked lips. No dropping to her knees to talk him into it with a blow job. Just a heat, raw and intense, unlike any he'd ever felt before, simmering under her skin, authentic and true.

"Yeah."

"Good," she said simply. "Let's do it."

Perfect, because the exhaustion lurked at the back of his brain, waiting to take him down. Tonight his role came easily, a little badass, a little rough, very intense. He reached for the loose, off-kilter knot of hair behind one ear and worked his fingers into it, the better to hold her mouth exactly where he wanted it. He tasted white wine and scorched-sweet custard as his tongue swept into her mouth, then he dragged his lips across her jaw, getting that first taste of skin. She shuddered when he closed his teeth over her jaw, but he didn't let go of her hair, just walked down the hall with her feet inches off the floor, and tumbled them onto his bed.

She gasped when she landed on her back, again when his hand delved under the folds of her skirt to skim up her thigh. He brushed his thumb over her mound as he came down on top of her, then with the hand still fisted in her hair urged her head back to expose her throat. He licked and bit his way down her neck to the swell of her breasts above her bright copper neckline.

"Get this down," he growled. She blinked at him, her eyes still so shockingly catlike. It took his hand at the zipper at her back for her to get the point, then she arched into him, her hands fumbling for the tab. The zipper rasped down. He nuzzled into her firm, lush breasts, then flicked his tongue over her nipple, sparking another gasp, this one with a shuddering little noise at the end.

Her hands touched down at his waist, the pressure light until he found the right combination of teeth and tongue to make her slowly writhe under him. Then her grip tightened, tugging his shirt from his suit pants, then unbuttoning his shirt from the bottom. He solved the problem of too many clothes by kneeling on the bed and yanking two shirts and his tie over his head.

With one hand he took both of her wrists and pinned them over her head as he took in her disheveled state. Her hair was coming loose from the knot, streaming over his sheet, her pale breasts tipped with nipples reddened by his mouth. Her skirt had climbed to her thighs; with the other hand he smoothed it up, revealing black lace briefs. Still watching her face he tugged them down, baring her to his gaze.

When he slid his fingers into her soft folds, her eyelids fluttered. Her panties held her legs closed, and she made a soft, panicked noise when he found her mostly dry. Still holding her gaze, he brought his middle finger to his mouth and licked it, then started slow circles around her clit. For long moments her only response was long quivers running from breasts to thighs, then the nub began to swell under his finger. When he dipped lower, seeking the better lubrication of her own juices, this time he found her damp. One leg draped over hers, he rubbed against her hip as she quivered under his touch.

She wasn't ready. Getting there, but not ready, so he tugged her panties all the way off and slid between her thighs. But when he worked his hands under her ass, she struggled up on her elbows.

"No," she said. "Just . . . I want you inside me."

Something was off here, her responses out of kilter, either lagging behind or rushing, but her impatience spurred a very typical, very male response. He unbuckled his belt and freed his cock, rolled on a condom, then braced himself over her, his hands above her shoulders, his knees spreading her thighs even wider.

"Look at me," he said.

Her eyes widened but she did as he said as he aligned himself at her entrance and slid into her until he bottomed out. Tight. Jesus. So fucking tight, wet, tense, and trembling under him. He worked in and out of her, watching the tension grow in her face and body. Her hands gripped his upper arms, her eyes feral and unreadable, her breathing catching sharply as he moved harder, then faster. When her eyes slid closed, he said more sharply, "Look at me."

Her nails dug into his upper arms as her knees drew up, clamping around his hips. "Ben," she gasped.

Friction unmoored her hair from the loose bun as he fucked her, the strands glinting in the light from the parking lot coming through his windows. Her soft breasts bounced with each thrust, and the heated rush of sexual energy seared his veins. He wasn't a little drunk. Neither was she.

She was burning him alive.

He dropped to his elbows, gripped one leg, and opened her a little more. She gave a trembling, gasping laugh. He shifted his angle, but while he was on the edge, she was somewhere near it. In the vicinity. Not quite there.

Not too proud to ask for directions, he said, "Help me out here, Rachel," as he slowed.

Her hand clamped down on his nape as she bit the tendon in his neck. He froze, then her tongue traced a warm path up his neck to his ear. "Don't stop," she whispered, then bit the lobe. The unexpected pressure and sensation raced along his nerves, straight to his cock. With a long, low groan he plunged deep inside her one last time, then shuddered hard against her as he came.

And she didn't. She was trembling under him, still in that no-man's-land of near release.

"When I said help me out, that's not what I meant," he said when he got his breath back.

"It's fine," she said.

The relief he heard in her voice set off warning signals in his brain, but there were half a dozen reasons why girls came home with a cop, and getting off wasn't the only one.

He pulled out and rolled onto his back, stripping off the condom as he did. He dropped it in the trash can beside his bed, then lay there. Exhaustion hit him like a roundhouse punch so that when the bed tilted slightly under him for a split second he thought he was on the rescue boat, heading into the harbor. But it was just Rachel, getting to her feet. Zipping up her dress. Finding her panties in the wreck of his suit on the floor.

"You okay to drive? You can stay," he said.

"Oh, I couldn't possibly," she said when she straightened, black lace in her hand.

He wasn't one of those assholes who kicks a woman out the

second the condom hit the trash can, he thought, then realized in his stupor he'd actually said the words.

"I'm fine," she repeated, and backed out the door. "I'll lock up behind myself."

A pause by the dinette set where he assumed she was putting on her panties, the rustle of her purse and keys, then the sound of the doorknob.

The oddest fucking date of his life. He should at least get up and hang up his suit, then take a shower, but the bed sucked him down. The last thing he heard before he dropped into darkness was the click of the latch as the door closed.

Chapter Three

Rachel couldn't stop trembling. Unpredictable little tremors ran through her body, shoulders to toes, although whether they came from losing her virginity or the sheer waves of emotion crashing from Ben Harris, she didn't know. An uncertain little laugh stuttered from her throat.

Did I just do that? Did I just drive alone to meet him at a restaurant, unchaperoned? Did I just drink alcohol? Did I just break bread with him, go back to his apartment, kiss him? Because I kissed him first. I kissed him, I helped him take off his clothes, I spread my legs for him, and I had sex with him.

That wouldn't go in this week's letter to her father.

Did I just take a man not my husband into my body?

Then leave?

Did I just do that?

She knew it was unlikely for her to reach orgasm the first time she had sex, but still it had been intense, visceral, a full-body experience that left her shaking from the promise of something left unfulfilled. Two steps behind him every step of the way, she wished she had known how to tell him what she needed. It was probably for the best that she couldn't. Surrendering to the fever pitch of climax while awash on the waves of masculine energy pouring from Ben Harris would have blown her mind.

I did do that, and it was good. Oh dear Lord, it was good. I will do it again.

She'd fooled him. Thank goodness for Jess and her rack-by-rack knowledge of Galveston's secondhand stores. Her entire life, Rachel wore print blouses and full-length denim or khaki skirts, fabric that covered the shape of her body yet clearly marked her not only as a woman but a justified, righteous woman from Elysian Fields. She'd never chosen clothes because she liked the color or cut, or because they made her feel a certain way. But she'd loved that dress; the bright, shimmering copper color; the silky soft fabric; the way it covered her from collarbone to knees but clung to her at the same time. A dress with nuances led to feeling sexy, desirable. Normal. Just a woman . . . on a date . . . with a man.

The man who'd taken her virginity without a backward glance.

Shame should be making itself known now. She'd lain with a man outside the bounds of wedlock, without even a relationship. He was essentially a stranger. She should feel ashamed, but she drove through the darkness back to the farm with only a rising fury for company.

They'd kept this away from her. Her father, her pastor, all the male leaders of the community, the women who guided and taught her had kept this intimate, vibrant, shocking thing from her, and that made her furious. Or maybe some of the energy pouring from Ben still reverberated through her, lingering pings of sensation as parts of her body she'd never thought much about before took center stage in her awareness. A faint tingling from the scrape of his teeth over her nipples subsided as she left Galveston's brightly lit streets for two-lane highways, but the stinging sensation between her legs didn't ease.

Time, darkness, and solitude gave her space to process what had happened. Her lips throbbed from the pressure of his mouth. Ben's kiss was hard, demanding; as hard as the body she'd seen so briefly, thin skin stretched taut over muscle, sinew, and bone. She'd never seen an erection jutting thick and swollen from a nest of darker brown hair, and she'd certainly never felt one push into her body. Access to the Internet, which was tightly controlled at Elysian Fields, enabled her to familiarize herself with the things men and women could do together, but knowing and experiencing were worlds apart in this situation.

It was casual, and violent in a way she'd never expected, the way he held himself above her as he thrust, the way his hips slapped against her inner thighs. He held her where he wanted her with hands in her hair and hips spreading her open and the strong glide of his shaft into her body. It was unspeakable, and incomprehensible.

But that interested her, because that rough touch made her muscles coil like hot wire. She'd felt hot and achy and needy, a dark, *so-right* urge to cling to him as he moved.

It was hers, and hers alone. Authentic. Real. Not filtered through older women's whispered descriptions, older men's decisions or expectations. *Hers.*

She drove past the farm's main entrance to the dirt road leading to the employee parking and the rambling bunkhouse the interns shared each season. Jess's car was still gone, as was the truck shared by the two boys getting their degrees from Texas A&M. A single light burned over the bunkhouse's front door. Getting out of the car made her wince, but there was no one in the combined kitchen, dining area, and living room to notice her discomfort. She hurried into the room she shared with Jess to shed the dress and wrap herself in her cotton robe, then grab her shower caddy and head for the girls' bathroom.

Light from the full moon poured through the window, illuminating pine walls and faded linoleum. Once in the shower, she stood for a moment, head tipped back, eyes closed, and let the hot water stream over her. She lathered up her facecloth and washed her face until no traces of makeup remained, then soaped up again and gently cleaned the sore skin between her legs. A smear of blood lingered on the cloth, then disappeared under the spray.

She dried off and pulled her nightgown over her head, then risked another glance at the mirror. There was her face, the wide brown eyes and curved cheekbones, the sturdy chin and full mouth she recognized from her previous lifetime. She looked no different. A woman's most precious possession, according to her pastor and every other male authority figure in her life, the thing valued higher than rubies, more treasured than gold, was gone forever, and all she felt was a longing to know more.

Jess sat on her bed in her sleep shirt when Rachel walked back into their shared bedroom. "Hey," she said avidly. "How did it go?"

"Well," Rachel said. "The restaurant was really good."

"You went out with a hero, you know."

"I did? I thought you said he was bad news."

"Maybe he's both. He walked into a robbery in progress at a gas station. The guy had a gun and Officer Harris, an eight-year veteran of the department with an assignment to the SWAT team," Jess said, mimicking a newsreader's intonation, "punched him out. The guy had a gun and three hostages, and your date clocked him, like something out of a movie! The video is all over the Internet!"

Oh. Oh, oh, oh. And he'd told her about the poor homeless man instead. She let out a little laugh. Nuances. Unexpectedly, her "bad news" had them.

"What's so funny?" Jess asked.

"He didn't mention it. He didn't even hint at it."

"Weird," Jess said, then blinked expectantly, but Rachel said nothing more. She might still be living in a communal setting, but her body and mind were now private. Instead, she switched on the oscillating fan that was their air-conditioning, set the alarm for 4:45 a.m., crawled into her bed, and curled up under the thin sheet. When she closed her eyes, flashes of the night came back to her. Ben's smile. Flickers of lightning down low in her belly, hinting at the possibility of so much more. She'd gotten what she wanted, but now she wanted more.

Ben awoke to sunlight pouring through the open shades, and a bitch of a headache. The wicked cocktail of adrenaline, the post-fight crash, alcohol, and sleeping later than usual resolved into what felt like a posthole digger slamming away behind his left eye. He needed water, aspirin, and based on the lingering scent of Rachel's skin on his, a shower.

Rachel. Something about her, what happened, tapped away at his brain with about as much subtlety as the hammer.

Squinting against the bright light, he snagged a bottle of cold water from the fridge, then swallowed four aspirin, started the shower, and brushed his teeth in the dark. The toothpaste cut through the thick fur lining his mouth, and as long as he didn't move his head too quickly, the water and aspirin were cutting in, opening space for memories of the night to surface.

He wasn't usually that out of step with a woman, but then again, Rachel wasn't like most of the women he saw. He knew female cops.

He talked to the women at No Limits, and sometimes he fucked them. Rachel was neither cop nor No Limits girl. The expression on her face after he told her the story about the bum startled him, like she was thinking through all the angles and consequences for everyone, the clerk, the bum. Him.

Good thing you didn't tell her about what happened earlier.

Steam filled the bathroom as he bent over to rinse and spit. When he straightened, a darker stain on his shaft caught his attention. He blinked, but it didn't go away, so he turned on the light.

Dried blood ringed the base of his cock.

"What the fuck?" he said to himself, and strode back into the bedroom to peer into the trash can. Blood smeared down the side of the white bag lining the can where the condom dragged along the plastic. "Jesus Christ."

He'd woken up smeared with girl-juices and lube, with chocolate syrup and cherries. He'd woken up tangled up with one woman, two women, one girl and another guy. He'd woken up hungover, still drunk, battered and bruised with two broken ribs after a bar fight, and on one memorable occasion, when he'd fallen down a cement stairwell, drunk as fuck and trying to get some in a parking garage, he'd woken up in the ER getting stitches.

He'd never woken up to a woman's blood on his body.

He dredged his memory, searching for clues. He'd been a little fast, a little rough, but he'd done nothing, *nothing*, to make her bleed. She'd seemed unhurt, so . . . had she started her period? That would explain the hasty exit. Except . . . it didn't fit.

Except . . . there was another reason for a woman to bleed during sex. By the time he toweled off and dressed in jeans, boots, and a snap-front shirt, he'd decided to spend his day off driving out to Silent Circle Farm.

Probably she'd started her period.

Probably wasn't enough.

He braked hard in the same No Parking space because it was closest to the barn, and apparently karma wasn't going to fuck with him today, because Rachel emerged from the shade of the farm stand as he stepped out of the truck. Some dim part of his brain noticed that she looked like she had at the auction, jeans clinging to her ass, the neck of her thin green T-shirt dipping low, her hair held back from her face in two thick braids, like the woman from last night didn't exist.

Her eyes widened when he strode toward her. She didn't look happy to see him. He read faces for a living, so he knew.

"You still can't—" she started.

He cut her off by slamming the truck door. They met in the dusty space between the stand and his truck. "What the *fuck*?"

Her shoulders straightened. "Excuse me?" she said tartly.

"What happened last night?"

"You know what happened," she said.

He peered down at her through his aviator shades, knowing the sunlight winked off the mirrored glass. "I found blood this morning, Rachel," he said, but he wasn't going to offer her the easy out. He wanted to hear the truth from her. "I've been at this a long time, and I've never made a woman bleed before."

At that she looked away from him, then turned as if she was going to walk away. He knew. Was this who he'd become, a man who didn't notice a virgin in his bed?

He grabbed her upper arm, but dropped his hold as soon as she stopped moving. He took a deep breath, dug his fingers into his hipbones as he stared down at her. "Talk to me."

She looked around the parking lot, then said in a lowered voice, "I was a virgin. I didn't think you'd be able to tell. Most women don't bleed. I'm sorry I made you worry."

She turned to walk away, and he grabbed her arm again, because the implications stung like rubber bullets. "Wait a goddamned minute. You were a virgin and *you didn't tell me*?"

"I don't want to discuss this here," she said, glancing around the parking lot again.

"We're discussing it here," he said. "How virgin?"

"There are degrees of virginity?"

Well, yeah. A friend of his dated a girl who wanted to be a virgin on her wedding night but went wild for anal and could suck the leather off a baseball. The look in Rachel's eyes answered his question and kicked his brain into high gear.

Pure virgin.

And he stripped her, spread her legs, and fucked her. If he'd known, if he'd had any idea, he would have gone about things more gently.

Liar. If you'd known you would have sent her home right then and there. Then you would have texted someone who wouldn't leave a trace in your apartment, let alone on your body.

Who was a virgin at her age? He'd lost his at fifteen to a friend's older sister. Fifteen years ago. At least he could still remember her name. Sharlene. And why would a woman who'd stayed a virgin as long as—

Oh, sweet Jesus. "How old are you?"

Her chin lifted. "Twenty-five."

Relief nearly buckled his knees. But . . . why would a woman in her midtwenties bid on a bachelor at an auction to lose her virginity?

Fuck *why*. He didn't do *why*. The right thing to do, the logical, sensible thing to do was to put her behind him and go on with his life. Such as it was. She looked at him, those odd, whiskey-colored eyes so disorienting, and while he didn't look away, he dropped back into his head. He'd learned the trick a long time ago on his father's ranch, seeming to be present, interacting, even thinking, when he really wasn't there. Going through the motions.

Possible outcomes and consequences danced a crack-the-whip in his head. While he would have stopped if she'd changed her mind, some guys didn't. Some guys would have been even more oblivious than he'd been, made her do things she clearly wasn't ready to do. She could have been hurt, physically, emotionally. She could still be hurt, if she didn't learn what this was all about. "What the fuck were you thinking, auctioning your virginity to a total stranger?"

"Technically speaking, I wasn't auctioning my virginity to you. I was buying your experience."

Memories of *yeah, I go that far* echoed in his head. He looked aside, shook his head. "It was stupid, not to mention dangerous."

Usually people backed up when he talked like that. She met his gaze head-on. "It was mine to do with as I pleased."

He wasn't going to argue with that, not when she used that razor-sharp tone of voice, but still. He lashed down his temper. "You didn't think I should know."

"I didn't think you *would* know. Or care," she added, as if now was the time for brutal honesty. Maybe she'd seen more than he thought.

A tasty, dark cocktail of inexperienced virgin and his anger over being set up sizzled in his veins. He studied her, well aware of his physical response, not sure if he should act on it or not.

The fuck you're not sure.

In his peripheral vision he saw a man standing in the open door of the barn, a border collie at his side. Ben recognized him from the auction as the Silent Circle's owner. He gave him a short nod, then said, "I want another shot at it."

Rachel's eyes widened. "Did you really just say that to me?" she said tartly.

"After last night you're going to have a hard time convincing me you're after sweet talk and roses," he said. Her gaze narrowed, but he didn't think he'd insulted her. More like hit the nail on the head. "That's good, because I don't do sweet talk and roses. What I do is what you need."

"I am *not* your responsibility."

The concept of anyone being his responsibility was laughable, but the words echoed in his brain. It took a moment, then he remembered. Sam said the same thing to him the summer they turned sixteen. He flashed her the smile, the only one he had left, and said, "Damn straight you're not."

She bristled at his smile, the one various girls called annoying, shit-eating, cocky, arrogant, and asshat. "You don't know what I need," she said as she glanced toward the barn. The dog and the man were making their way up the dirt path toward the parking lot.

"I remember," he said without lowering his voice, "how you were shaking under me at the end. Look me in the eye and tell me you don't need more."

She went still again, stiller than he thought possible. The man, Rob Strong, was almost within earshot, and based on Rachel's tense posture, she didn't want to have this conversation with him around.

He lowered his voice just a little. "I want an explanation. You want to do it again. Longer. Slower. Hotter. This time we'll both get what we want."

Her face flushed. He paused, because Rob and the all-business border collie were within earshot, but the implication was there. He did owe her, and while she might be willing to let him off the hook, he wasn't.

"Officer Harris," Rob said, but he wasn't asking. He offered his hand, and Ben shook it. Ben ignored him until the dog looked up at him, then held out his fist for inspection. Tail drooping, the dog sniffed his hand. "Is there a problem?"

Rachel watched the collie with a small smile on her face, and when the dog turned to her, she got an enthusiastic tail wag and even a little jump. "Hey, George." She crouched to ruffle the fur behind his ears. "Everything's fine, Rob," she said then looked up at Ben. "So I'll see you tomorrow night?"

"Great," Ben said without missing a beat.

"I can't leave until seven, after milking, and I can't go far. The does are getting close to their due dates."

Rob and George watched this interchange, and Ben didn't want to stick around to argue.

"I'll pick you up," he said. "I know a place we can go that's close."

Chapter Four

"Off you go, Irene."

Rachel gently patted the pregnant goat's side, then released the stanchion holding Irene in the milking stand, where she'd trimmed her hooves. The goat trotted off the stand and out into the goat yard, giving Rachel a shake of her tail before rejoining the herd. Rachel collected her tools and headed for the barn, taking care to securely latch the fence leading into and out of the goat yard. Rob named the predominantly female goat herd after devastating hurricanes for good reason. One improperly latched gate or gap in the fence meant hours tracking down and reclaiming loose goats, although the neighbors usually knew whom to call by the ear tattoos. Irene, however, was known by sight all over the county.

Rachel wandered through a medley of spring on her way to the barn, birds chirping as they mated and built nests in the cotton-woods, the scent of sweet, dry hay rising into the sun-warmed air, the rich, not unpleasant aroma of manure worked into the various fields. While she loved the clear spring sunrises and the booming, elemental thunderstorms rolling across the plains, she wanted to be able to walk to a coffee shop, work a regular schedule, travel. Never again would she be isolated, alone, dependent on someone else, an older woman or a man of any age, for her living.

Ben Harris seemed as intent on teaching her as she was on learning.

Inside the barn's cold room she replaced the trimming shears in the equipment room, then began the process of rinsing and washing the dairy equipment, left over from the morning milking. Rob hoped the yogurts and cheeses produced by the herd of goats would become a cornerstone to his growing business, so they carefully monitored the milk for taste and quality. She'd done much the same thing at Elysian Fields, which ran a similar co-op between the families living on the property. Her father coordinated the care and production from the co-op's goat herds, although the women and girls in the various families did most of the day-to-day work. But it would be too easy to fall into routine here, and the price she'd paid to leave home was too high to settle for anything less than what she'd set out to find.

"How much did we get this morning?"

She looked up from the hot, soapy water to find Rob standing in the doorway, laptop in hand.

"A little less than yesterday," she said.

"Hmmm," he said absently.

His shaggy hair blended into the hay spilling from the loft overhead, but his hazel eyes stood out even in his suntanned face. They were the eyes of a man much, much older, projecting a calm self-assurance she found familiar. While he had every right to be in and out of every barn, pen, and field on the farm, Rachel suspected Rob showing up here and now had more to do with their unexpected visitor than the goat herd's milk production.

Ben was the last person she had expected to see late Monday morning, but a Ben prowling with tightly leashed energy shocked her. He wasn't supposed to be there, demanding to know what happened, demanding a second chance. He was supposed to be a player, not interested in a solemn, shy woman who was by most standards little more than plain. But the emotions crashing over her from the moment he slammed the door to his truck swept her away.

"I mailed your letter," Rob said.

"Thanks," she replied.

"Submit your app yet?"

"No."

"When's the deadline?"

"A couple of weeks," she hedged. "I'm still not sure my science classes are up to the school's standards."

"What did the admissions counselor say?"

"They make decisions on a case-by-case basis, and I could always take summer classes."

Rob smiled at her, so easy and assured. "So you apply and see what happens. That was your date from the auction, right?"

She nodded.

"How did things go?"

She couldn't think about last night in front of Rob, so instead she thought about Ben's heat and energy radiating at her like the Texas sun in August, the tense, clipped phrases, the emotion humming from him, the intensity under those watchful eyes. The little zing that zipped through her when he identified exactly what she wanted. "Fine," she said.

"Did he treat you right, Rachel?"

Rob had an old-fashioned sense of honor. She thought about how best to answer that question before saying, "He was a perfect gentleman. You should up the ration of concentrate. They'll need more nutrition as they get closer to kidding."

Rob closed the laptop's lid, then smiled at her, a crooked, understanding smile that respected her privacy and her boundaries. But Ben didn't. He'd smashed through her boundaries as effectively as he'd held her off at the auction. She didn't buy that she owed him an explanation. What made her agree to his demand for a second chance was Rob walking out of the barn. Her single encounter with Ben gave breadth and depth to her inexperience, something she'd naïvely assumed would disappear once she had sex. She'd have to explain that to the next man, and the next man would be like Rob, caring, compassionate, making a big deal out of her background and her inexperience.

Ben knew. Knew what she needed, and wanted her to have a better time.

"Hey, George," she said as she rinsed the last piece of tubing and laid it in the drainer to dry. The dog trotted into the room and leaned against her calf, peering up at her as she emptied the sink. "Okay, I'll pet you."

She crooned nonsense words at him while scratching the soft fur behind his ears. After a moment he nuzzled into her hand, then took himself to a spot where he could keep an eye on both Rob and the activity in the parking lot out the big, wide-open barn doors, and sat down to wait.

"He won't usually sit still for petting," she said.

"Maybe he thought you needed it," Rob said with a smile. "I was pretty surprised when you bought one of the men from the auction. Are you ready to date—"

"Oh, I'm not dating him," she said, cutting him off.

Rob lifted one eyebrow. "You're seeing him again tomorrow night."

"It's not a date. It's . . ." She cast around for a reasonable explanation for a man like Ben to drive thirty minutes out of town then ask her out again, one that didn't include a second shot at sex, and came up blank.

Silence stretched between them. "When you're ready to date, let me know," he said, giving her a slow smile completely unlike Ben's slashing, seductive grin, yet no less potent. Heat flooded her cheeks and danced low in her belly. He was handsome, gentle, kind. Good with animals. Everything she was supposed to need and want, and yet he saw a fragile girl. Ben saw . . . what? "I like that we're friends," she said. "I need friends."

When she left Elysian Fields she hadn't left just her father, but an entire extended community of friends, prayer partners, accountability partners. Women she liked, even loved, and respected. She'd gotten exactly what she asked for: independence. But independence was terribly lonely sometimes.

Disappointment flashed momentarily in Rob's eyes, then was replaced with his usual good humor. "I thought I'd head up to the stand and help get ready for the evening rush," she said.

"Good plan." He snapped his fingers for George and took himself off into the fields, while Rachel walked up the hill. A week ago, she'd had no men in her life. Now she had one man who made her feel alive, and another who made her feel safe.

You've chosen to live. No more fear. No going back, not until you know why you should.

And no more deception. No more fancy dresses or sultry eye makeup or even lipstick. Tomorrow night she would go out with Ben Harris as herself, nothing more, nothing less, and explain herself to him.

• • •

The sun hung low in the sky when Ben's truck pulled into the Silent Circle Farm parking lot. A plume of dust rose in its wake, turning the light a dusky orange. Rachel hurried up the path leading from the employee bunkhouse to the parking lot and stepped through the picket gate, grateful he was a little late. She'd needed the time to shower and change into a plain cotton blouse and skirt. Ben rolled down the passenger window. Mouthwatering aromas of fried chicken, biscuits, and mashed potatoes drifted to her nose. Mirrored shades hid his eyes completely, but his mouth was set in a firm line.

"You sure about this?" he asked.

"I'm sure," she said.

The lock clicked. She opened the door and settled into the passenger seat, then carefully secured her seat belt. When the car didn't move, she looked at Ben, and let her gaze linger on all the places she wasn't supposed to look. He wore another western shirt unsnapped partway down his firmly muscled chest, this one in a faded blue pattern, jeans pulled tight across his hips and thighs, a brown leather belt, and boots. The ever-present shades hid his eyes again, and he hadn't shaved since the morning. Dark stubble lay along his jaw, around his full lips. Heat cracked low in her belly as she looked her fill, flickered to flame when his mouth softened ever so slightly. Like he was thinking about kissing her, or better, thinking about her kissing him.

When the truck didn't move, she spoke. "Is something wrong?"

"You have a curfew I need to know about?" he asked with a nod out her still-open window.

Rob stood in the open door to the hayloft, one arm braced against the frame, the other hand on his hip. George sat on the barn floor one story below him, ears perked and head cocked in a similarly vigilant posture. She lifted her hand and waved tentatively. Rob gave her a short nod in response. George didn't move.

"No," she said to Ben. "I don't have a curfew. The chicken smells delicious."

"It's from a hole-in-the-wall diner near the station. You hungry?"

"Very. Rob sent one of the A&M boys into town to pick up the Truck Garden. Jess took his place in the fields, and I was alone at the stand. It feels good to sit down."

Without taking his gaze from the highway stretching in front of them, he reached into a big white paper sack in the backseat and pulled out a cardboard tray of fried cheese balls. "Help yourself. We're going to be driving for a little while."

She popped a cheese ball in her mouth and bit down gingerly. The flavor of bread crumbs, jalapeños, and mozzarella cheese spread over her tongue. "Hot," she said, fanning her open mouth, then took the bottle of water he extended, cracked the seal, and swallowed.

"Too spicy?"

"I wasn't expecting that," she said, and ate the second one more gingerly.

He gave her a crooked grin and plucked a couple of larger curds from the container, but didn't say anything else. They drove farther north and west from Galveston, into Hill Country. Ben seemed to know exactly where they were going, braking to turn off the state highway onto two ruts through pastureland that gradually descended down to a creek bed. What appeared to be shrubs from the road were actually cottonwood trees. Ben parked the truck in a gap in the trees, nose pointing toward the nearly dry creek bed. Thick trunks rose around them, the branches arching in a canopy over-head, gilding the thick, humid air in greenish gold.

"Where are we?" Rachel asked.

"The back pasture of the Bar H ranch," Ben said, and turned off the truck's engine. "*H* as in Harris. This is my dad's place."

The leaves rustled in the breeze, the noise amplified when he powered down the windows. "Why are we here?"

He gave her that smile again. "I lost my virginity here," he said. "The summer I was fifteen. A friend's older sister had the keys to her daddy's truck. She used to sneak out, pick me up at the end of the driveway. We'd park down here. Good memories. I thought maybe we'd make you a good memory here. But you're hungry, so we should eat first."

He snagged the bag of food and got out of the truck. She met him at the truck's tailgate, where he handed her the food and unlatched the tailgate while her stomach growled. He took the food from her and set it in the bed, then turned to her and put his hands on her waist. "Up you go," he said, and boosted her onto the tailgate.

Heat from the truck's undercarriage swirled around her feet. She gripped the edge of the tailgate and waited while he hopped up next to her. She reached for the sack of food, but he held it out of reach.

"You're not dying, are you?"

"What?" she gasped. "No, I'm not dying. Not that I know of, anyway. Why would you think such a thing?"

He shrugged, then set about laying out the food between them. Crispy fried chicken, mashed potatoes with a container of gravy, corn, baked beans. "I didn't know if you liked tea, sweet tea, beer, or water, so I brought them all."

"Tea, please," she said. "Why would you think I was dying?"

"Because in the movies women who stay virginal until they're twenty-five, then suddenly go wild, are usually dying of cancer or some other disease where they get attractively thin and pale."

"I didn't decide to have sex because I'm dying," she said firmly.

"Good."

He handed her a bottle of tea and a paper plate. She helped herself to a smallish breast piece and a little bit of everything else, attempting to eat the chicken with the tips of her fingers and her flimsy plastic fork until it became clear the only thing to do was tear it apart. She pulled the skin off and ate it, sneaking glances at Ben while she chewed. He ate without seeming to notice her interest, until he cut her a glance as he tipped back his second bottle of beer.

"So, Rachel Hill, why were you a twenty-five-year-old virgin?"

No polite small talk to ease her into anything, just a demand for the explanation she owed him. He'd walled off, as if the place was good for her, but not him. The scent of clean sweat rose from his skin to mingle with dirt and water and tree. She finished her mouthful of baked beans and said, "Because I was saving myself for marriage."

He looked at her. "We're not married, so keep going."

"Because I believed premarital sex was as much of a mortal sin as murder," she said.

A huff of laughter, but no more. "Religious?"

"Very."

"But now you're not."

That was a very, very good question. She missed some of it. The singing that used to permeate her days and dreams. The certainty. Who was she outside the beliefs and community that defined her entire world? "I'm not sure," she said honestly. "Not like I was. Are you?"

He gave a short, hard laugh. "With the exception of weddings and funerals I haven't been in a church since I moved out of the house to go to college."

She nodded, and selected another piece of chicken. In the sheltered world of Elysian Fields, everyone went to Sunday services. In the outside world, almost no one she knew went to church. Jess and the A&M boys went back to bed after morning chores. Rob disappeared in the middle of the day. Rachel didn't know what to do with herself. Working felt wrong. So did church.

"Did you grow up around here?"

"Are you familiar with Elysian Fields?"

One eyebrow lifted. "The Fundamentalist community west of Rosharon? Yeah."

"I lived there until six months ago."

Both eyebrows lifted at that. He finished his mouthful of chicken and swiped at the grease left on his chin before saying, "Huh. Why did you leave?"

Most people didn't ask that question because they assumed any sane person would bolt from a community like Elysian Fields. They wanted details about wearing only modest dresses and skirts, about a homeschool education, about the blessing she knelt to receive from her father at the end of every day, about her daily routine in the kitchen or on the farm. They wanted to know why she'd never cut her hair above elbow length, and how she'd never been alone with a man other than her father and her pastor. She'd spent the first couple of months in the world feeling like a sideshow at the circus.

Ben asked the hard question, the one she didn't have a good, simple answer for. *They needed me to be someone I am not. They expected me to surrender all choice and control in my life to God, and if God's direction wasn't clear, my pastor or my father would explain it to me.* But on the days when she felt some winged creature inside her, talons latched around her heart, beating its wings against her ribs, safety and salvation seemed distant, and untouchable. "I didn't fit in anymore," she said.

"That can't have been easy," he said noncommittally.

"It wasn't." She thought of her weekly letter now making its way to the community's shared mailbox. "Science was the downfall. I'm willing to grant that the complexity of the natural world is a gift from God, but science is science. I wanted to know and understand, to dissect and analyze, but when I pushed I'd run into roles that functioned like walls. I didn't need to take chemistry or physics or biology because my role was to be a wife and mother. Not that I don't want to be a wife and a mother, but I want other things, too. I'd reached the point where leaving was easier than staying," she finished, as if either option were easy. "I still don't know what to do with myself when chores are finished on Sunday mornings. The whole day feels wrong."

He said nothing, as if her story of leaving rubbed him the wrong way, or maybe he was just the strong, silent type. A few minutes later he'd made a big dent in the box of chicken, and she'd finished off her first helping.

"Outside of the auction, a girl like you wouldn't have anything to do with me," he said, giving her a sidelong glance as he cleaned his hands on the wet wipes from the bottom of the bag.

"And here I was thinking you wouldn't have looked twice at me if I hadn't bought your date."

He did them both the courtesy of not denying her assertion while he sorted the leftovers from the trash. She came with too much baggage, and she knew it. That's why she'd bought a man at an auction to lose her virginity. "Thank you for dinner," she said, "but you don't have to go through with this."

Ben slid off the tailgate and turned to face her. The look in his eyes made her heart thump against her breastbone.

"So, Rachel Hill, former virgin of Elysian Fields, before you and I had our date, what had you done?"

Chapter Five

Fingers firmly gripping the tailgate edge again, she inhaled, slow and deep. "Nothing."

"Nothing?"

"Purity of mind, body, and soul were paramount, so boys and girls were never alone together. When couples started courting, their relationships were supervised. In most cases they didn't even hold hands before they married. I wasn't courted."

His eyebrows drew down, as if this was somehow a slight to her honor. "Why not?"

His genuine bemusement at this made her smile. "I asked too many questions."

He stood in front of her, long legged and lean hipped, broad through the shoulders, his dark brown hair smoothed flat against his forehead. Sweat shone in the hollow of his throat. He wasn't smiling when he said, "What do you want to do?"

Emotion crystallized into a word. *Desire*. "I want to kiss you."

Something like amusement made his eyelids droop and the corners of his mouth lift in a grin far less dangerous than his flashing, slashing smile. The tailgate remedied the difference in their heights. Sitting down she was slightly taller than he was, standing on the uneven dirt ground sloping down to the trickling creek behind him. He braced his hands on the tailgate, not quite touching her but nonetheless amping up the vibrations resonating in her chest. "So kiss me."

No hesitation, no guidance. He expected her to know and take what she wanted, assumed she had the courage and strength to do just that. She bent forward, and paused. She smelled dry grass, the faint dampness coming from the creek, dust, oil and gasoline from the engine, but mostly she smelled Ben's skin and sweat rising from the open collar of his shirt. The closer she leaned the more concentrated it got, and the heat of his body intensified it.

His mouth was closed, but she got the sense it wouldn't take much pressure to open them. His restraint gave her the courage to close her eyes, lean in, and brush her lips over his.

Sparks fired under her skin.

He still didn't move, so she did it again, grazing her mouth over his again and again, getting lost in the skittering sparking sensation in her lips, the way it spread down her throat, slackening her jaw as it did. He mimicked her, opening his mouth slightly, and now his breath mingled with hers.

So intimate, those soft exhales right into her mouth, faintly yeasty from the beer, a hint of residual heat from the jalapeño poppers. As if the memory of the spice made her want more, she hesitantly touched her tongue to the tip of his.

A short but definite halt to his breathing. She paused, unsure of herself, afraid to look at him.

"Keep going." Low and rough. An intimate command. This time she slipped her tongue between his lips straightaway, and stroked his once, twice. When she pulled back, his tongue followed hers into her mouth, and suddenly she couldn't breathe. Her pulse pounded, blood heating.

This time he pulled back. Without thinking she lifted her hand to brush her thumb across his lower lip.

"You like?"

She nodded, then put her hands on his shoulders and kissed him again, more sure of herself now, frankly eager for the heat. The rush. The kiss deepened as he followed her lead, never insisting, always tempting. Her fingers curled into his shirt collar when his teeth closed gently on her lower lip. She drew back to look into his eyes. Unapologetic desire simmered there, so she did the same to him, nipping hesitantly at his lower lip, coming back immediately for a sharper bite. Then, driven by an impulse she couldn't name, she licked the reddening spot.

A low groan rumbled in his throat before he swallowed it. "Jesus," he said.

His hard shaft strained against his faded jeans. She opened her knees to him. With both hands he gripped her bottom and slid her forward, plastering them together from hips to lips.

She got a little lost in the kissing that followed, as if the gilded spring air seeped through her skin and into her blood, drugging her. His teeth clacked against hers as his tongue brushed the roof of her mouth, setting off a teasing sensation that emerged as a gasp when he dragged his mouth from hers and laid openmouthed kisses along her cheek to her ear. His hands left her hips for her jaw, cupping her ears so that her heart and breathing sounded like waves. She curled her fingers through his belt loops and pressed against him. With each quick inhale his abdomen brushed hers, while his chest pressed firmly against her breasts and his shaft notched between her thighs. Hard to her soft, everywhere.

Ben paused, hands on her jaw, breathing deeply, and for a moment her attention crystallized on the heat between her legs, the sense of longing. One hand left her jaw to skim down her back and press against her tailbone. The pressure sent sensation crackling through her, and she gasped.

"What is this?" she asked. She wanted to rub up against him. She wanted to see him, touch his bare skin. She wanted . . .

He gave a low laugh she felt rumble in his chest as much as heard in her ears. "Chemistry," he said, and lifted his head to look at her. "This is some kind of wicked chemistry."

His mouth was swollen, wet from hers, and the thought that she'd used her mouth to make it that way sent heat wicking through her.

"Still with me?" he asked.

Yes. Oh yes. "I want more."

A smile quirked the corners of his mouth. "Come on," he said, and helped her down from the back of the truck. Sliding the passenger seat as far forward as it could go, he climbed in the back bench seat and sprawled out with his broad shoulders wedged against the window.

She took the hand he held out and clambered awkwardly into the space to kneel beside him. "Is this okay? No one will see us, right?"

He shook his head and pointed out the windshield at the dirt tracks curving up the hill. "Private property, in pastureland that's fallow, plus I can see any vehicle that comes over the hill. C'mere."

Looking into those spectacular blue eyes as she parted her legs and straddled him felt as intimate as the hot, licking kisses. She looked at his pulse, thumping at the base of his strong throat. "Can I touch you?"

"Sure," he said.

She bent and put her hands on his shoulders and her mouth to the side of his neck, just below his ear. Lips open, she touched him with the tip of her tongue. She'd never used her tongue to taste and touch at once. The skin just below his rough jaw was surprisingly soft and damp with salty sweat. A groan reverberated soft in her ears, and against her mouth, then his hands settled on her hips. Another long, vibrating moment while she scraped her teeth ever so gently against the tendon, then his big hands tightened. She filed his response away, and moved on.

Desire expanded inside her, and when she moved to his mouth she felt a matching response in the hot, slow kiss. She slid her palms over his shoulders to his pectorals. Heat and strength radiated through the cotton, into her skin as she toyed with the pearl snaps running down the length of his chest and abdomen to disappear behind his belt buckle.

"Go on."

The click of the snap releasing sounded loud in the truck's cab. Heat flared in her cheeks, but she didn't stop. He leaned forward when she spread the fabric so she went all the way, tugging his shirt down his arms and off.

Her breath scudded from her throat. The scent of clean skin and sweat, his taste lingering on her tongue, the sound of his breathing. She trailed her index finger from the hollow of his throat down his breastbone, over abdominal muscles covered with the thinnest layer of skin to his belt buckle. His hand covered hers, held it flat against his button fly. Heat and hardness strained against her palm.

"Not yet," he said. "My turn first."

He went to work on the buttons of her blouse, his touch very matter-of-fact, and in a few moments the shirt hung open, revealing her basic beige cotton bra. One dark brow lifted, and she nodded, not trusting herself to speak. He reached behind her, unhooked the fastener, and in seconds she was bare from the waistband of her cotton skirt to her hair. Then he unfastened her braid, first tugging the elastic from the end, then working the sections loose to send it tumbling around her shoulders. Her hair, as long and thick and straight as a horse's tail, slid forward into her face, sheltering her a little. Based on the way his shaft flexed against her, he liked the peek-a-boo game it played with her breasts. Heat flickered to life between her legs, and she shifted.

Call-and-response, her body to his and back again. Layers upon layers of pleasure and sensation.

He wove his fingers through her hair so the ends protruded like the bristles of a brush. Then, his gaze locked with hers, he stroked the soft undercurve of her breast, the touch gentle, slow, his rough knuckles a hard counterpoint to each caress. Her mouth went dry and her nipple hardened. He wrapped more hair around his other hand and did the same thing to her other breast until her eyes drooped, then closed, and her breathing shallowed.

Crickets chirped, the leaves rustled in the trees, and what little water flowed through the brook burbled under the breeze as her attention slowly focused to the *strokestrokestroke* of her own hair on her flesh. Molten heat coursed along newly awakened nerves, then pooled in places she didn't know could hold such desire.

His hands cupped her breasts, not nearly as shocking with her skin already sensitized, her body growing hot, needy. But when his thumbs slowly brushed her nipples, back and forth, back and forth, her head dropped forward, sending her hair into her face.

"Talk to me," he said.

She tipped forward and rested her open mouth on Ben's. His tongue flickered out, caressing her lower lip, then dipped inside to touch hers before retreating again.

"It's good," she breathed. "So good."

His lips moved under hers. "Yeah," he said. The word came out knowing, confident, masculine.

His palms cupped her knees, then slid up her thighs and under her skirt to grip her bottom. A few moments of shifting and he lay back on the bench seat with Rachel draped against him. The precarious position rolled her nearly full length against his body from chest to knees, her bare breasts to his exposed torso. He cupped the back of her head with one hand and held her mouth to his for kiss after hot, wet kiss. She flattened her palm against his abdomen. Hot, damp skin stretched over shifting muscle.

His fingers worked her skirt up to her hip, then slid into her panties to gently stroke her belly, then the damp curls at the top of her sex. She shuddered, and his movements slowed. "You'd never been touched here."

"No."

"No wonder you didn't want me to go down on you."

Her eyes opened enough to meet his blue gaze. He wasn't apologizing, or justifying, or blaming her. Just stating facts, calmly and certainly, as his fingers spread her soft folds. The first time she'd been unprepared for the hot flashes of pleasure expanding under his fingertip. This time she knew, anticipated, needed.

"I wasn't paying attention to you. But I am now," he said as his finger arrowed in on a particularly alive spot.

Her breath caught as she shuddered, and the flames leapt higher in his eyes. Her thighs clenched and her hips shifted forward, into his hand. She rolled forward and rested most of her weight against his body. One finger dipped lower, and this time when his finger slid against that bundle of nerves, moisture eased his way. He set a slow rhythm, taking his time, careful and measured, and heat built between her thighs. He kissed her and he touched her, tongue and finger and body working together to draw her down into the vortex.

But she was taking more than she gave. "I still want to touch you," she said.

This time when she reached for his belt buckle he didn't stop her. The buckle was a straightforward silver, the seams and pressure points of his button-fly jeans nearly as white as the clasp. She fumbled with the buckle but the fly opened easily, the button holes frayed and worn. As she moved down the placket the backs of her fingers rubbed against something hot and hard and still foreign.

She flicked him a glance. His gaze was still relaxed, heavy lidded, sensual. He lifted his hips, and she tugged his jeans and cotton shorts down just far enough to release his shaft. The wind pushed air through the truck's open doors, over their bodies. Her hair lifted, then caught on her mouth.

"May I?" she asked as she tugged the strands free.

"All yours, honey."

She gathered her wayward hair and swept it behind her shoulder, then trailed her fingers down his ridged abdomen to the shaft straining up from the thicket of brown hair between his legs. Hesitantly she wrapped her fingers around it, squeezing, exploring texture and hardness, the softness of the sac below. After a few moments his hand covered hers. He looked deep into her eyes as he taught her how to touch him, gripping the shaft more firmly than she would, cupping his testicles, then back to the shaft, where he set a slow rhythm. Then he lifted both hands to her head and drew her mouth down to his. This time she took the lead kissing him, and learned yet another way to build the pleasure. He jerked under her as she licked the soft curve of his mouth and moved her hand up and down.

Finally his hand landed on hers, halting her midstroke. His hand slid back into her panties. With two fingers he circled her soft opening, but when the fingers delved inside, she inhaled sharply.

His gaze searched hers. "Hurt, or surprised?"

"Surprised," she said. "Don't stop."

Those winter-sky-blue eyes never left hers as he gently, slowly worked his fingers in and out. His thumb brushed her clitoris with each subtle movement. Before long her eyes closed, so she felt his hand slide into her hair to cup the back of her head and hold her mouth to his. He didn't kiss her, just let the sweet, tantalizing promise of his mouth brushing hers provide the counterpoint to the smooth stroke of his fingers inside her. Then his fingertips slid over a hot, electric spot inside.

This time the noise was part gasp, part throaty moan. He did it again; again and without conscious thought she responded. Arched her back so her aching nipples brushed his chest. Touched her tongue to his. Undulated in his grasp. Her sex brushed his shaft as she moved, the heat and promise teasingly close, never far from her body, her mind.

"Feel good?"

She gave a half laugh, half gasp, because it felt like nothing she'd experienced before.

Nuances. Nuances would be the death of her.

He withdrew his hand, and she opened her eyes. Moisture gleamed on his fingers and she watched, dazed, as he touched her nipples, transferring the juices to her skin. Then he lifted his head and licked them. Between the muscles in his chest and abdomen flexing and the sensation of his tongue and teeth on her nipples, every nerve in her body lit up. She was past the point of need she'd reached the last time. Her blood slipped hot and thick in her veins, and sensation simmered between her legs.

"Why did you stop?"

He groped on the floor for his wallet, opened it, and extracted a condom packet. "Because when you come I'm gonna be inside you," he said as he opened the packet and rolled the latex down his shaft. His hands gripped her hips as he centered her over his shaft. "Slow," he cautioned.

This time the stretch was delicious, a promise fulfilled. She sank down, pausing when the burn threatened to become pain, felt her body clench around this unfamiliar thickness, then lifted up again, slid down. He wasn't all the way inside her, but it felt good. Powerful, something to claim, not hide from, or reject out of hand.

"Tilt your hips back," he said. His voice seemed to be part of the descending twilight, deep blue and as smooth as the rhythm. She did as he suggested, and on the next descent his shaft glided over that hot spot inside.

"Oh. Oh yes."

His fingers tightened on her hips. She couldn't tell if he held her to prevent her from rushing or because he liked the feedback of feeling her slide down his shaft, but the next time she took him all the way inside.

"Go on," he growled. "Take it."

Yes. This. Oh yes, this. Keep it slow at first, feel heat and pressure build. Feel your head drop back. Feel your skin heat up and glow. Feel him inside you, yours for the taking. Feel want grow into demand, demand swell into need.

Feel.

She was gasping, trembling, overwhelmed, unsure what was coming or how to get there, knowing only that she had to have it. Ben flattened one hand at the base of her spine while the other skated over her hip. Once again his thumb pressed firmly against her clitoris. With her next downstroke her skin tightened and on the next, fire raced from her core along her nerves as she tipped over the edge, her swollen walls clenching around Ben's length. Soft cries echoed in the truck's back seat. Only when the release began to ebb did she realize they came from her.

When she opened her eyes she blushed, hard, because based on his face he'd watched . . . everything. She ducked her head to let her hair slip over her face.

"No," he said, and tucked it behind her ear. "That was hot. That was very, very hot. Now do the same thing for me."

The demand made her blush harder, but she eased back into the rhythm, and studied his face for cues. Faster, or slower? Hard, or soft?

Sweat trickled from his temple to his jaw. She remembered his response to her teeth, leaned forward and licked the bead from the stubble, then closed her teeth on his jaw. His big body shuddered under her, so she did it again, testing the edge of her teeth along his jaw, then more gently on his lower lip, and all the while she took him into her body with no other goal than returning the pleasure back to him, of making him feel what she felt.

His shaft throbbed inside her and his hands closed hard on her buttocks. His head tipped back, exposing his throat. She took advantage, biting the straining tendon before licking the hurt to soothe it. Emboldened, she braced her hands on his shoulders and dug her fingernails into the taut muscles. A shudder rolled through him. He'd held himself entirely still under her, but with the sting of her nails his hips lifted into her as she slid down.

Now she got it. Slow, but hard. Impact like hammer strikes with body and mouth, and she could make him lose control like she did. Her next moves matched his intensity, and moments later a blood flush bloomed on his cheekbones as he fought to keep his eyes open. Reveling in the delight and desire coursing through her body, she rode him until his arm locked around her hips as he pulsed inside her.

She eased forward to lie against his heaving chest until the tension in his muscles eased. There was so much power to this, female power.

No wonder this wasn't allowed.

"Off," he said.

Their bodies disengaged when she sat back on her heels at the far end of the bench seat. In one smooth motion he shifted upright, then out of the cab. His motions were hidden but she assumed he was removing the condom. He added something to the sack of trash generated by their picnic, then jerked his jeans up and buckled his belt.

Modesty kept her from leaving the truck until she found her bra and blouse on the floorboards and put them on. He turned his back to her, running his hand from crown to forehead before buttoning his shirt. She stepped into her panties, tucked in her blouse, smoothed down her skirt. Hands on his hips, he gazed across the creek at the fallow pastureland.

"Do you want to say hi to your parents? It's a long drive out here without stopping in for a moment."

He looked at her. A muscle jumped in his jaw. "No."

For the first time that night an embarrassed flush swept up her neck, into her cheeks. Of course he wouldn't want to stop in and say hello to his folks with the woman he'd spent two hours rolling around in the back seat of his pickup truck.

"I could stay in the truck," she offered, trying to make it better.

A long moment passed, then without looking at her he slammed shut the tailgate. Metal clanged against metal, shocking the silent night air and startling her nearly out of her skin.

"Sorry."

"It's fine," she said. The breeze tossed her hair into her face; without thinking she quickly tamed it into a loose French braid she bound off halfway down her back. Arms braced on the tailgate, he watched her, but this time there was no pleasure in his eyes. Now they were the color of the sky during an icy cold snap. Blue frost.

"Ready?"

"Yes," she said.

She opened the passenger door and climbed inside. He stepped up into the driver's seat. They drove back to Silent Circle, music from an alternative rock station filling the silence between them. She directed him to the next driveway down, the direct road to the apprentices' bunkhouse, and gripped the door as they jounced through the potholes.

"You're angry," she said. It was a guess, more than anything else. Elysian Fields didn't just restrict choices in hair or dress or sexual activity. Everyone spoke with soft voices, said only kind words. Harsh feelings were reason for prayer, and certainly weren't vocalized. Not that Ben was actually speaking. But whether he realized it or not, emotion carved the line of his jaw, the thin set of his mouth, the rigidity of his shoulders. And while he'd looked much the same thirty minutes earlier, just before she brought him to orgasm, this was different. Very different.

"Nothing to say."

"All right." She opened the passenger door. Hot air rushed from the truck's undercarriage up her calves as she slid out of the truck.

He stopped her before she could close the door. "Rachel."

She turned to look at him over her shoulder. The interior light cast his square jaw and forehead in planes and shadows. "You're going to confuse it with love. It's not. It's sex."

"Actually, I don't think I will," she said. "I know what love feels like. That wasn't love."

He looked out the windshield, then gave a little laugh, the flashing, daring smile's dark and jaded cousin.

"Why did you do this?"

"Because I could," he said with a shrug.

Her eyes narrowed slightly and her lips pursed as she considered this.

"That pisses off most girls, you know. It's supposed to piss you off."

"My train of thought derailed back at the idea of having sex just because you could. I'll think about that for a while," she said. She slid down to the parking lot's dirt. "Thank you for a nice evening," she said, and closed the passenger door.

By the time she opened the bunkhouse's door, Ben's truck was raising dust on the dirt road back to the highway.

Chapter Six

Ben stood outside No Limits watching the bouncers handle the door. A line contained by a red velvet rope stretched from the front door along the brick exterior to the corner nearest the parking lot. The door staff, both muscle-bound bruisers, maintained an orderly line and for the most part kept things under control in the bar. Ben and his partner Steve, another off-duty Galveston cop, were there for when things got really out of hand.

Nothing that happened at No Limits was as dangerous as setting foot on the Bar H for the first time since he moved out. He'd taken Rachel out there because it was private and quiet, and to prove to himself that the ranch meant nothing to him. As casual as he'd been to her, he'd been facing off with danger down by the creek, in more ways than one. She smelled like danger, like thunderstorms and lightning and abandonment, a scent he'd learned to be wary of on the Bar H.

The door opened to let patrons out into the parking lot, and club music thumped into the hot night air. Ben glanced up, using eight years of experience to assess the sobriety of five women leaving the club. Four of the five teetered on their heels, but the one who shepherded her friends to a Jeep Cherokee and got behind the wheel was sober. Until Linc Sawyer bought the bar two years ago, No Limits had had a reputation for sex acts both inside and outside, and a higher-than-average number of DUI arrests and accidents for people leaving the premises. GPD logged more calls to No Limits than any other bar in the county. But Linc had fired the manager and all the bartenders, implemented strong policies about cutting off drunks, hired bigger bouncers, and added off-duty cops for consequence while improving the sound system and marketing the hell out of the place. As a result, the city's hottest nightclub had the fewest number of incidents related to alcohol while gaining a reputation as the place to go for a hot hookup.

Most nights the work was five hours of boring punctuated by the occasional ninety seconds of action. Stand outside and use the uniform to discourage fights, drunk driving, and parking lot hookups. Steve relieved the tedium with a Facebook addiction. Ben scanned the line, then the parking lot, keeping his behavior-detection skills sharp.

A familiar blonde, tall, slender, and dressed in a halter top and tight black skirt, detached herself from a pack of similarly dressed friends, ducked under the rope with considerable grace for a woman in heels and a microskirt, and had a short conversation with the bouncer. He nodded, then when she headed across the parking lot for them, gave Ben and Steve one raised eyebrow. Ben didn't need special training to determine her intent. Every cop on the force knew Juliette, or a woman like her.

"Incoming," Steve said under his breath. "Say yes this time."

Ben didn't move a muscle, just watched her walk, tugging down her skirt as she moved. Legs to her ears, and as the Gulf breeze caught the silky fabric of her halter, flashing hints of perky curves. With her lifted palm turned outward she brushed her hair away from her cheek, the gesture simultaneously feminine, vulnerable, and flirtatious.

He couldn't imagine Rachel doing anything that calculatingly female. Then again, he'd completely misjudged her. Twice.

"Hi," Juliette said when she drew near, stretching the single syllable out.

"Hi," Steve said in response, checking her out from heels to hair.

"I heard about the gas station," she said to Ben, then looked back at the pack of girlfriends she'd brought to the bar. "My hero. After we close this place down we should party."

"Sounds great," Steve said.

Ben's phone vibrated against his thigh. He pulled it from the side pocket of his cargo pants, saw the text disappearing into the background.

You alive?

His brother, asking a question he already knew the answer to, but Ben keyed in an answer anyway. Sam knew Ben was alive the same way Ben knew Sam was. While the connection wasn't as tight as it was in high school, he still knew when Sam burned himself with the welding tool, or when he had a close call with a semi on the highway. Sam was the first person to call after the gas station incident, hours before it made the news. He knew. He just knew.

Yes.

"Maybe," Ben said.

The corners of Juliette's gleaming red lips lifted. "The SWAT team guys party, Ben. You're not going to get in trouble for staying out late."

He gave her an A for persistence, but there was the text from Sam, and then there was Rachel. He shrugged and turned back to the parking lot.

"I'll be there," Steve said again.

Juliette turned to Steve. "Bring a friend," she said, with a side-long glance at Ben. "One who likes to party."

"No problem," Steve said.

"Come on, Juliette!" Her friends, now standing in front of the door, waved her over.

"I'll catch you later," she said, then ran, in those heels, to the door and disappeared into the wall of noise inside the bar.

"Why the hell not?" Steve asked.

"How many guys in the department has she fucked? Four?"

"Five, last I heard, and six tonight, if things go good." At Ben's snort, Steve added, "You never turn down a piece of ass that hot."

And hot she was, in all the right ways, with a thing for badges, but just because he could didn't mean he would. Cops got all kinds of perks, and he'd played football for Texas before he was a cop. He'd been there, done that, and while Juliette hadn't handed him the T-shirt afterward, the women who had were indistinguishable from her.

"I'm not interested in lining up behind half the department," Ben said. He ran his thumb over his cell phone screen, keeping it awake, waiting for Sam's return text.

"You feeling okay?" Steve said.

"Fine," Ben said. Just fine. Rachel and Sam and the Bar H, and spring thunderstorms rolling in from the Gulf every other fucking night. "I'm fine."

Steve sent a couple of texts then went back to Facebook, and for the next hour, the typical Saturday night at No Limits continued. Normally Ben drifted with the music, noise, laughter, but tonight flashes of Rachel punctuated the noise with silence. Crickets, the leaves in the trees, the faint sound of water over rock. The hot, involuntary sounds she made when his touch brought her alive. The look in her eyes, dazed and astonished and oh-so aroused when he swept her hair over her breasts.

She'd been nearly silent the whole time, dropping deeper into sensation, into herself as he showed her what her body could feel and do. He loved to talk dirty during sex, but the image of Rachel looking over her shoulder to say *oh yeah, you like that baby?* while he fucked her from behind made him huff out a soft laugh.

He almost wished she had. She wasn't what he expected for an almost virgin, and she certainly wasn't his typical, experienced lay. When he told her to make it happen for him he expected her to just ride him. Bite her lip tentatively, maybe. Be uncertain and ask for guidance. Not that sex was rocket science, or getting a guy off after an hour of foreplay was all that difficult.

Instead she'd given him the hint of slow, sweet pain that drove him crazy. The edge of her teeth. Her nails, stinging in his shoulders not because he was driving her to the edge but to hold him where she wanted him. She'd taken him apart then set him on fire.

His response was to practically shove her out of the truck like a one-night stand he regretted. He never treated women like that. Never.

Three guys left the bar, no big deal, but the two girls they supported between them caught his eye. The women had come in alone a couple of hours earlier and now they were leaving, stumbling drunk. He didn't need special anti-terrorist training to read the looks the guys exchanged. He stepped off the curb and crossed the lot, intercepting the group at a Challenger.

"Evening," he said. "You know these ladies?"

"Yeah, sure," two of the guys said, trying to keep the women on their feet while the third said, "No."

"Which is it?" Ben asked as he reached out and tipped one woman's chin up enough to see her glazed eyes, dilated pupils.

The two who said yes shot the third a glare. "We met them inside. We're taking them home."

"Conscientious of you," Ben said, then turned back to the woman. "Ma'am? What's your name?"

The woman's head turned to him, moving like it was on a slow, rusty crank. The man standing next to her tried to remove his hand from her arm, and she sagged at the knees. With a curse the guy held her up again.

"What's her name?" Ben said.

"Sharon," her escort replied.

"I'm Sharon," the other woman slurred.

Ben quirked an eyebrow. "Where do they live?"

In the silence that followed, not-Sharon hunched forward and threw up. "Jesus," the big one said, stepping away.

"Right," Ben said. "Get them over against the side of the building." After the men all but dragged the women to a sitting position on the curb by the bar, he said, "She has to be sober enough to consent. No, you're done," he added when the guys walked back toward the bar. "Go home."

"You can't stop us from going back in there."

Ben gave a sharp whistle. The bouncers and Steve all looked up. "They're done," he called and got a single nod in response. "Sure I can," Ben said easily. "Get in your car and go home."

"Asshole," one of the guys muttered under his breath.

"Step over here and repeat that," Ben said.

The smaller, smarter guy urged his friends into the Challenger, but not before one of them spat on the ground at his feet. Ben just smiled.

He stayed by the women until the cab arrived, then helped the driver pour them into the back seat and gave him the more sober woman's address from her license. The rest of the shift was uneventful.

Until Juliette and her posse emerged as the bar closed. "You sure you don't want to come over? Marta and I have something special in mind for you."

This was what he did. Comfortable. Routine. Same old same old.

His phone vibrated. He pulled it out to see his brother's response: *Prove it.*

"Got something to do," he said to Juliette. "Another time."

Galveston's streets were near empty as he drove up Seawall Boulevard to the Kempner Park neighborhood. He passed a patrol car driven by a young, yawning cop, who raised one finger in response to Ben's half wave. Sam's house was dark when he backed into the driveway, but the garage-turned-workshop at the end of the driveway was lit up. Ben strode up the driveway, along the paving stones arcing to the workshop door, and let himself in.

Sam shot three final nails into a sheet of drywall, then rose from his crouched position. The last time Ben had been here Sam was working on a couple of new pieces of metalwork art, but those materials and tools were neatly arranged at one end of the workbench. Electrician's tape, wiring, outlets, and plate covers now occupied center stage, with more drywall stacked at the back of the space. Sam wore jeans and a short-sleeved shirt, and tiny burns marred the skin of his forearms.

"My brother, conjured out of the dark," Sam said lightly as he crossed the workshop to stand in front of Ben.

They were so identical their mother couldn't tell them apart.

People asked if standing in front of Sam was like looking in a mirror. It wasn't. Mirrors only showed the external similarities. Standing in front of Sam was like being known. Being seen. Sam was true north, gravity, air.

Or had been, back when they were kids.

"Beer's in the fridge."

"Thanks." Ben helped himself, then sat down on the cement floor with his back to the exposed studs. His breath eased from him as his back sang with relief at the absence of weight. He tipped back the Shiner Bock can. Ice-cold beer slid down his throat, into his stomach.

"Long night?"

"The usual," Ben said.

"What time is it?"

"Three."

"Hope I didn't keep you from something."

"Just bed."

"Your own bed? Alone?"

He huffed. "Yeah."

"Call Gawker."

He slid Sam a look. "You were no better." Until Chris. Sam now wore his ring and his monogamy like badges of honor. Given that he and Chris had to go to Massachusetts, where same-sex marriage was legal, Ben understood wearing the ring.

Sam shrugged. "The right one is all it takes."

Silence. Ben knocked back another slug of beer, then looked around the garage. Old sheetrock lay stacked in one corner, while rolls of new insulation and coils of wire lay in another. "What's with the demo work?"

"We're rewiring the garage to 220-volt so I can run more stations when the kids come for art therapy."

"Got a contractor?"

"It's no big deal," Sam said. "Take out the old wire, install the new."

Chris had worked in renovations and contracting before switching to landscape design, but he wasn't a licensed electrician. Sam was a psychologist. He'd met Chris on job sites working his way through college, then grad school. Ben bit back his natural response, which was that every year Galveston EMTs transported some guy who electrocuted himself trying to save a buck. They were usually DOA.

Sam didn't even need to look at him to know what he was thinking. "The last time the social worker was here, she looked at all the exposed wiring in the garage like we were letting Jonathan frolic with knives and scorpions," he admitted.

Jonathan. The kid who'd been removed from his meth-addicted mother's house at one, and shuffled through several stints in foster homes in the last five years. The kid with attachment issues and behavioral problems. The kid Sam and Chris had fostered for six months and were determined to adopt. The road still wasn't easy for anyone, especially gay couples.

Ben saw the hope in his brother's eyes, the exhaustion lining his face, and his heart clenched hard. "I get it," he said. "Just be careful."

"Coming over for brunch later?"

Sam and Chris hosted a weekly Sunday brunch attended by a revolving door of people—fellow artists, neighbors new and old, strays they found God only knew where, including some of the homeless people Ben picked up in the city parks and drove down to the shelter. He had a standing invitation, but rarely made it to the potluck madhouse that stretched from just before noon until the sun went down. "Mom and Dad going to be here?"

His brother's shoulders stiffened as he carefully laid the nail gun on the bench at the back of the garage. "Probably," Sam said. "And Katy, and Alan, and the girls. Our *family* will be there. All of them."

Their sister, a year younger, had married right out of college, and was now raising two blond little girls who wore so much pink they looked and smelled like bubble gum. "I'll probably be sleeping," he equivocated.

"Still on Katy's shit list?"

"Yeah." His sister lived in a world of sweetness and light, where a steady stream of juice and hair bows, cookies and cooing smoothed everything over. Ben dealt with black and white. In his world, some things were unforgivable. Including their father driving Sam out of the house at sixteen when he came out of the closet. Sam had disappeared onto the streets, and for two years Ben had lived with not knowing where his brother was. Sam was gone, escaping a father who thought his son's homosexuality could be cured by a summer at a gay reeducation camp. When Sam left, their father never mentioned his name again. It was as if Sam never existed. Which meant Ben didn't exist, either.

Thanks to a tight twin connection he knew Sam was alive. Sometimes he knew when Sam was in danger or trouble or pain. When that happened, not being able to help or protect him drove him nearly insane.

In December of his freshman year at college, Sam had turned up outside Ben's dorm in Austin. He wore ripped jeans, a silver-studded belt, a flannel shirt, no-name shoes with holes in the toes, half-empty army surplus duffel at his feet. He was thirty pounds thinner than when he'd left, with a nervous twitch and a smoking habit that took him years to quit. They talked about where he'd been, a little. Never what he'd seen. Never what he'd done. Ben pieced most of that together in high-def nightmares that got worse after he got through the Academy and started working the street.

No fucking way was he forgiving their father for what he'd done. When he left the house the day they turned eighteen, he'd sworn he would never go back, not even for the old man's funeral. "For someone who thinks I should be more forgiving," Ben said, "Katy's got a death grip on a grudge."

"Withholding forgiveness is like drinking poison and hoping the other person will die."

What a semi-load of bullshit. Sometime later, when Sam was in college or early in grad school, Sam had reconciled with their father, but he'd always been able to see the good in someone. "You'd think you were a psychologist or something," Ben said not-so-lightly.

Sam refused to be drawn into the argument. He lifted the cooler's top and pulled out a beer, then sat down across the garage from Ben. "What've you been up to?"

Another shrug, another smile. "Went to a bachelor auction last weekend."

"Be still my beating heart," Sam drawled. "What the fuck for?"

"I was on the block."

"Get out."

"I was," Ben protested.

"Why?"

"When I got SWAT Rogers moved to my spot in Vice. He had to work the night of the auction, and since I beat him out for the team, he said it was the least I could do."

There was a long moment while Sam tipped back his beer, then looked at him. "I hope a skinny blond chickadee with enormous tits and the sex drive of the Energizer Bunny bought you, because you're into that kind of thing."

"Not exactly," he said wryly, thinking of Rachel. Barely a handful anywhere, humid electricity on the outside, razor-sharp and dangerous inside. Shuddering in his arms as she learned what sex was. She'd just be learning about the ache that came a day or two after a really good fuck, the desire to do it all over again. Scratch the itch once and it never really went away.

"You can't catch a break these days," Sam said.

Ben finished his beer and pondered what he *had* caught, a dark-haired, whiskey-eyed virgin who abruptly left everything she knew. Decision made and executed. Time to lose her virginity? Man purchased, decision made and executed. Except . . . she wasn't cold or unemotional. In the back seat of his truck she'd felt everything. She'd explore sex with the same single-minded focus.

She came with the intensity of a lightning strike. By now she'd want it again. Bad.

Hot, dirty possibilities bloomed in his mind. He could show her how good sex could be, that indescribable moment of luscious wet heat when his cock breached her soft opening, teach her to kiss, covering the nuances from a good-bye peck on the cheek to a mouth-meld that meant *I want to fuck you now, yes right-goddamn-against-this-wall now* to the heated connection that came from kissing and fucking until the pleasure melted your brain. He'd imprint himself on her body, in her body, deep in her mind, teach her how to be female to a male.

He wanted more. He was the only man who knew what she'd been, and he surely knew exactly what she faced. A native guide, as it were, to the land of disposable.

You're so civic-minded, Harris.

He picked up his phone and sent her a text. Maybe she'd see it, maybe she wouldn't, but he wasn't calling her like this was a date or something.

11 a.m. my place if you want something to do on Sunday morning.

He sent his address in a second text, then got to his feet. "I can't make it tomorrow," he said. "I've got plans."

"Sure," Sam said, a bite under his easy drawl. "Another time."

"Another time," Ben repeated, stepping back before Sam could hug him. He headed for the door, remembering how they'd slept in the same bed until they were ten, curled around each other like puppies in a box. Their father had destroyed more than Sam's childhood.

"Later, my brother," Sam said.

Ben strode out to the truck and found Sam framed in his rear-view mirror when he pulled out into the street. Sam was his mirror, but the mirror was cracked.

Chapter Seven

"Not already," Jess muttered when the alarm went off at five thirty Sunday morning. She rolled over, the thin cotton sheet tangled in her bare legs, and buried her head under her pillow. Tangled white-blond hair barely showed against the white pillowcase.

Flat on her back in the opposite bottom bunk, Rachel murmured in agreement. They'd spent Saturday evening in the Strand, a shopping and nightlife district of Victorian-era buildings in Galveston, at a Carrie Newcomer concert in a coffee shop/bookstore called Artistary. Glowing with the sheer emotion of the music and laughter she'd shared with Jess and the A&M boys, she'd taken a flyer listing future open-mike nights and concerts. Between dinner, the concert, the discussion, and coffee and dessert afterward, none of the Silent Circle Farm apprentices had gotten home until after midnight.

The late night ensured she'd be tired enough to nap part of Sunday away.

Getting up at dawn every day of the week was the only life Rachel had ever known, but Jess grew up in a wealthy suburb of Austin and wasn't accustomed to the daily routine of chores that never ended. Leaving Jess to untangle her sheets, Rachel pulled on yesterday's jeans and T-shirt, made a quick stop in the bathroom, then headed down the dirt path through the wildflowers to the goat shed. The simple tune for "I Believe" played in her mind as she walked. Katrina, Irene, and the rest of the does were waiting for her in a cluster of warm bodies by the gate. She gently used the gate to create enough space for her to slip into the pen, then greeted each doe according to her rank in the hierarchy. She fed them, changed their bedding, swept up the floor, then milked the does who gave birth in the fall and had weaned their kids. By the time she finished the sun skimmed the tops of the cottonwoods, and she could see Jess outside the chicken enclosure. They met at the end of the path leading back to the bunkhouse. The boys from A&M joined them where the path took a sharp left to the main barn.

"Waffles? Pancakes?" Toby asked as he transferred dirt from his palms to his jeans.

"Pancakes," Jess said decisively. "Buckwheat pancakes."

"With blueberries," Brian added.

"And eggs," Toby said, and held the bunkhouse door open for the women. "And cottage cheese and fresh peaches."

Smiling, Rachel picked up her phone and purse from the farm-house table, where she'd untidily left them the night before. Intending to put them away in her room, she stopped when she saw a text from Ben.

11 a.m. my place if you want something to do on Sunday morning.

She brushed her thumb over the screen to keep it from going dark. Three twenty a.m. He was up late.

"Sounds great," Rachel answered absently.

Inside the bunkhouse she opened all the windows and switched on the ceiling fans to circulate the cooler morning air. The bunkhouse was a simple plan, with four bedrooms separated into twos for men and women. A single room served as the common area, with the kitchen along the back wall, and a big farmhouse dining table separating the kitchen from the mismatched sofa and chairs and bookshelves comprising the living room. She hurried into the bathroom to wash the smell of goats from her hair and skin, then changed into a cotton skirt and white eyelet blouse. Her hair would take twenty minutes to dry with the hair dryer, or hours without, so she towel dried it as much as she could, then parted it on the side and loosely braided it. When she emerged Jess was cracking eggs into an ancient Pyrex bowl while Toby poured pancake batter onto a cast-iron griddle.

"Where are you off to?" Jess asked as she added a hefty dollop of milk to the bowl and began to whisk the eggs.

"Just doing some visiting later this afternoon."

A clomp of boots against the porch floorboards drew her attention. She opened the door to find Rob drying his hands on the towels hanging over the sink at the far end of the porch, George waiting beside him, already panting in the day's heat. "Just the woman I wanted to see," Rob said with a smile. "Good morning."

"Good morning," she said. "Everything looked fine this morning."

"Thanks," Rob said. He leaned against the porch railing. "Are you interested in staying past the kidding season? The Truck Garden's taking more of my time than I thought it would. I didn't anticipate raising enough money this year to get the outreach program off the ground, and I'm short an apprentice."

What she *should* do and what she *wanted* to do were two different things. "I can do that," Rachel said reluctantly, "but I can't commit past the summer."

"Sent in the vet tech school application?"

"No," she said, not willing to lie about it. But she knew how things like this went. She'd promise to stay one more season, or through one more winter, and the next thing she knew she'd be three years older but no more herself than she was when she left Elysian Fields. She wouldn't give Rob reason to depend on her. "Not yet. But I will."

"That's fair," he said. "If you take summer classes we can work around that. I'll make the time when kidding starts, too."

"Good," Rachel said firmly.

The screen door swung open and Jess peered around the weatherbeaten frame. "You coming in for breakfast?" she asked.

"Smelled Toby's pancakes all the way up at the barn," he said easily, "so I hope I get an invitation."

Jess opened the door even wider. "Come on in," she said.

Rob held the door open for Rachel. They settled down to stacks of pancakes, scrambled eggs, and platters of the farm's sausage, cottage cheese, and honey spread on thick slices of the bread Rachel had made earlier in the week. She left most of the conversation to Jess, who had much to say about raising food humanely and seasonally. When Rachel rose to stack plates, Rob got up as well and ran water and dish soap into the sink. "I'll help you with those."

The A&M boys disappeared as if they'd been vaporized. Rachel tied an apron over her blouse and skirt and washed all the dishes. Rob dried and put away. Jess hung around, wiping down the table, straightening the living area as she burbled on about their evening at the Artistary.

"What did you think of the concert last night?" Rob asked in a quiet moment. The look in his eyes reminded her of the look on his face at the auction. Had he been looking at Jess, or her?

"She has such a beautiful voice," Rachel said.

"You should have come with us," Jess added.

"I heard her in concert last year," Rob said and accepted a platter to dry. "She's the perfect blend of message and medium. You look pretty nice for a lazy Sunday lying around this place. Where are you off to today?"

She refused to blush. "I'm going into Galveston to visit . . . someone. Do you need me to pick up anything while I'm there?"

He shook his head and gave her a warm smile. "Drive safely."

More than willing to make way for Jess, Rachel decided to leave early. She settled into the Focus and rolled the windows down to clear out a week's worth of stale air as she headed down the dirt road for the highway leading southeast, crossing the causeway to the island an hour early. She spent the time at Artistary, drinking tea and reading a book she'd picked up the night before, then drove to Ben's apartment.

The clock in her dashboard read 10:55 when Rachel pulled into Ben's parking lot and braked to a halt in a spot marked Visitors. She cut the engine and got out of the car to look around. Three three-story apartment buildings all faced a parking lot, and the doors opened to common stairwells. Some balconies had plants, deck furniture, and wind chimes or cute little flags on them. The one she identified as Ben's held a single plastic chair, and the blinds were drawn across the sliding glass door to block sunlight and prying eyes. There was no personality visible from the parking lot, no hint of life inside. Maybe he was still asleep.

She checked her watch—10:57—then checked her gut. The indifferent text didn't seem to require a response. Show up or don't show up. No roses or sweet talking. Just sex. Take it or leave it. Her heart thudded in her chest, an unfamiliar anticipation shimmering in her pulse points, an unfamiliar heaviness in her breasts and between her legs.

She wanted. She now knew what it meant to want, what it meant to choose to satisfy that want. She would walk up to Ben's door, walk inside his apartment, lie down with him.

Spring sunshine and heat cascaded down to pool on the asphalt as she smoothed the pleats of her skirt across her abdomen, then closed the car door and clicked the locks. She checked her watch again—10:59—then crossed the lot, climbed the concrete stairs to Ben's door, and knocked. Long moments passed, then she knocked more sharply.

Finally the door opened to reveal Ben, wearing a pair of black cotton shorts riding low on his hips and a hooded, sleepy gaze, and nothing else. He blinked at her like he had no idea who she was or why she was there.

"Hi," she said, struggling not to stare at the broad expanse of his chest and abdomen. "You texted me. Remember?"

Another slow blink, then without a word he stepped to the side and let her into the apartment. He hadn't bothered to turn on the lights that night after dinner, so she'd seen only moonlight draped over shapes. Now sunlight filtered through the blinds, illuminating the space. The door opened into an eating area with a dinette set, mail stacked at one end, his utility belt slung over the chair nearest the hall closet. His gun sat beside the belt, and a key ring laden with keys lay beside it. Through the large pass-through window Rachel could see a kitchen. To her left was the living room, occupied by a brown leather sofa, glass coffee and end tables, and an enormous flat-screen television on a stand. The space was tidy and clean but lacked feminine touches like area rugs or artwork on the walls.

Beside her Ben rubbed his palm over his face and jaw. The sound of hard skin rasping against stubble sent heat trickling along her nerves. She remembered how that stubble felt against her lips, her breasts, a visible sign of his male to her female, harsh and rough to her softness.

"Why did you text me? I didn't think I'd hear from you again after you dropped me off."

"Why are you here?" he replied.

She tilted her head and let her purse drop to the floor at her feet. "You know," she said simply.

"I don't think I know anything about you."

"You know how inexperienced I am."

"That's why you're here?"

"I want more experience," she admitted.

His smile flashed, startling her. "Give me a couple of minutes."

He walked back down the short hallway leading to the bedroom on the left and the bathroom on the right. Rachel waited until the bathroom door closed, then stepped hesitantly off the square of linoleum doing duty as the foyer, into the living and dining area, then far enough down the hall to see into the galley-style kitchen. A white stove and fridge lined the wall, with a stainless steel sink and counter space under the pass-through to the eating area. The space lacked more than a woman's touch. It lacked personality. He lived here, ate occasionally based on the cardboard frozen meal containers neatly folded against the side of the recycling bin, slept based on the unmade bed visible through the bedroom door, stowed his stuff based on the dinette table dumping ground.

The water running in the bathroom ceased, and the absence of sound startled Rachel. She turned away from the kitchen and crossed into the bedroom to sit on the edge of the king-sized bed that dominated the room. No point in pretending she'd come here for anything else, like coffee or breakfast or conversation.

Ben opened the bathroom door, saw Rachel sitting on his bed, and paused for a second. Then he turned away from her. She heard the fridge door open, the sound of a bottle top twisting off, then he reappeared holding a bottle of water. One shoulder holding up the doorframe, he drank half, then looked at her as he wiped his mouth with a knuckle. He couldn't possibly look less interested in her, or for that matter in sin, but as he watched her, his eyes changed. Heated. Without a word the air picked up a charge. That skittering, sparking electricity made her grip the edge of his mattress.

He crossed to stand in front of her and set the bottle of water on the nightstand. A tuft of dark brown hair peeked from the elastic waist of the shorts, and the scent of sleep-warm skin drifted into her nostrils as she looked up his long torso to his face. To her surprise he went down on his knees in front of her. He said nothing, the sound of her shallow inhales running in counterpoint to his even breathing as his hands gripped her ankles and rose slowly up the backs of her calves, along the sides of her thighs. His thumbs met, brushing one after the other over her mound, awakening nerves before his fingers slid into the elastic at the top of her white cotton panties and tugged. She lifted her hips and he slid them down and off. Then he wrapped his arm around her hips and lifted her backward as he planted his other hand and shifted them back to the center of the big bed. As they shifted her hair, loosely braided halfway down her back, caught and she winced.

Without a word he settled easily on top of her, one hair-roughened leg between hers, her skirt rucked up to midthigh, his hard, bare torso pressed against hers. Braced on one elbow he reached under her back, found the end of her braid, and tugged the elastic free, then began loosening the plait.

Intimacy encompassed so much more than just sex, she thought. On her back, in his bed, she watched his face as his rough fingers worked away in her hair. Memory bled into the present as images of him using the ends of her hair to tease her breasts flashed in her mind. Without thinking about it she lifted her hand and rested it on his hip, gently rubbing her thumb on the ridge of bone exposed by his shorts. When he finished loosening her hair he cupped the side of her face. His thumb brushed across her lips, and it took her a minute to realize he was moving his thumb in the same slow rhythm she was. Curious, she dipped her thumb into the elastic waist of his shorts. In response he pressed gently on her lower lip, opening her mouth slightly. Then he bent his head and kissed her.

The taste of toothpaste, fresh and minty, quickly dissipated as the kiss grew heated. His hand roamed from her thigh, over her skirt to her waist, then up to cup her breast, back down again to tease her mound, then down to her thigh. Anticipation built, heat simmering in her lips, her nipples, in her sex, pressed firmly against Ben's hard thigh.

Still, the light, teasing brush of his fingertips as they trailed up her thigh, taking her skirt with them, made her tremble. But he continued the motion, up over her tummy, catching the hem of her blouse and working under it to cup her breast. He gripped it firmly and pinched her nipple. Sensation made her gasp and tear her mouth from his even as she lifted into his hand.

"Tell me again why you're here."

"I want to be with you," she said.

"What does that mean?" he said, his voice slightly amused, slightly mocking, then answered his own question. "You want to have sex."

"Yes," she whispered.

"Say it."

"Why? You know what I mean."

"Because *be with you* is kind of lame. Generic. Like watching a sunset on a date," he said, still amused, still mocking. "Guys are dense. The next one might need specific instructions."

She waited, her heart pounding hard against the palm cupping her breast. "I like watching sunsets, and I want to have sex with you."

A rough chuckle tumbled into her ear. "This won't be like watching a sunset. Be more specific," he said. "What do you want me to do to you?"

The world contracted, encompassing only their bodies, the mattress at her back, the sunlight filtering through the blinds. His bedroom was like a wolf's den, hidden away from prying eyes, safe and dangerous at once.

This wasn't about what she wanted him to do to her. It was about what she wanted to do to him, to feel with him, starting with his torso against hers, so she sat up. Together they got her blouse and bra off, and this time when they lay back down she wrapped her arm around his bare back, flattening her palm at the small of his back and pulling him closer. Her fingers explored the hard bumps of his spine, the muscles flexing and ridged along either side while he kissed her. Mouth, jaw, cheek, ear, throat, collarbone, each impact light, teasing, the scrape of his stubble striking sparks over each hot spot raised by his mouth. Her nipples hardened in anticipation when his mouth reached the top of her breast, but he ignored them, instead gently scraping then licking, rough then hot and smooth, then chilly as he worked his way into the valley between her breasts, teasing the undersides.

Then he flicked his tongue against one stiff nipple. She shuddered, felt as much as heard that low, dark laugh before he did it again. Tongue, teeth, then another slow tour of her breasts while she floated in desire, her nipples tight and sensitized in the cool, dim room.

"What do you want me to do?" When she hesitated, he dropped hot, openmouthed kisses down her breastbone to her belly, then flicked her a hot glance. "Say it."

"Kiss my breasts," she whispered.

He gave a low, rough growl-laugh, then ran his tongue up the underside of her breast to her nipple. "Like that?" he asked, licking the hard tip.

"Harder," she said.

He rewarded her daring with the pressure of teeth holding her nipple for the slow stroke of his tongue. Heat and light sang in her veins, spreading with her heartbeat, pooling between her legs. She undulated against his hard thigh, the rhythm slow, subtle—unlike her hands tightly gripping his shoulders as the air simmered around them. He brushed his cheek against the full sides, then slid up her body to hold her jaw for an explicit kiss. His mouth was wet, hot, lips swollen. She responded with abandon, her breath shuddering as she inhaled the scent of skin and sweat and arousal.

"Keep talking."

"Why?"

"Because you need to learn what works for you. Don't rely on the man to take care of you. Know what you want and how to ask for it." His scythe-smile flashed in the filtered sunlight. "Because it makes me really, really hot when a woman talks dirty in bed."

She blinked. He tucked a pillow under her head, then left a trail of kisses down her breastbone to her waistband. "Lift," he commanded.

The slight angle allowed her to watch him unfasten button and zipper, then slide the skirt down to toss it to the floor. He settled between her parted legs, blue eyes holding hers as he skated his palms up calves to knees to inner thighs. Vulnerability melded with desire, and she kept her legs as closed as she could with a big, broad-shouldered man kneeling between them.

"You said no to this the first night."

She nodded.

He loomed over her, dark hair, lust-dark eyes, scruff on his jaw, broad, tanned shoulders gilded by the weak sunlight pushing through the blinds, and without any movement at all she tightened again. He worked his big, rough hands under her bottom to curve around her hips. One palm flattened on her belly. The fingers of the other hand stroked her mound before he bent forward to press an openmouthed kiss to the top of her folds. "Say yes this time."

"I'm not sure I'm going to like that," she said.

"It's intimate," he murmured, hot breath against her sex, his stubble ever so slightly grazing awakening nerve endings. "More intimate than sex. Sometimes it's easier for a woman to get off this way. Close your eyes."

She did as he said. Her awareness of touch heightened. Sweat slicked her thighs where his shoulders held her open and where his palm lay against her belly, just above her mound. The fingers of his other hand curled around her hip. After a moment a slow stream of air blew gently against the top of her sex. She tensed. It stopped, but that faint pressure hinted at something more. When she relaxed again her thighs relaxed a little more. Her inner folds parted, the sensation heightened without the visual distraction of his dark face between her legs. The next time he blew gently, the air flowed over her clit.

Her breathing shallowed, and her hips tilted ever so slightly. Not enough. "Ben," she whispered.

"Say, *lick my clit*."

Her clit fluttered at the words as warm breath whispered against needy flesh. "Lick my clit," she said.

"Look at me and say it."

She opened her eyes to find him studying her. A shocking heat flashed from her nipples to low in her belly. "Lick my clit, Ben."

He was smiling when he pressed his open mouth to her sex. His tongue slowly circled her clit, sending heat streaming through her veins. The slick, smooth pressure was easier to take than his rough fingertips. She learned as he explored. One side was more sensitive than the other, and steady circles around the increasingly distended nub tightened her muscles. The pleasure ebbed with the cessation of contact, and she moaned and lifted her hips.

When she opened her eyes again, he said, "Still think you're not going to like this?"

"Don't stop."

He widened her legs with his shoulders, then used his tongue and very, very gently, his teeth until she was gasping. The build to orgasm still startled her, so demanding, so shockingly powerful. She gripped the pillow behind her head with one hand, threaded her fingers through Ben's hair with the other, and lifted her hips to his mouth. Gasping little breaths tripped into the still, quiet air, then she stopped breathing entirely. Then the wave crashed over her, pushing her deep into the void.

The rasp of palm over stubble brought her back into the room. She opened her eyes to find Ben wiping moisture from his jaw. Her moisture. "Kiss me," she said without thinking. When he hesitated, she said it again. "Kiss me. I want to taste that."

Chapter Eight

How in the name of sweet baby Jesus had this woman stayed a virgin for so long?

Broad damned daylight, she was naked in his bed, legs splayed for him, the sex flush still pink on her cheeks and throat. Ten minutes ago she didn't want him to go down on her. Now she wanted to know how she tasted?

This wasn't going according to plan. His cock hung heavy and rigid between his legs, balls tight to his body because talking dirty did turn him on. Rachel Hill talking dirty made him hard enough to pound nails. Her peremptory tone also did it for him, not quite a command but definitely leaving no room for him to refuse.

"Yes, ma'am," he said, and crawled up her body, using his knees to keep her thighs spread. *Make her feel the emptiness, the need. Don't hold back, and toss your expectations about delicate sensibilities out the window.* He nuzzled into her jaw, let her smell the musk clinging to his chin and lips, then brushed his mouth over hers. Her tongue flicked out to lick first his upper, then his lower lip, and somehow she'd rewired his brain so the touch of her lips against his mouth sent five thousand volts straight to his cock. He let out a soft little groan but stayed poised above her while she nibbled and sucked and licked, torturing himself until she wrapped one leg, then the other, around his to pull him down to her. She worked her hands under his elastic waistband and gripped his hips, pulling him closer.

"How do you like me now?" he said. Even to his own ears the words sounded rough, like she'd abraded his throat with sandpaper.

"Very, very well," she said.

"Gonna trust me to know what you need?"

"Maybe," she said.

She flattened her palms on his hipbones, one hand on either side of his erection, and eased his shorts down. The only thought left in his brain was how badly he wanted to hear Rachel Hill ask him to fuck her.

He sat back and opened the nightstand drawer to grab a box of condoms. "They teach you about safe sex at that church you went to?"

"Only that safe sex is married sex," she said.

Jesus fucking Christ.

He tore one condom from the strip, handed it to her, then shoved his shorts down and off. A muscle jumped in his jaw as he pushed back onto his heels, his knees spread wide. "First safe sex lesson. The guy always wears a condom. Always. Guys will use every line in the book to go bareback. It's non-negotiable until you see test results from a doctor."

She opened the packet and withdrew the condom. "I know," she said as she studied it. "I read up on safe sex before we went out on our date."

So there was a limit to the stupid risks she'd take. She'd buy a stranger at an auction, but know enough to make him use a condom. In some fucked-up way that passed for a plan. "Put that on me."

She slid him a look under her lashes, but settled on her knees in front of him, then rested the rolled-up condom on top of his shaft.

"Like this," he said, turning it over to show her how it unrolled.

His hand guided hers as she sheathed him all the way to the base, then turned her wrist so her hand cupped his testicles, gently squeezing until he showed her exactly how much pressure they could take, and the sensitive patch behind them. His breathing stuttered, then he wrapped his arm around her hips and bore her back onto the bed. Braced on his elbows he aligned their bodies from hips to chest, lowered himself between her thighs, and nudged into place.

He was looking in her eyes as, slow and steady, he pushed in until his hips were seated against hers, taking care not to abrade her overstimulated clit. Her inner walls adjusted in increments, muscles tightening, then softening to cling to his length. She adjusted under him and he lifted enough to let her move, but remained firmly embedded inside her.

"You okay?"

"Of course," she said. "It's not like this is my first time."

The unexpected flash of humor made him smile. She blinked, then smiled back. His heart gave an odd thump. In that moment he wanted to kiss her curved lips, so he did; slow, hot, sliding kiss after kiss, all the while buried deep inside her, unmoving. She lifted her hips, but he just kept kissing her until she writhed under him.

"Ben," she whispered when his mouth slid along her jaw to her ear.

"What?" he murmured. "Tell me what you want."

"It's a little ridiculous, if you think about it," she said distractedly.

He had to agree. Thanks to the job, he'd seen more than his share of porn. He'd had more than his share of sex, multiple partners, in front of every reflective surface you could imagine. Yes, it looked ridiculous, spread legs, hunched bodies, breasts bouncing, hips thrusting. The noises. It was ridiculous, until it transformed into something else. Something intimate. Hot.

"What is?" he asked, playing along as he pulled out, then slid back in. Keep it slow, but inexorable. Pitch his hips forward and glide into soft, clinging, slick flesh. He'd never thought about it before, but there was something hot and dark in that possession. Something as erotic as the taste of her juices on his tongue.

"You," she blurted.

This time his smile was slow and knowing, mirroring the withdrawal and thrust. "You mean my cock."

Heat rushed up her neck, into her face. "Yes."

"Say it."

The command held a compelling undertone but her upbringing held firm. "You want me to say your . . . your . . . is ridiculous?"

He withdrew again, then slid back inside, studying her face as he did. "No," he said easily. "Just say *cock*."

"I don't use language like that."

He paused as if he were going to pull out, but then didn't. Ensnared in need, she moaned and squirmed again. "Try *ride me. Pound into me. Make me scream*. Or go for the one that means all three. Try *fuck me*."

"No," she said. "Why are we having a conversation while we're doing this, anyway?"

As he withdrew he bent his head to her ear and murmured, "Come on, Rachel. You know it turns me on."

To tempt her he stroked in again, then paused. Her toes curled, her pussy clenched around him. The scent of steamy, electric risk filled the air, and he could almost see her glowing, like he was standing outside during an electrical storm, and her response—*I want to but*—died in her throat as it closed.

"Oh," she said faintly. "Oh."

"We're having the conversation . . . look at me, Rachel." Her eyes opened partway, the lids dragged down by the undertow now swirling in her body. "We're having this conversation because if you can talk this much, I'm not doing it right."

The rhythm was the same, slow and steady, making her feel every inch of his shaft sliding back and forth, but now he'd found the right angle so each stroke slid over sensitive nerves inside and out. Her eyes lapsed into soft focus, then closed. He could do it, make her say the words, but for now it was enough to teach her how desire grew, transformed into need. He noted the way her fingers tightened around his biceps and her toes curled, how her legs drew up and her heels dug into the backs of his thighs, opening her even more.

"Good?" he asked.

"Yes." The word came out as a whimper, though, high-pitched and breathy.

Each stroke of his shaft into her body heightened the contrasts, how soft and slick and swollen she was around his hard length, the way each thrust both drew his orgasm up his shaft and sent pleasure coursing back into his body when he bottomed out inside her. He bent his head so his morning scruff rasped over her heated cheek, and his mouth found hers, lips barely brushing hers, soft gusts of air marking his breathing before his tongue touched hers.

Her eyes opened. The look in the languid, pale brown irises sent heat and light into spaces left too long in cold and dark.

Ben stopped abruptly.

"Don't . . . *Why did you stop?*"

No light, no heat, no tenderness. If she wasn't going to play along, make it sexy and hot and dirty, then he'd do it. He sat back on his heels and tugged on her hand to help her into a sitting position. "Because we've done that before, and there are a dozen different ways to do this. Turn around."

She went to her knees and gave him her back. He snugged up close behind her, his erection sliding against her bottom until he smoothed his palms up her inner thighs to open her, then urged her up, guided her back, and slid back inside her.

"Oh," she said again. "Oh my."

The benefits to this position were many. He lifted both hands to her face, sliding rough palms along her cheekbones to gather her hair, sending it streaming over one shoulder. Then he smoothed his hands up her throat, under her jaw, tipping her head back to his shoulder before he cupped her breasts and gently pinched her nipples. She tightened around him and swiveled her hips on his erection.

"That's right," he said, as if she'd spoken. In a way, she had. One hand stayed at her breast while the other lifted to her mouth. The tip of his middle finger slipped between her lips and she licked it. Then that hand skimmed over her soft belly, between her legs, to circle her clit.

"You do it," he murmured in her ear.

She began to tip her hips back and forth, using the powerful feedback loop to refine her movements until she found exactly the right angle to rub the hot spot inside her against his shaft. He grunted and wrapped his free arm around her ribs, holding her hard against him because the way she writhed dropped him straight back to reptile brain.

The heat was building again, flaring hotter and higher than before. Apparently she didn't know what to do with her hands. They lifted, searching for something to cling to before one settled on his nape and the other on the forearm flexed like a steel band against her ribs. As the pleasure built she spread her knees, opening to him, and he shifted as well, slid a little deeper.

It was surrender and possession all at once. She couldn't break his grip but she also held him deep inside her, and he didn't want to think about that.

"Work for it, Rachel," he said, and matched his circling fingertip to the swiveling motion of her hips. She glowed, gasping, striving for something that seemed as impossible to attain as it was to do without.

And then it broke over her. Her body arched in his arms, breathy, astonished cries escaping her lips as the tight convulsions rhythmically gripped his shaft. He pulled out and thrust back in, the motions subtle and shallow, intended to keep him on the edge while drawing out her orgasm.

She was gripping his arm and neck so hard she'd dug her blunt nails into the skin. "I'm sorry," she said.

"So am I," he said.

Before she could ask him what he meant, he tightened his grip at her waist to hold her close, then braced his other hand on the bed and tipped her face-first into the sheets. Her hair tumbled over her face, buried in her forearms. He hunched over her and powered in, hips slapping against her ass. He'd done this the porn star way before, one hand on her tailbone as he watched his cock disappear into his partner's soft female flesh. But this time wasn't about *yeah baby you like that?* This was about the sheer, deep need to bury himself in Rachel Hill.

He was out of his mind. That was his last thought before orgasm blasted through him like a freight train, obliterating his mind. He shoved deep inside her, grinding against her hips, shaft throbbing as he jetted into her.

A soft little sigh eddied into the bed. The muscles in his arms and hands trembled as they relaxed, and his legs weren't exactly steady as he withdrew from her body and went into the bathroom. Out of the corner of his eye he saw her ease down on her side and close her eyes.

This should have been simple. Teach a virgin what she needed to know about sex so she seemed experienced. He splashed water on his face, then looked in the mirror as he dried off. If you knew what to look for, he looked as shell-shocked as Rachel. If you didn't know—and Rachel didn't—he looked like he always did. Square jaw, blue eyes, blank face. Some guys learned that look on the streets. He'd learned it long before he applied to the Academy. Just like Sam did, in fact.

Eventually, Rachel would look like this, too, like Juliette and Steve and everyone else he knew. If she were a good student. She'd learn to say and move and do what men expected, to make sure she knew what she liked and knew how to get it.

Back in the bedroom she still lay in a ball on the bed. He bent down and started separating clothes into two piles. Her white cotton panties. His black shorts. Her skirt. She pushed herself into a sitting position and followed his lead, tugging on panties, then skirt before claiming her bra and her blouse from the floor on the other side of the bed.

"What do I say afterward?" she asked as she buttoned her blouse. "Thanks?"

The offhand remark startled a laugh from him. "Depends on how good the service was," he returned.

Another silence. He never minded girls spending the night, having no desire to send a woman back onto the streets at three in the morning, too sleepy to drive defensively against the drunks and the teens. Telling a woman she could stay when he was awake was a completely different story.

"I should go," she said.

Yes, she should. No, she shouldn't.

He didn't move, his elbows and body blocking most of the door. The scent of sex and sweat rose from her skin, heightening that uniquely Rachel scent. "Want to do this again next Sunday?"

Her hair slid over her shoulder when she looked up at him, so she reached back and coiled the heavy mass, then twisted the coil into a knot at the nape of her neck. She slipped her feet into her flats and stepped toward the doorway only to come up short when he stayed where he was.

"Only if you answer my question," she said.

He frowned. "What question?"

"Why did you text me?"

He really didn't like *why*. "Because someone's got to teach you what you need to know." And there wasn't much that made him hot anymore.

"And it might as well be you?" she said.

He gave her a short nod that wasn't an answer.

"What would this involve?"

How did you explain water when you were a fish? He settled on, "What to do. What to expect. How to act. How to protect yourself."

A moment's silence passed, then she said, quite gently, "Excuse me, please."

He stepped to the side, allowing her to walk through the door without sidling past him. She picked up her purse from the dinette table. "See you next week," she said, opening the door.

In the silence that followed, still ringing with Rachel's helpless cries, he wondered what would happen when she'd learned everything he had to teach.

Chapter Nine

Nearing midnight on Saturday Ben stood outside No Limits, watching the scene. He'd spent enough time at a place where sex was all but for sale, and he'd learned to read the clothes, the bodies, the messages. Intention. Except for a few oddballs, everyone who came to No Limits had the same reason for making the drive. Party. Get drunk, get laid. Have a good time. He knew there were people who stayed home, cooked gourmet meals, and played Scrabble on a Saturday night, his passionately monogamous brother and Chris among them, but in Ben's world, *this* was the norm.

Tonight he watched it through new eyes, picking up tips to offer Rachel. Wear a short skirt or a halter top that exposed the soft bumps of her spine, or better yet, the black leather corset and skin-tight pants one of the women waiting in line wore. Her pink hair was cropped, spiky around ears and nape, giving her the appearance of a dominatrix anime elf. She turned and looked right at Ben, and with a shock he realized he'd gone home with her three, no four, months ago. Her hair had been jet black then, worn sleek and short, making her a dead ringer for Carrie-Anne Moss in the *Matrix* movies. He'd always had a thing for Trinity. She lifted an eyebrow at him in greeting, then went back to her phone.

The rules weren't complicated, but he'd never really thought about how much of his sex life depended on the woman going along with them, thereby making things so much easier for everyone involved. No harm, no foul in the full-contact sport of hookup sex, but sleeping with Rachel brought them into stark relief

"Juliette asked about you last weekend," Steve said.

Ben said nothing.

"Who you were seeing, or at least fucking. Was it serious? That kind of thing. I told her I had no idea. Because I don't. Three years we've been standing outside the club twelve hours a weekend and I can't name a single girl you've dated."

Because he didn't date. "You complaining?"

"Just stating a fact. Juliette said she liked the strong, silent type, so you're welcome."

Ben stayed focused on the line. "Who helped her get over the disappointment?"

"No one," Steve said.

Ben cut him a look.

"No lie," Steve said. "I offered, Carl offered, but she stayed at Tina's. Slept on the couch."

"How do you know?"

"Because I fucked Tina and Juliette was asleep on the couch when I left."

"You slept with Tina after Juliette turned you down?" Ben said.

"She said she had a condom in her bedroom with my name on it."

"Jesus Christ," Ben said. He tried to imagine Rachel announcing she had a condom with his name on it, and failed. "You were with the State Patrol, right?"

"Gave back four years in pension when I left," Steve confirmed.

"Ever catch a call out at Elysian Fields?"

"Yeah," Steve said without looking up from his phone.

"And?"

Steve transferred his attention from his phone to the line. "What are we calling a group of like-minded isolationists these days? A cult? A commune? A community? They've withdrawn from the sinful world. Thirty years ago a bunch of families bought land together and started farming. Subsistence stuff, mostly. Eventually the world caught up with them and got interested in organic meat, milk, products like that. They homeschool the kids, who tend to marry other kids from similar communities in the South. Big extended families. Women dress in those long skirts and long-sleeved shirts, or ugly dresses. Men run the households, the Church, the businesses. Women cook and clean and do chores and have babies. Lots and lots and lots of babies. I've never seen so many kids in one place in my life." He looked back at his phone. "Calls were petty theft, mostly. Vandalism. Kids from the local school used to spray-paint gigantic cocks on the barns. That kind of thing."

"Abuse? Drugs? Drinking?"

"Sure on the drugs and drinking, but usually kids and they usually wanted to handle it internally. Abuse . . ." He looked at Ben. "Physical, probably. Nothing we got called on or saw when we were there. Emotional and mental? Depends on whether you call indoctrinating people with a systemic theology that justifies your position in the world and sending your kids to special camps for extra discipline *abuse*. Why?"

"The woman from the auction used to live there."

Steve whistled. "She got out?"

"What do you mean?"

"Those women, they're under the men's thumbs. No real high school, no college. No jobs except as relates to the farm. They're raised to be obedient wives and mothers. Most of them don't have access to money. They don't talk back, they don't question the men."

She'd gotten out. People assumed virgin meant weak, naïve, insecure, even ashamed. Not Rachel. She was aware, thinking about what she did and why she did it, and strong enough to ask questions, plan, execute a course of action that left her alone in the world. She'd be easy to teach, easy to toughen up and prepare for casual sex in the modern world.

The thought process left him edgy.

His phone rang. He pulled it from his cargo pants pocket; his heart rate shot up when the number for dispatch flashed on the screen. "Harris."

The dispatcher, her voice several notches higher than usual, read off an address. "I'm ten minutes away," Ben told her before hanging up.

Steve knew what the call meant. "I've got this. Go."

Ben sprinted for his truck. Flashing lights guided him to the scene from blocks away. He parked at the rendezvous point and slid out of his truck. In front of him the rest of the SWAT team pulled on gear, the special vest and flame-resistant clothing, his brain tuning out everything else as the lieutenant ran down the situation.

A simple service of an eviction notice had turned into a hostage situation when the deputy surprised a felon with outstanding warrants. The deputy took a bullet through the shoulder before stumbling out of the house and calling it in. Hostage negotiator, a K-9 unit, and about five dozen other LEOs were on scene.

"We've cleared the surrounding houses, secured the neighborhood. The negotiator's trying to talk them into letting the female hostage out, but they're not listening." Lieutenant Jake Williams flattened a roughly drawn diagram of the house used in the earlier raid and directed his team to their positions. "Montgomery, Harris. Here, here," he said, pointing with one thick finger.

His task in this was a simple one. Wait for the signal to rake and break, then secure his room. In this case, he'd break the window into the back bedroom and order anyone inside to lie on the floor, hands palm-up, and essentially hold them at gunpoint until other officers arrived to handcuff them. Ben pulled down his mask, shouldered his rifle, and followed Montgomery through the neighboring house's side yard. They took up position and waited. Hours passed as the hostage negotiator tried to get the woman out of the picture. He could hear her crying until a loud slap silenced her. He clenched his teeth, exhaled slowly through his nose to calm his heart rate and breathing, and waited.

Inhale, exhale. Listen to the radio traffic coming through his hands-free headset. Inhale, exhale. Stay absolutely alert but conserve strength and energy. Inhale, exhale. After three hours of negotiation the woman was allowed to leave. Based on the sounds—a door opening, *get the fuck out, bitch,* and the cry and thuds of someone falling down a set of stairs—the hostage had been summarily shoved out the front door and into the waiting arms of the officers outside.

Hold your positions.

Once things escalated this far there was no backing down. Clouds cast the eastern sky in dull gray when the order to take the door came. The loud bang of a concussion grenade followed by what sounded like a hail of gunfire worthy of a full-on military assault. He'd broken the window on the back bedroom, and Montgomery was moving up the back porch when the back door flew open and caught him full in the face. Despite considerable forward momentum Montgomery slammed back into the rickety railing, which shattered under his weight, sending him tumbling onto the packed dirt at Ben's feet.

The suspect took the stairs in a flying leap and sprinted for the neighbor's yard. Ben took off after him, adrenaline fueling his muscles. Breath coming in short bursts, he caught the suspect in a flying tackle that took them both to the ground. Ben took a punch before he jammed his knee in the guy's kidney and wrenched his arm high enough up behind his back to make him shriek like a little girl.

Other officers pounded up behind him. Seconds later the suspect was spread-eagled, one knee in his lower back, another between his shoulder blades with his hand helpfully forcing his face into the dirt while Ben finished cuffing him. Two guys hauled him up as Ben swiped at his bleeding nose with the back of his hand.

"Nice tackle. What position did you play again?" one of the other officers asked Ben.

"Linebacker," Ben said, eyeing the suspect.

"Hear that, asshole?" the officer said cheerfully. "It's your lucky day. A former Texas linebacker just took you down."

"Motherfucker," the guy spat at Ben.

Ben flashed him a grin made gory by the blood trickling from his nose. "Work on your wind in prison. You're slow."

"Fuck you."

They hauled him away. Ben rounded the corner of the house where an EMT tried to hustle him to an ambulance. He ignored her until Williams pointed at the back of the bus.

Inside, Montgomery swore low and vicious while an EMT manipulated his wrist. Ben winced as another EMT pressed her thumbs to either side of his nose. "It's not broken," she said, then broke out the alcohol wipes to clean up the blood.

"Any of that his?" his lieutenant asked.

"No, sir," Ben said. "He caught me with an elbow when I took him down."

Williams watched the EMT wipe blood off Ben's face for a second, then said, "Nice tackle. You hear me calling you off?"

Ben looked at him. "No, sir."

"That's why we have Hera," he said, pointing to Ryan Sanchez, the team's K-9 handler, and Hera, his Belgian Malinois. Hera looked pissed. Ben made a mental note to give her a wide berth when he left. "When they run we send Hera after the bad guys. She hauls them down, makes them piss in their pants, then we arrest them."

He hadn't heard a thing after Montgomery landed in a heap at his feet. Not a thing except his own breathing. "Yes, sir," he said.

"Fuck it all, Harris!"

The EMT had been on enough calls to know when to make herself scarce. She packed cotton up Ben's nostrils, handed him an ice pack, and found something else to do.

Williams got right in Ben's face. "*Yes sir, yes sir, yes sir.* That's what your patrol lieutenant and the captain said you repeated like some kind of fucking jacked-up parrot after the gas station incident. You think this kind of stunt is why we wanted you on SWAT? It's not. We took you despite this, because your speed and strength beat out the other candidates. What you did at the gas station almost, *almost*"—Williams held up his surprisingly elegant fingers a millimeter apart—"got you booted off the team. You hear me?"

Ben knew better than to say anything other than, "Yes, sir."

"You've got the physical skills of a world-class athlete and the judgment of a sixteen-year-old kid."

"Yes, sir."

"Stop saying that, Harris." Williams studied him for a long, painful moment. "You got someone to go home to? A girlfriend? Wife?"

Prudently, Ben just shook his head.

"Just someone you call when you want to lose all of this in a warm body."

It wasn't a question, so he shrugged.

His lieutenant gave an impatient grunt. "Someone regular? The same warm body? Or just a list of phone numbers you got at that bar where you work?"

Ben cracked the ice pack against the side of the bus to activate it. "You ordering me to get a girlfriend, Lieutenant?"

"I'm making a suggestion. You're eight years into the job. As far as I can tell, you've got nothing but the job. You need a reason to go home in one piece at the end of the day. We've got too much money invested in you for you to burn out in a year."

"Sir," Ben said, an acknowledgment that his commanding officer had spoken, nothing more.

"I mean it, Harris." The lieutenant put his finger too close to Ben's aching face for comfort. "Get a hobby. Get a dog. Do something. We all want to catch bad guys, but if I get any more calls from your sergeant about you doing stupid shit because you're so adrenaline-jacked you don't think straight, we're going to have words."

Ben extracted the packed cotton from his nose somewhere in the second hour of paperwork, finished up around ten, then hauled himself home to shower. Only when he saw his neighbors leaving dressed for church did he remember Rachel would arrive at his apartment at eleven. At least he didn't have to text anyone to help him work off the adrenaline rush. Rachel would show up in thirty minutes with nothing more on her mind than sex.

He left his filthy clothes on the bathroom floor, swallowed Tylenol for the dull ache threatening his shoulder and the throbbing across the bridge of his nose, and stepped into the shower. As the water coursed over his face and shoulders, flashes of the night came back to him. The call. Suiting up, breaking the glass, seeing Montgomery go ass over teakettle through the railing. That undeniable thrill of taking off after a felon. The impact of his body against the runner's, their bodies against the ground. Life was a full-contact sport, and sex was a part of life. Didn't need anything but the job.

There was an inevitable reaction to the stress of the job. Warm water trickling over his cock only heightened the reaction. He braced both arms on the wall under the showerhead and let his brain work over all the possibilities for a morning with Rachel. Last time he'd made her ask for what she wanted. This time she'd see how she dealt with a man with one thing on his mind.

When he saw her little dented Focus pull into the parking lot, he unlocked the door, then sat on the arm of his sofa. She pushed the door open. Her eyes widened when she got a good look at his face, but she closed and locked the door before dropping her purse and crossing to stand in front of him.

"What on earth?" she asked.

"SWAT got called out," he said.

"I'd hate to see the other guy," she quipped. "I can come back another time."

"You're exactly what I need." He didn't say anything. He just sat there, a bottle of water dangling between his knees while Rachel studied him with those unreadable whiskey eyes. When her gaze became too much he leaned forward, wrapped one arm around her waist, and hoisted her over his shoulder. In the bedroom he knee-walked to the center of the bed, then put her down with her back to the plain wood headboard. He straddled her legs, then worked his fingers into her hair, pulling out pin after pin until he lost count and the sleek mass streamed down over her shoulders and brushed her cheeks. "I want you to use your mouth on me."

She didn't move or react in any way, and he wondered if he'd just thought the words, not actually voiced them into the sunlight filtering through his blinds. He was prepared to explain himself, to justify the demand by saying guys liked it, they'd expect her to know what she was doing. But without moving she reached for his hand and lifted it to her mouth. Her soft, hot breath on his abraded knuckles sent his nerve endings into high alert.

That wasn't what I meant, but oh, fuck that's hot . . .

"What happened?" she asked before she flicked her tongue into the sensitive skin between his fingers.

"He ran," he said. "Must have scraped my knuckles when I tackled him."

She turned his hand and kissed the inside of his wrist. "Why did he run?"

He paused to savor the sensation of her full mouth on his inner arm. "He was trapped. No one wants to be trapped."

She flicked him another look, then put her mouth to his shoulder. Slowly, her mouth covered his chest with kisses as her hands smoothed down his ribs. He inhaled short and sharp when she found a sore spot. Again she bent forward and this time she used her tongue to trace the ridges of muscle in his chest before she hesitantly lapped at his nipple. This time his shaft pulsed between her legs, so she kept it up, her confidence growing with each pass of her tongue over his flat nipples.

"Jesus," he said when she leaned back. He straightened, bringing his abdomen in line with her face. She looked up at him, dark hair highlighting her pale face flushed with heat, and those mysterious eyes, then put her mouth just below his navel. The touch of her lips, wet and gentle and teasing all at once, made his cock feel like it was hardened steel. He'd felt this before after a good day on the job. He usually worked it off drinking, dancing, fucking.

Never before like this. Never before knowing that what she'd do for him was the first time she'd done this for anyone.

Her breathing was even but shallow when she lifted the elastic waist of his shorts over the head of his cock. It bobbed free at mouth level. She gripped it, stroked down to the base, then bent forward and licked the precome from the tip. Her lashes fluttered upward. Barely breathing, he stared down into her eyes.

"Keep going."

She licked the tip again. Traced the outline of the head with her tongue. "Tell me what you like."

Heat seared through his balls. He leaned forward and braced one forearm on the wall above her head, then used his index finger on the spot just below the flared head of his cock. "That's a good spot. Work your tongue over it. Harder," he added when she hesitantly lapped at it.

She focused on that spot, then closed her lips around the tip and swirled her tongue around the head. She developed a rhythm of tongue and lips, sucking and licking, her eyelashes black curves against her pink cheeks as he looked down at her. Her face was bare of makeup, no mascara, no lip gloss or color of any kind, and the simplicity of it all made him groan low in his chest. No facade, nothing for her to hide behind.

"So hot," he murmured.

The words rasped into the air and she looked up. For a brief moment he thought he might come then and there at the sight of Rachel's lips stretched around his cock as she peered up at him. Then she straightened, taking a moment to work her jaw and spread her saliva down his shaft. Muscles in his abdomen flinched as she jacked him.

"Again," he said. "Harder."

This time he reached down and moved her hand in tandem with her mouth, showing her how to stimulate every inch. When she developed the rhythm he wound his fingers in her hair, resisting the urge to cup her head. He already had her backed to the wall, already felt his orgasm seething in the tip of his cock. He was holding back from thrusting into her mouth when she leaned back and gasped.

There was probably a trick to breathing through a blow job, but he didn't know it. She flashed him a smile as she looked up at him, her hand moving up and down his shaft, and the hot look in her eyes told him everything he needed to know. He reached down and opened her blouse and bra, spreading the fabric to the side to expose her breasts. Her nipples were hard and rosy, while a paler pink flush glowed on her collarbone.

She watched him stare at her breasts like he'd never seen any before. When he looked at her face again she had a little smile on her mouth. "I want to make you come."

"Here?" he asked as he smoothed his thumb over her lower lip, feeling the hot, swollen flesh, the slickness inside. "Or here," he added as he trailed his abraded hand down her throat to the tops of her breasts.

How far would his former virgin go?

In response she leaned forward and took him deep inside her mouth. He groaned and leaned forward, thrusting into her mouth as deep as her fist around his cock would let him go. She didn't just let him do it. She sucked and licked and with each stroke he coiled more of her hair in his fist until his entire body was rigid with need.

"Rachel," he growled. "Rachel, now—"

Release exploded at the base of his spine, pulsed out into her mouth. In some dim corner of his mind he knew she'd startled under him, knew she had no idea what to expect. But then her fingers tightened on his hip, holding him in place, taking it all until he slumped back on his heels, arm still braced against the wall, shaking hard enough to reverberate through her body. He looked into her eyes, trying to decipher her emotional state as he brushed his thumb across her wet, swollen mouth.

Raw emotion poured from Ben in hard, crashing waves, breaking over Rachel from the moment she walked in the door. His face was battered, a black eye forming, his nose slightly swollen, and his gaze held a conquering warrior's heavy-lidded, imperious look. Some primitive place, buried deep at the back of her brain, sent molten need streaming down her spine and into her sex while he took what he needed from her.

Now he slumped over her, arms braced on either side of her head, his temple next to her cheek as he breathed in deep, hard exhales intended to make space for the oxygen his body craved. He smelled like sweat and soap and sex. She turned her head and touched her tongue to his cheekbone, feeling a day's worth of stubble rasp as she added salt to the musky, somewhat bitter taste on her tongue. She never would have done that if she'd not been carried away by Ben's transformation into hard, rough male. She hadn't been thinking about being pure, being chaste, being holy. She'd only felt.

Rachel the virgin was long, long gone.

More of his weight settled against her thighs as his muscles continued to relax. One hand still at his hip, she lifted the other to squeeze his biceps. He turned his head to look at her. Her heart skittered in her chest at his intense blue gaze, the satisfaction etched around his mouth and eyes.

"You okay?" he asked.

Not really. She wanted sex. Now. Not oral sex or his hand

between her legs, but him inside her with all of that raw intensity back. Ben, however, was in no condition to provide it.

"No," she said.

He sat back, going from satisfied male to alert protector in the blink of an eye. "Fuck," he said, then swiped his hand over his eyes. "I thought . . . you didn't . . . I . . . *fuck*."

"No, no," she said quickly. "I wanted to do that. I just . . . wanted more."

His brows drew down. "You think we're done?"

"We're not?" she said.

A little huff of laughter, then he said, "The hell we are."

He sat back and unwound his hand from her hair, then pushed back off the bed. She pulled together the edges of her blouse as he did, the scrape of cotton over aching nipples pure torture.

"Stay put," he said, glancing at her now-covered torso, then strode into the kitchen. He came back with two bottles of water, cracked the seal on one and handed it to her. She swallowed gratefully, pulling her knees up and to one side as he leaned back against the headboard next to her.

"You okay?" he asked again.

"I liked that," she said. She would *not* deny what she did. How it made her feel.

He tilted back the bottle and stretched his legs out. The focus of so much attention and energy now lay half hard against his thigh. "Why?"

She thought about how to phrase this. "It was real. Authentic."

He looked at her and smiled. "Yeah."

"Explain what just happened."

He shrugged. "Adrenaline," he said. "Fights, chases, tough take-downs, the daily ups and downs of the job. It all feels like fight or flight to the brain. All that energy has to go somewhere. In men, it goes straight to their cocks."

"But you didn't want to have sex?"

He choked on the last swallow of water. "Feeling a little neglected, sweetheart?" he drawled.

Neglected wasn't the right word. Needy, demanding, desperate all came to mind, not to mention unsure how to handle the teasing. She pushed herself higher against the headboard. "Yes, to be honest," she said. "You were very aroused and I wanted . . ."

"Tell me."

She slid him a glance out of the corner of her eye. "I wanted to be under you. I wanted to feel what you felt. Inside me."

He pulled her to straddle him. "And I wanted to take the edge off before we had sex," he said.

One quick look showed he was hardening again. His pulse thumped in his shaft, lengthening and thickening it. She looked at him, noting the changes. His mouth looked as soft and swollen as hers felt, his gaze heavy lidded and intent. Twin red flags stood high on his carved cheekbones, as if passion etched away part of the mask he wore.

He smoothed his hands from her shoulders to her wrists before lifting each palm to his mouth and kissing the center. Nerves fired when the combination of hot, soft lips and rough stubble scraped her skin. She wasn't sure if the electric jolt to her senses came from the touch, or the knowing look in his eyes as they met hers. He kissed the pads of her fingers, each in turn, then her inner wrist before she tugged her hand free.

"You do that so easily," she said.

"Do what?"

"Arouse me."

He shrugged. "It's not me. You're a natural, honey."

"Do all women respond the same way to the same things?"

"No," he said. His hand lifted to her nape where his fingers trailed lightly over a patch of skin. She shuddered. "That's a sensitive spot for you. I'd bet, with enough time and attention, I could get you hot just from kissing your neck. We'll try that some time."

"Good," she said, her voice made husky by the slow, hot honey slipping along her nerves.

She traced the edge of his mouth, keeping the touch light, her gaze alternating between the captivating image of her finger at his lips and his eyes, where the secrets of arousal were most easily read. His breathing was even until she pressed the fingertip between his lips, to the tip of his tongue. His eyelids drooped for a moment, then he licked the fingertip as he looked right at her.

Eye contact turned the heat up a notch. She trailed her fingertip down over his bristled chin, along his throat to the point where stubble gave way to surprisingly soft skin. Then she bent forward and kissed that very spot, brushing her lips back and forth between scrape and silk. His pulse picked up under her mouth and the hand resting on her hip tightened momentarily.

She made a little sound of pleasure at having discovered a secret hidden in his skin, then licked the spot before continuing down to the hollow at the bottom of his strong throat. A hint of salt dissipated on her tongue when she dipped it into the depression between his collarbones.

With her head cocked she studied his face again. His lowered eyelids matched the flush on his cheekbones, and his mouth was set with intention. Purpose. Still straddling his legs, she put her fingers to her buttons and took off her blouse, then her bra, then unfastened her skirt and slid it down. He cupped her breasts, then brushed his thumbs across her nipples.

It was the give and take, she decided, the immediate, visceral response to her action that spurred his action. Heat flashed between her thighs, on her cheeks. She read her own passion on his face.

"Your turn," he said.

This time, when she rolled to her back on the bed, she spread her legs willingly. This time, when he put his open mouth to the top of her sex, she arched to meet him.

This time, she knew what was coming.

"Jesus," he said after one hot, wet circle of her clitoris.

She knew what he meant, could feel desire simmering between her legs, the slick moisture pooling there. "I guess I liked doing that," she said.

A velvety little humming noise, amused, aroused. "Anytime, honey," he said.

Then neither one of them talked. He worked his mouth between her thighs with a devastating focus, and the slow, tight circles around her clit drew her deep into herself. Oh yes, she knew what was coming, felt the sensitive flesh burning under his knowing mouth, felt the fist tightening in her belly until release bowed her back and made her cry out. His big hand flattened on her tummy, holding her down as the spasms passed.

She lay limp while he crawled onto the bed, to the nightstand for a condom. He put his hand on her hip. When she felt the thick length nudging inside, she eased herself down. Eyes closed, lips parted, head tilted back, she took him all the way inside her, stretching her, awakening nerves into hyperclarity.

"Gonna take you for a good, long ride."

The blunt words, murmured into her open mouth, should have shocked her, embarrassed her, but instead they sent a lightning bolt of electric heat cracking through her. Heat flowed from the place where they were joined, pulsing slowly out to the edges of her body.

"Yeah?" he asked.

"So good," she gasped back, unable to form a more detailed answer than that.

The simple words seemed to be enough. His hand tightened on her hip and his legs spread, drew up. His exhales shortened and tightened, huffing hard against her lower lip and chin. Pleasure fisted again as she strained after the release she now craved. She kissed him, her tongue stroking his each time she took him deep. Briefly she opened her eyes and caught him studying her, lust and need etched on his face, but then he closed his eyes. Orgasm pulsed through her, hot, sharp bursts of heat and light radiating from her core, through her skin.

The driven, intense way he pounded into her in search of his own release triggered another, subtly different sensation inside her, more primitive and female than even her orgasm. He was taking her, she thought. Again. Taking what he wanted, needed from her body, and when he grunted and went over, grinding his release deep inside her, it was absolutely, elementally erotic.

Sweat slid from his ribs to hers, slicked the contact between his face and her cheek. His heart raced against his rib cage, slowing as his breathing evened out and the tension ebbed from his muscles. She loosened her death grip on his shoulders. As soon as she did, he lifted himself off her body, pulling out at the same time. While he was in the bathroom she curled up on her side, her bent arm under her head.

Female. That's how she felt. Not womanly, but female to his male. All she wanted to do was curl up on the bed, his body still hard against hers, and nuzzle into his throat. She'd never seen such a thing done, but the impulse was there.

He appeared in the bedroom doorway, hands on hips, unabashedly naked, and flashed her a hotter, softer version of his smile. "How do you like me now?"

It was the second time he'd asked. She told him the truth. "I don't really know you."

The smile vanished.

"I'd like to, though," she added. She sat up on the bed and tucked her legs under her. Her hair slid forward, shielding her body.

He snagged his shorts from the floor and stepped into them. "What do you want to know?"

"Anything. Hobbies? Interests? Things you do with your free time?"

"Between the off duty and on duty, I'm working sixty hours a week. SWAT workouts the rest of the week. Sleep, eat, repeat."

The terse description matched the interior of his apartment. "Tell me about your family."

He cut her a look as sharp as his smile but without any of the charm. "Just a family. Mother, father, brother, sister."

The idea of Ben with a brother made her smile. "Does he still ranch with your dad?"

His face was utterly still, arms once again folded across his chest. "No."

"Oh. Does he live here in town?"

"Yes."

This felt like playing Twenty Questions on a long car ride to church camp but without the sense of playfulness. "Do you see him often?"

"I'm due at his house in a couple of minutes."

"Oh," she said again, and scrambled to her feet. "I'm sorry. I didn't mean to keep you."

Fortunately her clothes lay in a pile at the end of the bed. He didn't say anything as she dressed, but when she began to search through the twisted sheet and beige carpet for the U-pins necessary to hold her hair in place, he joined her. In the end she sat on the bed and used the comb she pulled from her purse to smooth her hair while he hunkered down to pluck pins from the carpet and lay them in a pile beside her. Elbows across knees, he watched her coil the length into a bun at the nape of her neck and use the pins to secure it.

"It's thick," he commented.

He'd had his hands in it more than any other man, so he would know. She'd taught herself to braid it after her mother died because her father had no idea how to brush, let along style, a young girl's hair, and working with it reminded her of her mother. "I can't do anything fun with it," she said as she inserted the last pin. "It won't hold a perm, much less curls from a curling iron."

"We've had plenty of fun with your hair," he said.

And there was the flashing smile. She smiled back, but didn't miss how he'd turned the conversation away from his family, back to sex. It was a mistake to make anything more out of this. "I suppose we have," she said as she tucked her comb back in her purse, then got to her feet.

Ben followed her to the door. "Same time next week?" he asked.

She paused in the doorway and looked at him, trying to understand the causes and consequences of desire. He wasn't trying to trap her or second-guess her, or even protect her. All he offered was a chance to experience something intoxicating, radically thrilling. For now, it was enough.

"All right," she said.

Chapter Ten

The following Friday traffic at the farm stand picked up as people got off work and started their weekend grocery shopping. When the A&M boys returned from town to help handle the rush, Rachel told Jess she was going to do the milking, then followed the dirt trail through the wildflowers to the goat yard. She milked the does, then turned to the nightly chores, mucking out the bedding hay and dumping it in a wheelbarrow to transfer to the compost pile, transferring the previous day's waste hay for clean bedding, adding forkfuls of new hay to the trough. At the plastic storage bin she measured out each goat's ration of concentrate based on where the doe was in the cycle, and dumped it into her feed bucket. The sounds of their communal munching, hooves rustling in the straw, used to make Rachel smile. Lately all she felt was a growing impatience to move on with her life.

Once again she inhaled deeply, this time getting lungfuls of sultry evening air, goats and manure and the unique scent of the concentrate. Underneath it all lay the faint scent of Ben; sex layered over sweat layered over soap, unique and distinct, something she couldn't get out of her nostrils. Not that she really wanted to. When she closed her eyes she saw his square jaw, felt his hard body against hers.

It was stupid for her to daydream about Ben Harris while she walked back up to the farm stand, stupid and naïve, something she tried hard not to be. He wouldn't tell her anything about who he was outside his bedroom. Based on his reaction last Sunday morning, there was far more to being a cop than black-humored stories about taking drunk men to a shelter. He'd been out on a SWAT call Saturday night. He'd been up for probably thirty hours, and on duty for most of it, by the time she showed up at his apartment. What happened between them was raw, intense, and to her, exceedingly intimate, and yet he wouldn't tell her what his hobbies were.

Jess stopped by the cash register to slip a check under the drawer. "I think I've figured out where you're going on Sundays," she said.

Rachel made a noncommittal noise and scanned the shaded stand for a customer who might need help. It was truly shocking how many suburban women came out to the stand, then had no idea what to do with the array of produce offered.

"You're seeing *Officer Harris,*" Jess said.

With Jess the teasing edge to her voice could tip into friendly girl banter or serious snark. She might be relieved Rachel wasn't interested in Rob, or there might be something to ridicule about dating a cop Rachel didn't know about. "What makes you think that?"

"You shower before you leave, and you shower when you get home. That usually means sex happened in between. But you don't wash your hair, which smells like his cologne."

"He doesn't wear cologne," Rachel pointed out as she wove through the customers to a woman staring at the carrots, no more than two hours out of the ground, laid out in bunches in a flat. "Can I help you find something?"

"I'm looking for baby carrots," the woman said uncertainly.

Behind her Rachel heard the irritated sniff that went with Jess's patented eye roll, and stepped in front of her fellow apprentice so the customer wouldn't see the derision. "Baby carrots are made from regular carrots," she explained gently. "The processing company shaves off most of the carrot and uses the gratings in bagged salads. What's left are those little baby carrots. Our carrots are fresh from the field today," she said.

She helped the woman choose a small selection of different vegetables to try, then added a sheet of paper with basic recipes, and sent her on her way.

"Can you believe how distanced the average American is from her food?" Jess said. "I mean, come on. She has to know that food grows in dirt."

Making the customer feel stupid wouldn't help. "Knowing isn't the same as understanding. We're all distanced from something basic," she said. For the customer, getting food from a stand, not a sanitized store with pretty packaging was a disconnect. For her, sex. For Ben . . . emotions. How could a man that intensely alive be so out of touch with himself?

"He wears something," Jess said, as if she knew what Rachel was thinking about. "I smelled it when he walked by me at the auction."

Rachel tried to remember what was on top of the dresser in Ben's bedroom and came up with nothing more than loose change, receipts, and pens. Something uniquely Ben lingered in her mind.

Soap. His skin. Sweat. Maybe detergent from one of those faded western shirts he favored, and opened so easily when she wanted a good look at his torso. Memory sent a rush of heat through her body.

Wasn't smell the most potent sense of all?

"I'm kind of surprised," Jess said. She straightened the remaining rows of beans and peas, moving opposite from Rachel, who did the same on the other side of the table. "He doesn't seem like your type."

"I'm kind of surprised, because I don't seem like his," Rachel replied.

Maybe sex was his hobby. Maybe he spent what little downtime he had doing exactly what he'd done with Rachel. "What is my type?" she asked.

"Rob," Jess said flatly. "You're perfect for each other. You're into the same things. You're so good, and you'd slip right into the farm's operation."

"I'm good?"

"You never yell or argue or even get impatient and bad tempered." Jess eyed her across the mounded sweet corn. "I've never known anyone like you."

She didn't yell because she'd never been permitted to raise her voice in anger or frustration or impatience. Those emotions were seen as signs of disobedience and disrespect to her father, her elders, and God. In the days after she left, the social worker at the shelter pointed out that there was a wide range of human emotional experience, and expecting a person to only feel joy and gratitude was a form of abuse. Rachel was now allowed to feel everything. Anger at what had been expected of her, taken from her. Sadness over what she'd risked and lost. Fear for her future. Humiliation at the sidelong looks when she wore the wrong clothes, or said the wrong thing. But while the farm felt like a refuge to Jess, it felt too much like home to Rachel.

"I like and admire Rob, but I don't want to help him run Silent Circle Farm," Rachel said.

"If you get into vet tech school, you'd be more valuable to the farm," Jess pointed out.

Rachel shook her head. "Rob has a vet. A good one. A farm like this doesn't need a full-time person on staff, just someone with decent knowledge about animal care, and you can get most of that with a season or two of experience and a good book."

Jess had arrived at the farm two months after Rachel. She'd graduated from college but rather than getting a job she'd come straight to the farm, searching for a meaningful way of life, yet not hesitating to call her parents when her laptop broke. "Where did you grow up?" Jess asked, as if the thought had just occurred to her. In all likelihood, it had.

She was saved from answering when Rob crested the slight rise, George by his side, panting from the heat. Like water flowing downhill, Jess drifted along the rows of tables in Rob's direction. Rachel went back to the faucet and ran a bowl of water for George, who lapped at it, then immersed his whole snout in the bowl and snorted, splashing water everywhere. Rachel laughed and rocked back on her heels, away from the playful dog. When she looked up, Rob and Jess were both watching her.

Feeling awkward, she patted George and shooed him back to Rob, tucked a loose strand of hair back into her braid, then picked up a flat of strawberries to carry to a customer's car. With the groceries safely stored in the back of the car, the woman pulled away and revealed a minivan Rachel knew very, very well. It belonged to Reverend Carlton Bayles, her pastor.

Her former pastor.

A complex swirl of emotion rooted Rachel in the dust as men got out of the vehicle. Four, no five of them, all leaders in the Elysian Fields church hierarchy, all dressed in khaki slacks and button-down shirts. All wearing identical expressions of horror when they saw her form-fitting T-shirt, the neck scooping low to reveal her collarbones, and her jeans. Tight tops and pants were expressly forbidden to women at Elysian Fields, for fear they would enflame men and encourage women to act like them.

In all her hours with Ben, his naked body against hers, inside hers, she'd never felt as dirty and ashamed as she did when the men who used to rule her world judged her in the Silent Circle Farm parking lot.

"Good Lord have mercy," the deacon intoned.

"At least you haven't cut your hair, Rachel Elizabeth," Reverend Bayles said, shocked.

She almost laughed. Instead, she stopped herself from crossing her arms over her torso, standing straight and tall. "What are you doing here?"

"Our duty. We've come to bring you home, Rachel Elizabeth."

"I'm not going back," she replied, at the last second changing *home* to *back*. But even in her defiance, she stayed out of arm's reach.

"Your father misses you," Reverend Bayles said.

"He is welcome to come see me anytime," she said.

"He cannot countenance your disobedience. The commandments admonish us to honor thy father and thy mother. Exodus chapter twenty verse twelve," he added automatically. "Your actions disgrace your father and shame us all in God's eyes."

Her heart pounded in her throat. "I disagree," Rachel said carefully. "I prayed for months about what I felt called to do. I believe I'm living out my life as God intended."

"By tricking your accountability partner into thinking you were reading at a Christian bookstore, then running away? You should not have been allowed to remain unmarried," Reverend Bayles said. "A woman needs a husband and babies to keep her mind focused on her role. He was sentimental, keeping his only daughter close."

"My father respected my wishes, and I'm grateful to him for that," Rachel said, trying to find common ground.

"And this is how you repay him?" He gestured at her clothes, the farm. "He's seen the error of his ways, and prays daily for God to forgive him for this lapse."

He wouldn't answer her letters, telling her without words that his love depended on her meeting the community's approval.

"Your eternal soul is at stake. God judges every thought, word, and deed on this earth, Rachel Elizabeth. Based on what I see in front of me, you are in grave, grave danger."

She was shaking too hard not to wrap her arms around herself. She'd fly apart if she didn't. Her stomach surged up her throat, because if God watched her with Ben Harris, wearing jeans and a T-shirt were the least of her concerns now.

"It's my soul to risk," she said, her throat tightening. "Mine. Not yours, not my father's. Mine."

"Until you marry, you are your father's responsibility. If your father dies and you are still unmarried, you are the Church's responsibility. We'll wait while you pack whatever things you have left that will be appropriate for your return to our community."

"I'm not leaving with you. Not now, not ever."

He straightened and thrust out his chin. "Rachel Elizabeth, I hoped it wouldn't come to this, but if you don't pack your bags and get in the car, I'll be forced to report you to the police for stealing your father's money."

It was an empty threat, as the community rarely invited outside authorities into their concerns, but anger flowed hot and acid in her veins. Thank God for the lawyers who volunteered at the shelter where she'd lived. "I spoke to a lawyer after I left. That was a joint bank account," she said. "I worked on the farm as many hours as my father. I'd earned half that money. I took one-third for fifteen years of work. I left him the rest, including my mother's family land, which was deeded to both of us. So you go ahead and call the police. I've done nothing wrong."

Rage suffused Reverend Bayles's face, then all five men switched their focus from Rachel to someone behind her. She turned to see Rob standing just off her right shoulder, with Jess lingering a little distance away. Embarrassment crawled along her nape. This was the last thing she'd wanted anyone to see. Other than Ben, she'd told no one where she'd come from, and she'd told only Ben because when he showed up in the parking lot demanding an answer, she figured he deserved to know.

"What's wrong, Rachel?" Rob asked.

"Who are you?" Reverend Bayles demanded.

"Rob Strong. I own this farm," Rob said, but he didn't offer his hand.

The men looked at Rob's left hand, then at Rachel's. No rings. Then they looked at Rachel, wide-eyed disbelief and horror on their faces.

"What is your relationship to this girl?"

It seemed like a reasonable question. Rob opened his mouth.

"Don't answer that, Rob," Rachel said.

He closed it again. Her tone and Rob's obedience weren't lost on the five men from her former life. No woman of any age or experience spoke to a man in the tone of voice she just used.

"My relationships are none of your business," she said clearly. "I am not a girl. I am not your responsibility. I am not leaving with you. Now, or ever."

Rob looked at the five men arrayed in a semicircle in front of Rachel, and jumped to the right conclusion. "Leave. Now." Beside him, George let out a low growl.

She'd never heard that tone of voice from Rob, or a growl from George.

"This isn't your concern, young man," Reverend Bayles started.

Rob cut him off. "You have sixty seconds to get in your car and get off my property or I'll call the State Patrol, give them your license plate and tell them you were harassing one of my employees."

Reverend Bayles stared steadily at Rachel, who stared right back. "Your rebellion is killing your father. Body and soul. He believes he's failed as a father, as a Christian, as a man."

Rachel's diaphragm stopped working, leaving her not breathless but entirely without air. When she could speak again, she said, "I can't be his salvation. I love him, but I can't be what saves him."

"Pray on that, Rachel Elizabeth."

She was shaking when the minivan circled the rest of the cars in the parking lot and pulled out onto the dirt road leading to the highway. Beside her, Jess let out a low *wow*.

"Rachel," Rob said quietly.

She was shaking, her stomach in acid-coated knots, with fury and shame and humiliation. She looked at him and shook her head. "Not now."

I am not a victim. I am not pitiable.

"I should get back to the stand," she said.

"Take the rest of the night off," Rob said quietly.

"I'm fine."

Rob reached out, very slowly and carefully, and lifted her hand from her waist and held it palm down in his. Her fingers trembled in his big, calloused palm, mirroring the muscles spasming up and down her entire body. Her heart raced, and she felt embarrassingly close to tears. In the raw, vulnerable wound all her old training raced back. Anything other than happiness and gratitude was rebellion, and a sin.

She was a sinner. An ungrateful, disobedient sinner.

No.

Her head spun, and she swallowed hard. "It's the Friday night rush," she said.

"You're in no condition to work," Rob said. "We've got this, me and Jess."

A spot on the team assured, Jess nodded eagerly. "No problem. Treat yourself. Eat a big scoop of ice cream or a slice of the gluten-free cake I made yesterday."

"Okay. All right. I will," she said, because she had to get away. She hurried toward the path leading from the farm stand to the employees bunkhouse, nestled at the bottom of the hill near the creek, but once she got inside, she couldn't stop shaking.

What did it mean to be whole? She had no problem with surrendering herself into a relationship, even secretly longed for that. But she drew the line at willingly giving herself to a man who used her to shore up his identity.

She paced through the bunkhouse. The air inside held all the warmth of the day and wouldn't cool off until after dark when the outside air temperature dropped. In the kitchen she opened the freezer, but one of the A&M boys must have finished off the ice cream because the carton was gone. The cake sat on the counter, but Rachel knew she didn't want cake. She wanted to rage and scream and clench her fists. Doing that in the communal environment of Silent Circle Farm, in front of Rob's customers, was impossible.

A long walk beside the creek to the back pasture currently

housing Rob's sheep herd would settle her down. She'd taken many, many long walks in the months before she left Elysian Fields, trying to reconcile what she felt with who she was. When she burst through the screen door and saw her car, another thought bloomed in her mind.

You aren't limited to long walks anymore. You've got options. Specifically, one very hard, very edgy option who knows exactly how this feels and what you need.

Ben's busy. He's getting off work at his first job and heading to his second.

So what? If he's not home, you'll enjoy the drive.

She snagged her keys from the hook by the front door, jerked open the car door, and got in. Seconds later she was spewing dust and gravel behind her on her way to the paved county road, toward Galveston.

Chapter Eleven

Ben's truck was in his parking space. Rachel took a deep breath and closed her eyes, searching for that bright inner space she used to live within. All she found was darkness, heated by desire, rich and loamy, like the fields after Rob plowed them. She got out of the car and hurried up the stairs to Ben's door. She knocked, heard footsteps, then a pause while she assumed he peered through the peephole. The door opened to reveal him shirtless and barefoot, wearing only his uniform pants. Two lines etched into the skin on either side of his mouth. When she dragged her gaze up from his broad, bare chest to his face, he quirked one eyebrow at her.

"Are you busy?"

"Just got off work," he drawled. "I've got an hour to shower, eat, get to No Limits."

His guard was up, his face tight with tension that didn't ease when he saw her standing there. He didn't ask why she was here, and this was a mistake. Sundays only, that's all he agreed to. "Never mind," she said, and turned to go.

He braced his shoulder against the doorframe. "You here to talk about hobbies, Rachel?"

She flushed at the teasing tone, but looked back over her shoulder anyway. "You know I'm not."

With a tip of his head he gestured her inside. The apartment was warm, the air-conditioning working to cool the space after he'd been at work all day; between the sunshine and the heat threatening to set the air on fire, heat crept along her nerves.

She already felt better.

"What do you want?"

Her gaze drifted from his sweat-dampened hair to his bare feet. "Let's take a shower."

He gestured her down the hall, into the bathroom. While she watched, he reached past her to slide open the shower's glass door and turn on the water. One dark gray towel hung from the rack on the door. He opened the linen closet built into the wall behind the bathroom door, flicked a glance at her hair and got out two more, then worked his fingers under her T-shirt's hem. The warm skin of his fingers brushed ribs and breasts as he drew the T-shirt up and off, and she got the message. He didn't want to know what was wrong, what brought her here.

Steam lifted over the top of the shower door. Ben reached for the knob and dialed the temperature back toward the cool side, then unzipped her jeans. She stood still, her back to the wall, and let him undress her. His touch was somehow both devastatingly intimate and impersonal at the same time.

Exactly.

He braced himself with his forearm beside her head, then his hand slid up her arm to cup her nape, just under the intricately coiled bun she wore. One pin dropped to the floor, then another before she said, "Leave it up." Her eyes were still closed because his fingers were stroking that sensitive spot on her neck, sending shivers racing across the top layer of her skin.

He bent to kiss her, his bare chest skimming her breasts with each irregular breath. His mouth left her cheekbone for her earlobe, then stopped at the sensitive hollow behind her jaw. Without thinking, she put her hands to his waist. She felt warm skin, hard muscle and hipbone, the combination of belt and uniform pants, all under her hands as she unbuckled, unbuttoned, unzipped. Taking what she needed.

His hard shaft thrust out thick and heavy as he reached for her wrist. When she didn't open her hand, he simply ran her knuckles up and down the underside.

"You want that?"

"Yes," she said.

He used hands and hips and shoulders to shift her into the shower. He stepped in beside her and shut the door, and suddenly the damp air clogged her throat, stung her eyes.

I am not dirty. This is not wrong. I am not a bad person. I am a person, a human being, with a body, with emotions. I am not dirty.

The water seemed to whisper this refrain to her as droplets pelted his shoulders, then streamed down his chest and abdomen in rivulets that quickly soaked the thick thatch of dark hair around his jutting shaft. The water plastered his hair forward on his head, emphasizing his hard features. Without a smile he looked almost brutish, and when he moved, all shifting planes and hard muscles, lightning struck between her thighs. A day's worth of stubble framed his mouth, which was soft, yet somehow exuding sexual purpose, and his eyes had gone storm blue and heavy lidded. A blood flush stood high on his cheekbones, throwing his face into a purely masculine relief.

Her breathing quickened from the weight, the heat, the humid, water-laden air, the way he crowded her against the wall. Eyes narrowed, brows lowered he pinned her with his body and slid one hand between her legs. She shuddered once, then again when he circled her clit with his fingertip. Using teeth and tongue, lips and fingertip he drew her under the surface of desire, into the hot depths. Water streamed over his shoulders, running between her breasts and down her hips as heat seared fast and hard between her thighs. In a matter of moments he flung her over the edge.

"More," she gasped. Pushed to the edge emotionally, she added, "Fuck me."

It felt right, so right. That's what she wanted. She wanted Ben Harris to fuck her, and she wasn't ashamed to demand it, either.

A low growl rumbled under the water pounding in the enclosed space. He reached for the condom he'd set on the ledge, leaning into her to keep her pinned as he smoothed it on. "Say it again," he demanded.

She gave a skittering little laugh. "Fuck me."

He lathered up his hands, then transferred the bubbles to her back. He stepped into her body and slid one arm under her hips to lift her. With her hands on his shoulders for balance, her skin slid easily against the shower stall, up to position his erection, then a pause.

"Again. Use my name."

Somehow, like this, male prerogative rubbed her exactly the right way. She looked right into his eyes and said, "Fuck me, Ben."

And *down*. His shaft slid into her, nerve endings popping and firing as the hard length stretched her, opened her. Not sure what to do, how to help, she reached out, grabbing first at his shoulders, then the top edge of the shower stall, trying to find something to help him support her weight.

He tipped his head back and looked into her eyes. "Just hold on," he said brusquely.

She wrapped her arms around his neck and her legs around his hips, and suddenly it all worked. All she had to do was open to him, cling to him, and let him take her, slowly at first, teasingly gliding in and out until she locked her ankles behind his back to better open herself to him.

"Harder," she said.

His next thrust impacted with enough force to send her a couple of inches up the wall. He adjusted his grip, bracing his forearm beside her head, fingers curled around the top of the stall so the next thrust sent her into his elbow. It was hard and rough and absolutely inescapable. In response she sank her fingernails into his shoulders. He just laughed. The sound, combined with another hard stroke, sent fire pulsing out from her core, curling her toes, tightening tendons and muscles until she cried out with need.

He was pounding into her now, using her defenseless position backed to the wall, entirely dependent on him to stay upright, showing her exactly how hot this could get. Each driving stroke shoved her a little deeper into the blackness, until the hot fist low in her belly flung open. Wave after wave of pleasure crashed through her, and as if from a distance she heard her desperate cries. As if her release triggered his, Ben thrust in once, twice, then held himself hard and deep inside her.

Water coursed over them, between them as he straightened, set her on her feet, and disengaged their bodies. Tremors raced along her nerves and her knees weren't quite steady, a problem he also seemed to face, because while his arm slipped from under her bottom, he leaned his weight on the forearm still braced on the wall. His free hand scudded up her wet arm to cup her jaw, and he bent his head to rest his forehead on hers.

A fresh wave of intimacy flowed through her. This one had nothing to do with sex, and everything to do with the way he leaned into her, his breathing slowly evening out, his fingers trembling ever so slightly. She got the sense he didn't do this often, lean on someone else for any reason at all, much less lean on a woman after sex. She waited for a long, sweet moment. When he didn't move, she gently stroked his nape. Bristly buzzed hair gave way to hot skin, each caress slow enough to be stealthy. To avoid spooking him.

Every sense was alive, the emotions tamped down to cooling embers.

He breathed deep and stepped back. Without meeting her gaze he opened the shower door and stepped out to deal with the condom. Cool air flooded the stall. When Ben rejoined her he turned her so she stood under the spray. He adjusted the showerhead so water rained over her back and shoulders, and only the spatter from the droplets misted in her hair as they shared the soap and water. Her brain was entirely empty, except for a line from Genesis that floated up into her consciousness.

And your desire shall be for your husband . . .

Desire she had in spades. The husband she did not have, did not want. But oh Lord, she wanted Ben.

"All set?" he asked.

She nodded, and turned off the water. They bumped knees and elbows and hips as they dried off. When Ben went into the bedroom she heard drawers opening, then fabric against skin. Rachel wiggled back into her jeans and T-shirt, clothes she'd been forbidden to wear. Farm work was so much easier in jeans and a lightweight shirt. Safer than a long skirt around heavy machinery, too. She'd removed most of her hairpins when Ben, now dressed in the same clothes he'd worn the night of the auction, leaned against the vanity and watched the heavy mass tumble around her shoulders; she gave it a quick towel dry, then smoothed it back and coiled it up again.

She would smell like him when she went back to the farm. Jess would know where she'd been, what she'd done. How out of character it was for her in the first place.

"What brought that on?"

"The pastor from Elysian Fields showed up at the farm. Now everyone there knows where I came from. How different I am."

He watched her comb her hair from ends up to the roots before he spoke. "What happened to make you leave?"

"Most girls in our community are married by twenty, twenty-one at the latest. I wasn't. I was looking after my father and his house. He managed the animal side of the farm's operation, and I helped him there, so it was good for the farm. I kept records for the vet who tended our animals, and after a few years, I knew more than the men. When I offered suggestions or input or new ideas, I was behaving in an *unwomanly fashion*. Stepping out of my place in the world, and once I did that, I had to step back into it. Except I couldn't. I withdrew fifteen years of minimum-wage earnings from our joint bank account, took my mother's watch and my birth certificate, and told my accountability partner I was going to the Christian bookstore. Instead I went to the shelter."

"You didn't tell them you were leaving? You just disappeared?"

She paused in the middle of combing from roots to ends. Something about this upset him. Everyone else complimented her on her bravery and daring, but Ben's blue eyes were as hard and flat as paint chips. "I called from the shelter the next day," she said mildly.

A muscle popped in his jaw. "Rob Strong didn't ask for references when he hired you?"

She shrugged. "He likes to teach people about farming, so he's used to hiring people with no experience, but after ten minutes of conversation he could tell I knew more about goats than he did. No one else asked, and I didn't tell them."

"Why not?"

Working slowly, she started a loose French braid at the back of her skull. "I spent two months living in a shelter before I found the job at Silent Circle Farm. There I was a victim. I needed a social security number, and a driver's license. I have a certificate of graduation from a homeschool institute, not even a GED, so I had a hard time finding a job other than fast food. I know what I want. It isn't much," she said with a laugh. "I want to work as a veterinary technician and have an apartment of my own. I'm tired of being a combination of a tragic figure, the oppressed refugee from a fundamentalist community, and a circus side show. Now everyone knows."

Ben just stared at her. That violation of her privacy was impossible to explain to someone who'd never known what it was like to have nothing for yourself. Not your body or your heart or your emotions. Reverend Bayles exposed her to everyone on the farm.

Intending to finish the discussion, she said, "They said they were there to take me back home. I told them I was never going back. I think they got the message."

In an instant Ben grew bigger, broader, as if some of her anger transferred from her to him. "Take you back? Kidnapping?"

She remembered how they arrayed themselves in front of her, how convinced of their moral superiority and rightness they were. "Their tactics involved guilt and shame," she said. "Not kidnapping."

"File a restraining order."

"It's not necessary," she said. "They hinted I'd stolen money from my father when I left, but my name was on the account and I'd earned that money. I didn't even take half of it."

"How much money?"

She got the sense the question was automatic, a cop reflex. "Enough to buy a date with you," she said lightly. When he didn't respond, she added, "I have enough to get me through vet tech school. I need to work to pay my living expenses, books, that kind of thing. It's not much, but it's enough."

She looked up at Ben. Clearly he thought with family back at Elysian Fields, they'd stop at nothing to get her back. Perhaps he thought she was wavering. "I'm never going back. I know that already. I just underestimated how long it would take them to let me go. Frankly, I didn't think they'd find me worth coming after."

"Some families don't let people leave without a fight."

"I didn't leave him," she said simply. "I write him every week. If he would write me back, even open my letters rather than returning them immediately, I'd go see him. Until then I'm not going back. This fight is over," she said.

He looked at his watch. "I won't keep you," she said, and went to grab her purse from beside the door.

"What would you have done if I wasn't home?"

"I don't know," she said. "Gone back to the farm and gone for a walk, probably."

"You should swing by No Limits. Hottest pickup bar in town, and the best place to blow off steam."

"I can't see myself at a nightclub," she said. "But I'd love to do something else with you."

The words hung in the air, never to be retrieved, before she remembered he worked there. He wasn't inviting her on a date. She opened her mouth to take back what she said.

"Like what?" he said.

His neutral tone didn't give her much hope. "There's a coffee shop and bookstore on the Strand called Artistary. They have concerts, book discussion groups, conversation nights, and open-mike nights on Tuesdays for poets and local musicians. They have sandwiches and salads, if you want to get something to eat."

It sounded dumb as soon as she said it. Ben wouldn't want to eat a salad, drink tea, and watch people read poetry or sing songs. *Think of it as another lesson,* she told herself. *You're learning to ask a man out. You're going to get rejected.*

"Okay," he said.

"Okay?"

"Okay." The blade of a smile flashed. "I can handle anything for a few hours. I'll pick you up, but I can't guarantee what time. I'll text when I leave town."

"You don't have to pick me up," she said. "It's two extra hours of driving for you." Half an hour out, half an hour back, repeat after the show. Or the sex. Whichever took longer.

"It's a date," he said. "I do know how dates are supposed to work."

She hesitated, then nodded because arguing with him seemed pointless and he had somewhere to be. "I'm glad you're coming with me. See you Tuesday."

She let herself out, down to the parking lot, an odd mix of emotions tumbling inside her. Bright flashes of desire mingled with that disquieting emotion she couldn't name, tenderness, perhaps, or affection. Simple happiness that he wanted to do something else with her. Anticipation for Tuesday.

Something new. It took her a minute to identify confidence. Today she'd stood up to the Elysian Fields leadership and initiated sex with Ben. More important, she'd reminded herself of how far she'd come, and how far she had yet to go. She closed her car door, pulled her cell phone from her purse and opened her Drafts folder in her email. The carefully written email with her application to the local vet tech school, admissions essay, and scanned transcripts sat in the folder.

She opened it, and touched Send.

Done. All she could do now was wait, and pray, and mull over another pressing question.

What on earth was she going to wear for a proper date with Ben Harris?

Chapter Twelve

Three a.m. Even after a shower and a night sweating in Galveston's humid spring air Ben could still smell Rachel's unique scent, rain and risk and an increasing element of longing. Steve seemed to have an ongoing thing with Juliette's friend Marta, but Ben drove not to Juliette's for a party but to his brother's house.

Fidelity to Rachel had nothing to do with it. He just couldn't see anything at one of Juliette's things topping what happened a few hours earlier.

He waited until Sam finished the cut on a sheet of drywall, turned off the saw, and tossed the safety glasses on the workbench. He'd expected silence but instead music filled the air. "Shine" by Collective Soul, but an a cappella version. As he watched his brother sing along, a big hand reached into Ben's chest and squeezed everything tight. Heart, lungs, stomach, gut.

Sam had such a great voice, textured, raspy, a channel for

everything he felt. He'd won the lead in the school musical his freshman year, the same year Ben started at linebacker. They'd grown apart those first two years of high school, Ben following the easy road through sports and girls to popularity while Sam struggled with his identity. Or rather, how much of his identity to show in a rural Texas high school that lived and breathed football.

He watched Sam sing and felt the hair lift on his nape.

To shake it off he looked around the half-finished garage. Drywall covered two of the three walls. Loose wiring hung between the beams of the unfinished wall, just one more hurdle to jump to get Jonathan.

It was unlikely to happen. Ben knew it, and Sam did, too, even if he wouldn't admit it. That didn't stop Sam. Nothing had, when Sam made a decision.

Sam caught sight of Ben out of the corner of his eye and spun into a crouch. "Jesus *Christ*!" he said as he straightened.

"Common spelling?" Ben said wryly.

Sam blinked. "What?"

He'd told Rachel that story, not his brother, the person he used to tell everything. "Never mind. Sorry I didn't knock."

Sam sat back against the workbench. "Two visits in less than a month. It's a miracle."

"A miracle would be Sunday brunch," Ben said.

"The answer to my prayers," Sam agreed. He opened the fridge and tossed Ben a beer. "How you been?"

Good question. In the couple of weeks he'd gotten verbal reprimands from two different superior officers, thoroughly debauched a formerly virgin refugee from a fundamentalist cult, then agreed to go to an open-mike night with her. He wasn't sure what was worse, expecting her to suck his cock like she was a No Limits veteran, or taking her out on a date. He settled on, "Fine."

"Staying safe?" His brother's blue eyes glinted like shards of a broken mirror.

"Not my job, Sam."

"I heard about what you did."

Sam already knew about the gas station so he had to mean tackling the tweaking violent offender. "How'd you hear about that?" The situation made the news, but his role was limited to *we apprehended the suspect*, which was just fine with Ben.

Sam looked at him like the idiot he was. "There are gay cops, Ben. Gay cops go to gay bars, where my friends hang out. Someone told a friend to tell me to check on my brother because while he's always had a reputation, he's not acting like a smart cop."

So much for the thin blue line. "I'm fine."

"She was worried about you."

"I'm fine," he repeated, because repeating it would make it so. "Is that why you texted me?"

"Yes." Sam chucked an empty at the recycling bin that held only empty bottles of organic orange juice and Coke Zero cans, with a few Shiners thrown in. A very few. "Stop being stupid or I will kick your ass."

Ben actually took that seriously. Somewhere in the two years he was missing, Sam had learned street-fighting moves that didn't spare eyes or throat or nuts. When he fought, he fought to maim. "It's not stupid. It's my job to go after guys like that."

"There are rules and procedures for calling for backup, or letting the dog take down the big crazy tweaking drug dealer. Jesus Christ," Sam said again, and this time a laugh huffed out. "What the fuck were you thinking?"

He'd never been able to resist Sam's laugh. "Fuck if I know," he said. "He was built like a goddamn tank, and he knocked Montgomery right through a railing. Hitting him was like hitting a brick wall. Good thing he tripped over his own fucking feet."

"And despite this, you're going home alone again?"

Ever since he'd met Rachel. Normally everyone understood the rules. Going home with him wasn't dating him. No one had any claim on him, and he gave the same courtesy. Whether a girl he'd slept with Friday night showed up at No Limits on Saturday with a male friend or a pack of girlfriends made no difference to him. He got booty calls, and considered them fair trade. When it was all over but the leavin', usually the woman gathered up all the peripheral bits of her image. She'd slip on a watch, rings, earrings, find something to pull her hair back. Grab her purse and shoes and maybe a jacket. Then she'd walk out the door. Rachel was exactly the same whether she wore a pretty dress, jeans and a T-shirt, or nothing at all.

Rachel had asked him to go on a date. Or hang out. What the hell was it?

Dating was part of what she had to learn about. Good dates, bad dates, rejections, they were all part of the scene she knew nothing about. It was just like teaching her about sex. Except it wasn't.

"You're taking an awful long time to answer that question," Sam said.

Ben shrugged. "Yeah."

Sam cocked an eyebrow, but went back to Ben's errors in judgment. "She said you've always been reckless, but it's been worse lately."

The song ended, and Ben changed the subject. "I haven't heard you sing in a while."

When his brother sang, everything he'd ever felt or seen or done swirled on the surface of his skin, then flowed into the air. When Sam sang, everyone in the vicinity stopped what they were doing to watch. Ben had learned to play guitar so Sam had someone to accompany him, and to his surprise, actually liked it.

Sam shrugged. "I fill in for a friend in a band every so often. Ever since we got Jonathan I want to stay home. How about you? Played much lately?"

After Sam left Ben had put his guitar in their closet on the ranch and never picked it up again. Sam knew that, so the question rankled. "Too busy."

"How busy are you October nineteenth?"

"Why?"

"You know why, you stubborn motherfucker. It's Dad's fifty-fifth birthday. We're throwing him a party."

Sam hadn't forgiven their father by his fiftieth. Now, because he had, Ben was supposed to forgive and forget? No fucking way.

He chucked his can at the recycling bin. "I'll probably be working."

"That's not a weekday, or a Friday night, or a Saturday night. It's a Sunday afternoon months from now. You ask for the time off."

"I'm on twenty-four/seven call with the SWAT team."

"And you don't get to ask for days off?"

"It's SWAT, Sam. I have to be out of the state to not get called."

He was lying. He knew it, and despite the effort he made to control his face, Sam knew it. Sam knew him.

"I'll take that as a yes, unless the state decides to serve warrants on violent offenders on a Sunday afternoon."

"Don't count on me. Sunday's a great day to serve warrants."

Sam didn't find this funny. "You'd better be there, Ben. What happened is in the past, and this is months from now. Know who's going to be there? Me, Chris, Jonathan, Katy and Alan and the girls, Mom, all her sisters, all of Dad's brothers and sisters, and damn near everyone else he knows. You'd better fucking be there."

The silence between them vibrated until Ben heard a ringing in his ears. Sam huffed out a laugh. "Bring whoever this girl is who's removed your screw-around gene. I'd like to meet her."

"There isn't anyone." It was just timing, and a virgin. A former virgin. A woman who chose him because she thought he wouldn't care.

Was that what he'd become?

"I'd believe that if your reputation wasn't the stuff of myth and legends."

"You know better than to believe in myths and legends."

"The thing about them, Ben, is that they may not be literally true, but they're always true. That's why they last as long as they do."

Ben had slept through World Religions. "Yeah. Okay. Whatever," he said, and turned to go.

Jonathan stood in the doorway, his bony knees sticking out from the hems of a pair of gray cotton shorts with blue sharks printed on them. Even Ben could tell the kid was half-asleep. Jonathan looked at Ben, then at Sam, then back at Ben. He'd done the same thing the first time they met—looked at Sam, looked at Ben, looked back at Sam—then said, "He's not like you."

For a kid who supposedly had attachment issues, he was a pretty sharp judge of character.

"Hey, kiddo," Sam said. He crossed the garage to hunker down in front of the boy. "You remember my brother, Ben."

Jonathan nodded.

"What are you doing out of bed?" Sam said, his voice gentle.

"I wanted a drink."

Sam straightened and held out his hand. "Okay, let's get you a drink. Hang around for a minute," he said to Ben in a low voice.

Ben leaned on the workbench and watched through the lit kitchen window while Sam got milk from the fridge. A couple of minutes later he disappeared from the kitchen window, then reappeared in the upstairs hallway. Enough time passed to tuck Jonathan in again, then he reappeared in the hallway window before pushing open the screen door to the backyard, taking the deck steps at a lope.

"What's up?" Ben asked, looking down at his folded arms.

"Do you know anyone at DPFS?"

He looked up into his brother's face, into his own face, and read real anxiety there. "Not well. Why?"

"They're stonewalling us again on the adoption papers. I thought I'd see if you knew anyone who could tell us anything."

"Besides the fact that they're overworked, you're gay, and this is Texas?" Ben said.

"Yeah. Besides that."

Ben huffed and shook his head. "I'll see what I can find out."

"Thanks," Sam said. "He's an amazing kid."

Stranger things had happened than Sam and Chris being allowed to adopt Jonathan, but Ben didn't know how Sam could keep doing it, keep caring and loving and committing himself when he knew how much pain came from it. "I'd better get some sleep." The buzzing in his head was back, intermittent, like a fly battering itself against a window, trying to get out.

"Me, too." Sam closed the garage door after him. "Don't be a stranger."

He drove home thinking about how laughable it was to label Rachel Hill a victim. He understood the obstacles she faced, a labyrinth of paperwork just to get the documents and identification everyone else in the world took for granted, but he had no doubt she'd make it. Taking her to open-mike night was just something else to teach her. A date. A simple date. He could do that. Do that right, he amended. With a little effort, he could make this first time better than the last.

Chapter Thirteen

The setting sun painted the windshield of Ben's truck in reds and oranges as it crested the top of the hill, then disappeared in the valley sheltering Silent Circle's farm stand. Only a dust plume and the engine noise signaled his arrival before he made the left turn onto a dirt driveway sheltered by cottonwoods. Rachel was waiting for him on the bunkhouse's front porch swing. She rose as he got out of the truck, carrying a wedge-shaped, paper-wrapped object in his left hand. Behind her laughter and talk rose from the poker game going on in the apprentices' bunkhouse. Jess and a friend from Austin were beating the A&M boys pretty handily.

Rachel had taken time with her appearance, including a shopping trip into Galveston with Jess, who was all too happy to help her shop after the scene in the parking lot. The dress, straight from the spring sale rack at Walmart, was made of white eyelet with wide shoulder straps, and daringly fitted to her curves at breast, waist, and thigh. As she walked down the stairs, wide pleats flipped around her knees. Her flat brown sandals closed with pink buckles brighter than her lip gloss. She'd loosely French braided her hair and tucked the end under so the plait ended between her shoulder blades; the relaxed style, gloss, and a hint of mascara and eye shadow softened her features just a little.

Ben's steps faltered as he took a long, slow look, and for a moment she thought she'd disappointed him somehow with the lack of color and revealed skin. Then his gaze met hers, and she saw a hint of wonder over a very masculine appreciation, as if his own response surprised him.

"You look really nice," he said, his voice low enough to blend with the dust settling behind his truck.

"Thank you," she said. "So do you."

He looked like he always did, dressed in faded jeans and a western shirt. The shirt stretched over his broad shoulders and was open at the throat and cuffs. The hint of tanned wrist made Rachel's stomach do a slow loop.

He seemed to remember he held something, then offered the package to Rachel. "These are for you."

She smiled and blinked as she accepted the paper. A peek through the stapled paper showed roses. Pink roses. "You brought me flowers?" she said rather stupidly as her smile grew.

Color stood high on his cheekbones. "Yeah."

This simple gesture made up for yet another returned letter. "Thank you. Come inside while I put them in water?"

He followed her up the bunkhouse steps and through the screen door. The poker game chatter stopped when Ben ducked his head and stepped inside. He stopped by the door, his back to the wall, thumbs hooked in his belt. Rachel introduced everyone as she hurried to the kitchen, opening cupboards in search of a vase large enough to hold what turned out to be a dozen roses surrounded by baby's breath and greenery.

"Color me surprised," Jess said in a low voice. She'd found a vase at the back of one of the lower cupboards.

Rachel thought about this as she emptied the food packet into the cool water. "I'm not," she said. He knew the moves. He just didn't *do* the moves.

"You should be," Jess said, but added nothing else as she snipped the stems at an angle under running water before handing them to Rachel to arrange them in the vase. She set the vase not on the dining table, where it would be in the card players' way, but on the battered oak coffee table that sat between the couch and two rocking chairs in the living area. Ben opened the screen door for her. Impulsively, she plucked one of the stems from the arrangement before she left.

"You want me to check the does at one?" Jess asked, a hint of mischief in her voice.

Rachel flushed and looked at Ben. He gave her an almost-imperceptible lift of his eyebrows that was no answer or guidance at all. This wasn't a Sunday sex lesson.

"Oh, no," Rachel said. "We're going to open-mike night at Artistary. I'll be home by then."

"G'night," Ben said to the rest of the apprentices.

He gestured to the truck with his hand and opened her door. After she stepped inside, he closed the door and rounded the hood. Once inside he rolled up the windows and turned on the air-conditioning. "What's with the flower?"

Rachel traced the stem of the single bloom she held on her lap, carefully skimming the thorns. "No one's ever given me flowers before," she said. "I didn't want to leave them all behind."

"No one's given you flowers." The truck roared up the dirt road to the highway and turned south, toward Galveston.

"We grew them in the garden, so I'd cut them and have them on tables around the house," she said, using her side mirror to watch dust lift in their wake. "But brought me flowers? No. I wasn't in a room alone with a male, boy or man, other than my father and my pastor, until I left. We weren't supposed to even think about the opposite sex, so we would keep ourselves mentally pure for our future husbands."

He didn't say much on the trip into town, but she was used to silence. "Do you know where you're going?" she asked when they reached the outskirts.

"The Strand." When she nodded, he added, "I've been a cop for eight years. If I can't tell you the best way to any given address in the city, I don't deserve the badge."

She looked at him. He hadn't shaved, so sunlight glinted off the dark stubble that covered his jaw and his eyelashes. The right word was *brooding*, she realized. Light seemed to glance off him, unable to penetrate the darkness shrouding him.

"Because speed matters?"

"Speed matters because if I get a call, bad shit is going down somewhere. No one calls first responders for a backyard barbeque unless a guy pulls a deer-skinning knife on his ex-wife and threatens to gut her in front of their kids."

Her eyes widened a little. "Is that a real example?"

"Yesterday," he said.

She made a little noise to indicate she'd heard him as she studied him. He was tense, strung tight, but not as tight as she'd seen him. Something else lay under Ben's terse response.

The Strand's streetcar rumbled by as Ben parked in the lot behind Artistary and came around to her side of the truck. When he opened the door he held out his hand, and Rachel put hers in it.

"No," he said, then nodded at the flower.

Confused, she handed it over.

He pulled a pocket knife from his jeans, deftly trimmed first the length of the stem, then the thorns. He held out his hand again. "Out you come."

Clutching her purse in her other hand, she gripped his fingers and set one foot on the running board, then the other on the black-top. Heat simmered up her bare legs, but it wasn't hot enough to stop shivers from running down her spine when Ben set his hand on her shoulder and turned her. He gently worked the rose into the loose braid, his fingers brushing her nape, ensuring the stem wouldn't scratch her skin. When he seemed finished she lifted her hand and checked to be sure the flower was secure.

It was. "Thank you," she said as she turned to face him. "I can smell the scent."

"I'm surprised you can smell anything over the asphalt cooking," he said dismissively.

She went on tiptoe and kissed him, just a sweet brush of lip on lip. "Thank you," she said again.

"You're welcome," he said more softly.

They stepped into golden evening sunlight gleaming on the original hardwood floors. Bookshelves lined three walls and stood in neat rows in the back half of the store, while windows along the front wall rose from knee height to the loft ceilings, tiled with historically accurate white tin. In one corner glass cases held sandwiches, salads, fruit-and-yogurt cups, and an array of desserts ranging from flourless chocolate tortes and custard pies to truffles. Bench seating lined the front half of the store, and square wood tables and white-painted wrought-iron chairs clustered around the performance space created by speakers and a microphone. Only a few were unoccupied. Beside the stage artists carrying notebooks, iPads, guitars, and a wide range of other instruments checked in with the emcee.

"Grab a table," Ben said behind her. "What do you like?"

"Anything but the egg salad or the roast beef," Rachel said. She claimed the empty seat and put her purse on a chair for Ben. She peered over her shoulder, watching Ben order at the counter from the woman who owned Artistary. He carried over two sandwiches, three different kinds of salads, and cups of fresh fruit, more food than she could possibly eat, even if she was responsible for just half.

He hitched his chair around and sat down. "So you don't like egg salad and you don't like roast beef."

"I like both," she said as she examined the sandwiches. Thai chicken. His plate held ham and Swiss. "But I want to try something different each time I come."

Without saying a word he swapped half his sandwich for half of hers. Rachel added a bit of each salad to her plate, and studied the emcee, still lining up the acts.

"How does this work?" Ben asked as he twisted the top off a bottle of beer.

She finished her mouthful of salad before she answered. "Anyone can play or perform. You put your name in with Kent," she said, nodding at the emcee. "He introduces each act, and then you perform."

"How do you know people are any good?"

"You don't. This isn't about being good enough to have a paying audience. It's about having the courage to get up on stage and perform."

Ben looked around, then shifted his chair again. "Everything all right?" Rachel asked.

"Fine," he said, then he shot her a wry look. "Next time you pick a table, go for one that's against the wall, or at least at the perimeter. I've got this thing about sitting in the middle of a crowd."

And they were right in the middle of the crowd. She'd snatched up the seat because it was the best place in the room to watch the performers. Craning her neck to scan the room, she asked, "Do you want to move? I see a table at the back."

"Yeah," he said.

They settled into another table at the back of the space. The performances started not long after Rachel finished her half of the Thai chicken sandwich. After that, she ate absently, focused on absorbing a series of poets and musicians. An hour later the emcee gave the audience a break to pick up dessert or more wine.

"What do you think?" she asked, conscientiously trying to be a good date.

He collected their dishes on the tray and slid it under his seat, then leaned back and draped his arm over the back of her chair. "It's okay. Tell me why you like coming here."

She considered this for a moment, working through answers in her head. "I like watching them," she said. "I can tell that some of them are scared, but being brave. Some of them are so confident I'm envious. Emotion is so close to the surface here. They've chosen the song or the poem or whatever because it's meaningful, so there's that. Then there's all the emotion that goes into going up on stage and performing. Fear, dread, anxiety, hope, pride, shame, humor, everything."

He was silent for a moment, then said, "I don't get it."

People were returning to their seats carrying desserts, wedges of the cafe's specialty carrot cake, crème brûlèe, or truffles. She used the increased noise and activity to cover the length of time it took to gather her thoughts.

"Everyone thinks the worst part about being at Elysian Fields was the superficial things," she said, keeping her voice low. "Not being fashionable, or keeping my hair long, or not going to college, or not having sex. And it was bad . . . although I didn't know that until later. What I did know is that any time I felt sad, or angry, or hurt, I was chastised for it. Anything but a joyous countenance is considered being disrespectful to parents or authority figures. Even a sin. Everyone assumes I left to have sex, to choose my own husband, to direct my own life. And I did. But I left because I'd been disciplined when I felt anything else. I wanted to feel. To have experiences that made me feel."

She shook her head in frustration. It was impossible to explain to someone from the outside who'd always lived with a wide range of emotions available to them. "I wanted to go to things like this, with someone like you. I wanted to get angry, sad, happy, pleased, hurt. It's so simple, and yet it's so complicated."

He didn't respond as the first act of the second round, two brothers who played guitar while one sang, took the stage. It slowly dawned on Rachel that Ben had moved them not only because he didn't like sitting in the middle of crowds. He'd distanced them from the stage. She watched emotion ripple under his skin, watched him try to hold it back. She was in no position to name what he felt, but the look in his eyes broke her heart.

When the emcee called the next break, Rachel looked at her mother's slim gold watch, something she wore only for special occasions. "We should head back fairly soon," she said quietly.

Ben glanced at his phone, then looked at her, eyebrows raised. "It's not quite ten," he said. "You want to go back to my place."

Another question phrased as a statement. "Yes, please."

He took her hand and they rose, making their way through the crowd to the parking lot exit. She expected him to drop her hand once out in the warm night air, but he didn't.

"This is a pretty tame group," he said, looking at the orderly crowd. "You want to see people pushing to the edge, you should try No Limits on a Saturday night after Texas wins."

The bar again. She smiled. "Or I could just have sex with you." One corner of his mouth lifted as he held her door for her. When he got into the driver's seat, she asked, "Do you play an instrument?"

She asked because while he'd maintained a facade of indifference for most of the performances, when guitar players took the stage, he changed. The poker face, the mask hardened, protecting something. There were no longing wistful looks, just the sense that he was forcing himself to not give anything away. She recognized that particular demeanor, the look of a person trying to ignore a hole in their soul. She'd lived within it most of her adult life, pretending not to care about things that mattered to her, pretending that a life lived in service to the Lord and denial of the self was enough.

"Ben?" she said quietly when he didn't answer.

He flashed her that slashing smile, warning of unbearable pleasure and danger. "You ready to feel?"

"Yes," she said. "Please."

Chapter Fourteen

Ben rolled his shoulders to work out the tension brought on by sitting through a painful reminder of what could have been. It wasn't difficult to imagine him and Sam up on that stage, if things had worked out differently. At the same time he wracked his brains to come up with something that would make Rachel Hill feel something.

It wouldn't take much, because Rachel still looked like she'd taken a tackle on her blind side every time she had an orgasm. Every time he had an orgasm, for that matter. She took none of this for granted, and when you didn't need new and different to get a kick out of sex, what should he do?

What did she want?

No fucking clue. Or was he just clueless about how to give her what she wanted?

When he saw her on the bunkhouse porch, dressed in white and looking like something out of a country music video, he'd forgotten the basics of driving, like braking before he ran into a building, and had to slam on the brakes to stop the truck in time. As he got out of the truck, anticipation had overwhelmed him and he'd flashed back to the nights when he used to pick up a girl, eager for the night to get started. When he'd tucked the rose she held the whole way into town into her soft, loose French braid, a hint of perfume and warm skin drifted from her nape to his nostrils. The comment about the cooking asphalt was a lie, intended to cover the odd hitch of his heart.

When was the last time he was eager to go out with a woman? Hell, nowadays he wasn't even eager to get laid. It would happen, and if it didn't, his phone held a long list of numbers to text in search of a warm, willing body. He knew when he'd stopped feeling. He knew why. For over a decade he'd set up his life on autopilot, substituting adrenaline for emotion.

The woman beside him wanted both. For good reason. People went without sex all the time, but to punish this beautiful, alive, curious woman for any emotional expression outside joy and contentment was like locking up the falcon she resembled.

That's what she reminded him of—a bird of prey, tawny eyes, a dozen shades of gold and brown like feathers in her hair, fierce and beautiful and strong. Capable of locking talons around a vulnerable creature and carrying it away.

She'd chosen him for the way he made her feel physically, nothing else. From the very beginning she'd chosen him because he wouldn't care. She knew who he was. What he was.

Great. She likes you, and you brought her flowers and went on a date with her, asshole. You're confusing things, not her. She's going to think that's a relationship.

No, she wouldn't. She'd get emotional support elsewhere. Maybe from Rob Strong.

Another emotion surged in Ben's gut, as unfamiliar as the antic-ipation. It took him a second to recognize jealousy. Rather than relieved, he was jealous at the thought of Rachel turning to another man for help or guidance, or even just a listening ear.

How are you going to feel when this is over?

He battled green all the way to his apartment complex, where he parked and walked around the hood to open Rachel's door for her. He put his hands on her knees just as she slid off the passenger seat, shifting his hands up her thighs, lifting her skirt as his fingers curled around the firm curve of her ass. After the first date she wore plain cotton underwear, something he hadn't seen on a woman since he went to college. No thongs or boy shorts or cheeky panties. Plain cotton briefs. Usually white.

The sensation of warm cotton on warmer skin sent heat flaring along his nerves and hardened his cock. He shifted her along the truck as he stepped into her body and aligned them from chest to thigh. She wrapped her arms around his neck and buried her face in his shoulder, her breath quickening against his chest. He slipped his finger under the cotton, then gently parted her soft folds and found slick heat. In response she widened her stance ever so slightly and made a soft noise.

"I like the skirt," he murmured. The scent of the single rose in her hair melded with the heat rising from her bare shoulder, almost crowding out the electrified scent of rain. He wanted to crawl all over her, growling, nipping, nuzzling, until she opened to him and let him in. He worked his free hand into her hair, weaving his fingers into the braid and flower stem, tugging her head back so he could look into her eyes.

Heat rose in the golden brown depths, transforming them into aged whiskey. When her soft pink lips parted, he couldn't help himself. He bent and kissed her, lightly at first, using heat and the merest pressure to tempt her to open to him, then touched the tip of his tongue to hers. She shuddered from head to toe when he did, and he edged her panties down a little farther to the tops of her thighs. He turned his wrist and purposefully sought her clit, swollen and slick at the top of her pussy. Circled it. Kept his touch as light as the pressure of his tongue on hers, soft, tempting, seducing. Emotion trickled along his nervous system, more notable for what this lacked than what infused it. The music at the club had lowered his walls. After a night at No Limits he was jacked up like a prizefighter, ready to fuck, unbreachable defenses up against whomever he was with. Tonight music made him vulnerable, and Rachel slipped into his bloodstream like a drug.

His heart pounded against his rib cage as he watched her succumb to the pleasure. His cock throbbed in response, and he rubbed against her hip in time to his finger's movements. Blood hammered in his ears, his breathing a distant rush while hers echoed soft and breathy against his neck.

A car pulled into the lot, the lights sweeping across the truck in a wide semicircle as the driver parked in front of the opposite building. Rachel pushed at his shoulder, so Ben withdrew his hand and stepped to the side, using his body and stance to block inquisitive gazes. She shoved her skirt down, then tugged her panties back into place through the fabric.

"Upstairs," he said even as she said, "Can we go upstairs?"

She hurried up the stairs in front of him. When they gained the relative privacy at the top of the stairwell he plucked the rose from her braid and spun her, then slid it into the cleft between her breasts and buried his face in her collarbone as desire swamped him. He could do this. He could let emotion swamp him, drown them both.

The scent of the rose and Rachel's skin was stronger here, the flower crushed by his cheek and releasing its scent into the dark, secret valley between her breasts. He backed her into the door and tugged at the skirt with one hand as he tried to free his keys from his pocket with the other. "I want to fuck you so bad," he said.

The door swung open and they stumbled into his dark apartment, shedding clothes as they went. She ripped open the snaps on his shirt and clawed it down his arms to puddle on the floor by the kitchen, then went for his belt. His vision narrowed to white-clad, panting Rachel as he tugged her panties to her knees, and gravity did the rest when he spun her around, hoisted her with one arm and bore her backward onto his bed. Two feminine gasps echoed into the moonlit air of his bedroom.

Two. That wasn't right. In the past, sure, but tonight? No.

His eyes snapped wide open to see Rachel flat on her back, her head inches away from the unmistakable curve of a woman's ass, resting on her heels in the middle of the bed.

There was a woman already in his bed.

Adrenaline shot through his veins just as Rachel went wild under him, shoving at his shoulders and squirming to get free. They both scrambled backward like cats jumping out of a bathtub. On the bed a woman struggled to regain her balance as the mattress dipped and lurched, her efforts hampered by her kneeling position and the handcuffs restraining her hands behind her back. The black ball gag in her mouth turned her words into garbled nonsense, but Ben got the horrified gist.

Juliette shook her hair back out of her face as best she could and stared at them, and for a long horrible second no one in the room said anything. Then Rachel clapped both hands to her mouth just as Ben found his voice.

"Jesus fucking *Christ*! What the *fuck*?"

"Lord have mercy," Rachel whispered through her hands.

He recognized an automatic stress response when he heard one, or two. Ben gripped her shoulder and spun her to the door, then down the hall, into the living room. Away from his bed.

"Sit," he commanded, all but shoving her into the sofa. He stood in front of her, ran both hands over his hair, then reached down and did up his buttons and buckled his belt.

"Ben," Rachel said, still talking through her hands. Her eyes were the size of saucers. "Who is that?"

"She's . . . Jesus . . . she's a woman I know," he said as puzzle pieces began clicking into place. "From No Limits. Don't go anywhere," he said.

Still covering her mouth, her eyes alight with horror and fascination and what might just be the saving grace of amusement, she shook her head slowly.

He spun on his heel and stalked down the hall, where he snagged his shirt from the floor, then into the bedroom. Yanking the sleeves over his arms, he looked at Juliette, and it didn't take a psychologist to see the humiliation in her eyes. Still keeping his gaze locked above the collarbone, he fumbled in her hair for the buckle to release the ball gag.

"There'd better be a fucking brilliant explanation for this," he said as he examined the handcuffs. He and Steve both used the brand issued by the department. These were a different brand, and his key wouldn't open them. Trust Juliette to have law-enforcement quality cuffs but not the ones carried by the GPD.

"Where the hell have you been?"

Teetering on the edge of something meaningful with a woman who wouldn't find this funny. *On a fucking date.* "Where's the key?"

"I don't know!" she said. "I think he took it!"

He took a deep breath. "Where are your clothes?"

"He took them, too," she said again, and this time he heard tears in her voice.

He pulled his cell phone from his pocket and was scrolling through his contacts on his way out the door to get Juliette a towel or something, since she was cuffed and kneeling smack in the middle of all the bedding he owned when Rachel appeared in the door, his lightweight POLICE windbreaker in one hand, her face averted. "Would this help?" she asked.

Ben took it from her hand and thanked her, but she was already gone. He draped it over Juliette, making sure the jacket covered her bare ass and pulling the edges together. She turned so her long blond hair hid her expression. Ben connected a call, listened to the ringing.

"Hey!" Steve yelled over the noise at No Limits. "Did you find the present I left for you?"

"Where's the key to the cuffs?"

"You don't need the key," Steve said, laughing. "Just tip her over and dive on in. Her idea, man. You can thank me later."

Later he'd find out how Steve got Juliette into his apartment. He tried to remember if the door was actually locked or if Steve left a bound, gagged, naked woman in an unlocked apartment. He turned to the corner, doing all he could to make sure Rachel wouldn't hear him. There wasn't much he could do about Juliette. "Get your ass over here and get this girl out of my bed."

"You're done already?" Steve asked incredulously.

Steve wouldn't hear him over the noise and Ben was too furious to find Steve's bewildered tone funny. "Now."

He hung up on Steve's question and tossed his phone on the dresser, then bent his head and rubbed the headache forming above his right eye. He could unlock the cuffs, no problem. Parlor tricks every magician knew. All he had to do was ask Rachel for a bobby pin.

He squared up, snapped up his shirt, and strode out of the bedroom, into the living room. Rachel had resumed her position on the sofa, this time with her hands pressed together, her index fingers against her lips. She looked up when he approached, her gaze locked on his as he hunkered down in front of her.

"I can't decide if I'm supposed to be amused or appalled," she said. "What's the usual reaction to something like this?"

"Screaming fury." Then he added, "I'm sorry. A guy I know left her here."

Something he prayed was humor gleamed in her eyes. "That was . . . thoughtful?"

"I need a bobby pin."

"What for?" she asked.

"My key won't unlock her cuffs. They're a different brand than I use, and he took the key."

Without breaking eye contact she reached up into that knot of hair as big as his fist and pulled out a single bobby pin.

Back in the bedroom he snapped the pin in half, bent the end to form a little hook, then dispassionately lifted his windbreaker just enough to reveal the cuffs, freeing Juliette. She immediately shoved her arms through the windbreaker's sleeves and wrapped it around her body, hunching in on herself. Ben folded the cuffs and tossed them on the bed, then dug in his dresser for a pair of cotton shorts and a T-shirt, then dropped them next to the cuffs.

The pink rose Rachel wore all night lay on the bed. It must have tumbled from her cleavage in her scrabbling haste to get away from Juliette. The petals were crushed against his unmade, rumpled bed.

"I'll be in the living room," he said, still not looking at her.

"Ben," she said.

He stopped, but still didn't look at her.

"I'm sorry."

He cut her a glance that silenced her. "This was a stupid stunt.

How long were you sitting there? What if I hadn't come home at all?"

Color rose in her face, and she looked away. "Steve said he'd come back in a couple of hours."

"Get dressed," he said curtly.

A car door slammed in the parking lot, then Steve's boots thunked against the cement risers. Ben strode to the door and hauled it open before he could knock.

"Fucking stick up your ass," Steve began. "Since when are you so fucking picky about who you—"

His voice cut off when Rachel rose to her feet. Ben hadn't bothered to turn on the lights. In these circumstances, darkness was his friend. Her white dress glowed in the light from the parking lot. "Hello," she said politely.

Ben kept his face expressionless as Steve looked from Rachel to him, and let the silence stretch long enough for a dull brick red color to cover Steve's face. "Sorry," he muttered.

Juliette emerged from his bedroom, dressed in his shorts and T-shirt, her arms wrapped protectively around her middle and her hair shielding her face. She hurried to the door, then paused in the doorway to look directly at Rachel.

"I'm sorry," she said clearly.

"So am I," Rachel said with a faint smile. "A difficult night all around."

Everyone was sorry, after the fact. He waited until Steve turned to follow Juliette out the door, then stopped him. "How did you get in?"

"Got the super to open the door," he muttered.

"It wasn't locked when we got here," Ben said. "You left a helpless woman handcuffed in my unlocked apartment. Never again."

Steve's eyes widened ever so slightly at the silky tone of his voice. "Yeah. Fine. Whatever."

When the door closed, energy drained from his body through the soles of his feet. He shoved his hands over his hair again, then folded his arms across his chest and looked at Rachel. "I'll take you home."

"I think that's for the best," she replied.

It was as if a cold front roared down from the northern plains, dropping the temperature forty degrees in an hour, freezing the air between him and Rachel. All the passion, all the heat and longing was gone, and he couldn't bring himself to lay hands on her, much less lay her down in the bed Juliette just left, not with the other woman's perfume hanging in the air.

Fifteen minutes outside of town the silence got to him, so he turned on the radio. Rachel said nothing on the drive home, something that frankly scared him, given how she processed the world. She just continued to stare out the window, into the dark night. The dashboard lights illuminated her profile against the glass, her full lips, the curve of her cheek, the line of her jaw.

When he turned into the bunkhouse parking lot, all the lights were off in the building. "Is it locked?"

"I have a key," she said.

"I'll wait until you're inside," he said.

She opened the passenger door, then turned to him. "Thanks for coming with me," she said. "I had a good time."

His breath huffed from his lungs. "Until the end."

"You know how I feel about new experiences," she said slowly.

In the dim glow, the overhead light highlighted the flush in her cheeks, but it was the low tone of her voice that sent heat pooling in his groin. Suddenly it became clear to him. The submissive position and the cuffs intrigued her, but she was too innocent to say it. "You want to try that?"

She didn't blush or refuse or play coy. "I want to think about it," she said. "I'll let you know on Sunday."

"So I'll see you Sunday," he repeated rather dim-wittedly.

"Of course," she said.

Air eased from his lungs. He didn't realize until that moment that he'd been holding his breath, braced for the end because this visible evidence of his lifestyle, a life she didn't fit into, would make her break things off.

The sense of relief floating up from his gut, into his chest, didn't make things any better.

Chapter Fifteen

A boom of thunder yanked Ben straight from sleep to heart-pounding, adrenaline-jacked awareness. For a moment he was nothing but a racing heartbeat and sharp breaths, totally disconnected from time and consciousness. Rain slapped at the window like pebbles, the rivulets coursing down the pane giving the air an unearthly gray hue. He turned to see if the noise woke Sam, but all he saw was a sliding closet door caught on a jumble of dark blue sleeves.

Where was Sam? *Where was Sam?*

Lightning cracked, then another boom directly overhead jolted Ben back into time, into his body. His apartment. His bed. Sunday morning, and the emptiness of that horrible morning was fourteen years in the past.

Except it wasn't. It was still inside him.

He hunched over, forcing his breathing to slow and steady. When it did he scraped both hands over his hair, then got in the shower.

Eventually the steady pattern of hot running water drowned out the memory of chilly rain, thunder, flash floods, darkness barely pierced by his flashlight.

He heard her car pull into his lot five minutes early, but the car door didn't close and her quick, light steps didn't start up the stairs until one minute till eleven. The sounds jerked him out of a fog of sexual anticipation, into the now. He wondered what she thought about while she was waiting outside, if she had to psych herself up for what they were about to do. Somehow he didn't think so. He was showered and dressed this time, perched once again on the arm of his sofa, his cuffs waiting on the nightstand.

Fuck, did he need this today.

He'd left the door slightly ajar, but she knocked gently anyway, then pushed it open and peered in. Today her hair hung loose, with just the sides twisted away from her temples and held back from her face with a dragonfly clasp that looked like a jeweled insect had landed in a fall forest, golds glinting among every shade of brown from light through chestnut to near mahogany. Raindrops clung to the strands, spattered her white sleeveless tank top that buttoned up the front. She wore a thin woven scarf in pastel shades of pinks and purple, and a soft blue skirt that flared around her knees as she stepped into the dining area, then turned to close and lock the door.

Thump-thump-thump. His heart rate picked up, and he exhaled long and slow, using his breathing to slow his pulse. She dropped her purse on the dinette table with a solid thunk, then she walked over to stand in front of him. He looked up at her, studying her face, searching for any signs of distress, any hint of a distance he usually relied on to keep things casual. But this time he didn't want to see distance. He wanted to see Rachel.

He did. Her pretty eyes held nothing more or less than simple calm as they studied his face.

"Good morning," she said, as if it weren't storming like God's own wrath outside.

Air huffed through his nostrils as one corner of his mouth quirked up. She was so hard to read, so completely self-contained and self-aware, that she always managed to surprise him. "Good morning," he said, then got to his feet.

She didn't step back when he rose, so the movement aligned their bodies and made it easy for him to cup her jaw and lower his mouth to hers. He brushed his lips gently over hers, once, twice, felt them soften, part, and her tongue dart out to taste him.

Oh, *fuck*, did he need this today. "Ready?"

Her head tipped to the side, giving him access to her cheekbone and ear. "I've been thinking about that," she said.

He lifted his head and looked at her while his fingers combed through the thick waterfall of hair streaming over her shoulders and back, then wound it around his fingers for the pleasure of feeling the strength of the strands. He brushed her shoulder and collarbone with the thick ends and watched goose bumps eddy across her rain-streaked skin. It didn't matter to him what they did, or so he thought. She couldn't possibly get more vulnerable to him than she already was. The cuffs were a game, a distraction, a trick.

"And?"

"I don't want you to use them on me."

"It doesn't have to be like it was for . . . what you saw," he amended. "I won't gag you. I won't do anything you don't want me to do, and if you want to stop, just tell me to stop."

She nodded. "I trust you. But that's not what I want to do today. I want to restrain you."

Heart to full stop. He stared at her, not sure he'd heard her correctly. He bit back his automatic response of *fuck, no*. "Come again?"

"I'm very used to feeling helpless. I know all about being restrained, not by handcuffs or rope but by expectations. A view of the world, who I am in that world, how I'm supposed to behave. I want to feel what it's like to be in control."

Three floors down in the parking lot, a car door slammed. The engine turned over, then receded as the driver left the complex. In front of him, Rachel waited patiently for his response. That was Rachel. Everything was serious. Nothing was a game. She was awake, aware, alive, the opposite of drifting from one superficial distraction to another.

"No."

"Why not?" she asked calmly.

"Because I don't want to do it."

"I understand," she said. "That's fine."

"That's not what you say, Rachel."

She blinked.

His heart was pounding again, hard enough to drown out her low voice, so he focused on her face, watching for nuance. "Talk me into it. Negotiate. Persuade me."

She considered that, and the scent of danger grew stronger in his head. She didn't just memorize, repeat by rote what he'd done. She improvised. "Why don't you want to do it?"

"Because, in general, cops have a thing about control. I've got this thing about a total amateur using my handcuffs on me. Something goes wrong and I'm the laughingstock of the department."

Amusement danced in her golden eyes. "I see. You did open them with a bobby pin on Tuesday. I may not be an expert with handcuffs but I am an expert with bobby pins," she pointed out.

"No cuffs." Blunt. Flat. Final.

"All right," she said. Holding his gaze, she reached for the scarf and tugged it loose from her neck. The movement revealed the strong length of her neck, the dip where throat met collarbone, and sent blood pounding south. "What about this?"

He considered it. "Do you like it?"

"Very much," she said. "A friend wove it for me and I miss her terribly. The colors aren't really my thing now, but she made it with love."

Fuck sentiment. "If you can't get the knots loose you're going to have to cut it."

She looked at the fabric dangling from her hand. "You don't have a scarf?"

He laughed. "If I want to get kinky I use the cuffs."

"Neckties?"

"One."

"I'll tie loose knots," she said seriously.

Silence. He didn't want to do this. He didn't want to say no, either. A gaping maw opened inside him, widening the distance between the man he used to be and the man he was with Rachel.

"How am I doing?"

An A plus so far, given that they were still talking about it. "Tell me you'll make it good for me." His voice was low and rough, like he'd forced the words through gravel. "Tell me why I'll like it."

Tell me you'll stop the rain.

She slid her hand under his shirt, cupping his hipbone, then around to flatten at the base of his spine. The move, confident and sure, brought her close enough to bring his hardening cock against the gentle swell of her belly. "Has anyone ever set out to satisfy you? Focused only on giving you pleasure?"

He didn't understand what she meant. He got what he wanted. Sometimes he took it but he was never an asshole about it. He shrugged, unwilling to admit ignorance. "You don't need to tie me up to do that."

"If I don't, you'll take charge," she said.

He laughed. "Bet your sweet ass."

"Trust me, Ben."

She'd gone on tiptoe so the words drifted into the rough skin on his jaw. Her tongue followed, licking so close to the corner of his mouth that the sensitive spot tingled in response. Muscles in his neck bunched as he almost sought her kiss, but the words stopped him.

Trust her. It was just sex. No big deal. She tied him up, did whatever she was going to do until it ended, then she turned him loose. How inventive could she possibly get? He'd taught her everything she knew. If anything, all he had to do was not act like it felt awkward, like she wasn't turning him on.

In other words, be kind.

Don't make such a big fucking deal about it.

The hand not resting at the base of his spine drifted from his shoulder down his biceps, along his forearm to his wrist. Her gaze fixed on his, she wove her fingers into his and tugged. Three steps took them from the living room to the dining area, where she turned a chair away from the table so it faced the living area.

"Not in the bedroom?" he asked.

She shook her head. Her face was serious but a small smile danced at the edges of her mouth as she pointed at the chair. "Trust me, remember?"

He eased onto the seat. "You don't know anything about this, remember?"

The words came out sharper than he intended, because she'd guided his wrist to the bend where the curved metal was holding the back to the seat. She looped the scarf around his wrist and the brass, then repeated the maneuver on the other side. He tugged experimentally, and to his total shock the knots held. He'd expected girl knots.

When he looked up into her face, that small smile was back. "I tie up goats," she said conversationally. "Goats are escape artists. I'm good at knots."

No fucking doubt, because she'd tied his guts in knots. His heart rate careened between full stop and red zone. He didn't say anything, felt his face going blank as the realization hit. He'd seriously underestimated Rachel Hill.

"As for what I know," she continued, "I guess we're about to find out."

She slid her finger into the knot, testing the give between his wrist and the metal. "Not too tight?"

"No," he said through his tight throat.

If his brusque answer offended her, she didn't show it. Instead she reached for her purse, still sitting on the table at his back, and when she opened it, every muscle in his body went rigid.

"No cameras, Rachel. You take your phone or a camera out of that bag and this is over. Today and forever."

She blinked, and withdrew a small, cylindrical object wrapped in brown paper folded flat at the ends. The paper unrolled to reveal a jar of honey. Still standing to his left, she set it upright on her palm and showed him the label. One hundred percent pure honey, made from the busy bees at Silent Circle Farm.

"What's that for?"

"You'll see," she said.

Then she hiked her skirt up and straddled his lap. Her hair swung forward, hiding her breasts as she snugged up against him, notching his cock between her thighs. She made a greedy little sound, then lifted both hands to his jaw and kissed him.

She held him where she wanted him and took her time, brushing her slightly open mouth back and forth across his lips, striking sparks, sending rivulets of sensation trickling along nerves. Only when his jaw slackened and he opened his mouth did she lick first his lower lip, then his upper lip, adding wet heat to sparks. Lips on lips again, then another swift lick, again and again while his cock throbbed uncomfortably. He forced himself to stay still until he couldn't resist any longer and touched the tip of his tongue to hers.

She sat back a little. When he opened his eyes, she shook her head gently. "No. Not yet."

A tremor rippled through his body but he controlled it, his gaze flickering between her eyes, so calmly intent, and her mouth. She bit her lip, then, as if inspired, leaned forward and bit *his* lip, gently trapping the teased flesh between her teeth. She was slow, excruciatingly slow, holding his lower lip long enough for him to feel blood pulse and swell in it before letting go. Another slow swipe of her tongue, then it was back to the lip-to-lip pressure. His awareness collapsed to nothing more than her mouth on his, her weight anchoring him to the chair, and her shallow puffs of breath against his skin when she went for the sensitive corner of his mouth again.

What the fuck did she want from him?

He couldn't remember the last time he'd been kissed like this. Maybe never. Each heated kiss seeped into the unacknowledged seams in his armor, melting him with tenderness. He lifted his hands to cup her head, anchor her hips to grind against her, and felt the woven fabric bite into his wrists. A low growl reverberated in his throat, and Rachel pulled back again.

"Shh," she said.

If that was supposed to make him feel better, it didn't. If the last timeless minutes were indicative of the rest of Rachel's lesson, he'd never make it. She was proving herself on his body, then gauging his response. Methodically, passionately, taking him apart.

"Rachel. Kiss me."

"I am kissing you," she whispered against his mouth.

The hell she was. The last time he'd been so aware of his mouth was just after a resisting suspect landed an elbow. Adrenaline jacked into his system, hardening his cock painfully in his shorts. He shifted and Rachel sat back, reached into the waistband, and adjusted him to remove the painful bend. The confident caress had him gritting his teeth but she just snugged up against him again, close enough for him to feel slick heat behind the layers of fabric separating them.

Then she went back to his mouth, holding him and prolonging the moment until she made an impatient little noise. Her hands slid from his jaw to his shoulders, then down his arms to lace her fingers with his as she slanted her mouth across his and kissed him.

Passionate. Deep. Confident. She pressed against him from her pussy to her breasts, close enough for him to feel every beat of her heart, every breath, the way her fingers tightened on his. She smelled exactly like the night Sam left, like rain and dangerous lightning. His heart thundered in his ears like the rolling booms that night, ominous, accusing.

Then her mouth covered his, her hands holding his face where she wanted it, and the heat and need in the kiss immobilized him. It was complex, an intricate blend of tongue and lips brushing, nibbles and sucks to his lips, calling him out of the past, and when it ended he was in a state of sexual arousal unlike any he'd ever known. Maybe, *maybe* he'd taken this kind of time with a woman. Never had a woman taken this kind of time with him. Before he would have said there was no difference.

There was.

She reached to the floor beside the chair and picked up the jar of honey. The lid gave easily under her strong hands. Inside was honey in a nearly raw state, not like the processed stuff that poured freely from the bear's head, but thick, with a white rime and a subtle scent. With her thumb she wiped his mouth dry, dipped the thumb into the thick honey, and dragged it across his lower lip.

"Don't lick it off until I tell you," she said.

Sweet seeped along the taste buds on the sides of his tongue, the scent mingling with sweat and rain, but he restrained himself. He should have felt ridiculous, tied to his own chair, honey smeared on his lip, but all he could think was that if this was what Rachel came up with now, what would she be like in a year? What would she be like in his bed, forever?

Silent again, she stroked her hand down his throat, pausing where stubble gave way to skin, then unsnapped his shirt, working her way down to his groin. She spread the fabric and worked it off his shoulders until it caught between his triceps and the back of the chair. Her gaze lingered at all the usual places, shoulders, pectorals, abs, but in odd ones, too. The hollow where his collarbones met, for one, and the spot where jaw met ear met neck. He knew that's where she was looking because she set her hands on his ribs and leaned in again to put her mouth to exactly that spot.

Excruciatingly slowly she moved from that hidden spot down his neck, kissing and nipping with enough force to sting. The mix of gentle and sharp made his heart pound, something she noticed when she put her lips to his pulse for a heated moment, then kept going. Down, down, exploring skin over muscle and bone much as she'd explored his mouth, and when she could no longer hunch over and keep going, she slid to her knees, put her hands to his inner thighs, and spread his legs.

Once again adrenaline jacked through his system as vulnerability surged. He'd keep this in mind, oh yes, the next time he spread a woman's legs and settled between them. He could do things with this, with Rachel. His wide stance let her press against him, her breasts hot and soft against his aching cock as she resumed her exploration of his abdomen, and when her mouth reached his waistband, she casually unbuttoned his fly and tugged his jeans and shorts down just enough to release his aching shaft.

"Have you ever done this before?" she asked as she settled between his legs again. He felt more restrained than before, hands tied to the chair, shirt trapping his arms, jeans tight around his thighs. His cock ached, lifting toward her mouth. "Gotten oral sex while you were tied up?"

He spoke carefully, because the honey was softening on his lip. "No."

She made a sweetly satisfied noise. "While she was?"

Memory and the hot, slick pressure of Rachel's tongue from base to tip had his head dropping forward. "Yes," he said through the thick haze of pleasure building against his skin.

"Something for you to talk me into," she said.

Then she set out to destroy him. She used her mouth and her hands, one at the base of his shaft, the other cupping his balls, mouth and hands working in tandem to stimulate every inch of his cock, but slowly. So slowly. She took her time, lifted her mouth when he could no longer help himself and thrust up into her mouth. The third time he did that she teasingly licked the head with each grinding thrust while the pleasure ebbed in his shaft. The screws holding the chair together squeaked in protest.

"Cocktease," he said.

She looked up at him, no longer shocked by what came out of his mouth during sex, but rather like she'd learned something about herself, and she liked it. A lot. Then, just to prove she had all the power and he didn't, she held his gaze while she sucked him. He did his best to hold out against her, but when the pressure built in the tip again *fuckIwanttocomesobad* she backed off and blew on the tip.

He could fight brutality, but she was gentle. So gentle. He was drowning in hot honey. It saturated the air around him, was inhaled into his lungs, seeped into his mouth, down his throat and into his chest, where it glowed around his heart. He felt like all his nerves were coated in the golden, sweet substance. Amber sweetness everywhere, especially in Rachel's eyes.

She let go of his cock and tugged his jeans down and off. He was so turned on he writhed in the chair, then went still when her hands lifted to the buttons fastening her sleeveless top. Her gaze held his as the placket opened and the shirt dropped to the floor. Her skirt landed on top of it, then her bra, then panties. Her hair streamed over her shoulders as she straddled his thighs again, this time removing a condom from her purse. Breathing hard, he watched as she opened the packet, smoothed it down his shaft. Then she braced herself on his shoulder and straightened his straining cock with the other hand, centered herself, and took him inside her.

Inch by excruciating inch.

After the tip disappeared, he couldn't watch. His eyes closed with the onslaught of heat and pressure, the shimmying adjustments she made when he was buried inside, getting him that little bit deeper, until he couldn't tell where he ended and she began.

After a long, vibrating moment when nothing happened except the edges of his body continuing to blur, he opened his eyes to watch her trail the backs of her fingers along his jaw, picking up sweat that trickled through his stubble. With her thumb she caressed the skin under his lower lip, then sucked the melting honey into her own mouth. He shuddered hard, on the edge, but she stopped, breathing with him, impaled on him and yet somehow in total control, until against his will he eased into her unique torture. At any number of points in this exercise he would have taken her over the edge, maybe even followed himself, but as Rachel waited they sank yet deeper into the energy pulsing in the room.

When she'd cleaned the honey from her thumb, she licked the pad of her middle finger and flattened her palm against her abdomen, her finger gently circling at the top of her sex.

"Jesus Christ," he rasped. Her hand obscured much of his view, giving him only teasing glimpses of dark pink folds, gleaming with juices, the hard nub of her clit swelling under the same slow movements she'd tortured him with. She wasn't going to tease him and then get herself off. She burned in the same fire licking at the soles of his feet, his balls, his mouth.

With a helpless little whimper she lifted herself up, riding him, slowly at first, in time to her finger, then one hand settled on his throat, index finger and thumb on his jaw, pinkie by his collarbone while the other slid down his sweat-slick forearm to link with his fingers again. Then she kissed him. No teasing, no hesitation, just her mouth and his, honey on her tongue and his, sweet and sticky and hot and slippery all at once, and each tight, hard impact of her hips against his forced sound from his throat. Not words or groans, but stuttering little grunts he heard in the back of his mind, sounds he'd never made before.

He'd never felt like this before. He was going to come so hard and deep. When she let him; she showed no signs of rushing for a big finish. Hard and sweet and deep . . . and slow. Tension seethed in his cock, each stroke coaxing it higher, higher. Every cell in his body vibrated as he lifted into her next downstroke.

"No," she whispered. The word was sticky-sweet against his mouth, and her pace slowed.

He fought to keep his hips still, but couldn't resist the need to slide down in the chair, spreading his legs, flattening out so she could get him that little bit deeper inside. Her head dropped back, her hair brushing his thighs as she arched her back and ground against him. The scarf tightened around his wrists, rubbing tendons and ligaments against bone, but he didn't care because she made a little whimpering sound he recognized, the one that meant she neared desperation's edge.

Again she slowed, her head dropping forward, her mouth brushing his, hair sweeping over his bared abdomen. Blood pounded in his ears as he gripped the chair legs, something inside trying to claw its way free of his chest. His head dropped back as air huffed from his lungs.

What the fuck did she want from him? What did she fucking want?

He was past the point of thinking, because she owned him, slamming her hips against his until a hot, helpless cry broke against his ear. Reflexively he tightened up, held back until the shudders wracking his body and the chair frame subsided, then surrendered to the demanding grip of her pussy. Fireworks exploded in his brain and he strained against the scarf holding him to the chair, because all he wanted to do was grip her hips and hold her so tight, so tight, never let her go.

When he came back to himself, Rachel was disengaging their bodies. She lifted herself off him, then went to her knees on the floor at his side. "Oops," she said in that totally Rachel, totally matter-of-fact tone. This girl didn't giggle. "My legs aren't working quite right."

Neither were his. Nothing seemed to be functioning according to tolerances. His heart raced when it wasn't jittering in his chest, and his muscles gave odd little twitches. He focused on taking deep, calming breaths as awareness flashed bright in his mind. He'd expected to be ravished, girl style. Instead she took him apart with her lips and fingertips, left him shaking, utterly exposed to her.

Thunder boomed again, off in the distance. Rain still swept his sliding glass doors, but more gently.

Had he taught her that? No. What they'd just done was unique to Rachel, what happened when hot experience met gentle, implacable curiosity.

Rachel wasn't one to debrief a situation immediately afterward. The enameled dragonfly holding her hair back tilted drunkenly but maintained its hold. Without turning his head he looked at her, kneeling naked on the carpet next to his chair as she fumbled a little with the knots. They'd tightened during their escapade, but in a few seconds she freed one wrist. He yanked loose the knot holding his other wrist to the chair, tossed the scarf to the floor, and snagged his pants from the floor on his way to the bathroom to deal with the condom. He wanted to slip down the wall, sit with his head bent and catch his breath, find his armor and put it back on, but everything he was told him the only way to minimize the risk of Rachel Hill was to act like nothing had happened. So he got up and walked back into the living room.

Rachel remained on her knees. "How did I do?"

This was no badge bunny playing power games. Rachel genuinely wanted to know, and he had no idea how to answer her.

She'd reached into his chest and gripped his heart, but left it there, shattering Ben's sense of who he was. When it came to sex, he would have sworn he was past innocent, past even being shocked. Turns out he wasn't as jaded as he thought. Turns out . . . he could still be vulnerable.

Now dressed, hands on his hips, he looked down at her. "Fine. You did fine."

Still on the floor, she reached over and gathered her clothes, then stood up. "Fine?" she asked as she pulled on her panties and bra.

That was all she was getting. He turned for the kitchen, covered his shaking hands by opening the fridge and snagging two bottles of water. "That's not what women usually want a cop to do," he said as he twisted the cap off one.

Now wearing her skirt and carrying her blouse, she joined him in the kitchen. "I gathered as much."

It dawned on him, weeks too late, of course, that Rachel had no expectations of him because of the badge and uniform. The identity he wore like other men wore suits or hardhats or hipster clothes meant nothing to her. She saw right through it because she didn't even know it was there. She was aware and awake, two things he tried very hard not to be.

When he didn't speak, she did. "Thanks for letting me do that."

He shrugged. Refusing would show weakness, something he gave up a long time ago.

When he didn't reply, she turned for the living room. "I should go," she said.

He followed her, stopped her at the door with a hand on her arm. Without looking at her face he swiftly undid her buttons, aligned the placket properly, and buttoned up her blouse again. When he did look up, Rachel was both blushing and smiling.

"I'm a little blissed out," she said. "See you next week."

The casual way she said it sliced through him, so he didn't answer. But when she left he did sink to the floor, strings cut.

Chapter Sixteen

Promptly at eleven o'clock the following Sunday, Rachel knocked on Ben's apartment door.

He didn't answer. The kind of silence that signaled an empty space vibrated behind the door. She knocked again, leaning in to listen for movement. No signs of life, no television or running water. After a moment she walked down the open stairwell far enough to scan the parking lot. No big black truck hulking in Ben's assigned spot.

She looked at her phone. No texts, no missed calls, no messages. He'd stood her up.

Her heart shrank a little in her chest, and an odd hot/cold sensation slid down her spine. After what happened last Sunday, he'd stood her up this Sunday.

Maybe he'd been called into work. Even if he had, that didn't explain the lack of a phone call or even a text.

She knocked one last time with no response, then slowly

descended the stairs to her car and headed back to the farm. He'd been called into work. It was the only reasonable possibility, far more likely than him avoiding her because she'd done something terribly wrong last week. But the whole way home, she ran through her memories of last Sunday morning. The look in his eyes, desire warring with nerves, the way he trembled, then went rigid as he came.

Had she done something wrong?

Rob was working in the barn when she parked in front of the apprentices' bunkhouse, George sitting in the open barn door with his ears cocked in the direction of the goat yard. She swapped her skirt for jeans and boots, then followed the path through the wildflowers, past the fields, and up the hill to the barn, where the radio was tuned to the local NPR station. For a moment she listened to the local news for anything out of the ordinary, a hostage situation, a violent offender holed up in a house, then felt guilty for hoping for something terrible to explain why Ben wasn't home.

The radio wouldn't explain why there was no text or call.

The truck and trailer was parked in front of the barn. Rob hooked hundred-pound bales, transferring them from the trailer to the barn's interior where they'd be spread for bedding and used as feed. His hair and T-shirt were soaked with sweat, his bare forearms reddened and scratched by the sharp hay stems. "You're back early," he said as he slapped the hooks into another bale, lifted it with a grunt and carried it into the barn.

She had nothing to say to that. "I can give you a hand."

He shook his head. "These bales weigh what you do, and I'm almost done. I was going to pack a lunch and walk down the river a ways. You're welcome to join me."

"I'd like that," she said. "I can pack the lunch if you want to clean up."

He gave her a slow, sweet smile. "Meet you by the goat yard in half an hour?"

She nodded and hurried back down the path to the bunkhouse. In the kitchen she found a backpack and stuffed leftover fruit salad, a tub of the farm's yogurt, cheese, crackers, a jar of honey and some bread, and some of the cookies she'd made last week.

Rob and George were waiting in the goat pen, George sitting testily by the gate, no doubt in a sit-stay to avoid harassing the hot, pregnant goats while Rob checked each expectant mama. He wore clean jeans and a lightweight shirt like hers, with boots on his feet. His shaggy blond hair was still damp from the shower and curled against his tanned neck and cheekbones.

"No one's ready to deliver," he offered.

She shook her head. "Not yet. They're all just really, really pregnant."

He nodded in agreement and reached for the backpack. "I'm glad you're here. I needed your help with the does, but with the Truck Garden off the ground I really needed your help with everything."

"I needed the farm, too," she said. Uncertainty about Ben made her restless, an emotion she recognized from her early weeks after leaving Elysian Fields. Silent Circle Farm provided a familiar life without the restrictions. A home base for her explorations, but only making a choice and moving forward eased the inner turmoil.

He didn't say anything about the incident in the parking lot, just smiled. "Let's walk."

They followed the path through the fields and into the cottonwoods lining the river. George prowled through the tall grass to their left, weaving back and forth, black nose to the ground, always checking in with Rob. After a while Rob stopped at a spot where the path sloped down to a sandbank. Rachel slid down sideways after him. A bleached-out log made a nice spot to rest their backs against while Rachel spread honey on thick slices of homemade bread and Rob opened the yogurt tub.

"What do you think of it?" Rob asked as he bit into bread and honey. He'd added beehives to the farm this year in the hopes of selling honey and wax next season.

She thought it reminded her of sex. "It's really good," she said.

Rob wore silence like most people wore the armor of iPods and cell phones, sitting easily in the dappled shade, watching the river trickle by, as restless as the emotions jostling inside her.

"It's all so confusing," she finally said.

Rob accepted this non sequitur as a vocalized component of a continuing, silent conversation. "It sure is," he replied easily. "Everything's confusing, but what are we talking about in particular?"

"Sex."

He didn't flinch or blink or look at her, just finished a handful of grapes. "You're sleeping with Ben."

"I am," she said.

"Your first?" he asked, meeting her gaze.

She nodded. Something flickered behind his eyes, something she couldn't identify. Instead he turned back to the river and tossed the grape stems into the sluggish current.

"And it's confusing," he said.

"Sex is thrilling and amazing and astonishing and exhausting," she said. "I'm confused about how I feel about it. About him."

"What happened today?"

"He wasn't there. I think . . . last week I think I made him do something he didn't want to do."

Rob's laugh held the slightest hint of disbelief. "A man like that? A big symbol of power and authority, and you? Not possible."

Why was Ben the only person who saw her as dangerous? "So what is possible?"

He dug in the backpack and withdrew the bag of cookies. "For him . . . I don't know. For you . . . it's possible to have really amazing sex with someone you don't like or respect, and to love someone with all your heart and have lukewarm sex at best," he said. "Getting the heart and body aligned isn't easy."

"And you're speaking from experience?"

He zipped up the backpack and resumed watching the river flow past. "I am."

She returned the courtesy of not pestering him about his past. "What happens if your body wants someone who isn't good for you?"

He shrugged. "Eventually you have to choose. One thing will bring you alive, and the other won't. I'm not saying sex without love is the thing that deadens you. For some people that's all they need, or want." He paused for a second. "Or are able to take from someone else. Others choose love without great sex, because an hour or two a week doesn't outweigh the rest of their lives together. Most people muck around in the middle, trying for both. Only you know what's right for you."

They sat for a length of time, Rob lost in memory, George sprawled beside him on the sandbar, Rachel mulling over her time with Ben Harris. Getting to know Ben depended on studying body language, not what he said, and he was really good at not giving much away.

"You have anywhere to be anytime soon?" Rob asked.

"No," she said, and looked around. The water flowed by, the surface of the river nearly smooth, revealing the current when a stick or a log or piece of debris drifted along. "It's nice here."

Rob shifted lower on the sandbar, so only his shoulders and head were supported by the bleached log. He folded his arms across his chest and closed his eyes. George rested his head on Rob's hip and gave a grunt and sigh before closing his eyes. Rachel stretched out on the blanket and stared up into the irregular edge where the green cottonwoods met the cloudless sky. Shade and a breeze held back the heat of the day, but she still found herself drifting languidly, her brain meandering through her current life.

This was nice. A picnic, a slow Sunday afternoon. A friend, and a really great dog. It should be enough. It wasn't.

Beside her, Rob jerked in his sleep, hard enough to startle Rachel out of her thoughts and make George raise his head and study his master. When he didn't awaken, George settled again, leaving Rachel alone with one man, and longing for a completely different one. Ben had taught her body well, but Rob was mere inches away. His mouth was soft and full, and so very tempting surrounded by glinting blond stubble. Under the denim lay a work-hardened body, long legs stretched out nearly to the water.

Heat blended with the taste of honey in her mouth and dreamy drifting. In that dream she picked up his hand and kissed the palm, then kissed her way up the tendons running along his forearm to the soft skin inside his elbow. In that dream she pushed up his shirt and licked his abdomen, then unzipped his jeans—

"We can do that, Rachel," Rob said without opening his eyes. "Anytime."

She froze. "Do what?"

He turned his head, opened his eyes, and called her bluff without saying a word. All of the restraint he normally showed was gone. He wanted her, and if she said yes, he would take her.

An entire universe of longing opened up before her. It was possible to evaluate a new lover before leaving your old one. It was possible for your body to respond to chemistry your brain tried to counteract. It was possible to feel desire and not be able to assuage it. No wonder the leadership at Elysian Fields spoke out so shrilly about the dangers of sex. That way lay madness.

As nice as he was, as good and honest and giving, Rob wasn't Ben. That truth settled into her awareness. So far there was everyone else, and then there was Ben.

She almost took the coward's way out and closed her eyes on the fire in Rob's. Almost. "I can't," she said quietly.

"Because of Ben?"

She shook her head. "I don't know that he'd care, or even say we're together in any meaningful way," she said honestly. "I meant me. I hardly know who I am now. I don't know who I'll be if I sleep with two men at the same time."

His eyelids drifted down, the lashes brushed with gold by the sun. "You know who you are, Rachel. Whatever else you choose to do, you know who you are."

This time when Rachel closed her eyes, her brain mercifully shut down entirely. The sun poured through the cottonwood trunks, not the leaves, by the time she awoke to find Rob a few feet away, pitching bits of bark and leaves into the river. Uncertain of her footing with him, she watched him until he became aware of her gaze on him. The smile he gave her was slow and sweet, patient, without a hint of the human male desire she'd seen in his eyes earlier. Relief called an answering smile from her. He walked over and extended his hand to pull her to her feet. They shook out the blanket and packed up the leftovers and trash, then Rob shouldered the backpack. As they made their way back to the farm, Rachel felt rested, as if the nap in nature reset everything inside her.

She detoured through the goat yard, where all appeared well, then hurried up the path to the bunkhouse. Jess and the A&M boys sat on the sofa together, watching something on a laptop.

"Where were you?" one of the interchangeable A&M boys asked.

"Down by the river," Rachel said, purposefully not meeting Jess's eyes as she carried the backpack into the kitchen. A white envelope propped against the red silo salt and pepper shakers on the farmhouse table stopped her. She set the backpack on the counter and cleaned it out, sorting recycling, stacking containers by the sink for the person assigned to dish duty tonight. She wiped out the bag and returned it to the closet by the fridge.

Only then did she pick up the envelope and study it, holding it braced between thumbs and pinky fingers. PLEASE RETURN, SENDER UNKNOWN, written in her father's neat hand. Tears stung her eyes. She wiped the back of her hand along her forehead and tried to get her breathing under control.

"Were you alone?"

Jess stood on the opposite side of the table, her arms folded across her chest. Rachel slid the envelope into her back pocket and gave the other woman a smile. "I was with Rob," she said.

Jess followed her into their shared room. "For four hours?"

"We fell asleep," Rachel said, trying to make it sound like nothing more than two friends spending the afternoon together.

"Liar." She tossed the word at Rachel, her gaze skimming over Rachel's hair.

Rachel blinked, her hand automatically reached up to check the braid. Her fingers found bits of dried leaf. "I'm not lying," she said evenly. "I came home early. Rob was in the barn. He asked me if I wanted to take a picnic down to the river. We ate. We fell asleep. We came home."

"How could you do that to me?"

"Do what?" Rachel demanded. "Have a picnic with a friend?"

"Distract him. He can't stop watching you. When you're around, you're the only person he pays any attention to."

The back of her neck prickled hot and then cold, same as it had when she realized Ben was nowhere to be found. Hard on its heels came anger, searing her veins hot and clean.

"If you want him so badly, why don't you go after him?"

Jess's gaze flickered to the chambray curtains covering the window, then back. "Because unlike you, I've done this before," she snapped. "It's not always sunshine and roses. It's great in the beginning, but then you get hurt. They *always* hurt you." Her eyes narrowed. Rachel could see her processing what she knew about Ben, what she now knew about Rachel. "Did the cop stand you up? Did you think he wouldn't hurt you?"

It was Rachel's turn to look away.

Jess mistook her silence for assent, and hooted. "Did you think he'd fall in love with you, that your purity would somehow reform him?"

"Shut up."

Never in her life had she told another person to shut up. The words lashed out like a whip, and to her utter shock, Jess's mouth snapped closed.

"Not one more word," she added. "Take responsibility for your own life. If you want Rob, ask him out. He doesn't play games. He'll say yes, or he'll say no. Either way, stop blaming me for your situation."

She hauled the door open and stormed through the front room, where the Texas A&M boys were studiously pretending they'd heard none of this. With the heel of her hand she slammed open the screen door, heading somewhere, anywhere, away from Jess. She was wrong about what was going on between Rachel and Rob, but she was right about one thing.

Ben would hurt her. He already had, and whatever happened between them later on, it would hurt when it ended for good. She hadn't confused what she and Ben were doing with love. She knew love. Perhaps not all the nuances, the dark, passionate, dangerous ones, but she knew it, and knew it well. She didn't love Ben Harris, but she was falling for him, for the man who absorbed everyone else's emotions like a black hole, seemingly untouched by them. Falling for the vulnerability inside he wouldn't acknowledge. Falling hard.

"You wanted to feel," she said to herself as she paced in the parking lot, circling in her own dust, smoothing back her hair from her temples into the perfect French braid. "You wanted to feel everything. Here you go."

They weren't done. If he was going to end things with her because of last week, he'd have to tell her what she'd done wrong, then end things in person. She took the steps to the bunkhouse in one leap, hauled open the door, grabbed her purse from the row of hooks hanging beside it, and hurried to her car.

This was not over.

Whether out of a solid sense of self-protection or a genuine "family obligation" Steve was missing from the No Limits off-duty crew after the Juliette incident. A cop Ben knew only by reputation filled in for him, and between them they said less than ten words not related to work both Friday and Saturday nights. He'd been torn between finding Steve the second he got back to Galveston and beating the ever-loving fuck out of him, and acting like none of it was a big deal. Not Juliette in his bed two weeks earlier, not Steve's

frat-boy stupidity, not Rachel and what she'd done to him the following Sunday.

Especially not Rachel.

The hiatus dialed Ben's fury back to a simmer, but the heat
turned up when Steve joined him.

"Hey," Steve said when he joined Ben at the parking lot entrance.

Ben capped his water bottle and slid it into his cargo pants
pocket, then folded his arms across his chest and looked at Steve.
"Hey? That's how you start this conversation?"

"I said I was sorry," Steve said. He braced up and glared
at Ben. "Jesus, give me a fucking hint, a clue, that you're with
someone else, and none of this happens."

Ben shot him a look. "It better not happen again."

"Trust me, I lost my taste for surprises," Steve said. "Despite
the fact that it was totally her idea, Juliette ripped me a new one on
the way back to her car. I guess it's all fun and games until the shit
hits the fan."

"You should have said no."

Steve ignored this. "Juliette said you two were about ten seconds
away from hitting it when you came through the bedroom door."

"That surprises you?"

"No, but it surprised Juliette," Steve said. "Said she was actually
nice to her. Brought her your coat. I think Ju expected a screaming
match."

"That's not Rachel."

Steve studied the line meditatively. "Maybe I'll take a turn when
you're done with her."

Fury flared in his brain, bright, white-hot. Before he knew it, he
was talking. "Shut your mouth."

Steve must have seen something, because he actually took a step
back. "What the hell is wrong with you?"

Rachel was wrong with him. Rachel and her dark hair and golden eyes and her ability to shine a light on the protective shield he held up between himself and the world. Just showing him it was there, let alone what it meant, or how thin it really was. Making him feel things he didn't want to feel.

That little nugget of awareness sat hot and heavy right behind his breastbone. "She's not like Juliette."

Steve stared at him, connecting the dots. "Is that the girl from Elysian Fields? The one from the auction? Oh man," he said, not waiting for an answer. "What the hell are you doing?"

Genuine concern infused Steve's voice, which made Ben laugh. Everyone worried about Rachel, because they had no idea what she was capable of. He had no idea what he was doing with her, and after she tied him to his chair and took him apart, he wondered why he kept letting her come back. She didn't need him to teach her anything.

So end it.

"Leave it," he said. "Just fucking leave it."

The rest of the night passed in stony silence. Steve did his job. Ben did his. Juliette and her girl-posse were conspicuously absent, but his temper didn't improve as the night went on. That was the thing about being awake and aware. You couldn't unlearn something once you learned it.

He went home and went to bed, alone.

Sunday morning, he was showered, dressed by 10:20. He called Sam on his way down the stairs. "Tell me they're not coming today," he said when his brother answered his cell.

"By *they* I assume you mean Mom and Dad."

"Yeah."

A pause, then, "No. Spring barbeque at church. Why?"

"I'm on my way," he said, tossed his phone on the passenger

seat, and pulled out of the parking lot at 10:22. Thirty-eight minutes before Rachel.

Why are you doing this?

Because . . . ?

Because I can. Because it's what I do.

He stopped at the liquor store for beer, then drove to Sam and Chris's house. The street on both sides was already lined with cars, so he parked four doors down and got out. He snagged the beer from the back seat, but left his cell phone in the glove box.

He took the steps to the front porch and hauled open the screen door, automatically noting the double-takes from Sam and Chris's friends who knew Sam had a twin brother but never saw Ben at brunch, then took a sharp left into the kitchen, where Chris was frying peppers and onions for fajitas. "Hello, stranger," Chris said affably, pausing his conversation with a woman Ben recognized as their next-door neighbor.

"Hi," Ben returned, then hefted the beer. The clock on the microwave read 10:52. She'd be turning the corner onto his street right about now. "Where do you want this?"

"Fridge in the garage," Chris said. His brother's partner was his opposite in every way: shorter, blond, blue-eyed, even-keeled. Ben liked him because he was a good guy and because he treated Sam well, but under their friendly surface simmered the fact that Chris knew things about Sam that Ben never would. He gave Chris a nod and made his way through the crowd gathered around the mimosas, out the back door and down the path to the detached garage. Sam had made good progress on the rewiring project since he'd seen him last. Ben slid the beer into the fridge, snagged a cold one from the shelf, and headed back out into the yard to look for his brother.

And stopped. It wasn't too late to get his phone and send Rachel a text, but the scene playing out by the sandbox caught his attention.

His nieces, their blond hair pulled up in pink-ribboned pigtails on top of their heads, were playing in the red race car sandbox Sam and Chris built for Jonathan. That meant his sister Katy was somewhere in the crowd.

Jonathan was playing in the bare patch of dirt under the oak tree. Ben slowly crossed the yard, watching the kids. Five, no six, Barbies sat in the sandbox, several in swimsuits, two in shiny satin evening gowns, and the Ken doll in cowboy gear. The girls had parts of a tea set in there as well, their high-pitched voices tumbling over each other as they played.

"Hi, Uncle Ben," Callie said.

"Hey," he said as he hunkered down to watch them play, then turned his attention to Jonathan. The boy sat off by himself, almost hidden by the tree. Attachment issues. That's the phrase Sam and Chris used most often. He'd used a gardening trowel to scrape away the dirt barely covering the tree's roots, and had a line of Matchbox cars nosed into the shallow depression.

"What're you doing, buddy?" he asked.

"Playing."

"You don't want to play in the sandbox?" Ben knew all about this sandbox. The pressure-treated, red-painted sides held four hundred and fifty pounds of the finest white sand money could buy.

Jonathan didn't look up from his precise arrangement of cars. "I like dirt."

Ben walked over to stand beside him, then went down on his heels again, but a couple of feet away. Jonathan had been forcibly removed from his home by a uniformed officer. Ever since Ben stopped by one night after work in uniform, the boy had stayed away from him. "Why?"

Jonathan shrugged. "It's just better."

Ben remembered how he'd played at that age. He and Sam found a scraggly patch of dirt at the top of the pasture and over the summer months carved an entire ranching operation into the natural hillocks and channels. They'd spent hours out there, negotiating roles, arguing over what land to use for what operation, just like their dad did. It was a passionate, all-consuming game, one that occupied them for most of the summer between first and second grade.

Jonathan was going through the motions. He pushed cars around with his skinny fingers, but he kept an eye on the girls and the back door, too. So wary.

Ben looked at his watch: 11:06. Rachel would have left his apartment by now.

His stomach did a twisty little flip-flop. To cover it he said, "Have fun," straightened, and set off to find Sam.

The house's main floor was filling up with Sam's eclectic Sunday lunch crowd, consisting of neighbors, friends, artists, anyone who took the open invitation seriously. His sister gave him a tight nod while describing an upcoming surprise trip to Disney World they were planning for the girls. He returned the nod and kept moving.

Eleven fifteen. No Sam.

He swung back through the garage for another beer. The male couple making out against the fridge moved long enough to let him snag another beer and wander out into the yard. The noise subsided a little out there. A group sat around the fire pit built into the stone patio Chris put in a couple of years earlier, their feet up on the rim, arguing politics. A couple sat on the swings, talking idly and sharing a bottle of beer. Ben looked around again, then up at the tree house nestled into the limbs branching over the sandbox. Jonathan ignored him as he climbed up the slats nailed to the tree's trunk.

Sam lay on his back, a beer in one hand, looking up at the branches and leaves overhead. "Took you long enough," he said.

Ben settled onto the platform and swung his legs up, then lay down on his back, his head at Sam's feet. "First time I came up here I interrupted a sex act," he said as he closed his eyes.

Sam laughed. "And you didn't bust them?"

"Private property," Ben said, his eyes still closed.

"They ask you to join in?" Sam said lazily.

Ben huffed. "It was two women, so they looked at me like I was physically revolting. I got the feeling I totally killed their mood."

Sam laughed out loud. Ben grinned, lifted his head enough to tip the rest of the beer down his throat, then stared up through the leafy canopy at teasing glimpses of blue sky.

"I thought you had something going on Sundays these days," Sam said.

"Not today," Ben said.

"What was it? Some work thing?"

Ben stared up at the sharp points and veins in the leaves. "Not exactly," he said.

"Off-duty thing?"

"Not exactly."

"Fucking talk to me or I'm going back to my party."

He could tell Sam anything. "This woman bought a date with me at a bachelor auction. We went out on the date and after the date I fucked her."

"You know," Sam drawled, "like you do."

Ben ignored him. "Turns out she was a virgin."

His brother propped himself up on his elbows. "What?"

"I felt bad about deflowering her in what had to be the least sensitive way possible, so I offered to give her sex lessons on Sundays."

"I'm fucking speechless," Sam said finally. "You felt bad about screwing a woman?"

Ben slugged him, hard, but Sam slugged him back just as hard. "Where the hell did you find a virgin?"

"Like I said, she found me at the bachelor auction."

"That was weeks ago."

And this week it was over. "She's twenty-five, and five months ago she was living at Elysian Fields," he said, like Sam had asked. "She needs to catch up with the rest of the world in a hurry. She knew exactly what she was getting. She said she wanted to lose her virginity with someone who wouldn't care."

How did she see that? How did she know?

"Ouch," Sam said mildly. He knew. He always knew how Ben felt, what he needed. Who needed a mirror when you could look at your own soul?

Yeah. Ben tipped back his beer bottle.

"What's she like?" Sam asked.

She needs something I can't give her.

"I thought she'd be a blank slate," he said finally. "Innocent, sweet, kind of clueless. She's more like . . . It's like when we used to rehearse in the barn. Remember?"

Below the tree Jonathan murmured quietly to the cars. Ben and Sam had graduated from Matchbox cars and a pile of dirt to video games to jamming away in the barn. Katy even played with them for a while, pounding away at the drums like a punk rocker. But then Ben joined the varsity football team and got popular with girls, while Sam got quiet. When he wasn't singing.

"I remember," Sam said quietly.

"It's like that." He stared up at the branches. Together. When he was with Rachel he didn't feel alone. They weren't exactly making music, but he wasn't alone.

Sam shifted his gaze from Ben's face to the leaves. "She's got something going on today?"

Ben stayed quiet.

"Benjamin Eli Harris," his brother said. "You didn't."

"It's how the game's played," he said to himself. He glanced at Sam's wristwatch but the sunlight streaming through the tree house window cast a glare on the face.

He wasn't going to ask.

He wasn't.

"What time is it?"

"Eleven twenty-two," came his sister's voice from the ladder. "Why? You have somewhere to be? Shove over," she added as she clambered up into the tree house.

"Hi, Katy," he said.

"Hello, Ben," she replied formally, folding her legs to the side and smoothing down her skirt. "Long time no see."

"I've been busy," Ben said.

"And yet you're magically not busy on the one day Mom and Dad aren't here? Very convenient."

"Katy," Sam said wearily. "Leave him alone."

"No, I don't think I will," she said mock-cheerily. "Is that why you're here, Ben? Because Dad isn't?"

"No," he said. Katy's attitude and the unpleasant truth made him clench his jaw. He was here so he wouldn't be where Rachel's lips and hips and fingertips could lay him bare again. Avoiding their father was just a perk.

Katy started in on the argument midstream. They'd had it so many times she didn't need a reason, or even a word from Ben. "We've all moved on, Ben. All of us. Mom, Dad, Sam, me, Alan, the girls. Even Chris. We've all moved on."

"That's great, Katy," Ben said insincerely.

"You're the one stuck in the past."

Ben looked at Sam and saw what no one else saw, the pain hidden behind his brother's eyes. The lines around his mouth. The wariness. He wasn't stuck in the past. In this he was Sam's mirror, bearing witness to the destruction of a soul, and if that was too hard for the rest of his family, too fucking bad.

"You two don't need me for this," Sam said. He crawled past Ben's outstretched legs and lowered himself through the hole in the floor to the ladder. His soft, loving *hey, buddy* drifted up through the opening, along with Jonathan's less guarded reply. Attachment issues or no, the kid loved Sam wholly and completely. The thought of what might happen if things didn't go well made Ben's throat tighten.

"Dad's sorry," Katy said into the silence. "He's sorry, and he regrets what happened."

Regrets what happened? He'd driven Sam out of the house with threats of a reeducation camp for gay kids. He'd removed the carburetor from Ben's truck so he couldn't search for his brother, his own lost soul. And when he'd started to cry, his father said, *Don't you start. Don't you fucking start. Be a man, for Christ's sake.*

Ben kept his gaze locked on Katy's face. "What exactly does he regret, Katy?" he said emotionlessly. "Because the list of things he did to this family is too long for *sorry* to cover it."

"You're the one who's ruined family dinner and holidays for a decade. Not Dad." She shook her head. "You're just like him. Stubborn as hell, hard as hell."

"How do you think justice happens, Katy? You think it comes from being soft and easy? You have no fucking clue what happened to Sam, what he went through on the streets," Ben snapped. "I do. I see it every goddamn day. Sam's got to live with that for the rest of his life. Dad does *not* get to set that down and walk away with an apology."

He was halfway through the hole in the tree house floor when

Katy put her hand on his arm. "You're hurting all of us, Ben, but the person you hurt most is yourself."

"Sam never pulls that pop psychology bullshit on me, and he's a therapist, not a loan officer. You don't get to, either."

Eventually, as the day dragged into later afternoon he made his way through the mellow crowd and down the block. Inside his truck he turned on the AC and picked up his phone. Four twenty-seven. Not that he was checking the time or anything. He scrolled through his missed texts and calls.

None from Rachel.

Well, fuck. A laugh huffed from his chest. He didn't need to teach that girl any-damn-thing.

He picked up a pizza on the way back to his apartment. Dinner consisted of opening the box on the coffee table and eating in front of the Sunday night game.

The knock on his door surprised him. The last time someone knocked on his door on a Sunday night he'd ended up in a ménage. But the knock wasn't military firm. It wasn't tentative, either, and lightning didn't strike twice in the same place.

He opened the door to Rachel Hill, dressed in jeans and a white eyelet shirt that tied under her breasts, her hair in a French braid as thick as his wrist. From his taller vantage point he saw bits of dried leaf clinging to the strands. Emotion simmered in her whiskey eyes, too complicated for him to figure out. Anger, mostly. He recognized that, no problem. Concern that grew as she studied his face, which confused him. Today was what everyone did, a lazy Sunday brunch with family. No cause for concern.

The anger won. "An hour ago I lost my temper with someone, for the first time ever. It felt really good so I thought I'd come here and try it again. Where were you?"

"Sam's."

His answer made her blink hard and look away. "Oh," she said. "That's nice. Did you have a good time?"

He shrugged. "It's just a family thing," he said and left it at that.

"Why didn't you tell me you had other plans?"

"Because I didn't."

She worked through the implications, then settled on the right one. "That is not all right, Ben," she said. Her voice was clear and even, not hushed to prevent his neighbors from hearing. "If I did something wrong last Sunday, if you don't want me to come around anymore, then tell me and I'll find something else to do. But be honest with me. Don't make me guess."

"You didn't do anything wrong," he said. "Guys just stop calling. You won't know why. It's what you need."

At that she turned on her heel and took two steps toward the stairwell. The sight of a white envelope tucked into the back pocket of her jeans forced her name from his throat. "Rachel. Wait."

She stopped. Turned back to face him. "I'm done with people telling me what I need, Ben," she said firmly, as if that could cover the tremor in her voice.

"Okay. I get it. I do," he said and stepped back to open the door wide. "Please."

For a long moment she didn't move toward the stairwell, or toward him. But then she crossed the short distance, and turned sideways to slip past him, into his apartment. He shut the door, then picked up the remote and turned off the TV.

"It's so complicated," she said as she rubbed her forehead.

"What is?" he asked cautiously.

"Everything."

The look she gave him wrenched something out of alignment inside him. Indomitable Rachel, with tears in her eyes. Then she eased down on the arm of the chair next to the TV and pulled the envelope from her back pocket. "My dad returned my letter. Again. I don't know why it still hurts. I've sent him letters, one a week since I left, and he's returned all of them. Unopened."

Ben folded his arms across his chest and sat on the arm of the sofa nearest her. "And?"

"I applied to vet tech school. They have rolling admissions so I should hear soon, but the waiting is killing me."

"And?"

"Jess is mad at me because she thinks I'm after Rob, but I'm not. I'm not. I just like him. He's a friend."

"He'd be more than a friend if you wanted," Ben said.

"I know that," she said impatiently. "I was never stupid. I'm not even naïve anymore. He wants me. I want you. I don't know what you want. You're not my lover. You're not my friend. You're . . . It's a mess."

He crossed to crouch down in front of her but refrained from touching her. "Do you want me to be your friend?"

She reached out with her index finger and touched his lower lip, gaze fixed on skin-against-skin as she pressed gently. The sweet taste of honey bloomed unbidden in his mind, fading again when her finger traced down his chin to the hollow of his throat, then over his collarbone to tug aside his collar. The snap below her finger gave way, the sound of metal popping loud in the silence.

She slid off the chair's leather arm and slid down on her ass with her knees to her chest, between his spread legs. Gaze still fixed on his, her finger followed the upper contour of his pectoral, tugging open another snap in the process, then more directly moved down his sternum.

Click.

Click.

Click.

"Is that an option?" she asked.

Were they talking? He'd forgotten, because Rachel's finger brought his skin to life. All the nerves went on high alert in its wake, sensation coursing south to pool in his cock. The expectant look in her eyes triggered his memory. Was being friends an option?

Click.

His shirt gaped open. He watched her eyes flick between his face and his torso, and didn't answer the question.

Disappointment flared briefly in her eyes. He saw the moment, the exact moment, she settled for the sheer sexual heat simmering between them. She fisted her hands in his shirt and pulled his mouth down to hers. The kiss was hot, electric, an angry, sliding battle of tongue and teeth. He teased her, holding back his own emotional turmoil to heighten hers. *Get angry. Take it out on me. Make me feel something other than this festering knot of anger and abandonment.*

She got to her knees and reached for his belt, making quick work of buckle, buttons, and jeans while he tugged her jeans and panties off. He sat back on his heels, pulling his wallet from his front pocket both to ease the strain of his jeans pulling across his thighs and to get a condom. She plucked it from his fingers and rolled it on, a brittle edginess in her movements. He rarely worried about putting himself in a woman's hands, but Rachel was strong, and pissed. She rode the edge, though, handling him just roughly enough to make him insane.

He swallowed hard and wrapped one arm around her waist as she straddled his thighs, centered herself over his cock, then wound her arms around his neck. Her lips brushed his, and this time she was the tease, her tongue flicking at his lips, her breath heating nerve endings already sensitized to her kiss as she worked herself down his cock.

Then she rode him with none of the connection she'd created when she tied him to his dinette chair. It was hot and fast and completely focused on her own release. Based on the hitches in her breathing she took a perverse pleasure in leaning just of reach when he tipped forward to kiss her. Really kiss her. Swiveling and grinding on his cock, the end of her thick braid rhythmically brushing his forearm, slick little noises drifting under their erratic breathing, she closed her eyes and took exactly what she wanted from him, while giving him nothing. When she came she buried her face in his shirt while the contractions gripped the length of his shaft, but he was nowhere near coming himself.

This he understood. Taking and getting used in return. It was simple, uncomplicated, and unemotional. Who he was.

When her muscles slackened she shifted backward, clearly intending to push herself up and off. His arm tightened at her waist. "Where are you going?"

"I'm done," she said evenly.

"I'm not."

"Perhaps I don't feel very accommodating after being stood up this morning."

The words were both dead serious and testing. He felt one corner of his mouth lift as he looked at her, because he knew damned good and well the difference between *no* and *talk me into it*. "Perhaps I'll change your mind," he said, mimicking her precise cadence.

Keeping one arm tight around her waist he rose to his feet. His jeans sagged low on his hips but not low enough to hamper his progress to the wall between the kitchen and the bedroom. Her legs rose to clasp his waist, but that slight surrender didn't stop him from thudding her into the wall and driving in, hard, right through her breathless gasp. Her eyes widened as she studied his face. The concern was back in her eyes, he noted through the need raging inside him. Not concern that he'd hurt her or use her. Concern for him.

He'd heard the phrase *fuck her blind*, which was why he powered his hips and his mouth, ravaging hers, as he pounded her into the wall so she would stop looking into his soul. It was hard, fast, ruthless. Apparently the raw power worked for her because within moments her eyes closed and her head tipped back, exposing her throat. Her hands scraped the back of his skull, holding his mouth to hers. The air in her lungs, huffing out over his lips and jaw, was as erotic as her body tightening around his hips. Weight braced on one forearm, the other under Rachel's ass, he pounded his anger and frustration into her.

She took it greedily, urging him on, demanding more, until a strangled cry wrenched free of her throat. Her pussy convulsed around his cock, hot and slick and so fucking tight that he went over himself. With one final, deep thrust he nailed her to the wall with hips and chest, his face pressed against her cheek, and poured everything into her.

This time she gasped for air like she was strangling. His fault. He straightened enough for her to breathe more easily, and felt sweat trickle down his back and along his jawline.

"Better?" he asked.

"Yes," she said, but the word lacked complete conviction.

He stepped back and set her down, disengaging their bodies in the same move. She took a couple of tentative steps back to the living room, and by the time he'd ditched the condom she'd stepped into her jeans and panties. He pulled his jeans back up and buckled his belt, but didn't bother with his shirt.

"You've got leaves in your hair," he said.

"Rob and I went on a picnic down by the river," she replied.

It took only a split second to imagine the scenario that involved fallen dry leaves making contact with Rachel's hair. Jealousy roared through his chest and down his limbs to his fingers and toes. As if she felt the blast of emotion, she looked at him. His rational mind noted that she'd spoken the words without a hint of taunting or threat. She'd simply stated fact.

"It was just a picnic," she said wearily. "We fell asleep by the river."

He got the sense she'd said the same thing to Jess the jealous farmhand. "It's none of my business."

She shrugged, neither confirming nor denying his statement, but *it could be your business* lay under that shrug. She walked over to the dinette, where she'd left her keys, and picked them up. Keys, leaves, a lazy Sunday afternoon by the river, and a woman who wanted to feel blended in his mind.

Without thinking, he spoke.

"Let's go to the Pleasure Pier next Saturday night."

"Because our dates go so well you want to do it again?"

One corner of his mouth quirked up. "I promise this time it won't end with a woman gagged and handcuffed in my bed."

She shot him a raised eyebrow. "What *is* the Pleasure Pier?"

"It's an amusement park. Rides, carnival games, junk food."

"It's like you're speaking another language," she mused. "I thought you worked Saturday nights."

"I'll get someone to take the shift."

"Why?"

Because I'm jealous. Because I want what you're giving Rob. "I still owe you from the auction."

"You owe me?" she asked lightly, then added, "That's a change from wanting another shot at it. Sounds like fun."

This woman had no self-protective instincts whatsoever. "I'll pick you up at seven."

"You don't have to drive out of your way to get me," she started.

He cut her off. "That's how dates work."

She gave him a little smile, a real one, like maybe things were better than when she showed up at his door. "See you Saturday," she said. "Stay safe."

"You, too," he replied, and locked the door behind her.

Everyone was worried Rachel would get her heart broken if she didn't get a ring and a vow and a happily ever after right out of a movie. But Rachel needed something more, something he didn't know if he could give her. She had no shields whatsoever to protect her from anything.

Including him. The only thing he could teach her was how to harden her heart.

Chapter Seventeen

After closing the farm stand on Saturday evening, Rachel dashed up the bunkhouse stairs, accidentally slamming the screen door against the wall in her haste to get inside. Jess, reclining on the sofa with a book in her hand, startled. "What's wrong?" she demanded.

Those were the first words Jess had spoken to her since last week. She'd apologized the next day, but their conversations during the week were limited to work situations, and strained. "I'm late," Rachel said as she hurried past. "I never used to be late. Now I'm late for everything."

"You never used to go anywhere," Jess pointed out, her tone slightly amused. "Cut yourself some slack."

In the bedroom Rachel stripped, drew on her robe, and took a fast, cold shower, thinking more about getting various smells off her skin and out of her hair than making herself pretty for a date. Back in her bedroom she pulled on a clean skirt and blouse, then roughly towel-dried her hair and began the lengthy process of detangling it.

Jess leaned against the doorway and studied her fingernails. "You're going out?"

Rachel nodded. "Into Galveston."

A pause, then, "With who?"

She paused, the comb halfway up her hair, and looked at Jess. "Ben."

"Oh."

"Did you talk to Rob?" she asked.

"No."

"Why not?"

Jess crossed her arms over her chest, but her tone wasn't defensive. "It's not that easy. *I'm* not that easy."

Rachel charitably refrained from agreeing. "There's someone who will love you for who you are."

"For someone who's been dating for just weeks, you're pretty confident about that."

That was the truth. Confronting Ben and then having sex with him took the edge off her temper, but it didn't resolve any of the fundamental issues she faced. Another letter returned unopened, still no word from the vet tech school, and Ben's stress level made hers look meager. Was that how he coped, how he lived? In search of something edgy and raw to kill what he felt? Or numb it? Rachel lacked experience with emotional ups and downs, but even she knew feelings couldn't be killed.

Two hard knocks sounded on the screen door, echoed when the weathered wood kicked against the frame. Jess peered over her shoulder at the door while Rachel looked at the clock.

"Your date's here," Jess said.

Six thirty on the dot, not a smidge of makeup on her face, and he wasn't her date. "I need five more minutes," she said, pulling the wide-tooth comb through her hair.

"I'll stall him," Jess said, and reached for the doorknob.

Out in the living room she heard Jess invite Ben inside and offer him a drink. Ben declined, and based on the lack of footsteps, he stood just inside the door. Hair smoothed and coiled into an off-kilter knot at her nape, lip gloss and a bit of mascara applied, she checked her buttons and slipped her feet into her sandals. As she expected, Ben stood just to the right of the screen door, his back to the wall, his hands in his jeans pockets.

Rachel flashed her roommate a quick smile and got a lifted eyebrow in return. "I'll be home by midnight," she said, then turned to Ben to explain. "The does are due any day."

"I'll set the alarm," Jess said.

"Thanks," Rachel said.

She climbed into the truck. Ben closed the door behind her and came around the front. The setting sun winked off his wraparound sunglasses and picked up glints of blond in his dark hair. He hitched himself up into the driver's seat and reversed back to the dirt road. Despite the early spring heat, he wore yet another faded western shirt and jeans. The windows were open to the night air. Rachel turned her face to the setting sun and let the bluegrass music on the radio and the breeze settle her down.

"How was your day?" she asked after the first fifteen minutes passed in silence.

"Busy," he said.

"With what?"

"We served warrants on three felony offenders," he said.

"Which means what?"

"We surrounded their locations, took the doors, subdued the offenders, and hauled them off to jail."

He said it so matter-of-factly. She tried to construct a picture in her head of *taking a door*, and failed. "And you did this on a Saturday?"

"Police work is anything but nine-to-five. Some units work mostly nights and weekends. Gangs. Drugs. Vice. SWAT works whenever, and surprising the fuck out of a guy with outstanding warrants for armed robbery, assault with a deadly weapon, and attempted rape, while he's still in bed with a hangover beats the hell out of another hostage siege."

He was vibrating. Absolutely vibrating with an energy she couldn't name but was becoming so familiar with. From what she'd seen, Ben Harris had two speeds: jacked up and post-fuck. The time between the two, well, she didn't see that. "Have you ever thought about doing something else?"

"No. How about your day?"

And that was the end of that conversation. "Also busy. Today the Truck Garden made its first run into Galveston so we shined it up and loaded it before we opened the farm stand. The line was six deep at the register all afternoon. Plus the usual chores. The does are so close, and I mean *so close* to kidding. Rob's like a nervous father with fifteen expectant mamas in his care. I told him they're more likely to kid at night, when it's calm and quiet, but he keeps checking on them. Then there was milking, feeding, stalls, harvesting what's ready to sell, one of the barn cats had kittens in the tack room, a customer's car got a flat tire in the parking lot so the A&M boys changed that for her, and George got sprayed by a skunk."

He laughed, and the smile that lingered on his face held no sharp edges, no threats. "Damn."

"George was just thrilled with this new thing to chase, but then Rob called him a bad dog, and George practically crawled on his belly in apology. Poor thing. I think the smell was so tantalizing he just lost his head. He apologized with lots of wagging and licking, Rob apologized for shaming him, and then we mixed up a home remedy and Rob bathed him. And then I did afternoon chores. And shut down the farm stand. And showered. I did not take any doors."

Her too-bright tone must have registered, because Ben cut her a glance. "Another letter come back?"

"Yes," she said. At least she wasn't carrying it around with her.

"When are you going to give up on him?"

"Never," she said, astonished. "I'll send him graduation pictures, wedding pictures, snapshots of his grandchildren. I left Elysian Fields, but I'll never stop loving my father."

Silence held until they pulled into the Pleasure Pier's parking lot. They parked in the reserved lot and caught the shuttle to the front gates. Even from the parking lot Rachel could see the pier extending hundreds of feet into the Gulf, lights and sound bouncing off the water. The thunk and rush of the roller coaster, the whirling swing that sent chairs swinging out over the water, the screams echoing from the roller coaster's passengers. Ben paid for two unlimited ride passes and they walked into a wall of sound and humanity.

"How hungry are you?" Ben asked, his voice pitched to carry over the noise.

She turned slowly in a circle, taking it all in, the noise and lights and intermittent screams, the thunder and rumble of the roller coaster, the jangling music. She laughed out loud, delighted by the sheer intensity of the experience.

Ben stopped her midspin. "Food or rides," he said

"Rides," she said. "Definitely rides."

A slow, hot smile crossed his face. Without discussing it they bypassed the kiddie rides like the carousel and the teacups, continuing down the pier until they reached the Pirate's Plunge.

"You're going to get wet," he warned.

She took his hand and pulled him toward the line. When their

turn arrived they clambered into a hollowed-out plastic log decorated like a pirate ship. Ben leaned against the back of the seat and
braced his feet against the floor. Rachel sat between his legs, tucking her skirt down. His arm came around her waist, snugging her
back against his torso. "Okay?" he asked.

"A skirt wasn't my best choice for tonight," she said.

The ride started with a jerk, bumped along a coursing current
in the slide and ended with them shooting down a long, steep drop
into a pool. Water sprayed back into the boat, dousing Rachel's
white blouse and red-and-white checked skirt. She laughed and
slicked her hair back, checking her pins to make sure the bun was
still intact. "Told you so," Ben observed as they climbed out of the
ride.

"You're wet, too," she said, plucking her wet shirt away from her
breasts. The seat of his jeans and the thighs were soaked, and his
shirt clung to his torso. She stepped against his body, put her
hand on his abdomen and tilted her head up for a kiss. He wrapped
his arm around her waist, where she linked her fingers through his
and lifted his arm to tuck her neatly under his shoulder, then
brushed his lips possessively over hers.

The good mood held through the Sea Dragon, which rocked
them back and forth until they were nearly perpendicular to the
pier, and the Iron Shark roller coaster, on which Rachel was simply
too overwhelmed to scream. Her heartbeat thundered in her ears
and she couldn't hear her own breathing, or even much of the Pleasure Pier's ambient noise. An amused smile on his face, Ben firmly
took her hand and led her to the food court, where he left her
reserving a table while he joined a long line at the counter. To pass
the time she watched people meandering along the boardwalk.
Groups of young men and women studied each other as they passed,

parents ushered children from ride to ride, couples shared drinks and food. But as her pulse slowed and her breathing evened out, something about the energy bothered her, something she couldn't quite put her finger on.

Maybe it was the way the children seemed inured to the sights and sounds around them, the parents frantically cajoling them into enjoying the rides, the food, the games when they obviously needed a break from all noise, maybe a book to read in a quiet room. The dinging games, the flashing lights, the swoops and drops and heights, all combined to create an artificial high. The veneer of sound and lights cracked ever so slightly to reveal a desperate search for distraction or anesthetizing, for so much input the brain would shut down just to get some relief.

There was a thrill in doing something her body knew was bad for her, but there was a price to be paid, too.

Ben returned with a tray of pizza slices, cheese sticks, and a platter of spaghetti on the table. He unloaded forks, knives, and napkins from under the plates, then pulled a bottle of water from one back pocket, and a bottle of beer from the other.

"You okay?" he asked.

He'd picked up on the shift in her mood. "Fine," she said. She lifted a slice of pizza from a plate and bit into it. "Why do you like this?" she asked through a mouthful of cheese and crust.

He looked at her, gaze sharp. "You don't?"

"No, I do," she said. "I'm having a great time. I just want to know."

"It's fun," he said and bit off another mouthful of pizza.

"Why is it fun?"

"Why do you have to know why?" he replied with a smile that held an edge like a blade. "Does there have to be a reason for everything?"

She thought back to his workday. "I like to know why," she said. "When you know why you know something about the world, and yourself."

He gave a shrug that wasn't an answer.

"Too many questions?" she asked lightly.

"I don't know what answers you want," he said.

The blunt reply surprised her. "Sometimes I just want someone to ask the questions with," she said.

They finished dinner, then strolled through the arcade, heading for the Galaxy Wheel. Her steps slowed at a shooting game called Target Practice because a crowd had gathered around one young man, attempting to win a stuffed animal for the lady at his side. Excitement fueled the girl's pleased smile and the boy's endearing swagger. Ben pulled her close to his body as they watched, keeping her out of traffic.

"Let's give it a shot," he said when the young man failed to win the largest teddy bear hanging from the framework around the game. His girlfriend accepted the smaller bear and rewarded him with a kiss.

"Who's next?" the barker called.

"I'll go," Ben said, withdrawing his wallet from his front pocket.

"Think you've got what it takes?"

Ben just shrugged as he handed a bill to the man and hefted several of the guns, which were attached to the stand with extendable cords. Seemingly unaware that the crowd lingered to watch another showdown, he examined the sights, then chose his gun and nodded at the barker. Ducks fell backward but he missed as many as he hit.

"Not bad, not bad," the barker consoled as he offered Rachel a choice of key chains.

"Let's go again," Ben said, extending another bill. The barker's eyes widened ever so slightly at the shark smile, but he took Ben's money and reset the game. Ben squared up, feet braced, and this time when the timer dinged, he snapped the gun to his shoulder. It was as if everything about him clicked together perfectly, muscle and bone and weapon and deadly intention. He methodically mowed down ducks, moving from the right hand side of the game to the left, eventually taking targets the moment they emerged from the protective screen. When the buzzer signaled the end of the game, Rachel laughed out loud.

Ben lowered the gun in a slightly shocked silence. "You can keep the key chain," he said casually to the barker. "Pick your bear, darlin'."

Rachel examined all the bears carefully, then pointed. "That one." The bear she chose had mismatched fur and dark brown eyes. The barker hooked the bear and handed it across the counter to Rachel.

"You were sneaky," she commented as they made their way through the crowd to the end of the pier. "You let him think you were just like anyone else," she said.

"He knew what I was," Ben said. "Games like that depend on the barker being able to read the players. I helped him, too. Other guys will throw down their money thinking they can do the same thing."

They finished the night on the Ferris wheel, Bear sitting on Rachel's lap. When the wheel stopped with their car at the top, Rachel twisted around to look over her shoulder. Wave crests gleamed atop the shadowy water behind them, and the Pleasure Pier stretched out in front of them, the noise dampened by height and distance. She turned back to find Ben watching her take everything in.

He kissed her, his mouth the only steady thing in the gently rocking car. "Come home with me," he murmured against her lips. "Come home with me, Rachel."

The heat and promise in his voice sent her stomach into a slow roll, igniting a fire deep inside. "For more pleasure," she said seriously.

"Yes." Something unreadable glinting in his blue eyes. "For more pleasure."

When the ride ended they wove through the crowds down the pier and caught the shuttle back to the parking lot. He paused by the truck's passenger door and pressed her into the metal, his hard body pinning her to the equally hard metal for long, slow kisses. She climbed inside and fastened her seat belt, waiting until Ben navigated them out of the parking lot and onto the city streets before reaching across to flatten her hand against the bulge in his jeans. Rigid heat pulsed through the denim and she turned her wrist to cup him. He shifted under her hand and shot her a glance. When they pulled into his parking lot he killed the engine, then unfastened her seat belt and dragged her across the console to sprawl in his lap. As he undid the buttons on her blouse he lifted his chin, his mouth open, half invitation, half command to kiss him.

That was her delight, her private, secret pleasure, the way heat and longing coursed through her when her mouth met his. She brushed her lips back and forth across his, the light touch striking sparks until he lifted his head just enough to sweep his tongue inside. A firm pinch to her nipples at the same time made her gasp and try to spread her legs, but she didn't have room.

With a muffled curse Ben fumbled for the door handle. Night air and sounds rushed in, crickets chirping, the rise and fall of canned laughter from someone's television set, the salt-air scent permeating Galveston. "Out," he said.

She tumbled from the truck, her flat sandals skidding on the step, only Ben's hand around her upper arm keeping her upright. The next thing she knew, her back was to the wall by the steps leading up to Ben's apartment, the strain of his day, the night, and maybe something else in his rough kiss. His hand scudded up her thigh, lifting and opening her to accept the hard thrust of his shaft.

"Ben," she gasped.

"Sometimes you want it right-the-fuck-now," he growled into her ear. "Against the wall now."

"What if I don't want to?"

A rough chuckle, somehow both lazy and arrogant as his gaze searched hers, daring and taunting all at once. Something spurred her to duck under his confining arm but he caught her before she was halfway up the stairs. Arms outstretched, she went down hard on one knee, then he spun her onto her back and crawled up her body to pin her with mouth and hips.

It was like pouring gasoline on flickering flames. Heat exploded inside her, pulsing out through her skin, eddying from her throat on a long, low moan. She braced both hands against his collarbone and shoved, popping open the top snaps on his western shirt, but he didn't move, didn't even pretend to ease up. The edges of the stairs bit into her shoulder blades, lower back, and thighs. Ben had one hand braced beside her head. With the other he tugged at her skirt again.

It was wild. Insane. Thrilling.

"Right the fuck now, Rachel," he said.

She heard the command in his low, dark tone, heard it, and decided not to obey. Maybe he was serious, maybe he wasn't, but the heat of the chase, of being prey to his hunter, sent jagged lightning cracking deep in her belly. She knocked him off balance with a sharp jab to his braced elbow and a knee to the vicinity of his hip, and scrabbled backward. When she cleared the landing she got to her feet and dashed not down the hall to the other stairway that exited into the green space between buildings, but up again.

He caught her again on the stairs. This time he didn't drag her down to the floor but instead shoved her up against the wall. She expected him to try and trap her hands, but he let her struggle to move him while he worked his fingers into the thick knot of hair at her nape. Hairpins pinged to the steps as his fingers tightened, pulling her head back, back, until her throat was exposed and her jaw opened.

"Shh," he said, low and rough.

Her scalp stung until she stopped struggling. When she went limp his grip loosened just enough to let her attention focus on the steady progress of his hand up her leg again, bringing with it an air of vulnerability she'd never felt before. Her breathing shallowed as so many sensations registered in her awareness. His bare chest against hers. The unusual angle of her neck, and his breath, hot and slow against the unprotected skin. He raked his teeth over her pulse, a pure animal move that sent a shudder through her body. She twisted her head but he released neither her hair nor her hip, where his hand slid under her panties, the fingers delicately stroking her soft folds.

He could make her want to open to him, she realized. He could force her or he could seduce her. Or, he could do both. He could hold her, make her surrender to seduction.

His shaft was an iron rod against her hip but his fingers were so, so gentle as he parted the folds. Rachel shuddered again, involuntarily opening to him, her clitoris awake and pulsing in anticipation of his touch. But he didn't touch her there, simply circled his finger just inside her opening. The soft flesh pulsed and she shifted, trying to draw him in, increase the stimulation.

A car door slammed, followed by two more. Rachel froze, eyes wide open and staring into Ben's. Voices, raucous laughter underscored by giggles, and the footsteps sounded like an entire herd of people were making their way up the stairs.

"Ben," she gasped.

He just looked at her, his smile glinting in the darkness, his gaze completely unsympathetic. She squirmed, and got his fist tightening in her hair for her trouble. But the voices and steps moved along the second floor hallway, not seeming to notice two sets of legs intimately entwined on the stairway above them.

"Second-floor neighbors," he said.

"You should have . . . ," she began, but that finger circled again and the words trailed off.

"Should have what, Rachel? Should have fucked you on the steps while they stumbled around? Should have made you be quiet while you took my cock deep inside?"

She shook her head, as much response to the tumultuous cascade of sensation his words set off as negating his interpretation.

"Should have stopped?"

The whisper was dark, taunting. She nodded, felt the tug when his fist remained locked in her hair.

"Not gonna stop, Rachel." Two fingers slid inside her when he spoke, and a breathless little cry escaped her lips. "I want it right now, right the fuck now, against this wall now."

He did want that. She felt it in the rigid pressure of his shaft against her hip, the tension trembling in his muscles as he held her where he wanted her. "And you're ready for it," he continued. "No lie, you are hot and slick and ready. So no, we're not stopping."

This time when she jerked her head away her hair streamed down over her shoulders and immediately slid into her face. With most of her peripheral vision gone she couldn't see him as well, so his next move surprised her. He crouched and put his shoulder into her belly with just enough force to tip her forward, fanny in the air. The world spun crazily as he hoisted her without even a grunt and took the rest of the stairs two at a time. The door opened, closed, and the world spun once again when he set her down inside the door. In the split second it took her to recover from the momentary dizziness he shoved her blouse down her arms and stripped off her bra.

And backed her into the wall. He used his broad shoulders and chest to hold her while he popped open his fly, then yanked up her skirt and shoved her panties down. The only sound in the dim room was her high-pitched gasps and his low inhales, faint and hard to hear over her pulse, pounding in her ears. Because she wanted this, oh God, did she want this. It was the slow, clunking ride up the steep incline of the Iron Shark, fear and excitement together in a whirlwind spinning with dread and desperate need.

He left her hair alone this time, as if he knew the thick mass blinded and hampered her. Occupied with trying to get it out of her face, she was too distracted to think through what he'd be able to do with two hands. He wove the fingers of his left hand through hers and pinned the back to the wall just above her shoulder. With his right hand he lifted her skirt, then he stepped between her thighs and trapped her other hand. It took five seconds, maybe less, to completely subdue her. Half-blind, pinned, and with that hard, demanding shaft almost, almost inside.

He began to thrust, and in that moment she knew true helplessness. There was nothing she could do to stop the inevitable now. When he found the right angle, the right pressure, and he would, he'd glide into her and . . .

Moments slipped by, hot, elastic, saturated with lust. The world shrank to her hair in her face, his hard body pressed against hers. She gasped and spread her legs. He took his time working all the way inside, making her feel each and every inch as it stretched her swollen channel. He paused deep inside, then slowly withdrew.

When he shoved back inside her it was like the Iron Shark drop. No more anticipation, no more dread, just a nerve-screaming, pulse-pounding thrill ride that flung her off the cliff and into the red-hot void faster than she'd ever thought possible. His mouth slammed over hers, trapping her helpless cries, as her sheath convulsed around him.

He stepped back and pulled out in the same move. "What?" Rachel gasped just as he tossed her over his shoulder again and stalked down the hall to his bedroom. He dumped her on his bed.

"No condom," he said shortly.

Her eyes widened. "I forgot."

"We both forgot, or at least I did until I was inside you," he said as he sheathed himself. He came down hard on top of her. "Then it felt too fucking good."

Her reply was cut off by his take-no-prisoners thrust inside her. She clung to him, fingers digging into his shoulders, heels clamped to the backs of his thighs as he sought his own release. His entire body went rigid, from his jaw to his toes, as he ground himself inside her and shuddered in her arms.

"Sorry about that," he said.

She wasn't sure what he was apologizing for, the rough sex, the forgotten condom, the world in general, so she stayed soft and pliable, hoping he'd relax into her for just a little while. "I'm not worried about it," she said.

Her relaxed response seemed to ease something within him, because as the tension ebbed from his muscles, he didn't pull away. Shadows cast his face in planes and shadows as he loomed over her. Sweat dropped from his jaw to her collarbone.

An uncomfortable awareness grew inside her. It would look like he was feeling so much. Big games as a football player, big chases, death, accidents, daily banal sordidness. It was the perfect cover. He was doing good, difficult, selfless work. Nothing wrong here. Move along. Nothing to see. At first glance all you saw was a good-looking, hard-drinking, harder-partying Texas hell-raiser.

Until you scratched the surface, or slipped under his defenses. Then you got a second look at a dark emptiness, a shallowness that drove women away. Only a third glance revealed the pain in the darkness, the sure certainty, just as surely avoided, that sex and drinking didn't work to defuse the pain. He was strung tight, and he couldn't take much more.

"Ben," she said softly.

He looked at her, emotion shifting behind his eyes, under his skin. For a long moment she waited, breathless. Then his whole demeanor changed, brow furrowing as he shook his head once, then again. He buckled his belt, then felt in the pocket, then cursed and went to his knees on the floor.

"Ben?" she said. "What's wrong?"

Nothing. Then the phone rang, under the bed by the muffled sound, and Ben lunged for it. "What happened?"

Indistinct babble resonated from the phone. Ben turned away from her, and her body chilled.

"Chris," Ben barked. "Hang up and call 911. Now."

More babble, this time at a higher panicked pitch. She caught the name Jonathan, then Ben glanced back at her. For a brief moment the light from the parking lot fell across his eyes. Her heart froze. They held an adult's agony and an old, old bewildered terror, the emotion that lurked at the back of Ben Harris's eyes. Sirens wailed faintly through the open connection, and Rachel struggled to piece the fragments together. An accident. Someone named Chris had called 911, then Ben, a trained first responder.

Whoever was hurt meant so much to Ben that emotion actually showed in his eyes.

"I'm on my way."

Rachel pushed her skirt down and hurried after Ben, into the living room, where she snatched her blouse and bra from the floor. A muscle jumped in his jaw as he waited for her to get decent before opening the door and taking the stairs two at a time. Rachel clattered after him, reaching for the door handle as the lock clicked open. She tossed the teddy bear into the back seat and clambered up. "What happened?"

"I'll drive over," Ben said tersely. He jerked the truck through the parking lot, hitting the horn when a car backed up. Brake lights went on and Ben shot through the gap. "Take my truck back to the farm."

"Ben, what—"

"My brother."

He flagrantly ignored the speed limit on the main drags, slowing down only when he entered the residential neighborhood, turning hard on the heels of a patrol car. Flashing lights from an ambulance, a fire truck, and two other police vehicles marked off one house. All the lights in the garage and along the driveway were lit. Ben braked to a halt angled into the street and hurled himself out of the truck, leaving the keys in the ignition. Rachel turned off the engine, palmed the keys, and followed more slowly, taking in the scene as she crossed the lawn.

The EMTs had a body on a gurney and were wheeling it down the driveway at a good clip. A man wearing a T-shirt with the sleeves ripped out and paint-stained khakis ran alongside, a gangly, crying, dark-skinned boy jouncing on his hip, the other hand gripping the shoulder of the man on the gurney. When they passed Rachel, her heart lurched sickeningly in her chest.

Ben's mirror image lay on the gurney, blood staining his face and shoulder.

Brother . . . twin brother . . . ?

"Chris," Ben said.

When the man holding the child saw Ben, he turned to him, his face crumpled with agony, as if he could finally let go. "Oh my God, Ben. He wasn't breathing. He wasn't breathing for so long." He drew a deep breath and added in a rising voice, "The sound his head made when it hit the cement—"

"UTMB?" Ben demanded.

"Yeah," one of the EMTs said. "Move."

Ben visibly restrained Chris as the EMTs loaded the gurney into the back of the ambulance. "Shh, Jon," Chris said to the weeping child, but the tears streaming down his own face didn't help. "Shh, baby. It's okay. Sam's gonna be okay, I promise."

Twin brother . . . and . . . ?

Oh.

Both arms wrapped around her torso, Rachel edged along the sidewalk. Her mental image of Ben's family shattered and reassembled itself to form a completely different picture. The unconscious man on the gurney and child wheezing as he sobbed *Sam . . . Sam . . . Sam.*

The crying echoes glinted like shards in Ben's eyes. He saw her and stepped protectively between her and the ambulance. The set of his jaw and shoulders managed to be defensive, protective, and challenging all at once. Before she could say anything, the man turned to Ben as he pried the boy's arms from around his neck. "I have to go with him. I have to. We have power of attorney for each other, but I better call your parents just in case—"

Ben cut him off. "What about Katy?"

"Disney World, remember? I love you, Jonathan. Ben's here. Take him," he said to Ben. Between the two of them they pried the screaming child from the man's arms. Then he kissed Jonathan on the top of his head and sprinted for a car parked in the street.

Chapter Eighteen

Jonathan's heartbreaking wails were the soundtrack to Ben's voiceless dreams. The year they were five. The year they were sixteen.

The driver hit the siren as the bus bumped over the curb, startling him into the now. It wasn't supposed to be Sam who got hurt. It was supposed to be Ben. Stupid, adrenaline-junkie Ben, walking into robberies in progress, tackling a tweaking dealer. Not Sam, gentle, loving Sam who'd been through so much.

Ben couldn't hear himself think over the crying, let alone figure out how to stop it. Sam was gone. Chris was gone. As the first responders packed up, going through the routine they all used to distance themselves from the job, the EMTs, firefighters, and cops were watching with a mixture of sympathy and that oddly blank look he recognized. The only way to deal with what they faced was to block it out. Newer first responders still showed some expression, those and the truly empathetic.

Rachel's face showed neither. She stood in the middle of his brother's front lawn, his car keys in her hand, and he couldn't read her eyes. Dark hair, golden eyes, pale skin, a body he knew as well as he knew his own, but she was absolutely opaque to him.

For a moment neither of them moved, then he felt a warm wetness spread down his hip. Rachel figured it out before he did, hurrying past him and up the stairs to the front door. When Jonathan's cries shifted from anguish to shame, he got it.

"Christ," he muttered, and took the steps two at a time, Jonathan still wailing away. Rachel had the door open. Most of the interior lights were on. He brushed past her and headed upstairs, into the white tiled bathroom. Jonathan was sobbing brokenly now, tears wetting his shirt as he clung to him so tightly Ben couldn't break the hold to get his wet shorts and underpants off. He also couldn't find the distance that came so easily on the job.

Because this wasn't the job. He shut the toilet lid and sat down on it, shifting Jonathan on his lap.

"How can I help?" Rachel asked quietly from the doorway.

At the sound of her voice, Jonathan hid his face in the crook of Ben's neck. He warmed up to strangers slowly at best, often navigating the crowd in the house wearing a superhero cape and mask on his way to the tree house to deflect attention or comments. Sam and Chris prepped visitors by telling them Jonathan was invisible, but pretending didn't make it so, and deep down, Jonathan knew that.

"You can't help," Ben said. "Take my truck and go home. I'll have someone drive me out tomorrow to get it."

She gave him a level look, then turned and disappeared. Ben heard drawers opening in Jonathan's room, then she reappeared with a dry pair of Superman underpants and cotton sleep shorts. She set them on the sink. Then her flat shoes clapped down the stairs, and the front door closed.

"Come on, buddy," Ben said. "Let's get you changed."

Jonathan kept on sobbing. The kid's shoulder blades stuck out like bird wings from his skinny back. Ben could count every vertebra in his spine, see the knobs of his hips through the soft shorts and his ankle bones where his long legs dangled on either side of Ben's. He was basically skin and bones, his breaths wracking his body from shoulders to toes. Urine trickled down his leg and Ben's, and he showed no sign of moving, let alone wanting to get cleaned up and into dry clothes.

"I want Sam," he sobbed. "I want Sam."

"Sam will be back soon," Ben said, lying through his teeth.

"When?" Jonathan sobbed, his tone escalating. "When will he come back?"

Based on Chris's admittedly hysterical description of Sam's tumble from the top rung of the ladder to the cement garage floor, it was entirely possible Sam wouldn't come back at all. Hemorrhage, swelling on the brain, concussion, blot clots, the shock to his heart and nervous system—all the possibilities danced in Ben's mind. Not to mention the possibility that he lived, but in some vastly reduced mental capacity. All of that assumed no damage to his spine in the fall.

Ben's eyes burned. His throat tightened, and for a long moment his heart seemed to halt midbeat.

He'd waited too long to answer Jonathan. Crying, the kid shoved off Ben's lap and huddled in against the wall, emptying his soul into a void Ben knew didn't answer back, didn't give a damn that your world was coming apart around you. He was sweating, Jonathan was sweating, the room stank of urine, and the screams slashed like razors at Ben's eardrums. In the early days when Jonathan had come to live with them, Sam told Ben about the night terrors, the seemingly random screaming fits that happened anywhere from the backyard to the supermarket to the park, about how the only thing to do was to sit with him until he settled down.

It sounded easier than it was. He sat down next to the kid, but by the time Jonathan went limp against him they were both sweat-soaked, their clothes damp with urine, tears, and snot. "You ready to take a shower?" Ben said.

A sniff, then Jonathan nodded. "Don't leave."

"I won't," Ben promised. That he could promise. He wouldn't leave. He didn't leave.

To give Jonathan some privacy, he busied himself shaking out the fresh clothes while the boy shoved his wet shorts into the laundry hamper. Then he stepped into the shower, but the curtain slid open thirty seconds later.

"Use soap everywhere," Ben said without thinking, echoing what his mother used to say.

The curtain closed again. This time when it opened suds were dripping from the kid's ear, so Ben assumed he'd made at least a cursory effort to get clean. He held open the shark towel embroidered with *Jonathan,* and the kid dried himself off. As kids, they'd never had anything with their names embroidered on it. Sam and Chris were trying so hard.

Ben opened the door to head down the hall, into Sam and Chris's bedroom in search of a dry pair of shorts for himself.

"Where are you going?" Jonathan demanded.

"I'm going to go into Sam's room and get some dry clothes," he said.

"I wet my pants," Jonathan whispered, tears welling up in his eyes.

"It happens," Ben said matter-of-factly.

Still wrapped in the shark towel, Jonathan blinked then followed him, sitting down on the floor behind the bed to pull on his underpants and shorts while Ben rummaged through Sam's dresser. Jonathan scrambled to his feet to follow Ben back into the bathroom.

"Wait out here, buddy," he said.

The boy's enormous, red-rimmed eyes got bigger. "Don't close the door," he whispered. His breath clogged in his chest, no wonder given that he'd been bawling flat out for nearly half an hour.

"I won't," Ben said.

He stripped to his skin, took a thirty-second shower, then pulled on Sam's shorts and a T-shirt. When he was dressed he found Jonathan sitting on the floor outside the door, his attention focused on the stairs. Ben heard the rustling of plastic sacks.

"Somebody's here," he said.

He knew who was down there, but he said, "Let's go see."

Rachel stood behind the butcher block island, unpacking a plastic sack from the grocery store. Chocolate chips. Vanilla. Brown sugar.

"I told you to go home," Ben said roughly as Jonathan hid his face in Ben's side.

"Bear told me to make cookies," she said, then nodded at the bear, sitting at the kitchen table.

Ben and Jonathan both looked at the bear, like stuffing and fur were going to explain what the hell that meant, then Ben transferred his gaze to the clock set into the rooster's abdomen. "It's almost midnight," he said.

"Bears don't care what time it is when they want cookies," she told him evenly.

"What kind does he want?" Jonathan asked, his face still buried in Ben's borrowed shirt.

"He likes chocolate chip," she said. She wasn't looking at Jonathan, Ben noticed. "What kind does Sam make?"

Jonathan looked at her like she'd fallen out of the sky. "Sam doesn't make cookies," he said. "Chris makes cookies."

Rachel still wasn't looking at Ben, or Jonathan. "Okay, so what kind of cookies does Chris make?"

"M&M's," Jonathan said.

"Is that what Chris likes?"

"That's what me and Sam like. Chris likes oatmeal chocolate chip."

Rachel seemed to consider this. "Bear likes M&M's," she said. "We could make the oatmeal chocolate chip cookies and put M&M's in some of them."

Jonathan didn't say anything, and Rachel went ahead, opening cupboard doors for mixing bowls, drawers for measuring cups, the pantry for ingredients. "Can you show me where Chris keeps his recipes?"

A beat passed, then Jonathan slid out of Ben's arms and went to the shelf that held the cookbooks to remove a three-ring binder. He and Rachel paged through it while Ben pulled a chair back from the kitchen table and settled into it. An unexpected emotion surfaced through Ben's turmoil: gratitude. Her slow, calm movements caught Jonathan's eye but weren't frantic or even upbeat. She was doing something routine, giving the boy something that would anchor him in the present and distract him from what happened earlier.

She was doing what Ben couldn't. She was comforting Jonathan. Humming quietly under her breath she studied the recipe. "Want to help?"

He nodded. Together they measured out flour, sugar, salt. Rachel opened the bag of chips and sprinkled four or five into the batter.

"Bear wants more," Jonathan said.

Her eyebrows rose. "He does? Want to measure them for me?"

He nodded, found his stool, and carefully poured a cup of chips, then the bag collapsed and a bunch extra fell onto the counter. "Oops," Rachel said matter-of-factly. "Dump in what you poured out."

Jonathan did, then looked at Rachel. She sectioned off most of the spillage, swept them into her cupped palm, and added them to the batter. "The rest are for us," she said, and popped one into her mouth.

The silence had an odd note to it, as if the night's terrifying events took everyone somewhere they didn't want to go. Ben, Jonathan, even Rachel. "Who taught you how to make cookies?" Ben asked. That wasn't what he meant. He meant, *Who taught you to make cookies for terrified children at midnight?*

"My mama taught me," she said, talking to Jonathan. "But my daddy used to make them with me when I woke up with bad dreams."

Bad dreams. He thought about the Pleasure Pier and kinky sex and standing her up. Shame crawled up his spine.

"I have bad dreams," Jonathan said.

Rachel nodded. "What do Sam and Chris do?"

"We talk about it. Sam sings, sometimes."

Ben looked up at that. But Rachel just continued mixing the cookie dough. The little boy's chin trembled.

"What if I have bad dreams tonight?" he whispered.

Rachel flicked Ben a glance that read, *Do you sing?*

Not since I was sixteen.

He shook his head. "We'll deal with it if it happens, buddy," he said. Jonathan swiped at his eyes and went to sit with Bear, not Ben. Rachel dropped spoonfuls of dough onto the cookie sheet she found in the drawer under the oven. In just a few minutes the smell of baking cookies permeated the air. She stayed next to the oven, busying herself with tidying up. Wiping counters. Folding dishtowels and aligning them neatly on the oven door handle. Putting everything away, except the half-eaten bag of M&M's she'd found in the cupboard.

When the timer beeped she pulled the first batch of cookies from the oven, slid three onto individual plates, and topped one with M&M's. She poured Jonathan a glass of milk, and sat down across from them. Jonathan sat up and reached for the cookie.

"It's gonna be hot, sweetheart," Rachel said.

Jonathan waited, then bit into the cookie carefully. He ate it like it was the only thing keeping him from a horrible black void he faced far too often, slowly, carefully, staving off God only knew what. Terror, probably. Bedtime, for sure. The kid's eyelids were drooping even as he ate.

"Can I have another one?"

Rachel's eyes met Ben's. He shrugged. She looked back at Jonathan. "Not tonight," she said gently. "But you can have three more M&M's."

"Five?"

"Deal."

He ate those as slowly as the cookie, but when Ben stood he didn't protest at all. Ben carried him upstairs and laid him in his bed, surrounded by the kinds of soft things little kids loved. "Will you sit with me?" Jonathan whispered.

It had to be bad if not-Sam was an acceptable substitute, so he stayed while Jonathan wriggled his way into a comfortable position. Light picked out the bumps of his fragile spine, and after a minute, Ben stroked the smooth skin of his back, once. Again. Jonathan's eyelids drooped, then closed. Ben kept his hand between his shoulder blades until he twitched.

Back downstairs, Rachel was sitting on the sofa. She looked up when Ben dropped into the chair opposite her. "Why didn't you tell me about them?"

"Same reason you didn't tell me you were a virgin. We don't have a talk-about-family kind of relationship," he said, too strung out to filter to his words.

"You assumed I'd judge your brother for being gay," she said.

Fine, they'd go there. "I'm careful who I bring into my brother's home."

She looked around, at the house decorated like something out of a Pottery Barn catalog. "It's a beautiful home, but that's not what you're careful about letting someone into," she said quietly. "You assume I'm quite the hypocrite if I'll sleep with you in place of going to church and at the same time judge your family."

Ben just shrugged. "Good old-fashioned heterosexual sex with a cop on Sundays is totally normal. None of this is normal."

"I grew up at Elysian Fields, so I don't know much about normal," she said. "But I know love and compassion when I see it."

"Your dad made cookies when you had nightmares? Sounds like something a mom would do."

"My mother's death caused the nightmares," she said, still calm. "I'd wake up screaming for her, and when I got older I started dreaming that the cancer that killed her was inside me, eating me like it ate her. At the end she smelled like something rotting, and the smell was in my dreams. I was terrified to sleep. My dad made me cookies because the smell reminded me of better times with her, and after we baked, I could go back to sleep."

The words were a slap across the face. They spawned a hundred questions he had no right to ask and tilted his perception of Rachel's previous life entirely on its head. Because dads who made cookies for their scared daughters weren't the kinds of Bible-thumping repressive monsters daughters left behind easily. She hadn't walked away from unilaterally horrible. She'd walked away from people who loved her, people she loved.

He was in too deep, she was too deep for a man like him, and he didn't have anything left inside to give her. The way she studied him, the way her golden eyes peered right through him made him feel naked.

"Take my truck and go home," Ben said. "I don't know when I'll be out to get it."

Rachel considered this. "I'll drive it back into town when the Truck Garden comes tomorrow and catch a ride home with them."

With Katy out of town for who knew how long, he didn't argue with her. "Just tell me where you leave it," he said.

"I'll stay if you want me to," she said quietly. "If you don't want to be alone."

"Right now all I want is to be alone," he said just as quietly.

It should have been him. He should have been hurt. Not Sam. Never Sam.

He didn't mean it. She took him at his word, and left.

Chapter Nineteen

Spring sunshine winked off Ben's black truck, hulking over Rachel's Focus and Jess's VW Bug. Coffee cups in hand, Jess and Rachel stood on the front porch, contemplating this new addition to the apprentice parking lot.

"Why did you drive his truck home?"

"He had a family emergency," Rachel said, fairly sure that Ben Harris wouldn't want his family issues trumpeted to all and sundry. He'd been vibrating so hard she expected him to shatter at any minute. Probably she should have left the first time he told her to, but there was no way she was leaving that terrified child without trying to help him.

His screams took her back to a place no child should ever have to go and no adult ever wanted to revisit, and Ben's obvious heartbreak in the face of Jonathan's fear and grief nearly broke her heart. Doing the only thing she knew how to do to comfort someone wasn't an impulse. It was a need, a way to reconnect with the father who considered her dead, a way to help in the face of overpowering anguish. The grocery store was five minutes away. Sam and Chris must bake quite a bit because the list on the fridge included vanilla and chocolate chips. She picked up the milk and orange juice and whole-wheat tortillas because she was going, and she might as well.

Flinging her childhood terrors at him like scalding oil on what had to be one of the most difficult nights of his life wasn't in the plan, either.

Still eyeing the big black truck, Jess said, "Is he compensating?"

Yes, in a hundred different ways, but weren't we all? "For what?" she asked as she set her cup on the railing and picked up a covered casserole dish.

"You know. Big truck. Small dick."

"No," she said distractedly as another piece fell into place. Ben would drive the truck because it could handle anything. Nothing would stop him from getting to someone who needed help. The truck, the attitude, the muscles, the job . . . all of it fit together seamlessly to form the shell of Ben the Indestructible Protector.

Some piece of grit in Ben's soul formed that shell, the uniform, the weapon, the smile and the attitude, the truck. It was a life lived as impenetrable armor, invisible to the casual eye and like a character hidden in a cast of thousands, plain as day as soon as you saw it for what it was.

She wiped her thumb across her forehead, then glanced at the activity in the farm's parking lot. They'd loaded the Truck Garden and the A&M boys were ready to head out for the day. At the sharp whistle and wave Rachel carried the casserole dish and a bag of fresh-picked vegetables to the truck and climbed in, jockeyed it around until it pointed out the driveway, and led them onto the highway into Galveston, to Sam's house.

In the daylight she saw Craftsman-style homes with neatly

tended lawns and flowering shrubs. The Truck Garden pulled in behind her. "I'll just be a minute," she said when she parked on the street. A tall woman with pale brown hair holding hands with a long-haired blond man gave them a wave as they walked a dachshund down the sidewalk past Sam's house. She hurried up the front walk lined with flowering pots and knocked on the front door.

Ben answered. Cartoon noises drifted quietly from the television and Jonathan was asleep on the sofa, Bear clutched tight to his chest. The location of a Ben-sized dent in the cushions told Rachel Jonathan had fallen asleep on Ben's lap. Lines tightened Ben's eyes; he looked like he hadn't slept at all, but no expression showed on his face.

"Any news?" she said, keeping her voice low.

His gaze flicked over her shoulder to the Truck Garden, idling in the street. "Cracked his skull in three places, broke his collarbone. No spinal trauma. Until he regains consciousness they won't know for sure if he's got brain damage."

A lump formed in her throat at the even, unemotional recitation. She studied his face. On the surface he looked much the same as he always did, skin and muscles revealing nothing, but as she watched, something flared in his eyes only to be tamped down again. *Fear.* Gone. *Anguish.* Gone. *Bewilderment so similar to Jonathan's her heart broke.* Gone. "I'm so sorry, Ben," she said, then glanced past his shoulder to the boy sleeping on the sofa. "How is he?"

"Slept for a few hours. Woke up crying. Now he's sleeping again. I took today off. My sister's booking a flight back from Florida to help."

He was tense and tired, but that wasn't what caught her attention. Ben's typically sky-high energy level was stilled, like the odd silence when power lines went dead. "Ben," she started.

"What's that?"

She offered him the foil-covered casserole dish. "Macaroni and cheese," she said. "Just bake it at three-fifty for forty-five minutes or so. Fresh beans, peas, and a few tomatoes just off the vines."

He stared at the Pyrex dish before accepting it, as if he couldn't comprehend basic information about food. "Thanks," he said. "They're waiting for you."

She looked over her shoulder at the A&M boys, eyeing her and Ben with undisguised interest. "Ben, what can I do—"

He cut her off. "Thanks for the food," he said and stepped back inside.

Worn out from the season's busiest week yet at the farm stand, Rachel dragged herself down the path from the farm stand to the bunkhouse. Two envelopes were tucked between the red silo salt and pepper shakers on the farmhouse table. Rachel picked them up. One was addressed in her handwriting to Ronald Hill, once again marked PLEASE RETURN, SENDER UNKNOWN. The other was a plain business envelope with the vet tech school's stylized puppy-and-kitten logo and mailing address in the upper left-hand corner. Her heart pounding, Rachel looked around the empty house, then opened the envelope.

Dear Ms. Hill,
Thank you for your application. Unfortunately, we are
unable to offer you a position in our fall class. . . .

Disappointment forced a soft noise from her throat. One hand pressed to her stomach, she pulled out a chair and sat down to finish reading. *Largest pool of applications in the school's history . . .*

excellent grades in science and math characterized the admitted
class . . . all best in your future endeavors.

She found her phone in her jeans pocket and called the admissions counselor. "It's Rachel Hill," she said. "I just got the letter."

"I'm so sorry," the counselor said gently. "Your personal essay touched the committee's heart, and no one doubts your commitment to animals' health and well-being, or your determination. But several instructors were concerned that your transcripts lacked the biology and chemistry necessary to ensure your success in the program."

"Yes, ma'am, I understand," she said. "What can I do?"

"Take a couple of classes in the fall at a community college. Get your GED. I know you have a homeschool certificate, but shore up your transcripts and I feel very confident you'll win a spot in the next class."

"Yes, ma'am," she said. "Thank you."

Rachel hung up after the counselor's gentle good-bye and stared blankly at her phone. Okay. She could do this. It was a simple setback, easy to remedy. Take the classes and reapply. When the farm closed down for the season she'd get a job in Galveston, take the classes, find somewhere to live, someone to live with. She'd do exactly what she planned, except she wouldn't be in vet tech school. That goal was only postponed, not completely out of her reach.

Nonetheless, rejection stung. To her surprise it stung worse than never having tried at all. It was a completely different feeling from straining against the repressive role Elysian Fields forced her into. For the first time in her life she'd "put herself out there," as the career counselor at the shelter put it, been assessed and found wanting.

She gave a shaky sigh, then smoothed her hands over her hair, checking her pins, securing a few loose strands. She had the house to herself tonight. Jess and the current A&M boys were going into Houston to see a comedian. She'd take a hot shower to steam away the day's grime, make something easy for dinner, and sit in the meadow to watch the sunset. But when she got out of the shower a text from Ben was waiting on her phone.

Come into town tonight.

This was his first contact in a week. She considered texting back, but decided to call him instead. "Harris," he answered.

"It's Rachel. Why do you want me to come into town?"

"Do you have other plans?"

He didn't like why, so she didn't ask. "I was going to sit in the meadow and watch the sunset," she said. To mourn the setback. "Why don't you come out here?"

"Because I want to get drunk and have sex, not watch a sunset."

She may not know why, but she surely knew what he was thinking. "And what's in this for me?"

"Music. Dancing. Drinking. Me. Inside you."

Bold and brash, with a flat edge to the words. This wasn't the Ben she knew, but heat wicked through her. He was promising oblivion, and being with him certainly reset her emotional frame of mind. "Where?"

"No Limits. I'll text you the address." Then he hung up.

He kept saying she needed to go there, so why not? She looked up the bar's website, skimmed the pictures, and chose her wardrobe accordingly. Tight, dark jeans, a silky halter top that tied behind her neck, and glittery sandals. She dried her hair and brushed it to shining sleekness in a side part. It slid forward, obscuring her face much as it had that last wild night with Ben. Then she examined her reflection in the mirror hanging above the sink and did her best to re-create the look Jess designed for her bachelor auction date with Ben. Weeks ago she felt like her eyes looked out from a Mardi Gras mask, but tonight she actually recognized the woman looking back at her from the mirror, as if she'd grown into what had been a costume that first night. But had she grown into it, or had she learned to put on a shell, like Ben did?

Pushing the question from her mind, she got in her Focus and drove into town, pulling into the No Limits parking lot at five minutes to nine. Ben stood with the two cops stationed near the entrance but he wasn't in uniform. Instead he wore jeans, the ever-present western shirt, and boots. He kept talking to the two officers but his gaze followed Rachel as she nipped into an available space close to the entrance.

Arms folded, legs braced, consciously or unconsciously Ben mirrored the cops' stance as he watched her cross the parking lot. Something in his gaze sent heat flickering through her body, a shock heightened by the shift and slide of the satin halter top across her breasts. Without thinking about it, Rachel gathered her hair and slid the whole heavy mass over one shoulder.

The other two cops stopped talking, too, until one with a hint of concern on his face leaned toward Ben and said something. Ben ignored him, stepped off the curb, and walked to meet her.

"Hi," she said.

Ben took her elbow and guided her around the back of the building, out of the noise and regulated commotion at the bar's front door. He bent his head and kissed her, his mouth lingering on hers for just a second for a quick flick of tongue. "Very nice. Very sexy."

"Ben, tell me about Sam," she said.

"Still unconscious. He picked up a staph infection so he's running a fever," he said. His hand stroked down her bare arm, then toyed with the thick ends of her hair before his hand fell to his side.

"Why aren't you with him?"

"Because my parents, Chris, Katy, her husband, and her two kids are doing a round-the-clock vigil at his beside," Ben said, then leaned closer and murmured, "I want to be here, with you."

Her gaze narrowed. It wasn't true. Even an emotionally inexperienced person like Rachel could see the agony in his eyes. What he wanted and what he was doing were two entirely different things. "Why here?"

"Because it's time to take off the training wheels."

Once again she was missing something crucial. "I don't understand."

"Pick up a guy, go home with him, and fuck him."

Air left her in a soundless rush. It took a few seconds for her to regain the ability to speak, and those seconds she searched his gaze for any trace of the man she'd come to know over the last few weeks. That rakish pirate's smile firmly fixed on his mouth, he stared back, unblinking, unflinching, all walls and armor and step-back attitude.

The smile didn't reach his eyes.

She tried to imagine doing what he demanded: going into No Limits and choosing the next man she'd let into her body. It wasn't impossible. After all, she'd chosen Ben, but the thought that he could dictate this to her made her furious. "Is that what you want from me, Ben?" She leaned closer and whispered, "Do you want to watch?"

He froze. Six feet and two hundred pounds of lethally trained man went utterly still against her. She felt his heart beating, felt his breathing resume, and only then did her unintentional double entendre hit her.

She meant watch her choose another man. He thought she meant watch her *fuck* another man.

He said nothing, as if her response shocked him.

Let's see how far he would take this. "Fine. Let's go," she said, then ducked under his arm, still braced against the brick by her head.

A muscle in Ben's jaw jumped as he guided her past the line, right up to the front door. "Don't we need to wait in line?"

"They do. We don't."

She handed the bouncer her ID and stepped into the whirling noise and flickering lights that was like the Pleasure Pier times ten. The dance crowd bounced and sang along to a song about drunk sex. She made her way to the bar and ordered a glass of white wine, then stood there watching Ben while he ordered a beer for himself.

My God, he was broken. So broken, this frightening vulnerability protected only by pieces of bulletproof vest held together with razor wire, attitude, and a smile that broke her heart every time he flashed it. And something about the bar, the way the noise shut down all the clamor in her head, brought clarity unfelt since she made the decision to leave Elysian Fields.

She was falling in love with him, and he was so broken, so damaged, and trying so hard to hide it.

How do people do this? How do they offer everything they have, taking the risk that it's not enough?

"Who do you like?"

She looked around, considering and discarding possible candidates based not on looks but on demeanor. Too cocky. Too drunk. Too preoccupied trying to get his hand up a woman's skirt to even notice her.

"Come on, Rachel. Which one turns you on? Which face do you want to see above you as he pushes inside you?"

"Having you here won't help," she pointed out.

He tipped back the beer bottle, then flashed her the smile she was growing to actively hate. "You are still such a virgin," he said.

She walked away from him, making her way through the crowd, using the noise and crush of the crowd to shut down her brain as she looked around. One possible candidate stood in a pack of men at the opposite corner of the bar. He wasn't tall, but he held his shoulders with a straight-backed confidence she found intriguing. He put more attention into the conversation than into projecting attitude or scoping out women, which didn't bode well for her. She sipped her wine again, and when she looked up, she found him watching her. One corner of his mouth lifted in an easy smile.

The second time it happened, she smiled back. He detached himself from his group of friends to make his way through the crowd to her. "Hey."

"Hi," she said.

"I'm Seth."

"Rachel," she said.

"Buy you a drink?"

"Oh, I'm fine," she said, then looked at the group he'd just left. "You're here with friends?"

"Guys I work for," he said. "They just landed a big contract. They're celebrating."

"What kind of work do you do?"

"Security," he said. "You?"

"I'm . . . in school."

"So you're not an admin?" he said. "They need to hire an admin."

She shook her head. Conversation was nearly impossible in this place. The noise level both deafened and frightened her. Seth leaned close, and she caught the scent of cologne. "Want to dance?"

"Sure," she said. It was almost impossible to hear him over the music, talk, and laughter, and in any case this wasn't about talking.

She left her wineglass on the bar. Seth slipped his hand into hers and led her to the dance floor. While some of the dancers were clearly showing off practiced moves, others were immersed in the beat, eyes closed, hips and arms moving to the primal heartbeat she felt in her ears, low in her belly. That she knew. That she could do.

Apparently she did it well enough for him, because after a few bars he slipped his arm around her waist and drew her against his body. His strength and confidence carried over to the dance floor but despite the bump and grind he didn't light her up like Ben did. She remembered Rob's words, that it was possible to have amazing sex with someone totally wrong for you, and mediocre sex with someone you liked very much.

The knowledge tasted bitter, like honey gone rancid.

The song started to shift into the generic thumping drumbeat that signaled a change in songs. Seth tipped his head toward his group of friends and said, "Come on."

Why not? She followed him to the periphery of an entire group of people. He replaced her glass of wine, and she paid attention to the conversation, to the way they finished each other's sentences. Standing off to the side, she eventually pieced together that the men were former military, now working together here in Galveston, and Seth was a contractor. While their friendly banter and sense of community only heightened her awareness of what she'd lost when she left Elysian Fields, it did help block out the aimless noise of No Limits, the emotional high without any meaning, the emptiness of the looks, dancing. The distraction, desperation, and not just for someone to take home. Avoiding life.

She didn't want to be here. The knowledge slid sharp and sure along her spine. Even if Ben brought her here, danced with her, took her home, she wouldn't want to be here. The surface appeared wildly different thanks to the slick gloss of sex and skin covering every-thing, but underneath, No Limits was exactly the same as the empty rituals and routines of her life at Elysian Fields. She didn't belong there, but she didn't belong here, either. She didn't know how to do this.

She didn't *want* to know how to do this.

Seth's gaze sharpened just as a hand slid along Rachel's waist and a voice murmured low and rough in her ear. "Dance with me, darlin'."

Ben. She didn't even have to turn around to know it was Ben. His scent, his touch, that hard body at her back and she lit up like a live wire. In that instant she understood why wiser voices recommended delaying sex until marriage. Would any other man call that response from her body? Was she supposed to go to bed with her husband knowing this hot, sharp longing would never be hers again? Was she supposed to choose between all-consuming passion and a lifetime love?

"Actually," she said, evenly, "I was just about to leave."

"He's your choice?" Ben murmured in her ear as he sized up the other man. She knew what he was doing because Seth's expression shifted from assessing to pure challenge.

"You know this guy?" Seth asked.

"Yes," Rachel said.

"Protective," Ben said. The sharp bite of whiskey drifted to her nostrils as he spoke. His hand slid under the halter's hem and he stroked his thumb along her bare stomach. "A nice touch. But he doesn't do it for you like I do."

She didn't bother to deny it. "My goodness, you're charming when you've been drinking."

"Rachel," Seth said evenly, "if you want me to make this individual leave the premises, it would be my pleasure."

Ben's smile flashed in her peripheral vision. "He's a Galveston police officer," Rachel said.

"I don't give a fuck," Seth said, his smile not all that different from Ben's.

Just like that she was drowning in testosterone. "Thanks for the offer, but we have some things to talk about," Rachel said. "Enjoy your evening."

Ben's fingers encircled her wrist in an unbreakable grip. He towed her through the crowd, but she dug in her heels and jerked away from him. "What's the matter?" Rachel said, not liking the mocking tone in her voice. "You told me to pick up a stranger. You said you wanted to watch."

He put his hands on his hips, claiming space from everyone around them. "I didn't think you'd do it."

"Ben, have I given you the impression that I don't do what I say I'm going to do?" she shouted over the insane noise. His gaze never left her face. "I was leaving, but not with him. But eventually, I will. I will choose another man the way I chose you, and I will sleep with him. You don't have any right to have a problem with that."

"I do," he said so low she thought she'd imagined the words. She wasn't sure if he meant he had a right, or that he had a problem with her going home with another man, and she suspected he didn't know, either. "I do. You have to do this sometime, but God help me, I don't want it to be tonight."

"Then it won't be. You're like a stranger to me anyway," she pointed out.

Emotion flicked across his face so fast she couldn't name what she saw. "Dance with me," he said.

He led her through the crowd to the dance floor, and oh God, this was how it was supposed to feel, hot and slippery and electric. Relentless. He wove their legs together, snugging her up against his torso, pressing his hard shaft to her hip. It thickened as they danced, one hand flat at the small of her back, holding her close, the other sliding under her hair to loosely grip her nape. She wound her arms around his neck, used his strength to press herself against his body and let the percussive bass draw her under.

Everything left her mind, the words, the other people in the room, the music itself, except for the thumping beat and Ben. Her hair stuck to her arms, to his, slipped into her face so that when he kissed her, he had to smooth it back from her face. The shock of hot lips, quick breath, and then his tongue dancing against hers sent a bolt of electricity sharp and jagged between her thighs. His abdomen tightened, and he pulled her closer. One song became two, then she lost track of time and the relentlessly sexual lyrics.

A woman backed into Rachel, stepping on her heel and jerking her out of the hot haze. Ben looked as dazed as she did, desire etched into his face by the sweat streaking from his temple to his jaw. She reached out with her fingers, grazed the side of his face, trailed the tips along his cheek to his mouth. He bit the tip of her index finger, then soothed it with his tongue.

"If you think we're a good fit, stranger, I'd like to dance somewhere else," she said.

"I've got a room at the motel across the street," he murmured.

At this odd statement she pulled back, looked into his eyes. Torn halfway between fantasy and reality, she bit her lip and looked up at him. He leaned forward and used his teeth to tug her lip free, soothe the spot, then bite down on it himself. The heat and danger so tightly leashed.

"Let's go," she said again.

Chapter Twenty

Ben took her out through the storeroom, past a redheaded waitress in killer heels whose "Hi, Ben" got a curt nod as he opened the door to the alley. They wove through cars in the parking lot onto the sidewalk, then jaywalked across the street. The motel across the street had nothing to recommend it, a listing arrow of white neon with a red VACANCY flashing over two floors of doors facing the street. Ben led her up the stairs to the second floor and unlocked a door.

When she stepped inside, she saw a round table with two chairs, a single queen bed with a faded spread and thin pillows, and a dresser with a mirror hanging from the stuccoed wall above it. Ben closed the door on the streetlights and traffic, then stepped away from her, leaving her in the faint scent of industrial-strength cleaning products while he turned on the lamp above the table. When he closed in on her, all she could smell was Ben, heat and musk rising from his skin, almost as palpable as the tension simmering just under the surface.

He flashed her that smile she so distrusted, the one that meant he was stretched thin, the veneer of attitude barely covering the raw ache inside. Then he picked up a worn leather case sitting on the table, opened the snap, and pulled out a pair of handcuffs. He didn't ask, just opened them, the ratcheting sound loud in the still air.

"My turn."

She tilted her head and studied his face. He held her gaze with nothing in his eyes. She recognized that expression, had seen it in her own eyes those last tortured months at Elysian Fields.

"This is what you'd do with a stranger?" she asked.

The single lifted eyebrow, mocking, amused, was answer enough. She turned around, felt the awkward strain on her shoulders when she brought her wrists together at her tailbone. The steel, warm from his body, closed around her wrists.

Ben tossed the case on the bed, then rested his chin on her shoulder and his hands on her hips. His hard body shifted against her back and bottom, shoulder to shoulder, erection brushing her restrained hands, while his breath riffled the silky halter top. He unfastened the halter top's ties and the cups fell forward, baring her breasts. The backs of his fingers skated down the side of her breast, along her ribs, then he unzipped the side and worked the top down over her hips.

He walked around her in a slow circle, the heat of his gaze a physical caress on her bare back, ribs, and breasts. Aroused by memory and eager for his touch, her nipples peaked. One corner of his mouth lifted in response. He reached out and laid his big hand on her ribs just below her breast, then stroked the soft underside with his thumb. The pressure, so tantalizingly close to where she wanted it, made her eyelids droop.

It should have felt awkward to stand half-naked in front of him. Doing so in front of a true stranger would, but this was Ben, and all she felt was a little dirty. Not bad dirty, but the kind of dirty that struck sparks and drew dampness between her legs. The kind of dirty spurred by a connection between them so fundamental and raw she could hardly stand it.

A connection he studiously ignored. "Touch me," she said softly.

"Only if you watch," he replied. He wrapped long fingers around her upper arm and guided her over to stand in front of the mirror, but didn't look into the reflective surface. "You like to watch?"

The words were murmured into the slope where her shoulder met her neck; between his hot mouth and the shockingly carnal sight of his hands on her, a shiver ran through her body. They both knew she'd never watched this before. "Yes," she said faintly.

His hands were so dark against her pale skin. They started at her shoulders, flexed down her arms before turning slightly to brush the full sides of her breasts, then continuing down to her waist, then the curve of her hips before skimming back up her ribs to cup her breasts. He squeezed gently, almost distractedly but ignored her nipples, now hard for his touch. Instead he brought one fingertip to her mouth. She watched her tongue flick out and dampen his skin, then kept watching as that fingertip brushed over each peak. The wetness heightened the air-conditioned coolness, and her nipples tightened even more.

But his hands moved low again, this time to unfasten and unzip her jeans. He didn't push them down, didn't slide his hand inside, just left them open, and the dirty-hot sensation ratcheted up another notch. She was nearly naked to his fully dressed, restrained to his free, slender and delicate to his broad shoulders and heavily muscled body . . . a body she couldn't see.

"Take your shirt off," she said.

He just shook his head. "Watch yourself. Watch me turn you on."

As long, heated moments passed, she did just that. When his

fingers finally alternated between cupping her breasts and pinching her nipples, her head lolled back against his shoulder.

"Look at you," he growled. "So hot."

Her breath eased from her parted lips in soft, irregular pants. She couldn't control the shimmy or the slight whimper she made when his hands dropped lower to push her jeans to the tops of her thighs, revealing her mound. When his finger dipped into her hidden folds she tried to spread her legs but couldn't.

"Look at you," he said again. His middle finger skimmed up a little, brushing the side of her clitoris. "Watch while I get you off."

So she did, and as she did, she wondered at the back of her mind if this was the Ben other women saw. Slightly rough, slightly edgy, not all that dissimilar from the man she'd bought at the bachelor auction. The new Rachel looked back at her from the mirror, eyes alight with passion, cheeks flushed, bare breasts tipped with reddened nipples, a man at her back. His rough cheek snagged in her hair and sent it spilling over her shoulders. Then the stroking finger made her thighs clench. Her eyes slid to soft focus. Ben ground his hard shaft against her bottom as she undulated and gasped.

"Shh," he ordered without letting up on his ruthless touch.

Silence was impossible, because this was the hottest thing she'd ever done, slow and visceral, like straining time through honey, and she saw it all. Saw the sex flush bloom on her chest, the same color as the roses Ben brought her, saw it climb her throat and claim her cheeks. Saw muscles tremble and clench in her abdomen and thighs. Saw her throat work as she tried to stifle the desperate, pleading noises he called from her. Then, when the pleasure peaked and his hand slid up from her breast to cover her mouth, she let go. Waves of release pulsed from the slick spot where his finger stroked outward through her skin, into the room and beyond. Her knees trembled and she sagged against his body. As she watched, Ben bent over her, his forehead resting on her shoulder.

"Ready for more?" he asked her reflection, but he had to clear his throat to get the words out.

Her hair slid into her face when she nodded. He turned her to face him, tucked the heavy strands behind her ear, then crouched to push her jeans clear of her legs. He stepped back until his legs met the bed, then sat down. Springs squeaked and the mattress sagged. He put his hands on her hips and pushed. As she went to her knees she looked over her shoulder to find Ben centered in the mirror, all dark stubble and hooded blue eyes.

"You want to watch me do this?" she asked, and there was no hint of innocence in her voice.

He focused on her mouth, on her drawn shoulders, on their intimate, sexual position. "Hell yes," he said roughly.

He unbuckled his belt, popped open the buttons of his fly, then leaned back on his elbows, drawing his shirt up to expose his lower belly. The cheap polyester bedspread rustled under him. Rachel bent forward, firmed up the tip of her tongue, and traced the vein all the way up his shaft to the sensitive spot just under the head. Then she settled back on her heels and repeated the process, each time covering new ground but always, always finding the bundle of nerves. His breathing shallowed as his gaze flicked between Rachel's mouth and the show in the mirror.

He slid his palm under her hair to cup her nape and bring her head forward. She opened her mouth just enough that it gave him the edge of teeth scraping ever so gently as his cock slid into her mouth to the back of her throat. For several long minutes he set a slow pace, the slick sounds of her mouth and his breathing punctuated occasionally by her soft whimper. He gave her a breather, letting her swallow hard. His cock pulsed, then he dragged his hand from her nape through her hair to brush his thumb over her lips.

"Very, very good," he said. "Let's keep going."

He found his wallet and pulled out a condom, rolling it down his shaft while Rachel knelt between his legs. Then he pulled her up onto the bed. The ancient mattress dipped and swayed as he adjusted her position, on her knees and centered in the mirror. He wrapped one arm around her and guided her forward, face to the bedspread, ass in the air, and used his knees to spread her wide. She was blind until he gently collected her hair at the back of her head.

When he could see her face, he braced one fist on the bed by her right knee, and gripped her hair with the other, making escape impossible. He slid inside, torturously slowly. The contrast of his gentle stroke with his rough handling made her tremble. She needed to touch him. Even in this position she wanted her hands free to caress his leg or cup the nape of his neck. Whatever she could reach. She wanted that connection.

But he started to move, and within moments slow was long gone, the firestorm of lust roaring higher with each stroke. He hunched over her and took what he wanted, powerful strokes from tip to hips. The smacking sound was loud in the room. Then he bent forward, shifting his weight from his right hand to his left.

"Come on," he murmured. "Tell me what you like. Is that better?" he asked, widening her stance a little.

A faint whimper. "How about"—he adjusted the cant of his hips, sliding lower over the hot spot inside her—"that?" he asked, and did it again.

A hard shudder ran through her.

"Tell me," he demanded.

"Good," she gasped. "So good, but . . ." She undulated, her wrists straining against the cuffs, her hands reaching for something and getting nothing. She didn't want it to end like this, him deep inside her yet miles away. Her arms jerked again, desperate to hold him close, but orgasm reared up, poised to crush her. All she had left was his name.

"Ben," she cried out.

Then the wave crashed over her, drowning her in sensation. Ben thrust deep, his release jerked from his body as he ground deep inside her. When the last shudder ripped through him he inhaled a deep gasping breath, and curved over her. Instinctively sheltering her, and yet giving her nothing of himself.

Rachel's heart tore just a little.

When he straightened he immediately released her hands, then stepped away to deal with the condom. She pushed back to her heels, the muscles in her thighs and arms trembling with the effort, forcing her to tuck her knees to the side and sit for a moment to regain her balance. Ben tucked the cuffs into their leather case, then strode into the bathroom. Water ran in the shower, then the curtain slid closed.

For the first time, it wasn't enough. More honesty and intimacy infused their first night together than this, and if she'd learned anything in the last year, it was that doing what she'd always done in the hopes of getting different results was a waste of time and energy. Her body quivered, the hot aftermath sliding along her nerves as she found her clothes discarded on the floor and dressed. Ben didn't seem surprised to see her ready to go when he came out of the shower. He dressed in quick jerks, slipped his wallet, keys, cuffs into various pockets, then tossed the room key on the table.

"I'll walk you back to your car," he said.

"I'd prefer you didn't," she said quietly.

He cut her a sharp glance that flicked away as quickly as it landed, then folded his arms across his chest.

"I can't keep doing this, Ben," she said, gesturing around the hotel room.

He barked out a laugh. "You wanted a man who wouldn't care. I'm that man. Never expect a man to change. What you see the first time is what you'll get the last time."

"How disappointing," she said. How sad. How *tragic*.

"Lower your expectations."

"I meant for you," she said as gently as he'd been harsh.

One eyebrow lifted. "You can't fall in love with the first man you screw."

"You can't tell me what to feel," she said. "Because I could so easily fall in love with you. I'm halfway there as it is. You're strong and dedicated and you care so deeply, as much as you try to pretend you don't."

"I don't give a fuck about anything," he said easily.

"So you say. Life at Elysian Fields sheltered me from so much about the real world, but I did learn about men who wall themselves off behind the way things are supposed to be. You need me to treat this as casually as you treat it. You need me to be another plate in the armor you wear to defend yourself against feeling anything."

He somehow got bigger, broader, even more walled off. "Bullshit."

"Why aren't you with your family at the hospital? When was the last time you went to Sam's for brunch on Sunday with your parents?"

He went still. Totally still. "That's none of your business."

"I know," she said evenly. "It's no one's business, Ben, and that's the sad part. I don't want to learn what you have to teach me. I don't want to go where you're going. I sacrificed too much to become a stranger to myself." She looked around the cheap room, the cigarette burns visible on the bathroom counter, the cracked mirror.

"This isn't even your apartment. What's next? The back seat of your patrol car?"

He flashed her that shark's smile, the bright, flashing one that made the average woman's brain stutter to a stop. But not hers. "Lady's choice," he said easily.

"That's what breaks my heart, Ben," she said. "You told me not to confuse this with love, and I haven't. But it doesn't even hold the promise of love, or the chance. Sometimes it's not even affectionate. I can't keep doing this. I don't like who I'll become if I do."

With that she stepped out of the hotel room, into the open hallway running the length of the second story. She closed the door behind her and walked down the stairs and across the street to her car, still waiting in the No Limits parking lot. The noise and commotion coming from the bar remained exactly the same.

But the words *rent asunder*, heard so often in her previous life, took on new meaning. Her heart was rent asunder when she walked out of that hotel room.

He was falling. Tipping. Skidding. The floor trembled under his feet like the edge of Rachel's lip when she looked around the room. He had been from the moment Rachel surrendered. She should have looked a little bit ruined, cheap and awkward with her jeans around her thighs and no way to keep her hair out of her face.

Instead, she looked powerful. Like a comic book action heroine, the kind who could call down fire or summon the ocean to do her bidding. The kind who blasted through steel plates without blinking an eye. She took his breath away.

This isn't even your apartment.

He'd gone from the bare minimum of intimacy—conversation over a shared meal and sex—to a twisted, warped game, or tried to. The only reason a third man, a total fucking stranger, wasn't leaving this room with Rachel's scent on his skin was her innate, true, unbreakable sense of self.

At least she had one.

He'd known this was coming. All he'd wanted to do was the right thing, get her up to speed on how the world worked.

The thought sliced dull and deep, and he winced, shook his head once. *Get her up to speed.* Like she'd come late to a briefing for a tactical operation. Like the most important thing he could offer her was a crash course in how to separate sex and emotions.

Like *because I can* defined him, and therefore should define her. *That's all you have to offer her.*

Now that it was here he didn't feel relieved. He was shattered because he'd purposefully ignored every cue, every shudder, every plea for greater intimacy, for—*admit it,* he thought to himself—what they both wanted.

Oh God.

When he'd come out of the bathroom she was fully dressed. Her hair spilled like a dark waterfall against her cheeks and over her shoulders. Even thoroughly fucked, she was beautiful.

Then she'd called him on everything. Every fucking thing he did and every fucking thing he was and every fucking thing he lived for. She was so goddamn beautiful, the way things that could end you were. Guns. Knives. The tawny bird of prey she resembled.

Unnameable emotions reached into his chest and gripped his heart and lungs, trapping them against his ribs. With his back to the door Rachel had just walked out of, he laced his fingers behind his head, slid to his heels, and hunkered over. Trying to breathe. Failing.

But he knew this. He'd done this before, survived this before, hoped to never survive it again, and here it was. Familiar in its pain, sitting comfortably inside his rib cage, crushing his lungs, knocking away at his heart.

Eventually his body succumbed to the need for oxygen. Eventually it would demand food, water, rest. So, eventually he pushed to his feet and opened the door. Across the street a typical Saturday night at No Limits roared on, laughter and music and high-pitched chatter spilling out of the open door. Steve and the cop Ben got to replace him tonight stood by the entrance to the parking lot, glancing between cell phones and the line waiting to get into the club.

Ben scanned the parking lot. Rachel's hail-dented Focus was gone.

Walking came back to him just before he navigated the stairs, thank Christ. Hearing returned just before he walked in front of a bus, and the driver's startled honk brought back the armor that allowed him to walk up to Steve.

"Your girl just left," Steve observed.

"How'd she seem?"

"Better than you do, to be honest. Head held high. Went to her car, put her hair up, got in, and drove away." He looked at Ben, but Ben stared straight ahead. "You okay?"

He didn't even know what that meant. Okay. What did it mean?

"Fine," Ben said shortly. "Everything's fine."

He wondered how long it would take the cold black mass inside to recede again. He wondered if Rachel would make it home okay.

Mostly he wondered how long it would take Rob Strong to give her what she really needed.

Once again Rachel drove back to Silent Circle Farm in a daze, but this time she knew exactly what had happened. She'd had passionate, intense, boundary-pushing sex with Ben Harris, but the *why* eluded her. Complicated, tempestuous, emotional despite his best effort to keep it meaningless. Once again she'd left someone she cared about.

Her watch read shortly after midnight when she parked in the bunkhouse lot, so she decided to check on the does a little early. Using the full moon's silvery light to guide her, Rachel made her way down the path to the goat shed and found Irene in the birthing stall. She'd shown no interest in food for the last day or so and hung off by herself, away from the other does. But when Rachel quietly opened the door, Irene looked at her, a distant, unfocused cast to her liquid brown eyes. Humming quietly, Rachel stood in the darker end of the shed and studied the doe. The bones in Irene's hips and tail protruded more prominently and her tail jutted out from her spine.

"Okay, sweetie," Rachel said. "It's time."

She hurried through the wildflowers to Rob's small house and knocked on his bedroom window. Almost immediately his face appeared in the window, his hair a tousled halo around his head. "Irene's kidding."

Without a word he let the curtain fall back over the window. Moments later he opened the front door, jeans on but not buttoned, his shirt in his hand. "I checked her at ten and she wasn't in labor," Rob said as he followed her back up the path.

"She is now," Rachel said.

When they entered the goat shed Irene stood exactly where Rachel left her, in the corner of the pen, head down. Rachel gathered the kidding tote from the supply room and shrugged into the old flannel shirt Rob left there as protection against messier jobs. When she came back out, Irene stood head down, her sides rigid with the effort of pushing. When the contraction eased she looked at Rachel and nickered, as if to say *What's going on?* Rachel looked over the young goat, her hand sliding along her side, fingertips searching for clues to the kid's position. Rob scratched gently behind Irene's ears. But with each contraction a nose and one hoof presented, only to slip back inside when the taut muscles eased. She quickly washed her hands and pulled on the gloves, then slid her hand inside. "I found an ear," she said. "I can feel the rest of the skull, but the head's definitely twisted."

"Okay," Rob said.

"Grab some gloves," she said.

"Your hands are smaller than mine," Rob protested.

His hesitancy made her smile. "But next season I won't be here," she said. "You'll be fine." When Rob wore gloves and was up to his knuckles in the birth canal, she held Irene's head and said, "Fold one foot back and guide the head over that foot."

He took his time and with the next contraction the kid presented perfectly, one tiny black nose resting on two equally tiny black hooves.

"Pull," she said.

Again gentle but firm, Rob pulled as Irene pushed, and just like that, the kid slid from the doe's body, into the straw. Rachel and Rob got rags and a box lined with soft cloths, drying the kid off as best they could. After a moment Irene turned around and nosed the kid, licking the amniotic sac from its neck as Rachel used a clean rag to clear the nose and mouth. Eventually the kid scrambled to its feet, wobbling as she nosed at Irene's udders.

"Good job, new mama," she said. She disposed of the gloves, then offered Irene a treat of raisins and peanuts. The goat lipped the sweets from her hand and stood under Rachel's gentle petting while Rob washed up. Then Rachel washed her hands and arms, and came to stand by Rob outside the pen.

"I really hate to lose you," Rob said quietly.

"You might not. I didn't get into school," she replied. Was that only a few hours ago that she'd gotten that news?

He looked at her, and Rachel was grateful for the crescent moon and lack of light. The muscles of her face twisted into unfamiliar positions as she struggled to hold back tears and the onslaught of emotions. She blinked hard, cleared her throat.

"I'm sorry," he said with the same gentleness. "What did they say?"

"My essay was great, but I don't have enough science."

"That's fixable," Rob said.

It was. Totally fixable. She'd done the hard stuff. She'd left, lost her virginity. She could take high school science. At twenty-five.

"Are you worried about how you'll do in the classes? Because you'll do just fine. You're smart, and you work harder than anyone else I know. It's just a question of time."

What knotted her throat unbearably wasn't his kind words. She wanted to hear them from Ben. Not Rob. But Ben would never be there for her like that. Oh, if she needed to work off steam in a man's bed, Ben would be there for her, waiting just inside his door, all sleep rumpled and stone-faced. She wanted him to share the good times and the bad, not lock them away.

You foolish girl. You fell in love with him. You were warned, but you gave your body away and where exactly did you think your heart was?

She loved him, loved his strength and the wounded, damaged soul inside.

A sob escaped her. Rob turned to look at her. "Hey," he said, clearly a little alarmed, and reached for her.

Rachel turned her face into his shoulder, sobs wracking her body. Rob held her while she cried, both arms around her to keep her close, giving her strength while she had none. When her tears subsided she relaxed into his torso.

"Why do I think that wasn't just about the miracle of birth and vet tech school?" he asked wryly.

She let out a rough laugh and looked up at him. His gaze remained focused on the night sky. "Because you see more than you say? I broke up with Ben," she said, and swiped her sleeve across her face. "My first breakup, except . . . I don't think we were even together. Either way, it's harder than I thought it would be."

"I'm sorry. You seemed to really care for him."

"I did," she said, then tipped her face to the starry sky. "I fell in love with the first man I slept with. I wanted something passionate and intense and real. I knew it would hurt . . . just not this much. Now I understand why Jess is the way she is."

A low laugh huffed from Rob's nostrils, and he looked down at her.

"No virgins here," she said.

"Not anymore," he conceded.

They stood by the pen for a while before the day's events caught up with Rachel. She yawned, then used the stretch to step out of Rob's sheltering arms. "I should get to bed."

"You've got a knack for this," he said, nodding at the pen. "Things are going well this season. I'm going to branch out, add alpacas and sheep. I could use permanent help. The job's yours if you want it. I'll work around your class schedule."

She hesitated. This was the safe thing to do, stay at the farm. She wished it felt right, but it didn't. Maybe it was the events of the day. Maybe she'd feel differently after some sleep and some distance.

As if sensing her indecision, Rob said, "You don't have to tell me now. We've got the summer ahead of us. Let me know when you make up your mind."

Chapter Twenty-one

An entire week had come and gone without Rachel, without even the promise of Rachel. The pain permeated Ben's entire gut, like an infection he couldn't cure. He stood outside No Limits, watching the bouncer usher stragglers out the front door. Closing time on yet another night of wild, sexy fun. A carload of young women idled near the exit, waiting for Steve. "Go on," Ben said. "I'll finish up here."

"I can wait," Steve said. "Or you want to meet us later?"

He should, for the simple reason that there'd been no one since Rachel. Every night he'd gone home alone to sit in silence. He didn't want what he usually sought out, mindlessness. He wanted Rachel. Slow and passionate and deep as the ocean. But Rachel asked more of him than he could give.

Fuck dilemmas. Fuck rocks and hard places. The razor-sharp edge of who she was hovered over his paper-thin excuse for a soul. He didn't want that blade to fall. He couldn't bear to push it away, either.

"Not tonight," Ben said.

"How's your brother?" Steve asked.

"Home." Sam was sixteen pounds lighter, but he was alive, out of the hospital, expected to fully recover. The doctors said the headaches would taper off, and for God's sake, stay off the ladders.

"Glad to hear it," Steve said, then left.

The bouncer signaled Ben, pointing at two guys meandering through the nearly empty parking lot.

"Hey," Ben called, then whistled sharply when they ignored him. "Don't even think about it."

After some grumbling the guys sat on the curb, phones in hand, presumably texting sober friends or a cab company. Ben bounced on the balls of his sore feet, waiting for the bouncer to shoot the bolts, signaling the end of his night. Same shit, different day . . . except he was different, too.

The last person out the door was Juliette.

Her tight microskirt and heels highlighted her long legs as she crossed the lot in his direction. He watched her walk because he could. The skirt stopped at her upper thighs, and before Rachel he would have said this was what he wanted. Long blond hair, carefully applied makeup, clothes chosen to highlight breasts, legs, her flat stomach, and toned legs. A surface. A pretty one, sure, but a surface. Like the plastic cover on an iPhone. He had no idea who was underneath that surface, what she loved, what she dreamed about. Maybe nothing. Maybe something that would surprise him.

Like Rachel.

The bouncer tossed him a wave, then stepped inside and closed the doors. The bolts shot home just as Juliette stepped up onto the sidewalk. "Hey," she said quietly.

He gave her a nod.

"I wanted to apologize in person," she said. "What Steve and I did was stupid, and wrong. I'm sorry. Even if Rachel hadn't been there—"

"If Rachel hadn't been there, things would have turned out very differently and we both know it," Ben said. He flashed her the smile, the one he used to hide everything, the one that never fooled Rachel.

Juliette smoothed her hair away from her cheek with that familiar palm-out movement. Rachel's hair flashed into his mind, the matter-of-fact way she dealt with it, not using it to signal interest or availability.

Who the fuck have you become?

Get her out of your head, or you're going to go out of your head.

"How are things with Rachel?" she asked, only a slight artfulness to the question.

He gave her a look, because they weren't the kind of friends who inquired into personal relationships. He didn't even know her last name. "Over."

Juliette's eyes widened slightly. "Really," she said, as if he'd surprised her. He was struggling through what that single word in that tone meant when she shrugged, her bare shoulders lifting above her strapless top. "How 'bout we do that different ending tonight?"

It was the offer he expected, the perfect opportunity to pick up right where he left off, mark the last few months as a blip on the radar of his life. As if Rachel hadn't changed the way he looked at the world. But something told him Juliette wasn't any more into this than he was, and *because I can* made his stomach lurch like it had in the hotel room.

"I've got to be up early tomorrow," he said, letting her down as gently as he could. "Are you okay to drive?"

"Water only for the last couple of hours," she said. "But thanks for checking. I'm sorry you and Rachel are over," she added as she walked away. "From what I saw, it was something special."

She saw them thirty seconds away from fucking. What came through that made it special? Was it some kind of girl-radar that turned everything into the big moment, the happily ever after, like sounds only dogs and dolphins could hear, leaving the average man standing around, bewildered?

His phone buzzed. The text from Sam read, **i'm awake come over.**

Might as well. Ben climbed into his truck and drove to Sam's house. He found him in the garage cleaning up his workbench.

"Hey," Sam said when he opened the door. He nodded at the now-finished garage walls. "Thanks."

"I wasn't taking any chances you'd come back and try to finish the job," Ben said pointedly. He'd called in a favor from a contractor friend. She'd finished the job while Sam and Chris were living at the hospital. "How're you feeling?"

"No headaches for the last couple of days. You coming over tomorrow?" Sam asked.

"Probably not."

"Still got the thing with the virgin?"

"No."

"Why not?"

"She ended it a couple of weeks ago."

"She did or you did?"

He flashed Sam his battle-tested smile, the one that was all teeth and no eyes, then looked down at his phone. "She did. It was getting boring anyway."

Even as the lie left his mouth a fist came out of nowhere, landing hard enough against Ben's cheekbone to explode a supernova behind his eye and rock him off balance. He stumbled backward into the workbench, then scrabbled at the edge of the shelving unit, automatically trying to right himself when Sam slammed into him full bore. The air knocked from his lungs, Ben grappled with him, pushing his forearms in his face, just trying to keep Sam from hurting himself. Glass jars of screws and nails tipped over. One spun to the edge of the bench, rolled to the ground, and shattered, sending sharp metal and glass all over the floor.

"Jesus, Sam," he gasped. His brother landed an elbow to Ben's gut, another to the side of his head before driving Ben back into the cement. He twisted, taking the brunt of impact from both their bodies into his shoulder and head, which knocked against the floor, then wrapped one arm around Sam's torso, locking his arm at his side as he tried to contain the other.

"Knock it—stop—goddammit!" he roared as they grappled on the floor. "You're going to hurt yourself!"

The garage door flung open. "What the fuck is going on out here!" Chris demanded. "Jesus fucking Christ, Ben! You hit him? He just got out of the fucking hospital!"

"I didn't—" Ben huffed out from flat on his back, then ducked an elbow. "I didn't hit him!"

Chris bear-hugged Sam's waist and hoisted him right off the floor, then carried him a few feet back from Ben, but not before Sam's foot landed in Ben's diaphragm as he straightened. The kick knocked the wind entirely out of him. He went to his knees on the floor, trying to wait out the panic until his breath came back in one heaving gasp.

Inhale felt like prayer.

"What the fuck is your problem?" he shouted at Sam.

"Do I have your attention?" his brother demanded as he shook free of Chris's arms.

Ben fingered his temple, pulsing with his rapid heartbeat and already swelling. "Yeah."

"How long are you going to punish everyone else for what I did?"

He looked up at Sam. "What the fuck are you talking about?"

Hands raised, Chris stepped between them, then he pointed into the identical faces. "It's about fucking time you had this conversation, but keep your goddamn voices down," he said, his tone as smooth and quiet as a blade. "I just, and I mean *just* got Jonathan back to sleep. You wake that boy up and I will put both your asses back in the hospital."

What conversation? Ben swiped blood from his mouth and glared at his brother. With his brows lowered and furious intent in his eyes, Sam looked like a Neanderthal, which meant Ben did, too.

"Have you lost your mind?" Ben hissed. His head throbbed like he'd taken a hit from a sledgehammer. Sam didn't need hand-to-hand training. His brother learned to fight on the streets, and he fought dirty.

With Chris back in the house, Sam strolled up to Ben and gave him a taunting little shove. "G'on. Get mad at me."

"I'm not mad at you," Ben growled, refusing to get drawn into a fight with his brother.

"Why not? You should be. Going easy on me because I'm a faggot?" Sam punctuated the question with a not-so-gentle push. "Or because it's easier to be mad at Dad than me?"

Ben stared at his normally rational, thoughtful brother while fear sucked his stomach through the cement floor. Concussions and other brain injuries could bring on changes in personality, and Sam had been out for the count for days.

"Or is it because you're a fucked-up pussy?"

He'd let his brother get away with a lot, but that accusation hit too close to home. "Watch it," he warned Sam, bringing his arms out sharp and hard to knock Sam's next shove away.

"Bring it," Sam shot back, yelling in a whisper. "I'm not afraid to take risks."

"I take risks."

Another shove slammed Ben against the newly installed drywall at the back of the garage. "In situations where you end up in the hospital, sure. Get shot, get a pipe taken to your thick, stupid head, that's Ben Harris, tough man. When the consequences are adrenaline rush or death you'll risk everything we love to prove you don't give a shit about us or how we feel. But you won't risk loving someone."

The words landed with the same brain-stunning power as Sam's first punch. Wounded, shredded, his soul battered, he shoved Sam, putting his full weight into the move. His brother stumbled back. "I've already lost my heart, Sam. Someone I loved more than I will ever love another human being again walked out of my life without a word, and that someone was *you*. So don't you fucking talk to me about taking risks. Some of us don't have anything left to risk."

As soon as the words left his mouth he would have given his life to take them back because he knew it was a lie. He'd left Sam for football and girls and the safety of popularity long before Sam left home. He'd abandoned the brother who talked for him, taken for granted that the person who knew him best, who was him, would always be there for him.

Don't go. Stick it out until we're eighteen. Tone it down a little. It's not much longer. Two years. We can make it, then we'll be out of here.

But Sam had to be Sam, had every right to be Sam. Ben was the one who'd failed him, and therefore failed both of them. He couldn't take care of his own brother. How could he take care of anyone else?

Sam straightened, then folded his arms across his chest. Ben blinked, looked away, covering the flinch with another swipe across his swelling mouth and fingers testing his bruised eye. The bare bulb overhead hummed in the silence stretching taut between them. He was the one trained to wait out a suspect's silence, but faced with Sam and what happened all those years ago, he broke first.

"It's not your fault," Ben said. "I wasn't there for you."

"What?" Sam blinked. Shook his head like he hadn't heard him right. "What?"

Sam looked at him like he dropped out of the sky, his face in an expression Ben didn't recognize in himself, or in Sam. He shrugged to cover his reluctance to say this out loud, to confess his shame and failure. But in the end, he'd do more than that to keep Sam now. "I didn't listen. I kept telling you to just hold on until we graduated, to just tough it out. Stay safe. Don't take any risks. But it was the wrong thing to do. You had to go. I know that now. It just . . . hurt."

"Jesus God, Ben," Sam said, then swallowed hard. "Is that why you do this? Make it easy for people to leave?"

"Sam, don't ask me why," he said. "Do I strike you as even remotely self-aware?"

His brother rubbed his palm slowly over his jaw. A light dawned in his eyes, and the similarity to Rachel's clear, golden gaze made Ben's heart clench tight. "You didn't fail me. If you hadn't loved me so much, I wouldn't have had the strength to go. Knowing you loved me even though I was gay meant I was never alone. You were the only good thing. I was the selfish one. I couldn't take it anymore, and I left. I didn't email or call, because if I did you'd track me down. I knew you'd leave what you had for me. After a while I figured you'd hate me for what I'd done. I hated me. For leaving." He nailed Ben to the wall with clear blue eyes. "For everything I did after."

Ben didn't look away. It took all his strength to not look away from his brother when he finally alluded to what runaways did to stay alive on the streets, to numb the pain of the streets.

"And then I showed up outside your dorm and you got your football friends to let me crash with them off campus and you never asked—"

"I wasn't going to put you through it again." He swallowed hard, but even so, tears trickled down his face, into the cut on his mouth. "You were back. Where you were or what you did was completely irrelevant. All I cared about was putting you back together so you wouldn't leave again. I didn't know how to be without you, Sam. I still don't."

"Me, either." His brother swiped a hand over his eyes, then put his hands on his hips and met Ben's gaze. "You were there when I began. You weren't my other half. You were me. But I had to know who I was without you. As hard as those years were, my only regret was leaving you. Every time you come over I'm so happy to see you, and it kills me because I'm afraid, fucking scared to death, that you'll never forgive me for what I did. I left, but you never came back."

Ben eased to the floor, his back to the drywall. Sam sat down opposite him, mirroring his position. Knees up. Forearms dangling. They sat in the silence that was never really silence, instead a charged communication happening on the cellular level. "I'm okay," Sam said finally. "I am okay, Ben. I won't lie to you. I wasn't, for a long time, but you hear me? I am okay. Come home. Please."

Ben cut him a glance. "You'd think you were a psychologist or something."

"Apparently I suck at it. I didn't know you were blaming yourself."

"I thought I was blaming Dad," Ben said.

"Close enough. You're just like him," Sam said ruefully.

Ouch. "Katy says the same thing."

Sam blew out his breath. "I know it wasn't easy. Dad's said as much. But he's different now."

Ben rubbed his forehead. "I don't know, Sam. Do people really change?"

"Yes," he said with a quirky grin. "Let Dad off that hook. The only thing he wants, the only thing he prays for, is that you'll start talking to him again. He remembers when we used to walk the fence line together, back before all this started."

The thought brought fresh tears to Ben's eyes. He wiped his face on his shoulder to cover them.

"All anyone wants is someone to walk with them," Sam said quietly.

Rachel. So strong, and so alone. And he'd been teaching her to walk alone. He wanted to watch her do everything. Come apart under him, discover who she was now, who she'd be in a month, a year, a decade. He wanted to watch her live. Rachel was the kind of woman who'd be different every time he came home after a shift, and there was another thought he couldn't shake—Rachel in his apartment when he came home, or maybe in a house they bought together.

He'd tried to force her to disconnect, to treat life like he did, as a dip in the shallow end of pleasure. Meaningless. Empty. He'd done what he did with every other woman, made it hot and fast and rough, and she'd called him on it. His apartment was empty, missing even the promise of Rachel. His life was empty of that as well, and of Sam, even though Sam had been back for a decade. That's what was inside him. Emptiness.

"I made her leave," he said. "I really did."

"How?"

"I was me."

Sam, his brother, his twin, his heart and soul, knew what he meant. "So be someone better."

"I don't think I can make up for this." The cuffs. Shit. Fuck.

The way her hands jerked at the end. Like she wanted to hold him. *Fuck*.

"Be romantic," Sam said dryly. "Be thoughtful. Jesus. As many girls as you've been with, you must know something about romance."

"Romance wasn't what got me girls." The uniform and an empty smile got him girls. Before that, it was football. The night after the conference championship game was an alcohol-soaked blur, but he was pretty sure there was a blonde, a brunette, and a raven-haired girl all on their knees at one point.

Was that who he was?

Christ. This was hopeless. He bent his head and ran his hands over his hair before linking his fingers at the base of his neck.

"You know the story behind her name, right?"

Without looking up, Ben shook his head.

"Heathen," Sam accused without heat. "In the Bible, Jacob loved Rachel and promised to work seven years to earn her. On the wedding night, Laban swapped Leah for Rachel. Jacob didn't notice, did the dirty deed, and was married to Leah. Laban said he'd have to work another seven years to earn Rachel. Jacob loved Rachel, so he did."

"I'd notice," Ben said, all the while thinking about Rachel's father naming his baby girl something that would remind him of how precious she was, how special, how no man would deserve her. "I'm not that far gone. Fourteen years?"

"Fourteen years. Figure out romance and you can probably knock some time off."

If Rachel could leave behind life at Elysian Fields, then he could leave behind a life of aimless debauchery. "We're about to find out."

He got to his feet, crossed the garage, and held out his hand to his brother. When he was upright Sam didn't let go, but instead pulled Ben into a hard hug. "I missed you, man."

He relaxed into the hug, into his brother's heartbeat and breathing, familiar from the womb. "Yeah," Ben said. "Me, too."

They parted, and this time it was Sam wiping tears on his shoulder. "Help Dad with the fences sometime," he said. "Pick up your guitar while you're out there. Time we started playing together again."

His brother, as usual, was right. He had to get his house in order, air it out and sweep it clean before he invited anyone else into it. So he started with the obvious.

He deleted any contact from his phone that was a woman's first name only, or worse, a descriptive nickname.

He talked to Linc, made a couple of recommendations for replacements, and quit No Limits.

He lived with the great gaping hole inside him, dark and empty, oddly weightless but very specifically shaped, curving against the interior of his ribs, present with every breath and heartbeat. He carried it around, studied it, made peace with it. He went to briefings and did his job and let that darkness ride along. Because Rachel shouldn't have to save him.

As the summer progressed his awareness of it diminished, as if patience made it part of his lived experience when alcohol, anger, resentment, sex, and adrenaline only fed it. Then he went to where it all began. He went back to the Bar H to see his father.

He knew what he was getting into. His father was a hard man, a successful rancher, and Ben had been pretty unforgivable. If his father didn't throw him off the ranch, he'd spend all day out on the fence line with a man he hadn't talked to in over a decade, but driving past the turnoff to the creek reminded him what was at stake, strengthening his resolve. He'd dressed for the job in work pants and sturdy boots, his gloves on the seat beside him. When he pulled up the dirt driveway, his father was walking from the house to the barn, dressed in a worn denim shirt with patches at the elbows. Time had bowed his shoulders a little, and when he turned to see who was coming up the lane, Ben saw wisdom and pain etched into his face.

"You get a new truck . . . ?" His gaze widened, taking in Ben's broader shoulders and tanned face as he got out of the truck, and probably the wary look in his eyes. "Ben?"

"Dad," he said. When the silence stretched longer than Ben could bear, he added, "Sam said you were mending fences today."

Tears gleamed in his father's eyes, but what tightened Ben's throat was the way his father's firm mouth trembled. His father cleared his throat. "Yeah. I am."

Ben ignored them, and the ones stinging behind his own eyes. "Need some help? I'll drive."

His father loaded a new spool of staples into the fencing gun. Together they tossed the wire, posthole diggers, replacement posts, crowbar, hammer, and staples into the truck bed and climbed in. "South pasture," his father said, and Ben set off.

The smell of new grass and earth rose into the late spring sunshine while his father pried out the rotten posts. Ben dug postholes for the new ones. His father held the post while Ben hammered it into place and tamped down the dirt, then leaned his whole weight on it to test it. He gripped lengths of barbed wire in his gloved hands while his father stapled them to the posts. The work was physical, required two people to do it properly, and other than grunts and half-spoken instructions back and forth, mostly silent as they made their way down the fence line.

He kept waiting for the accusations, for the argument. Instead he got the quiet presence of a man who'd hurt, who'd learned lessons, who desperately wanted to make amends.

They were better than halfway done when his mother brought out lunch, steaming hot meatball sandwiches, fruit, chips, brownies, and fresh lemonade. The tight squeeze of her hand, dotted with age spots, made him duck his head as he thanked her. They sat on the pickup's tailgate and ate overlooking the creek.

"I always felt connected to this place," Ben said, thinking about Rachel.

"I hoped one of you boys might take it over," his father said.

Ben swallowed the last of his fresh lemonade before answering. "You never know, Dad. One of us might."

They finished the job as the sun set, bumping home over the hillocks as the sun bled red and orange in the rearview mirror. He stayed for supper. His mother brought him up-to-date on local gossip, but the only thing he remembered saying, over and over, was *I'm sorry*, words his father repeated while his mother wept.

He promised to be at Sam's on Sunday morning.

Before he left, he went into the room he shared with Sam for sixteen years. It was a craft room now, where his mother made scrapbooks and knitted toys for his nieces, but when he opened the closet his guitar case leaned against the back wall. He studied it, the stickers on the case, knew it would be out of tune and in need of repair. But it was a good guitar, the one Sam bought for him with money he saved doing chores for the next ranch over.

Could he be that man again? There was no point in playing the guitar if he didn't bring passion and love and intensity to the music, throw body and soul into a song.

He didn't know. He honestly didn't know.

It was time to find out who he could be.

Chapter Twenty-two

After crying in Rob's arms, Rachel didn't fall apart so much as disappear into the long, hot summer. More baby goats arrived as the weeks passed. Business at the farm stand picked up as the growing season progressed and the farm's reputation grew. She planted and harvested, sold and educated, cared for the baby goats and litters of kittens.

She continued to go to open-mike nights at Artistary, and used the long summer evenings to page through apartment guides, and browse roommate want ads online. Reinventing herself wasn't a one-time thing. Every success, every failure offered the opportunity to adapt, but it required awareness. Patience.

She avoided apartment listings in Ben's neighborhood.

One of the baristas at Artistary asked her on a date, so she went. She found she liked him, and so was relieved when the budding romance faded into friendship. When it became clear that Rachel wouldn't move on from Ben to Rob, Jess became much easier to live with.

"You don't change men like Ben Harris," Jess commented from across the root vegetable table as she unloaded another bushel of beets.

Rachel considered this while she jostled new potatoes in their sloped container until they found a precarious synergy. Jess wasn't jeering at Rachel for being naïve. If anything, she was commiserating. Except Rachel had known exactly what Ben was from the moment he strode into the auction tent.

"I didn't hope to change him," she said finally. "He's living on the fringes in so many ways. Always on the outside looking in."

"Housebreak him?"

She shot Jess a glance over the carrots. "He's not a dog."

"Tame him, then. He's a wolf. A lone wolf."

"Where are you getting these comparisons?"

"You lack an entire cultural framework," Jess said. "Look, maybe he likes life on the edges. No responsibilities. No obligations."

Ben carried the weight of responsibilities so heavy they'd break a lesser man. "Maybe he does," she said.

She worked her way back into the Sunday morning cooking rotation, made more of an effort to hang out with whichever A&M boys were sharing the bunkhouse. When the next term began she enrolled in biology and chemistry classes at the community college. True to his word, Rob worked around her class schedule, but the long drive took a toll on her. With fall coming she stepped up the search for a roommate and a job in town. Positions at clinics were few and far between, but she circled them and applied online.

One day she was in the goat pen helping the vet give the kids a round of vaccinations, when her cell phone rang. She lifted an eyebrow at the vet, in the process of laying out the drugs and syringes. He nodded and Rachel stepped into the tack room that now doubled as storage.

"Hello?"

"I'm calling for Rachel Hill." The accent was brusque, flat, and grating. A Yankee, and she didn't know any.

"Speaking."

"Rachel, this is Dr. Carly Weisen. I own the Dog Days clinic in Galveston, and I've got an opening for a receptionist. I understand you're looking for a position in a clinic."

Her heart stopped. She knew the names of all the clinics she'd applied to, and the Dog Days, one of Galveston's biggest, wasn't on the list. Had Rob called someone and not mentioned it to her? "Yes, ma'am," she said. "I am, but how did you know?"

"I have the contract to care for the Galveston Police Department's K-9 animals. Hera, the SWAT team's dog was in for her annual checkup yesterday. One of the officers with her saw the sign on the front door and said I couldn't hire a more committed, dedicated, hardworking individual."

Ben. Rachel sank down on a hay bale.

"I'm from New York," Dr. Weisen continued, "but I've learned that when a Texas man leans on a counter and plays up his drawl, he's charming you into something."

Definitely Ben.

"Or out of something, but in this case Officer Harris charmed me into giving you an interview. Tell me about your experience."

Apparently the interview was right now. Rachel ducked into the tack room and related her history and experiences with record keeping for Elysian Fields and Silent Circle Farm.

"Any experience with AVImark?"

AVImark was a common system to track appointments and patient records. She knew this from position descriptions but had never seen the software in use. "No, ma'am," she said, "but I'm a fast learner."

Rachel heard keyboard keys tapping. "He must like you very much," Dr. Weisen said absently.

"Yes, ma'am," she said. Was it true? Weeks and weeks of the summer gone without a word from Ben. No texts, no emails, no calls. Then this. Out of the blue. Totally unexpected.

Just a chance at the most important thing in her life.

"When can you come in so we can talk face-to-face, and you can take a look around the clinic?"

When Rachel arrived the clinic was quiet except for one little dog barking frantically in the kennels until Dr. Weisen took her out and held her. She showed Rachel the exam rooms, the lab in the back, the surgery, and the outdoor kennels. "We're open late a couple of nights a week. Any scheduling concerns?" she asked as they made their way back to the receptionist area.

"I'm applying to vet tech school. I was homeschooled so my science isn't quite up to standards but I'm taking night classes in the fall," she said steadily. "Once I get into school, I'll be in class during the day."

She glanced at Rachel's unpolished, blunt nails and tough hands. "I grew up on a working dairy farm in upstate New York. I'm the first person in my family to go to college. I know what it's like to work your way through the world." She gave Rachel a smile. "The job's yours if you want it."

"I do," Rachel said. "I really do. Thank you."

They settled on a start date. Outside the clinic Rachel pulled her phone from her purse. After a moment's thought, she sent Ben a text.

I got the job. Thank you.

The answer arrived while she was waiting at the light at the corner.

You're welcome.

That was it.

Suddenly change was in the wind at Silent Circle Farm. The sweet baby goats weren't so sweet anymore, instead capering around the pen and testing Rachel's knots. After deciding that farming wasn't for her, Jess took a position in the kitchen of an organic restaurant in Houston. The A&M boys all went back to school. Rachel found a roommate-wanted ad on Craigslist with the header *NO PARTIES! NO DRINKING! NO DRUGS!* She emailed the poster, had coffee with a no-nonsense nurse who worked nights, and rented her second bedroom.

On moving day Rob followed her into town with his truck and helped her purchase and bring home a single bed, dresser, bookshelf, and a desk. When all the furniture was assembled and arranged, he packed up his toolbox and gave the room one last look. It was just a room, with beige carpet, cream walls, and cream vinyl blinds covering the window, but it was hers, paid for with money she earned at her job.

"It's not exactly my own apartment," she said. "But I'll get there."

"I don't doubt it," he said. "I'm sorry things didn't work out."

She knew he meant more than her work on the farm. "Me, too," she said sincerely.

"Friends?" he asked.

She stepped into his embrace and gave him a long hug. "Always."

After Rob left she went to the Goodwill and bought scrubs decorated with puppies and kittens. Her first letter to her father from her new address and plans came back returned like all the rest. Alone in her bed, she dreamed about Ben, about his body, his hands, his scythe of a smile.

Small pleasures almost made up for the longing. The open-mike nights took a hiatus until later in the fall, so she took to studying at Artistary after the clinic closed. One late afternoon in mid-September, a group of men wearing dark blue cargo pants, bullet-proof vests, handcuff cases, and assorted weapons strapped to hip and thigh came into the shop. SWAT was printed above the badge symbols embroidered into the polos. Armed to the teeth, they stood by the counter, laughing and bantering with Ally, the barista who closed most nights.

Ben was with them.

First through the line, he placed his order, paid, and shifted to the end of the counter to accept two coffees, a big to-go cup of water, and two dog treats, which he carried back outside, all with-out noticing her at the table. Through the floor-to-ceiling windows Rachel could see an alert pair of dark brown ears swiveling like radar dishes. He stooped to set the cup on the ground in front of the dog, then remained outside, talking idly with another officer before he caught her watching him.

He blinked, and something seemed to ease inside him.

His eyes asked a question she answered with a nod. After a couple of quiet words to the dog's handler he straightened his shoulders, then walked back into the shop.

"Hi," she said. He remained standing, his eyes wary, as he returned the greeting.

"Is that Hera out there?"

He looked over his shoulder. "Yeah. She's still mad at me for stealing her takedown earlier in the spring. The water and biscuits are peace offerings."

Rachel smiled. "Can you sit down?" When he eased down on the empty chair opposite her, she asked, "How are you?"

"Good," he said. "I'm good. You?"

"Good," she said, then rushed on. "I'm so glad I saw you here. I can thank you in person for recommending me for the job. I love it. I don't know what you said to Dr. Weisen to get her to call me, but . . . thank you."

"I told her the truth. You're smart, work hard, are committed, with lots of experience and she wouldn't find a better employee."

"She said you charmed her."

He flashed her The Grin along with a slightly lifted eyebrow. "Maybe a little. It was for a good cause."

That grin, that flashing, slashing grin curving his full mouth, cut her to the bone as she considered the possibility Ben had charmed Dr. Weisen right into bed. "How's Sam?" she asked, remembering her manners.

"Fully recovered. Still has Jonathan. DPFS is dragging their feet on the adoption proceedings, but he's hopeful."

"So you're spending time with them?"

"Most Sundays," he said.

He looked different. The set of his jaw was softer, and he lacked the charming edge he'd held when they met. "That's good," she replied. "That's really good."

He studied her face. "I've been making these guys come in here for coffee for weeks, hoping to run into you. You study here a lot?"

"Most nights," she said. "I moved into town a few weeks ago. I've got a roommate and an apartment a few blocks from here."

He looked around, his voice studiously casual. "How are you spending your Sundays?"

She shrugged. "Doing this and that. Alone, usually."

"Let's go, Harris," one of the other guys called.

Ben didn't get up. He smiled, shades of the shark in the movement, his intense blue eyes studied Rachel's. "Not with Rob?"

Her breath caught, and for a moment she couldn't speak because as she watched, the smile shifted, the muscles in his face easing ever so slightly, transforming the shark's smile into something achingly vulnerable. He was afraid, afraid to ask the question, afraid of the answer. With a start, she realized why Ben looked different. He looked like a man who would care.

"It's none of my business," he said, backpedaling.

She overrode him hurriedly. "No. Not with Rob. Or anyone else."

His summer sky eyes cleared. "Okay. Good. I have to go. Maybe I'll see you around?"

"I'm here most afternoons," she said. "Including Sundays."

She watched him blend into the group as they left. The walls were gone. He was still big and strong and tough, but the attitude he used to wear like a suit of armor had changed somehow. Pieces were missing. He was still utterly confident in himself, his body, what it could do, the pleasure it could bring, but the shield of world-weary jadedness was gone.

After that, he stopped by Artistary two or three times a week. Rachel didn't doubt he could buy sweet tea anywhere else, nor did she doubt he chose Artistary because she might be there. Sometimes he wore a uniform, sometimes he wore regular clothes. He was seeking her out. Engaging in casual conversation.

Getting to know her. Letting her get to know him. He paid attention, not staying long if she left her textbook open and kept her pen in her hand, but staying for a couple of hours another time when she was reading a fantasy novel borrowed from the library at her roommate's suggestion for the few spare minutes she had in a week. The conversations weren't anything earth shattering. Family. Work. The weather.

"I miss sunsets," she said one day, watching the sky darken in hues of red and orange. "I'm in class, studying, or working late most days."

"That's a shame. We're having some pretty ones this fall."

"A year or two of missed sunsets is worth it."

That night during the break in class the next night she got an email from Ben.

To: Rachel Hill
From: Ben Harris

Date: September 23

Subject: so you don't miss it
    <Attachment sunset.jpg>

She sent one in return:

To: Ben Harris
From: Rachel Hill

Date: September 23

Subject: so you don't miss it
    Thank you . . .

Another photo arrived the next night, and the next, and the next. When she saw him at the coffee shop, she said, "You don't have to send one every night."

"Do you like getting them?"

"I love them," she said.

"Then I'll keep sending them. It reminds me to stop and look, too."

"Where are you when you take them?"

"Out at the Bar H sometimes. Sam's house. Wherever I'm working."

"I can see the emergency vehicle lights in some of them. What do the other cops think of you taking a picture of the sunset?"

That new smile spread across his face, as slow and hot as a Texas sunset. "I don't ask."

"Sometimes you're at your dad's?"

"If there's pasture and cattle in the shot, yes."

"That's good."

"I missed one with you that night," he said. "I'm trying not to miss more."

The next week Ben seemed restless the whole time they talked. She thought it was because she mentioned the open-mike nights starting up again, and kicked herself for bringing up something that probably still troubled him. When he stood to leave he reached into his back pocket. "I brought you something."

She accepted the paperback book with automatic thanks, then added, "Oh!" with genuine delight when she saw the title.

"It's the next book in the series you're reading."

"I know. I just finished rereading the first," she said, smoothing the cover. "Ben, thank you."

The tips of his ears reddened as he made a *no big deal* gesture with one hand. Awareness bloomed in Rachel's brain. The open-mike nights didn't make him uncomfortable. Ben "Because I Can" Harris was nervous because he was courting her in the most old-fashioned sense of the word. Bringing her offerings of the friendliest kind. Nothing expensive, nothing that would alter the balance of this burgeoning friendship, nor make her uncomfortable, but were sweetly meaningful. Using her responses to gauge whether or not she welcomed his attention. She got the sense the snail-slow pace stemmed not from his uncertainty about how he felt, but because he'd never done this before. He'd done everything else, but he'd never fallen in love.

She let him court her, not because she loved him any less, or had ever stopped loving him, but because Ben needed the same space he'd given her all those months ago, the space to explore who he was, and who he could be. She neither muted nor exaggerated her reactions to him, but gave him the gift of her honest, unclouded response.

Most nights she left the coffee shop feeling the adrenaline high of a woman taming a wild animal, convincing a panther to pace closer, then eat from her hand.

They kept the slow pace well into the fall, until one night when the temperature dropped rapidly after the sun went down. The shop's owner opened the windows to the ocean breeze. Without a jacket or a sweater, Rachel shivered in her thin scrubs.

"You want some hot tea?" Ben asked.

They'd been talking for two hours, and Rachel's fingernails were blue. Her choices were clear: drink hot tea or go home. "Yes, please," she said. "Chai."

Ally knew what Rachel liked for milk and sweetener, so she sent Ben back with a wide-rimmed white mug with a spiced-tea bag steeping in water and a splash of soy milk, and two packets of honey on the saucer with the spoon. "Smells good," he commented.

"You can try some if you want to," Rachel said in the act of squeezing the honey packets into the mug.

Ben said nothing. She looked up to find him watching the sweet liquid flow into the tea, swirling in a thick stream to the bottom of the mug. His face changed yet again, the muscles in his cheeks going slack, his soft, full mouth bringing a memory of sweetness without so much as a sip.

Honey.

A moment stretched between them, then he flicked her a look full of hot intent. Her heart jumped against her breastbone, sending electric sparks along her nerves to pool in her breasts, between her thighs.

She cleared her throat and used the spoon to dissolve the honey in the liquid. Each gentle clink of spoon against ceramic sounded loud in the silence.

His voice, when he spoke, was low and rough and desperate. "Why are you letting me do this, Rachel?"

Chapter Twenty-three

This question, Ben thought, from a man who habitually ducked any question starting with *why*. Turns out people could change. He could change.

"What do you think you're doing?" she asked gently.

"Courting you," he said. Watching honey flow into the tea sent pent-up heat from months of celibacy flowing through his veins and down his spine. "Trying to be good. Do the right thing."

Heat turned her cheeks red but she stirred her tea like the fate of the world depended on it. "That's what I thought, too. As for why I'm letting you do it, I'm trying to let you be good."

"I need practice," he admitted. "I was an asshole."

"I know," she said simply. "On the plus side, you didn't see me as weak or fragile."

He barked out a short laugh. "People do?"

"Oh yes," she said wryly. "It's usually the first thing people think. Poor Rachel Hill, locked up all her life by horrible, crazy religious fanatics, forced to wear ugly clothes, never allowed to have sex."

"They don't see you."

"You did."

"I took advantage of you, again and again, and you turned out to be the most dangerous woman I'd ever met."

"I liked that you saw me that way. Strong. Sexual. Alive."

"Dangerous," he repeated.

She lifted the mug to her lips and sipped, watching him the whole time. She didn't bat her eyelashes or lick her lips. She just looked at him with those honey-colored eyes, knowing the taste bloomed on his tongue as surely as it did on hers.

He watched her drink her tea as the barista closed down the shop, as desire unfulfilled danced through his body.

"Walk me home?" she asked.

That was new. He'd offered her rides or an escort home, but she'd gently declined each time. It didn't stop him from being a gentleman. This was the first time she'd asked.

"Sure," he said.

Ally locked the door behind them. Ben tugged his fleece pullover off and handed it to her, then picked up her book bag while she pulled the jacket on. They set off down the sidewalk at a slow pace.

"Tell me about Sam," she said.

Trust Rachel to go right to the heart of things. "Sam was me," he said simply, "and I was Sam. Mom couldn't tell us apart, and she worried about us because we didn't talk until we were almost two. I don't remember that, but I can imagine why. We didn't need to talk, and on the ranch we were isolated from other kids. When we figured out it mattered to people, we started talking, or Sam did. Sam said what we wanted or didn't want. What made us sad or happy, what we liked or didn't like." He shrugged. "I didn't need to talk, because Sam did."

"It sounds sweet," she said.

"*Sweet* landed me in a class for developmentally delayed kids when we started kindergarten," he said. "I talked in a hurry when I figured out I'd spend all day away from my brother."

She laughed, and slipped her arm through his. Maybe she was cold. Maybe she was giving him comfort in a completely nonsexual way. Either way, he kept talking.

"He was my mirror. Looking in one was always weird, because I saw me when I expected to see Sam. He was always the quiet one, but he was my center. I knew what we would do, where we'd go, how we'd play, but he knew what we thought, what we felt, right up until high school. Ninth grade, everything changes."

"When did you know he was gay?"

"I've always known, and never cared. Our father, on the other hand, was a homophobic, conservative bigot. *Was*," he emphasized. "Any signs of Sam being gay, he landed on him like a ton of bricks. He threatened to send Sam away to a reeducation camp, and Sam started talking about running away. Just pretend, I said. Stay until we graduate, then we can go wherever, together. But that's not Sam's way. It's the only thing we fought about. I wanted him to not take the risk. He just wanted to be Sam, and Dad made his life a living hell for just being Sam. The weekend we turned sixteen he ran away. I woke up one morning alone in our room, and I knew he was gone."

The emptiness in Sam's bed filled his soul with blame.

"Did your parents look for him?"

"No. My dad told me he was gone, and it was time for me to be a man." He shrugged. "So I was a man."

Rachel mused on this for a moment. "You lost your brother,

your anchor in the world, and your trust in your ability to take care of the one person you loved more than any other, all in the same day," she said quietly.

"I thought I drove him off, that what I said made it impossible for him to stay. I thought I failed him, after he'd always been there for me."

Rachel stopped. He didn't want to lose her touch, so he stopped, too, his gaze flicking from the streetlights to the corners to the shadowed doorways before settling on her face. Pained compassion softened her eyes. "Ben," she said gently. "You didn't fail him."

"That's how I felt. And because I couldn't admit how badly this gutted me, how badly I'd failed, I took it out on my dad."

She nodded, her eyes pools of compassion, golden, gleaming.

"By the time he showed up again, I was in college, and he was wrecked. I was so scared he'd leave again, I never brought it up. But I never got over it."

They'd reached her apartment complex, and climbed the stairs to the second floor. He handed over her bag, but she didn't fish her keys from the interior pocket. Instead she let the bag drop to the floor, flattened her palms alongside his face. The simple touch stopped his heart in his chest.

"You are a good man," she said. "A *good* man."

Then she kissed him. Her lips tasted of chai and honey, and he thought the surge of lust and love and long-simmering desire might drop him to his knees right there in the hallway. She was kissing him like she loved him. Like she'd walked into the worst of his life, into the self-destructiveness, the sex-like-a-handshake, looked around, and somehow liked what she saw. She knew the dark, dangerous places, the character flaws, and loved them anyway. He'd kissed Rachel through every nuance of passion and this was different, a whole new world of kissing. This was kissing with hope, with a reckless optimism, with faith. She kissed him with a faith that brought him to his knees.

Heat flared along his spine like flames along spilled fuel, then combusted. In his mind he hoisted her into the wall and ground against her, his hands on her ass, his cock notched between her thighs. In reality, he braced his forearms on the wall on either side of her head and kept his hips and chest a breath and a heartbeat away from hers, close enough to feel her breasts shiver with every inhale. He kissed her, and only kissed her, giving her the kiss she should have had the first night they were together. He infused it with hope and optimism, an offer of his soul and his future, everything he had and was and did was hers and hers alone. Because he could.

When she pulled back, she bit her swollen lip and looked up at him, the shock and wonder of tempered passion in her eyes.

She deserved that. She should have had that from the beginning. Invitation warred with hesitation in her eyes, so he stepped back. Put his hands on his hips. Took a deep breath.

"I'm not sorry about that," he said.

"I'm not, either."

He grinned at her, the new smile that was beginning to sit more comfortably on his face. "But we stop there."

Curiosity brightened her eyes. "Why? You know I go that far."

Maybe his stopping was enough for her, but it wasn't for him. He'd see pure, untempered want in her eyes the next time he lay down with Rachel Hill. Nothing less. "Because I can. And because this is what you deserve," he said, then leaned forward to give her a very gentlemanly kiss on the lips. "Good night, Rachel."

He jogged back to the now-empty coffee shop parking lot to claim his truck. Along the way he dialed Sam's number. "I feel like we're ready for our first public performance."

"When?" Sam asked without hesitating.

"Next Tuesday. Open-mike night at Artistary."

The first open-mike night of the season drew a big crowd. Artistary was packed on Tuesday night, and thanks to a dog who ate the remnants of a tube of chemotherapy ointment, Rachel was late. She'd held the cheerfully unconcerned canine while Dr. Weisen poured a charcoal solution into the dog's stomach and settled the animal overnight.

Then she took thirty precious minutes to shower and change so she didn't walk into the coffee shop in scrubs that smelled of dog. Instead, she walked into a packed house, every chair taken, people crammed onto the padded benches under the big windows and lining the walls and shelves. Standing in the doorway she scanned the room for a space, any space to watch even a few minutes, and found nothing. But then a small boy wormed his way through the tables and lurched to a halt in front of her. "Hi, Miss Rachel," he said.

"Hi, Jonathan," she said, surprised. "What are you doing here?"

"Sam's gonna sing!" he said. "We saved you a seat."

She recognized Chris at a table in front of the cleared area that formed the stage, standing and waving her over. Tucking her bag to her abdomen, she worked her way through the crowd to the table.

"We didn't get properly introduced," Chris said, offering his hand. "You make good cookies. Thank you for being there for Jonathan."

"It was my pleasure," she said as she sat down in the seat he'd saved for her. "How's Sam doing?"

"See for yourself," he said with a smile.

Jonathan balanced on Chris's knee, his attention focused on a stack of anime trading cards in his hand, while Rachel scanned the crowd for Ben, because surely he wouldn't miss his brother singing. The emcee arranged two microphones and stools on the stage. Rachel's heart stopped in her chest when Ben and Sam walked out, both carrying guitars. Ben wore faded jeans, a western shirt, and the brown, scuffed boots. Sam wore dark skinny jeans, a short-sleeved T-shirt from a gay pride event over a waffle-weave under-shirt, and Keds, his hair spilling over his forehead. Sam waved at Jonathan and Chris, then gave her a quirky smile. Ben focused on arranging the height of his stool and microphone, then hooked the heel of his boot in the stool's lowest rung and balanced his guitar on his thigh.

When he finally, *finally* looked at Rachel, she read everything in his face. Her heart crawled up to sit at the back of her throat and flutter like a trapped bird. He was so handsome, shoulders straining the shirt's seams, the planes and angles of his face illuminated by the spotlight, his blue eyes brilliant against the brown fabric back-drop with the coffee shop's gold logo.

Then he smiled at her, slow and sweet as skin-warmed honey.

"Hey, y'all," Sam said into the mike. The crowd quieted down. "I'm Sam Harris." He hooked a thumb over his shoulder at Ben. "I've never seen this dude before in my life but he was backstage with a guitar so we thought we'd go on together."

Laughter rippled through the crowd, and Ben shot Sam a clear, pure smile. Seeing them together like this Rachel understood all the old phrases. Two sides of the same coin. Two halves of a whole. Blood brothers. While they both had separate lives, being together clearly completed them in a way no one else could understand. She glanced at Chris, wondering if he harbored any jealousy, but his face mirrored what she felt inside. This was as it should be, healing and whole, Sam, Ben, the people who loved them, everyone they touched directly or indirectly. This was family as it was meant to be.

Ben said something Rachel couldn't hear to Sam that made him laugh. Sam adjusted his stool and microphone. "Okay, that's my brother, Ben. Bear with us, folks, 'cause we haven't performed together in a long, long time."

A hushed silence fell. Without so much as a glance the brothers began to play. Rachel's experience with pop music was limited, so she didn't recognize the song. The intensity and beat took up residence in her chest. Ben and Sam weren't playing gentle, sweet coffeehouse music. This was intense, driving, a demand in notes and beat, and when Sam began to sing, she recognized the song for what it was.

Prayer.

Give me a word, give me a sign
Show me where to look and tell me what will I find.

Oh yes. Prayer. She knew prayer when she heard it, recognized a plea flung into the air from the very depths of the human soul, and when Ben leaned forward and joined Sam's voice for the chorus, she knew she was right.

Neither man made eye contact with the audience. Sam's eyes closed as he sang, clearly a more polished performer than Ben, who'd somehow both disappeared into himself and shed what was left of the defenses shielding him. Sam performed, but Ben *was* the guitar. Emotion streamed from him like light shining down. In perfect unison they played a driving chord, then paused; in the split second of silence Rachel's heart thrummed in her ears. She'd never felt like this before, alive to the very surface of her skin, because *he'd* never felt like this before.

She was pinned to her seat, her muscles frozen, not even breathing, as Ben Harris laid his soul bare before her.

They played the same series of chords, another silence. Not a cough or a shuffle or a whisper in the coffee shop. Lyrics and guitar and voice blended into a throaty demand for presence, for mystery, for love. When Sam sat back to watch Ben's guitar solo, Rachel watched his abraded, reddened fingertips shift and press on the guitar neck. The placket of his shirt opened, exposing his throat and collarbone as he curved protectively around the instrument, calling vibrating notes and hushed, seductive nuance from the strings, voicelessly saying everything Rachel never dreamed she'd hear from him.

She imagined him practicing for weeks in the hopes this moment would come, using time with his brother to heal and to hope for the future. He'd excavated himself layer by layer from the strata of pain to have something to offer her, his brother, himself.

The song finished almost abruptly, then Sam smoothed his hair back from his face and looked at Ben. The smile they exchanged, exultant and secretive all at once, sent the tears building in Rachel's eyes spilling over.

There was a moment of stunned silence, then the crowd erupted into wild, stomping applause and whoops. Rachel just sat there, one hand pressed to her throat, the other across her belly, tears slowly trickling down her face. Ben's gaze skimmed the crowd as he gave a single, short nod, then looked straight at her. His blue eyes held a question.

Yes?

Yes. Oh yes. Always yes.

The applause had only begun to die down when Ben and Sam stood to make way for the next singer. Ben slid the guitar into its case, then held out his hand to Rachel. Without thinking about the invisible boundaries between stage and audience, men and women, her and Ben, she slid her hand into his and let him lead her into the dark brick hallway.

The waiting performers around them applauded and called out

their congratulations, but Ben kept moving, down the hallway, to the left, and out a door that led to the alley. It was clearly marked Fire Door but Ben just pushed through it, into the cool night air.

"Lord have mercy," Rachel said, and meant it. Hot, cold, lightning streaking through her veins, and breathing seemed to require thought.

Ben palmed the back of his neck and shot her a look as he paced. The full moon silvered his hair, the hard planes of his face. "Yeah."

When he passed in front of her she reached for his free hand and found his pulse. Thumping hard against tendons and skin, and racing. "Big rush?"

"You'd know," he said, startling a laugh from her. Because she did know. She knew what it meant to stop hiding and start living. He shoved his hand over his hair, then wove his fingers through hers.

"You were amazing."

"I'm glad you were there to see it."

"Me, too," she murmured. "Me, too."

The fire door opened again and Sam peered out. "Jonathan's too wired to go to bed so we're going out for ice cream. Want to come?" He glanced at Ben, then at Rachel, and lifted an eyebrow. "I'm guessing not," he said, answering his own question.

"Ice cream?" Ben asked her.

She shook her head, flashing Sam an apologetic smile.

"See you tomorrow," Ben said.

"We're hosting a birthday party for our dad, and you are most welcome to join us, Miss Rachel," Sam said, then looked at Ben. "Make sure she gets there," he called as the fire door closed.

Hands on hips, his blue eyes glinting in the early evening sunlight, he said, "How about brunch and cake with my brother, Chris, Jonathan, my sister and her husband and kids, my parents, and about forty other people tomorrow? No pressure. You don't have to come, but I'd like to introduce you to my family."

"I'd love to go," she said.

"Walk you home?"

She thought about heaven's light shining down, and the restraint in Ben's eyes. She thought about how much she missed him, and how much he'd changed in the last few months. She thought about what it meant to love, about what he'd given her. "My roommate has tonight off," she said. "She'll be up all night."

He lifted an eyebrow. "My place?"

"I'd like that," she said.

They drove in silence back to his building. She spent the ride wondering what would happen, but in the end, it was as natural as breathing to climb the stairs to his apartment, wait while he unlocked the door and opened it for her, then walk inside.

It was as natural as breathing to slip her hand into his, follow him down the hall, and stretch out on the bed with him. Her heart rate stuttered when he lowered himself down beside her, half covering her, using fingers that trembled slightly to brush her hair back from her face.

It was as natural as breathing to lift her head ever so slightly and brush her lips across his. Palms flattened against his rough jaw, she kissed him and kissed him, ravaging his mouth.

It was as natural as breathing to make love with Ben Harris. There were no gymnastics or dirty talk. Tonight Ben touched her like she was precious to him, baring her, stroking her, heating the contours of her soul and calling it forth from her skin. He held back, restraint in the way his fingers trembled as they skimmed her ribs, in the way he built the pleasure with purposeful touch. His big palm stroked over her torso, then his fingertips found her nipples. He followed with his mouth, down her neck to her breasts, then to her abdomen to settle between her legs.

Slow and sweet and tender. Each slow stroke of his tongue against her clit, each pause while the heat pooled in her hot spots, drove her wild until she fell over the edge, into oblivion. When she opened her eyes, he was braced over her, shuddering.

"Ben," she whispered. "Please."

He smoothed a condom down his shaft, then positioned himself between her legs and pushed inside her. The electricity skittering along hypersensitive nerves as he took possession of her body forced a cry from her throat and tightened her muscles. He stayed like that, hard and heavy inside her, for an eternity without moving. Eons passed, then he lifted his head from her shoulder and kissed her. Decades after that he withdrew and stroked back in, then groaned. The sound echoed into the room like it had been torn from his chest by an implacable hand. Her arms, legs, sex, all tightened to draw him in, close, so close to her.

Slow and sweet and tender, until hot desire and weeks of abstinence burned slowly to the ground. She wound around him like hot gold wire, welcoming every hard thrust, the force of his body against hers, hard planes to her soft curves. He braced an elbow above her shoulder to hold her in place. She gripped his lower back and closed her eyes against the onslaught.

Love. This was the love she never expected to find with a man who wouldn't care. They were making love for the first time, and the combination of emotion and pleasure shattered her. Sharp cries tore from her throat with each pulse of release. He held her to him, the move at once devastatingly protective and possessive.

When he found his own release it was in the sheltering circle of her arms.

• • •

Much, much later, he lifted his head from her shoulder. As her fingers traced lazy swirls up his spine, he spoke. "I swore I'd never fail anyone like I failed Sam. And I haven't. I've just failed people in other ways." He lifted his head and peered into her eyes. "I'm sorry for what I made you feel. Made you do. I hurt you, and I'm sorry."

She smiled up into his face. "That was a lovely apology."

He ran his finger along the piping on the bedsheet. "I worked on it."

"I accept your apology," she said formally.

A slow, sweet smile tugged at the corners of his mouth. "I love you, Rachel."

"I love you, too, Ben." Spurred by some wicked little demon inside, she added, "But maybe you shouldn't fall in love with the first woman you make love to."

One corner of his mouth lifted in a grin. He brushed her hair back from her temple. "Maybe I made love to her because I'd already fallen in love."

She slept the night through, waking the next morning to sunlight streaming through the cloth blinds and a warm, hard body next to her. She lifted her head to see Ben next to her, lying on his back, one arm tucked behind his head.

"Good morning," she said as she hitched close enough to temptation personified to rest her chin on his chest.

"Good morning." With his free hand he reached up to tuck her loose hair behind her ear. It slid forward almost immediately, grazing her jaw and covering one eye. A slight smile quirked the corners of his mouth as he tucked it away again. This time it stayed in place, so his fingers lingered on her jaw, her lips.

She lifted her hand and flattened it against his. Her fingers were almost as long as his but his palm was much bigger. After a moment she wove her fingers into his, felt his warmth and strength seep through her skin, into her bones. She turned their wrists so she could kiss the back of his hand, then flicked her tongue against the sensitive skin between his fingers. When she finished, he turned her hand to his mouth and mirrored her movements. The sensation of warm lips and tongue tracing the veins in the back of her hand made her eyelids droop. After long moments where the air temperature in the room rose to meet the heat in her blood, he draped her arm over his shoulder and wrapped his arm around her waist to pull her across his body.

His heart raced, she noticed at the back of her mind. He felt all the deeper emotions, desire, uncertainty, longing, anticipation, hope. Love. He loved, and let himself be loved.

She lowered her mouth to his. It was slow and sweet and tender, the way he kissed her, brushing lip against lip, waiting until she touched the tip of her tongue to his lower lip before opening his mouth to claim hers. "I have to go home," she murmured. "I can't show up in the same clothes I wore last night."

He gave a half-amused, half-frustrated growl, but let her go. "I'll drive you home and pick up the cake while you're getting ready," he said.

She dressed while he showered. He drove her home, where she undressed, showered, then pulled on the white dress she'd worn to their first night at Artistary. She wound her hair into a loose, off-center bun, slipped a cardigan through the handles of her purse, and was waiting for him when he returned.

"What will your parents think about me coming to a family

party?" she asked as he opened the door and held out his hand to help her up into the seat.

"They'll love you," Ben said. He dropped a soft kiss on her lips. "Don't worry."

So many cars lined both sides of the street they had to park five houses down from Sam's. When they started up the sidewalk to the front door, Jonathan barreled down the steps and hurled himself at Ben. He handed off the cake to Rachel and visibly braced for the impact of a hurricane-strength boy at full speed.

"Hey, squirt," he said.

Jonathan locked his legs around Ben's thigh and climbed up him like a fire pole. "Guess what!"

"What?" Ben said with a grunt. Rachel grinned. He shot her a pained smile, shifted Jon to his hip, and set off up the front walk.

"Gramma and Gramps brought me the police car Lego set. It's got a cruiser and an ambulance and a SWAT truck." He held it out, right in Ben's face. Ben leaned back to take in the details and nearly missed the first step up to the front door.

"The picture of athletic grace and poise. Good thing she's carrying the cake," Chris said as he held open the door. "Welcome, Rachel."

Ben tossed Chris a response Rachel couldn't hear, because the interior of the house was a whirl of noise and laughter. Balloons hovered over lamps and the newel post to the banister. A Happy Birthday banner hung over the entrance to the dining room, where guests lingered over a spread rivaling a restaurant buffet.

Mission one was to deliver the cake, so she turned for the kitchen and found Ben, Sam, and two people who could only be their parents behind the island. The boys had their mother's blue eyes and brown hair, and their father's squared-off jawline.

Ben's warm hands came to rest on her waist. "Mom, Dad. This is Rachel Hill."

She offered her hand, but Ben's mother pulled her into a hug. "It's so good to meet you."

His father followed propriety and shook her hand with a warm, callused grip. "Our pleasure, Miss Hill."

"Happy birthday, Mr. Harris," she said.

"It's a very happy birthday," he replied. She didn't miss the glance at his sons, standing shoulder to shoulder in the kitchen.

"Ben's told us so much about you, but not how you met," his mother said.

She accepted a glass of iced tea from Sam as she looked at Ben. He lifted one eyebrow, a smile tugging at the corners of his mouth. *Go ahead,* his eyes said.

Begin as you mean to go on, and all that. "I bought him at a bachelor auction."

Mrs. Harris's eyes widened. "Really?"

"I took one look at him and knew he was the man for me," Rachel added, in case Ben's mother was a romantic.

Sam turned a laugh into a cough, and the smile broke free on Ben's mouth.

"Well, what a sweet story," Mrs. Harris said, but the glance she gave her boys told Rachel their mother wasn't fooled.

Ben held out his hand to Rachel. "Come meet the family," he said.

The next few hours were a whirl of names and faces and relationships, reminiscing over plates of food, a loud rendition of "Happy Birthday," and cake and ice cream. Jonathan gave her a tour of the tree house; Chris gave her the latest on the adoption proceedings. As the sun set Ben left Jonathan playing with the Lego trucks in the dirt and joined Rachel on the swings.

"It was a really nice party," she said.

"Sam does it up right," Ben agreed, then nudged her sandaled foot with his boot. "Miss your dad?"

"Yes," she said. "But . . . the last three letters didn't come back."

"Hopeful."

"I told him about you. I think he'd like you." She shrugged at Ben's raised eyebrows. "You're very likable and I'm optimistic."

"A force of nature is what you are," Ben said. "We won't give up."

"No," she said quietly. "We won't."

His smile, soft and slow and sweet, promised her all the warmth and shelter she could want, along with all the independence she craved. She sighed with contentment. "I love you, Ben."

"I love you, too," he said. "Come on. Let's get seconds before Sam eats all the cake."

He draped his arm around her waist and led her through the deepening twilight, into the warmth and laughter inside.